About the Authors

Born in the UK, **Becky Wicks** has suffered interminable wanderlust from an early age. She's lived and worked all over the world, from London to Dubai, Sydney, Bali, NYC and Amsterdam. She's written for the likes of *GQ, Hello!, Fabulous* and *Time Out*, various YA romances, plus three travel memoirs – *Burqalicious, Balilicious* and *Latinalicious*. Now she blends travel with romance for Mills & Boon and loves every minute! Find her on Substack @beckywicks

A.C. Arthur was born and raised in Baltimore, Maryland, where she currently resides with her husband and three children. Determined to bring a new edge to romance, she continues to develop intriguing plots, sensual love scenes, racy characters and fresh dialogue; thus keeping the readers on their toes! Artist loves to hear from her readers and can be reached via email at acarthur22@yahoo.com

USA Today bestselling author **Kat Cantrell** read her first Mills & Boon novel in third grade and has been scribbling in notebooks since she learned to spell. She's a So You Think You Can Write winner and a Romance Writers of America Golden Heart Award finalist. Kat, her husband, and their two boys live in North Texas.

In The Spotlight

September 2025
Fame's Temptation

February 2026
Runway to Romance

December 2025
Chasing Stars

March 2026
Desired Melodies

January 2026
Written in Passion

April 2026
Prescription for Love

In The Spotlight: Prescription for Love

BECKY WICKS

A.C. ARTHUR

KAT CANTRELL

MILLS & BOON

All rights reserved including the right of reproduction in whole or in part in any form. This edition is published by arrangement with Harlequin Enterprises ULC.

This is a work of fiction. Names, characters, places, locations and incidents are purely fictional and bear no relationship to any real life individuals, living or dead, or to any actual places, business establishments, locations, events or incidents. Any resemblance is entirely coincidental.

Without limiting the exclusive rights of any author, contributor or the publisher of this publication, any unauthorised use of this publication to train generative artificial intelligence (AI) technologies is expressly prohibited. HarperCollins also exercise their rights under Article 4(3) of the Digital Single Market Directive 2019/790 and expressly reserve this publication from the text and data mining exception.

® and ™ are trademarks owned and used by the trademark owner and/or its licensee. Trademarks marked with ® are registered with the United Kingdom Patent Office and/or the Office for Harmonisation in the Internal Market and in other countries.

First Published in Great Britain 2026
by Mills & Boon, an imprint of HarperCollins*Publishers* Ltd
1 London Bridge Street, London, SE1 9GF

www.harpercollins.co.uk

HarperCollins*Publishers*
Macken House, 39/40 Mayor Street Upper,
Dublin 1, D01 C9W8, Ireland

In The Spotlight: Prescription for Love © 2026 Harlequin Enterprises ULC.

Tempted by Her Hot-Shot Doc © 2018 Becky Wicks
One Perfect Moment © 2018 Artist Arthur
The Pregnancy Project © 2016 Kat Cantrell

ISBN: 978-0-263-42159-0

Printed and Bound in the UK using 100% Renewable Electricity
at CPI Group (UK) Ltd, Croydon, CR0 4YY

TEMPTED BY HER HOT-SHOT DOC

BECKY WICKS

For my Mum.
Sorry about the sex scenes. Don't tell Dad.

CHAPTER ONE

THE RAIN WAS coming down harder than she'd ever felt it. Sharp, wet pricks to her bare arms sent mini-lightning bolts through Madeline's flesh and deep into her bones as she hurried along the London cobblestones, holding her umbrella over her as best she could.

The bolts, of course, were mostly due to the man her agent had arranged for her to meet—America's wealthiest and most inspiring flying doctor and a man most women would surely kill to meet—Ryan Tobias.

His name, now rolling around in her brain, sent further spikes of adrenaline through her body, along with the goosebumps now settling in with the cold. She'd left in such a hurry she'd forgotten her jacket.

'Don't be late,' Samantha had told her. 'He doesn't like it when people are late.'

But Madeline had been so caught up in her internet research that she'd gone and made herself late anyway. She'd been determined to have as much background information on him as possible before their meeting, and it had been near impossible to tear her eyes away once she'd started.

The internet seemed to have its own busy corner of photos, articles, videos and GIFs made from *Medical Extremes* footage—the show Ryan Tobias starred in along with his team of GPs and surgeons. She'd watched a clip of him walking across the glacier in Alaska to reach a stranded explorer at least five times, pausing on the moment when the camera had gone in for a close-up of his bearded, rugged face in front of the whirring helicopter blades.

She had no idea at all about what Samantha had in mind for her to do with this man, but she couldn't deny it was exciting. And *terrifying*.

Madeline's phone beeped, making her jump. She almost tripped over the cobblestones. Damn, she *had* to pull herself together.

'I'm nearly there,' she blurted hurriedly into it, just as she rounded the corner into Trinity Buoy Wharf.

Samantha was standing there in the doorway, waiting. She was in high heels, too, Madeline noticed. Were they both dressed to impress a man they knew almost never looked impressed?

'He's already here,' Samantha said in a low voice, taking the umbrella and ushering Madeline's wet body through huge green doors into the sandy-coloured building.

A flurry of filming activity assaulted her eyes as she swiped at the raindrops on her skin. Men were everywhere: lifting crates, unscrewing lighting equipment, packing things into cases. It was a studio, as she'd expected, but the hectic feel of the place, plus the knowledge that a good few pairs of eyes were now on her, threw a spanner into her already frazzled works.

'Over here first,' Samantha said, putting a firm hand to Madeline's soaked white shirt and starting off across the room.

She was a little too quick for her to keep up, however, and before she could stop herself her heel was catching on a cable stretched out across the floor. She almost went flying.

'Are you trying to kill yourself?'

The deep voice sounded out in front of her, just as she put her hand to the wall to steady herself.

'I'm so sorry. I'm...' Madeline trailed off, realising it wasn't actually a wall she was touching.

It was hard, undoubtedly, but it was breathing.

'Dr Ryan,' she blurted, straightening up instantly.

She removed her flattened palms from his broad chest, scanned his face up close and felt her cheeks flare from pink to beetroot as her heart started pounding in her ribcage. For a strange moment she felt just as if she'd fallen asleep at her kitchen table and woken up on the YouTube channel.

Ryan Tobias wasn't in his trademark *Medical Extremes* white shirt and jacket. He was wearing a black waterproof coat and jeans. His hair, just as it always was on television, was wild and windswept—as though the breeze over London's River Thames had as little respect for him as the wind in a Patagonian hurricane.

She'd watched *those* clips twice or more. Somehow they'd airlifted a pregnant, sick lady to safety, even though Ryan and the brave pilot had been the only ones willing to risk a flight in the storm.

He was taller than she'd expected, somehow, towering over her with a look of amusement mixed with something she couldn't quite read in his familiar grey eyes.

Madeline realised with horror that he must be taking in her rain-drenched hair and the small but noticeable coffee stain on her shirt. A woman had splashed her latte on her on the tube. What must he be thinking?

She glanced around her. Samantha had been ushered off to another corner and was now apparently deep in what looked like an angst-ridden conversation with a guy waving a flowerpot.

Ryan was still appraising her, she realised.

He coughed and crossed his arms. 'I'm afraid I don't know your name.'

'Madeline,' she said, flustered.

'Where did *you* come from, Madeline?'

'From a *much* less embarrassing situation,' she replied without thinking.

Surprise flickered in his eyes before he uncrossed his arms and laughed. A proper laugh that revealed his teeth, as white as snow-capped mountains—a laugh she was pretty sure she'd heard only two or three times on the television.

'Well, they do insist on blocking the walkways like this,' he said, motioning to their feet. 'Good thing you didn't twist your ankle in those shoes. I don't know which box my emergency supplies are in.'

'Guess I got lucky.'

He threw her a surreptitious half-smile. 'I prefer to live life on the edge of danger, too.'

'I've never seen *you* in high heels.'

She adjusted her handbag on her shoulder as he laughed again. A part of her couldn't quite believe she was making Dr Ryan Tobias laugh.

'Anyway, my agent Samantha, over there, kind of surprised me with all this, so...'

'Your agent?' Ryan's expression shifted before her. 'What do you mean?'

Shards of ice were stuck in his eyes now, and it was as if Madeline was alone with him on the peak of a snowy mountain, or maybe trekking over that glacier to reach another lost adventurer who'd been injured and needed his help. Either way, she was suddenly much colder.

'Agent for what?' His arms were crossed again.

'My writing career.'

His forehead creased into a frown.

'Sorry—sorry.' Samantha bustled up behind her, breaking their locked gazes apart. 'I see you've met Madeline Savoia,' she said, putting a hand to Madeline's shoulder. 'She's almost set to be your new ghost-writer, joining you in the Amazon. What did you think of her portfolio?'

Madeline spun her head around to face Samantha. Ghost-writer? *Amazon?* It was the first she'd heard of it.

Samantha had called her to the TV set at the last minute, saying she had the perfect opportunity for her with none other than the selfless, compassionate and dazzlingly good-looking Ryan Tobias, but she'd assumed she'd be assisting in an interview with him—maybe sending some tweets for the travel and entertainment website Samantha sometimes had her freelance for.

Ryan was unreadable now, standing solid as a rock.

'I see. How much experience do you have with malaria and spider bites, Miss Madeline?'

He didn't sound as friendly as before.

Samantha squeezed her shoulder. 'Madeline is a phenomenal writer, Ryan. You might have read her geopolitical romantic thriller—the one set in Madagascar?'

'Can't say I have,' he said. 'I don't get a lot of time to read.'

He was reading *her*. Madeline knew it. Scrutinising her like a beetle under a microscope. She felt the urge to cover herself, but realised it was pointless.

'She's a keen traveller and explorer, like you, *and* she's a medical professional,' Samantha carried on as Madeline's cheeks flamed. 'I thought she'd be the perfect fit.'

'What kind of medical professional?'

'I used to be a nurse, but I'm not any more...' Madeline let her words taper off. She didn't particularly feel like explaining why she'd quit nursing. The thought of it still shamed her, but she doubted the time she'd spent on the wards of St David's Hospital would help anyone who'd been mauled by a jaguar or hugged by an anaconda in the Amazon.

'Is this necessary, Samantha?' Ryan said, after a moment.

His tone was irritated. His arms were still crossed, tighter than ever.

Something in his icy tone made Madeline recall with a flash the other articles she'd uncovered on the internet. Ryan had lost one of his team members five years ago on a sponsored expedition. He'd been twenty-seven at the time. She remembered thinking that she and Ryan were the same age—both thirty-two now.

No one knew the finer details of how or why the young physician Josephine McCarthy had died suddenly out in the jungle. Ryan had clammed up—never shared it with the media. And the medical team with him at the time had also never divulged what had happened—if they even knew.

The rumour mill had been spinning ever since.

Most of what had been printed was hearsay, of course, but Ryan had spent a lot more time in the wild since then, setting up an HIV awareness programme in Africa, arranging vaccinations at schools in Nepal.

Apparently he hadn't particularly wanted the camera crew to follow him when the concept of *Medical Extremes* had first been discussed, but the money they paid him helped thousands of villages get the medication they needed. And besides, the world needed to see the importance of doctors operating without borders.

That was what had been announced in the press release, at least.

'I'm sorry, Ryan,' Samantha said, interrupting Madeline's thoughts. 'A contract is a contract.'

'I know... I know.'

His jaw twitched in annoyance as Madeline stood awkwardly between them.

'If you don't take Madeline with you we'll only have to send someone else you haven't even met, and we're running out of time.'

'Time has a habit of running out,' he replied, somewhat mysteriously.

He's incredibly moody—that was what she'd read. Those rumours must be true at least. Ryan Tobias spent his life touching the lives of many in the world's most remote locations, but he himself was untouchable. And now Samantha was somehow asking *her* to accompany him on his next televised medical mission to the jungle?

She wondered whether her telling Samantha that she was now single had anything to do with this. She suddenly regretted telling her agent how Jason had decided to pursue his burgeoning relationship with a young zoologist called Adeline.

'How can he want an Adeline when he has a perfectly good Madeline?' she'd said at the time, enraged.

'Ryan!'

Someone was calling him back towards a camera. He didn't move. Instead he shot Madeline a narrow look that rattled every nerve-ending in her body. She fixed her eyes on his, determined not to let him know she had a lump in her throat the size of a cricket ball. He didn't break his gaze—not that she was about to break hers either. She was damned if she'd let another moody man walk all over her, even if he *was* rich and famous.

'Well, as you say, a contract is a contract,' he muttered after a moment, sucking in a breath and letting it out so heavily that Madeline felt her damp hair ruffle.

'It'll be great for your profile,' Samantha told him matter-of-factly, and Madeline caught him rolling his eyes.

'We'll see about that. Good to meet you, Madeline.' He thrust his hand out at her suddenly. 'We can always do with another nurse around, I suppose.'

'Oh, like I said, I'm not a—'

'Ryan! We need you over here, please.' That voice again.

His face was expressionless as he engulfed Madeline's hand with his own, and for some reason another episode of *Medical Extremes* was flashing in her mind. Cambodia. The one where he'd eaten a fried tarantula. It had been a gift from the family of a man he'd helped to save.

Ryan Tobias was fearless—that was what everyone said. Well. She was damned if she'd let him scare her.

'I'm looking forward to working with you,' she said calmly.

'Ryan!'

'I'm *coming*, damn it!'

He dropped her hand, turned and strolled across the studio, and Samantha took Madeline's elbow, leading her to a sofa and coffee table in the corner of the chaos. Both were covered in sheets of paper.

'You did good. I'm so sorry to spring this on you.' She poured them both a cup of coffee. 'But this opportunity wouldn't have waited. I suggested *you* the moment I heard what happened to the last ghost-writer…'

'What happened?' Madeline realised just how dry her throat was.

'Fell down some stairs—cracked three ribs, broke one arm. Ironic isn't the word. Would you like a biscuit?'

She shook her head, glancing to her right. Ryan was walking towards a guy packing a camera into a very large black box on wheels, talking about some supplies he needed but hadn't seen yet. His voice still sent chills…or was it thrills?…straight through her.

Was she *really* going to the Amazon?

'He seems…nice,' she ventured, sipping her coffee.

'He's *very* nice, when everything goes to plan. So, Madeline, the long and short of it is that Ryan's contract states that he needs to deliver a memoir and his publishers want it released for Christmas. Only as yet he's been too busy to write it.'

'OK…'

Madeline gripped more tightly onto her cup and bit into her cheek. Ghost-writing wasn't exactly something she was thrilled about doing. Her last book—written under her own name—hadn't gone too well, though, due to her publisher having no marketing budget, mostly. Her sales had suffered horribly while she'd been out writing the next one in the middle of nowhere in Zimbabwe.

Apparently bad things happened to books if you couldn't spend twenty-four hours a day on Twitter, telling everyone about them.

Bad things happened to relationships, too, if you stupidly left your boyfriend alone for two months…

Madeline pushed thoughts of Adeline from her head.

Samantha sipped her coffee, then put the cup down on the messy table.

'Ryan is about to go and shoot the third season of *Medical Extremes*, as you know, and what with all his appointments he hasn't got time for the memoir, too. We need someone to help him write the book at the same time as he's filming—gather quotes, insights, interviews, you know? Am I right in thinking you're still free to take a week or two, probably three, out of London at the moment?'

Madeline nodded blankly. Ryan was so tall and so commanding without even trying. Everyone seemed to be in awe of him. And although she was a little loath to admit it, after the way he'd just acted towards her, it wasn't hard to see why.

As well as being the sexiest doctor since George Clooney, Ryan was a millionaire who gave selflessly to charities all over the world. He didn't have a lot else to spend his riches on, apparently. His father was a heart surgeon, famed for working with those less fortunate in the US. Ryan had taken things one step further by setting up his own non-profit organisation and flying all over the world with his team, crossing borders to reach people who'd never get help otherwise.

Samantha lowered her voice. 'Ryan doesn't write. Obviously his skills lie in other areas. But with you on board, plus his celebrity status, this book could be a bestseller. Easy. The publishers have a very impressive budget.'

'And Twitter?' Madeline said. 'How many followers?'

'Over four hundred thousand. He never tweets a damn thing, of course, but we have Amy from Middlesex University who's his biggest fan. She won the competition to be his Twitter manager. He just got done with a news team covering the story... BBC, I think. How are *you* at being on camera? You've got great cheekbones—I bet it loves you. And you speak several languages, I recall? Always useful.'

Madeline's stomach lurched. This was turning out to be a lot more than she'd bargained for. But it wasn't as if she had anything else on the cards.

She mused over the offer as Samantha kept on talking. She vaguely registered her agent mentioning Rio, a remote tribe—*'none of those weird neck rings or anything'*—parasites, anaemia… But after a minute she was only half listening, because she could feel Ryan looking at her again from across the room.

She straightened her back again, so that he could see he wasn't intimidating her in any way, and tried to look enthusiastic and excited. She had to play her cards right. This chance was too good to pass up and maybe Samantha was right. It could be a bestseller by Christmas.

We can both get something out of this, she thought, sending the thought across the void and straight into Ryan's cool, iceberg eyes.

CHAPTER TWO

'Did you know that CAN's first pilots were called the flag-bearers of the skies? That was in the early nineteen-forties.'

'I don't know much about CAN at the moment,' Madeline said. 'This was all a bit short notice, as you know. Maybe you could explain?'

She was trying her hardest not to let turbulence affect the way she was talking to Ryan. This plane was far too shaky for her peace of mind, but of course this man flew everywhere for a living and didn't even look as if he'd noticed they were bumping up and down in what felt like God's hugest tantrum since the last giant tornado.

'Correio Aéreo Nacional,' he said, picking up a packet of peanuts and running a tanned thumb over the seal without opening it. 'Their mission was to help integrate the most remote Amazon outposts with the rest of the country.'

'How did they do that?'

Madeline pulled out her notebook, wishing she'd put her laptop under her seat instead of up in the overhead locker. She could type much faster than she could write these days, but there was no way on earth she was climbing past Ryan. She'd rather not risk feeling his eyes on her again as she tripped, or did something else stupid as a result of her nerves.

There was something in his stare, she mused. It stayed with her even with her eyes closed. She'd seen it a thousand times in camera close-ups, of course, and it was part of what drew people in their thousands to watch him in action. It had the power to make you feel like you were the only person on earth. It also had the power to make you feel like an idiot.

Ryan smiled, apparently scrutinising her handwriting from his seat on the aisle. 'CAN transported isolated residents from riverside communities to places where they could be helped—usually the city. They had dozens of planes flying over the Amazon—more than they do now anyway.'

Madeline scribbled as fast as she could to get his words down, feeling thankful that she'd brought a Dictaphone for later.

When she looked up his grey eyes were fixed on her, and she found herself annoyingly self-conscious. At least she wasn't wet and covered in coffee this time—she'd put on a very respectable knee-length blue dress for the flight, one that accentuated her small waist, and she'd left her long hair down around her shoulders. Also, he seemed to be making a concerted effort to be friendly, for which she was more than grateful.

'The flying doctors were known as the Angels of the Amazon, is that right?' she asked him, reaching for her necklace.

'Correct,' he said, watching her fiddling with the silver chain as she slid the small crystal apple up and down on it. 'They *were* angels, Madeline. Still are. They deliver medical aid by aircraft. If they didn't these people would only get help after weeks of travelling on foot through the jungle, or by boat.'

'So, would you consider yourself an angel now, too?'

Ryan frowned, drumming his fingers on his tray table. 'I just do what's necessary—like *they* do,' he said. 'These people live and breathe the Amazon—a place most of us know little about, except that it's a living pharmacy essential to billions of lives on earth, right? They're the caretakers of the jungle and everything in it. By helping them and looking after their health we're helping the environment.'

The plane jostled them again and Madeline's tray table jumped.

'Do you know where we're going?' he asked, catching her notepad before it slid off.

'Caramambatai,' she replied quickly, hoping she was pronouncing it right. 'Your producer says it's an indigenous settlement...'

'The Ingariko tribe, yes. They're spread all over South America, but this camp is pretty much hidden on the border between Brazil, Venezuela and Guyana. It's about as remote as you're going to get. Legend has it people have been swallowed whole by thick morning mists in these parts. They're more likely to have been finished off by surucucu snakes, if you ask me. Highly poisonous, by the way. If you see one it will probably be the last thing you see.'

She realised, now that he was so close, that he had lines around his eyes—proof of laughter, perhaps, more than age. He'd been happy once. Happier than the media made him out to be now anyway. He looked sexier in person, too, she decided.

Then she caught herself.

Sexier? There was no way she was letting herself

think *that* again. She was here to do a job—and besides, as if *anyone* would go near her, let alone this guy. Her friend Emma had said she reeked of heartbreak, which wasn't particularly nice but was definitely true. Hardly surprising after what Jason had done.

Madeline could still recite every line of that love-struck email to Adeline she'd read by mistake after he'd left his laptop open.

I'm just trying to find the right time to tell her, baby. You know it's not her I'm in love with any more.

'So, how do we reach these people once we get to Brazil?' she asked, trying and failing to cross her legs properly under her tray table.

They'd been on the plane for four hours already, and she'd already counted at least nine things in her head that she'd forgotten to pack or research. She was hoping she'd have time to sort a few things out in Rio—where they were stopping for supplies before taking another flight to Saint Elena.

'We'll take a Cessna,' Ryan said. 'Either that or a Black Hawk—whatever the team have booked. Both are pretty good on the runways.'

'There are runways in the rainforest?'

'Well, they're mud strips, really.'

Ryan opened the peanuts and offered her one. She shook her head, trying her hardest to write without scribbling on the tray table instead. They were still bouncing up and down, as if the plane itself was on some sort of trampoline.

'The runways were carved out by the gold miners initially,' he told her. 'Illegally, of course, but they help us do our jobs so I suppose the *real* value of that gold just keeps on increasing—wherever it is. You can write that down.'

She realised her pen was hovering and that she was lost in thoughts of Jason again. But this time Jason was standing next to Ryan Tobias in the jungle, and being somewhat dwarfed by him.

She blinked to get rid of them both. 'Right, yes. Good idea.' She started to scribble, flustered.

'Whatever you do, stay close to us,' Ryan said suddenly, in a tone that pulled her eyes to his again like a magnet. 'People go missing out there all the time.'

Her breath caught as she saw an emotion she didn't recognise cross his face.

He continued without looking at her. 'Last time we found a burnt-out helicopter which must have crashed twenty years ago. No skeletons inside…who knows what happened to them? The jungle has a way of luring people in and keeping them.'

Madeline tried not to shudder. For some reason she knew he was thinking of Josephine McCarthy. What *had* happened to her, exactly?

'When were you here last?' she asked.

'Eight months ago. Five-day CAN mission. No cameras. We treated six hundred patients for minor infections, brought some ultrasound machines. We felt bad we couldn't help the guy who got shot, though.'

'Shot?'

'He did it to himself—his gun got all twisted. By the time we found him his leg had more larvae in it than a dead horse. We cleaned him out, worked on him a long time, but he didn't make it. So, like I said, don't go wandering off on your own, please.' He met her eyes, concern shining around his pupils. 'And watch what you do with your gun.'

Madeline realised she felt quite ill. 'Ryan, I wouldn't be comfortable with a gun, and I really don't think…'

She trailed off as she caught the smile creeping onto his face and felt her cheeks flush crimson. He was joking.

'Don't worry—you're safe with us,' he chuckled, nudging her gently with an elbow.

But just as quickly as it had appeared his smile was retracted, as if a memory had snatched it back again. Something stopped Madeline asking any more questions, though a million were fizzing on her tongue.

'I *feel* safe with you,' she said instead, meaning it. 'How could anyone not?'

Ryan leaned back against the seat, and looked past her, out of the window again. 'You'll be safe with me as long as you're smart. It's no one's job but your own to protect yourself out here, Maddy. Can I call you Maddy?'

'Sure.'

'The Brazilian military uses these trips to gather intelligence sometimes, so if we have any guests you'll know they're on to something and it's a sign to be on high alert.'

'What do you mean?'

'Cocaine trafficking, illegal gold mining—it's all going on in these parts. There were reports of drug runners in the area not so long ago.'

'Drug runners?' Madeline whispered quietly. 'They wouldn't touch you, though, those sorts of people—would they? Especially not with a TV crew… That would just be drawing attention to themselves.'

Ryan shrugged, pouring a handful of peanuts into his big hand as the clouds fluttered past their window. 'You never know *what* they'll do, but let's just say our carefully made runways are as good for transporting illegal drugs as they are for shifting real medicine. You wouldn't want to see the wrong thing by mistake.'

'Do you ever get scared?'

He seemed to contemplate this for a moment, popping the nuts into his mouth, running a hand over his dark stubble. She studied his lips as he chewed. She'd bet he had a million women after him. She wondered if he'd ever asked anyone out who wasn't some sort of celebrity...

'I wouldn't say I never get anxious,' he replied eventually. 'But if we don't take these risks, Madeline... Maddy...we risk a lot worse. We risk thousands of people dying unnecessarily. Sick people take risks when they hear about us. They walk for days, even weeks, to get our help in these places. If we suddenly decide *we're* too afraid we're failing them and we're failing ourselves. You can write that down, too.'

Madeline put her pen back on her notepad, realising with dismay that her handwriting was worse than a child's.

'So, is there anyone you need to stay in touch with while we're away?' Ryan asked her. 'You know there's no signal in the Amazon? Rio might be your last chance to check in for a while.'

'I'm single. My boyfriend and I broke up,' she said, tucking her hair behind her ear and trying not to let the anger register in her voice.

She'd bypassed the emotional phase a couple of weeks ago and transitioned smoothly into fury—an emotion that reared its head like a lion whenever she thought of Adeline's face. She wished she hadn't checked out the other woman's Facebook page now. It was worse being able to picture her.

'He started seeing someone else while I was away

working on my last book. He didn't exactly stop once I got back.'

Ryan was silent. When she looked up he appeared to be fighting a smile.

'I'm sorry to hear that,' he said, straightening his face quickly. 'But I actually meant for this book—do you need to send things to your editor while you're away?'

'Oh.' Madeline's cheeks were on fire. She kicked herself internally. 'Not for a while,' she managed. 'I just have to make sure we get our interviews in—and I'll shadow you, if that's OK.'

'However you think it would work best,' he said, resting his arm on the armrest and brushing hers accidentally. She moved as far away from him as she could, crossing her legs away from him.

'I really am sorry about your boyfriend,' he said quietly. 'It hurts to lose someone you're close with, however you come to part ways.'

Madeline closed her eyes. Something in his voice spoke volumes of his own loss.

'These things happen for a reason,' she said, as firmly as she could manage. She picked up her pen again. 'It'll be interesting to see your work with my own eyes. I've watched most of your shows—you really do amazing things for people.'

'Thanks...we try.' He nodded appreciatively. 'You're a trained nurse, as I recall?'

Her heart sped up. 'Yes, well remembered.'

'Why did you quit?'

She opened her mouth to reply, but shut it again quickly. She found it hard to vocalise exactly what had happened. She'd thrown herself into her writing instead; it was what her counsellor had told her to do.

'It's OK—you don't have to tell me.' Ryan put a hand on top of hers for a moment.

Two seconds, maybe three, of skin-on-skin contact and her heart was a kangaroo. She yanked her hand back—maybe too quickly. What had happened in the hospital almost poured out of her, but she bit her tongue. He was a relative stranger. And she was in no mood to go into the details of her past life—that was what it felt like sometimes anyway.

For the next few hours Ryan plugged himself into an action movie and left her to read her book. She couldn't help the odd glance in his direction, just to confirm she wasn't dreaming. And she was almost entirely certain he was sneaking a few at *her*. The next few weeks accompanying him and his *Medical Extremes* team were going to be 'extreme', to say the least.

CHAPTER THREE

RYAN STUDIED HIS face in the mirror. He liked to think he didn't really suffer with jet lag any more, but the truth was he probably threw himself head-first into every new time zone without giving his body the chance to react. This mission was going to be a particularly tough one—not least because he'd have Madeline Savoia on his trail.

He rested his hands on the sink, leaned closer to the glass and frowned at his reflection. His eyes looked tired. Madeline had distracted him from sleeping on the plane.

She looked a lot like *her*. The first time she'd all but ploughed into him in the studio he'd almost jumped out of his skin. His reaction had been poor, he knew. Angry... The way he always acted when confronted with something he really had no clue how to handle. He'd felt as if he'd seen a ghost.

Josephine.

The name popped into his head like a gunshot. He swallowed hard, jerked the cold tap on and ran his hand under it. Then he said it out loud, straight into the mirror, watching his lips make their way over the word in a way they hadn't for a long time.'

'Josephine.'

He rarely let her name past his lips. Every time he so

much as thought of her the guilt crashed over him like a tsunami. It had smothered him and almost made him tumble when Madeline's hands had pressed against him to steady herself. She hadn't realised, of course, but she'd kind of been holding him up at the same time.

Ryan splashed his face with cold water. The more he tried not to think about this, the more he *did*. It was something about Madeline's eyes. And her pursed lips. And the way she'd crossed her arms defiantly over that coffee stain she'd clearly been so embarrassed about. The way she'd lowered her head just slightly when she'd asserted herself, indicating her vulnerability.

A knock on the hotel room door made him jump again. *Dammit*.

'I'm coming,' he called, wiping his face on the towel and running a hand through his hair. It was getting long at the front again. He frowned at the few stubborn greys now making a permanent home in his stubbled chin.

Nothing he could do about it.

Salt and pepper looks better on you than on my French fries.
#DrRyanTobias

A fan of his had tweeted that the other day. He mentally rolled his eyes—such gushing usually went straight over his head. He had quite enjoyed that French fries reference, though. He liked to think years of torment hadn't marked him physically…at least not as much as they had on the inside.

He threw on a white button-down shirt and pulled on his smartest jeans as the knock sounded out again. 'Give me one second!'

He hopped across the patterned carpet, still doing his belt up, and pulled the door open.

'What's the emergency?'

'No emergency.' Madeline smiled. Her hand was still hovering in the air, as if she was about to knock on his face. 'Sorry to interrupt. You said to knock before I went downstairs.'

'What time is it?' he asked, flustered.

He was totally thrown now. She looked entirely different somehow in this light, with her round, beguiling eyes lined with kohl and a hint of green eyeshadow. His hand found his hair again, at the same time as the other started buttoning up his shirt.

'Almost five thirty,' she told him, with her gaze now fixed on his exposed chest. 'Doesn't the drinks thing start now?'

'Yes, yes—sorry, I got caught up. There was an issue with the supplies being delivered to Saint Elena, and I've been on the phone trying to fix it.'

'Is it sorted out?'

'Almost. I did all I could.'

'OK. Well, don't worry, I'm sure we can sneak you in late without anyone noticing. It's not like you're a VIP or anything.'

Laughter burst from his mouth as he hurried back into the room to pull his shoes out of his suitcase. The dryness in her tone tickled him. He'd always found the British sense of humour quite fascinating.

He grabbed his key card and wallet, turned the bathroom light out and let his eyes travel over Madeline's petite yet curvy figure as he walked towards the door again. She was wearing another dress, an emerald-green one this time, tied around her waist with a paler green belt. Her hair was up now, in a French braid draped over one shoulder, and her lips were glistening in a shade of burgundy.

'Were you writing?' he asked, for want of something to fill the silence.

'In my room? A bit.'

He nodded. He'd fought the urge, on the journey, to ask her more about her books, aware that he'd perhaps been a little rude about her passion before. It was just that when Samantha had first mentioned a ghost-writer he'd imagined for some reason someone older, greyer, crinklier. Perhaps an avid cat-lover or crochet aficionado. He definitely hadn't imagined...well. *This*.

He cleared his throat. 'You look nice,' he said.

'Thank you—so do you.'

'So, you recognise me OK without the *Medical Extremes* outfit?' He smiled now.

'You're kind of hard to miss.'

'Is that right? I thought I'd been watching my weight.'

It was Madeline's turn to laugh now. 'As if you need to. I meant you have presence.'

Ryan realised that her cheeks were redder than they had been five seconds ago. He hadn't exactly intended to get himself dressed in front of her...but, then again, they *were* headed into the jungle. Tribal villages in the Amazon rainforest weren't exactly renowned for their privacy.

He stepped past her, closing the door behind him, then put a hand to the small of her back as they walked towards the elevators, noting her shoes—summer wedges with green straps.

'You're a little better at walking in those,' he said without thinking, pushing the button.

'That tripping over in public thing? That was a one-off—don't worry.'

'I'd only be worried in the Amazon,' he replied as the doors pinged and slid open. 'Big black cables on the floor of the jungle have a nasty habit of not being cables.'

She raised an eyebrow questioningly.

'Snakes,' he explained, and she pulled a face that made him chuckle.

In the elevator, Ryan fixed his eyes on their reflections in the full-length mirror. She was at least a foot shorter than him; that was shorter than— He clenched his fist. This was ridiculous. Madeline was not *her*.

He was determined to count the differences.

Some of her expressions were similar, sure, but Madeline had bigger eyes, wide and unnervingly quizzical— even more so now, framed with make-up. Her hair, long and dark and shiny, was the same...but she was slimmer, perhaps. He didn't know much about women's sizes, but he knew when he could hold a waist with both hands without leaving too much room between his fingers.

The elevator doors swung open. The music in the hotel foyer took the edge off his discomfort slightly as he guided Madeline towards the restaurant, past a crowd of tourists in matching floral shorts, speaking hurried German.

'I'm sure you've been briefed about this,' he said, trying to regain an air of authority if only for his own peace of mind.

'Not really.'

He frowned, looking down into her sea-green eyes, then cleared his throat again. 'Well, this is basically a getting-to-know-you event for the new people joining us and the suppliers. We also have a new cameraman from here in Rio, and a local paramedic. It's about building trust as a team before we get out there, you know? That's when the real work starts.'

'It's a good idea,' Madeline said. 'So I'll introduce myself as your ghost-writer?'

Ryan felt his brow crease. How had he forgotten her mission? He felt that tsunami again at the thoughts of having to regurgitate any of those moments he'd been trying his hardest to bury for so long—of seeing them laid bare on the pages of a book...a book he'd eventually see someday in a bargain bin, with the forgotten demons that would surely plague him for ever tossed aside by a reader who'd lapped them up and promptly let them go, in a way he never could.

His hand found his hair, swept it from his forehead. 'About this memoir... We need everyone to feel secure in the fact that our attention is fully on the patients. Our work always takes priority.'

'I know that.'

'You're there to write the memoir, of course, but we might need you to help out as a nurse from time to time—'

'I'd really rather not be a nurse while I'm here,' Madeline interrupted.

She paused halfway to the table, where he could see the team already waiting, chatting away. She looked nervous again now.

'Ryan, with all due respect, I didn't come here to—'

'Madeline, I get your current role, believe me, but people will be needing you out there. Do you really think, after everything you've trained for, that you could actually walk away from someone in pain?'

She opened her mouth to respond, but shut it again quickly. Annoyance was flickering in her eyes. He was concerned that this wasn't looking very professional; people were looking at them.

'It's going to be fine,' he whispered in her ear, getting

a whiff of her floral perfume as he did so. Dear God, she smelled good.

'Ryan, my man! Good to see you—and who's this?'

The tall, sandy-blond-haired guy approaching them in smart black trousers and a purple shirt was Evan Walker—a trusted friend and doctor from Wisconsin, and a firm voice of reason on the *Medical Extremes* team. Viewers loved him for his sense of humour and equally for his ability to take charge at a moment's notice. He had his own online fan club and was also popular because of his award-winning wife's efforts in setting up a domestic abuse helpline.

'Madeline Savoia is my ghost-writer…for the memoir,' Ryan said calmly as Madeline dutifully held out her hand. 'But she's a nurse, too. I've explained that it's all hands on deck at times.'

He felt her eyes burning his cheek as he spoke, but he didn't turn his head.

'Excellent,' Evan enthused, throwing him a look Ryan knew only he could read. Evan knew everything about Josephine. And he hadn't said a word.

'I'm a huge fan of your work, Dr Walker,' Madeline said.

'Thank you very much. So, have you been out to these parts before?'

A waiter approached and guided them all to their seats.

'No, I can't say I have,' she replied.

Ryan pulled a chair out for her and motioned for her to sit down beside him. He'd noticed the way Evan was looking at her now.

'You know, you really look a lot like…'

'What is there to drink?' Ryan put a hand up for the waiter and signalled for a menu.

Evan seemed to take the hint. He took his seat and started pouring the three of them water from a jug full of ice and lemon.

'You're in for a treat, Madeline,' he continued, 'these are some of the nicest people on the planet. Always so grateful and patient. It's harsh out there, you know?'

Madeline pulled her glass towards her. Ryan noticed her nails were drumming slightly on the glass. 'So I hear.'

'And they live pretty differently to how we do. Most have no idea that all this is even here, and even if they did they'd probably hate it.' He gestured around him now at the opulent restaurant, with Rio de Janeiro's Ipanema in their direct line of vision through the windows.

Ryan gazed out with Madeline at the swirling cormorants and emerald hills in the distance. The beautiful side of the jungle, he thought to himself, feeling a sudden twinge of familiar guilt.

He forced himself to think of something else.

He couldn't help but wonder yet again what the story was with Madeline quitting nursing. Whenever anyone brought it up she looked as though she might run for the hills. He kind of understood how that felt, though. He'd been running for years.

He'd hidden behind deadlines and responsibilities, creating more work for himself than one man should probably have to deal with in a lifetime. But now it had caught up with him in the form of this woman—sent to spill his secrets to the world.

He motioned to the waiter approaching with the wine. 'White, please,' he said. He turned to Madeline. 'You?'

'Red,' she said. 'Just a bit, though, I don't want to fall asleep at the table. I'm trying to outsmart my jet-lag.'

He smiled.

Evan was still talking. 'Last time we were here we helped a little baby—just nine months old, I think. She had a temperature of one hundred and two and climbing...and she wasn't getting enough oxygen. She had pneumonia...she was malnourished. If we hadn't been there...if *Ryan* hadn't been there...she would have been dead in two days.'

Madeline turned to him as a starter of fresh fruit was placed before her on the table, and he was surprised to notice the glistening of tears in her eyes at the mention of the baby.

Casual conversation about supply checks and sleeping arrangements at the camp kept them going as their starters were consumed and everyone's glasses were refilled, and then, just as the waiters hovered on the periphery with their main courses, Ryan tapped his fork on his glass to silence the table.

He rose to his feet, dropping his napkin.

'Ladies and gents,' he said, smoothing down his white shirt and holding up his glass. 'I'd like to thank you all for coming on this brand-new mission with *Medical Extremes*. Let's welcome Pablo, our new cameraman from right here in Rio, who'll be joining us where thousands wouldn't and hopefully not capturing *everything* on camera. No one looks their best after living on bananas and tropical rain for a few weeks.'

He paused for laughter, which flittered around the table as he'd known it would.

'I'd also like to introduce Madeline, here. She'll be working on some writing and lending a hand wherever possible, so I'd like you all to give her the *Medical Extremes* welcome we give everyone and make her feel like one of the family.'

He raised his glass higher, but before she or anyone

could say another word, a noise from the kitchen made the entire room jump in their chairs.

'Fogo! Fogo! Fogo!'

The voice was female.

'Help!'

Ryan just had time to see Evan grab his medical bag before they were both off their chairs in a flash, running for the kitchen. He made it to the back of the restaurant just in time to see the blaze of orange fire running up a woman's sleeve—just before he plunged her arm into a nearby sink, under a gushing tap. She was sobbing.

'What happened?' he asked, and was flooded with a stream of Portuguese. The fire was gone, but a crowd of people in white coats and chef's hats were all talking at once.

Evan was behind him, pulling out a sterile bandage from his bag as Ryan moved closer to keep the woman's arm under the water. It was blistered and red, but he could already tell she wasn't going to need hospital treatment—thank God.

'I'll go tell everyone not to panic—you got this?' Evan said.

'All good,' Ryan told him, and watched him shoot back through the door.

'She was pouring pecans into the chocolate mix when her sleeve caught on fire. That's why they're all over the floor.'

Madeline.

Ryan had only just realised she was there, too. She was holding the bandage Evan had given her and translating every word. He took the bandage from her, noticing the pecan nuts under his feet for the first time.

'She says she's worried the dessert is ruined. It's been cooking too long now without being stirred.'

Ryan listened as Madeline spoke in Portuguese to the crowd and someone moved to stir the pot she was pointing at. She reached for a clean dishcloth, soaked it under another tap and handed it to him. On autopilot Ryan placed it over the woman's arm for a moment, before wrapping the bandage around it and fastening it behind her wrist. Her tears were subsiding already and she really did seem more concerned about her dessert.

'Can you tell her I'll give her some ibuprofen, and that she should go home and get some rest?' he asked Madeline, who promptly did as she was asked.

Back at the table, when the ibuprofen had been dispatched and the drama was all but forgotten, the party resumed its happy chatter while the glorious Rio sunset made way for a sky full of stars.

'You were pretty impressive in there, Nurse Madeline,' he whispered, when he couldn't keep it in any more.

He hadn't been able to stop thinking about it—the way she'd sprung into action and known what to do, and say. His Portuguese was limited, as was his Spanish. He got by—but mostly on charm and miming, he had to admit.

'I didn't do anything,' she said quickly.

He frowned. 'Yes, you did. It was instinctive.'

She shrugged, clearly uncomfortable with his eyes on her. Her jaw started pulsing and he knew not to say anything else.

He also knew without question that keeping away from Madeline Savoia was going to be impossible. Not only was she impossibly intoxicating—whether she liked it or not—she wasn't just a writer.

If he had his way she'd be helping him with medical duties so frequently that the details she really needed for the memoir to be a hit would be the last thing on her mind.

CHAPTER FOUR

THERE WAS SOMETHING about Rio de Janeiro, Madeline decided, that was quite entrancing. The streets were alive with the sound of market stall fruit sellers, and tourists examined cheap patterned sarongs and vibrant paintings of ladies dancing under starry spangled skies. The smell of coconuts and sunscreen permeated the air, and she'd seen more thongs, she mused, in the space of twenty minutes than she'd seen in twenty branches of her favourite high street store back in London.

Madeline had been wandering around in the sunshine for a couple of hours alone, trying to get some last-minute bits and pieces before they were due to catch the plane to Saint Elena at six p.m. The rush of the ocean in her ears as she strolled along the mosaic-riddled promenade, coupled with the whoosh of rollerblades, was like a musical symphony. It was hard to believe that just twenty-four hours ago she'd been climbing out of a black cab in the awful London rain.

Madeline was grateful for this time to herself while Ryan rushed about filming another segment for *Medical Extremes*.

'Go enjoy yourself in the sunshine,' he'd said that morning at breakfast. 'And don't forget Sugar Loaf Mountain.'

She wasn't sure she had the energy for Sugar Loaf.

They'd stayed around the table till the early hours last night, discussing the mission they were about to undertake, and perhaps, on reflection, she'd enjoyed a bit too much wine after that incident in the kitchen.

She'd noticed that Ryan had stopped at one glass, and she remembered reading somewhere that Ryan didn't drink much. Something about never knowing when he might need to help someone. She smiled, remembering the look on his face in the kitchen. He hadn't realised she was fluent in Portuguese. Then again, how *would* he have known?

What Ryan had said about her actions being instinctive had been playing on her mind. She'd told herself a million times that her nursing days were over, but he was right. Someone had really needed her and she hadn't been able to turn those instincts off at all.

'Mango!' a fruit seller was calling from her tiny stall.

Madeline shook her head politely. She'd avoided eye contact with Ryan all night after that. She knew without him saying another word that he was planning to demand her nursing skills in the Amazon.

'Pineapple?' another fruit seller called out as she turned another corner.

She smiled once again, holding up the plastic bag of fruit skewers she'd bought earlier.

Ryan had escorted her up to her room at around two a.m. By then she'd been almost asleep on her feet. She'd been acutely aware of his hand on her lower back over her dress as they'd left the dining room, and the sound of him clearing his throat in the elevator as he'd pressed himself against the wall opposite her. She'd felt his eyes on her in the mirror.

She'd pondered at the time that he might be trying to

stand as far away from her as possible in the enclosed space. She'd been doing exactly the same thing.

'Try to sleep in if you can in the morning,' he'd said, stopping with her outside her room. 'It might be the best sleep you'll get for a few weeks. The sleeping arrangements won't be up to this standard in the jungle. But I'm sure you've probably figured that out.'

'I'm looking forward to it,' she'd said, trying to sound as if she meant it. 'Thank you for tonight.'

'Thank *you*,' he'd replied softly.

'We should pencil in some time for us to talk. I was thinking regular slots, maybe one every day…'

'Let me see what I can do once we're out there,' he'd said, cutting her off quickly. 'I mean, of course we have to get this memoir written, but things are going to be really hectic for the first few days at least.'

He'd been looking at the doorframe as he'd said that—not once at her.

'I'll see you tomorrow,' he'd told her, and with that he'd leaned in and dropped a quick kiss on her cheek.

It had been as soft as a moth landing on a shadow. She'd felt the brush of his stubble on her skin, caught a whiff of his cologne. Then he'd turned on his heel and Madeline had watched his undeniably sculpted butt in his jeans as he'd walked the whole way back down the corridor and turned the corner.

For the first time in months, with questions she wanted to ask this mysterious doctor galloping maddeningly through her thoughts along with jet-lag, Madeline had eventually drifted off to sleep without thinking once about her ex. She was grateful for that at least.

Armed with sunscreen and mosquito repellent, plus a new bright yellow sarong and several colouring books and sets of crayons for the children she'd inevitably meet in the Amazon, Madeline reached the hotel again at four p.m.

She'd just arrived back in her room and was planning on changing, packing and heading down to find the team, when a knock on the door made her jump. She went to open it in bare feet, expecting someone from Housekeeping. Her insides performed an impressive somersault as she came face to face with Ryan.

'Hi. Everything OK?' she asked, clutching the doorframe and hoping she didn't look terrible.

'We're still waiting on some of the ultrasound equipment we lost track of yesterday,' he said.

She ran her eyes quickly over his blue denim shirt. The sleeves were rolled up over his tanned forearms and his practical, multi-pocketed khaki trousers made her smile. It was still a surreal dream, being face to face with this man.

She didn't miss him looking her up and down in return, in her knee-length, red strapless sundress. She hoped she hadn't dropped any fruit on it.

'Some of it's already halfway here, so unfortunately it means I'll have to stay another night.'

'Just you?'

'It only needs one of us to wait. The rest of the team will leave today and set up camp as planned. I was just wondering if...'

He trailed off for a second, seeming to contemplate his words. She detected the slightest trace of hesitation.

'I was wondering if you wanted to stay with me? I realise I've been a bit...well, aloof about this whole memoir thing, but I do appreciate you have a job to do. Maybe we can get to know each other a bit better over dinner. If you like. Just us this time.'

Just us this time.

Madeline stood up straighter. 'Yes,' she said quickly. 'I think that would be a good idea—before things get too crazy. Good thinking. I have some questions prepared that will help me get a good head start. I'll think up some more. What time should I meet you?'

She hoped she was sounding professional in this moment, because even as she spoke she was mentally unpacking her suitcase, looking for the right thing to wear to dinner.

Ryan shifted his weight onto his opposite foot and folded his arms. 'I was thinking we'd get out of the hotel. I know a restaurant nearby that does great tapas.'

'My favourite. Huge fan of olives.'

He nodded. 'Good. Shall we say seven in the lobby?'

'Seven it is.'

'Great. Well…' He paused again, uncrossed his arms and let out a long, almost relieved sigh. 'I'll see you then, Maddy.'

She shut the door after him, turning back to her room in a panic. She had precisely three hours to prepare a set of questions that wouldn't make Ryan Tobias fear talking to her about the details they both knew she needed, and in that little time she had to make herself look worthy enough to be out in a restaurant with the world's most famous flying doctor.

She rammed her hands through her hair again.

By the time seven p.m. rolled around Madeline was more or less satisfied that she looked OK. She'd opted for her second-favourite green dress—a casual maxi-dress that plunged at the neck in a V without revealing too much. She'd paired it with a long beaded necklace and left her hair loose around her shoulders. Silver-strapped flat sandals completed the outfit, and a hint of peach lip-gloss made her mouth shimmer in a way she hoped made them look plumper, too.

Gathering her green and silver sequined purse, she put her notebook and pen inside and took one last deep breath before reaching for the door.

Ryan was already waiting for her in the lobby. She felt as if the jet set of the insect world was throwing a party in her stomach as she approached him. She hated being starstruck—if that was what this feeling was. But at least it was taking her mind off her break-up.

'Green is definitely your colour,' he said.

His smile reached his eyes and she could tell it was genuine.

'Thank you.'

Ryan was still wearing his khaki trousers, but had chosen another white button-down shirt that highlighted his broad chest and deep bronze tan. The kind of tan only a travelling man had, she mused in appreciation.

Madeline caught his eyes lingering for a split second on the hint of cleavage she knew she was displaying behind her beads, but instead of feeling self-conscious she realised she was feeling quite empowered.

'Let's go,' Ryan said, patting his flat stomach. 'I'm famished.'

They walked outside together, through the hotel's revolving doors and into the balmy night. The breeze picked up her long hair and tousled it about her shoulders as she walked alongside him.

'Any more news on the supplies arriving?' she asked.

'First thing in the morning, so they said. We'll fly at two p.m.'

They passed a shirtless guitar player on the street—a beaming guy with huge, chunky dreadlocks. Ryan pulled some notes out of his pocket and dropped them into his upturned hat. The guy's hands stopped moving instantly on the guitar frets and his eyes widened at what was clearly a significant amount of money, but Ryan didn't stop.

The palm trees swayed rhythmically to their own calypso as they walked along the street. Tourists strolling towards similar reservations were either hand in hand or holding selfie sticks between them, taking photos. She thought back to her friend Emma's gushing email that morning, posing a million questions and demands of what she wanted Madeline to ask Ryan.

Are you single? seemed to be top of her list.

They were welcomed into the restaurant by a beaming waitress the size of a toothpick, who flicked her long, styled auburn hair over her shoulder as she raked over Ryan with eyes as wide as Bambi's.

'I hope this will be OK for you, sir,' she gushed in a thick Portuguese accent as they were led outside to a table on the terrace. She made a big fuss over arranging Ryan's napkin on his lap.

'Fine, thank you,' he replied, seemingly oblivious to the batting eyelashes an inch from his chest.

Ryan took the wine list. A candle flickered in the middle of the table in a mason jar and Madeline studied his famous face, now bathed in a soft, flattering glow in a way she rarely saw on the television. The surgery lights were always so harsh.

She placed her purse under her feet, careful to keep the strap around her knee. She'd been caught out once by a bag-snatcher in Peru, and these days she was disappointingly quick to suspect passing strangers of crimes they probably had no intention of committing.

All around them people were chatting and laughing amongst themselves and Ryan leaned back in his seat.

'Drink?' he asked. 'You might not get the chance again for a while. They don't have much in the way of vintage wine in the Amazon. How about a cocktail?'

'If you're having one,' she said. 'Or maybe just a gin and tonic?'

'Great idea—make that two, please,' he told the waitress, handing back the drinks menu.

'Coming up. I'll be back to take your food order, Dr Ryan.'

She tottered off on her high heels, and Madeline watched as Ryan took his phone out of his pocket and flipped it to 'silent'.

'Is it not weird that everyone knows who you are?' she asked. 'We're in *Rio*!'

He put his phone back and folded his arms in front of him on the table, unwittingly causing his biceps to bulge in his shirt. 'It's less weird than annoying.'

'I read somewhere that you hardly ever drink,' she followed up, training her eyes away from his biceps.

'That's true. I usually stop at one.'

'In case somebody needs your help and you need to focus?'

He grinned, thumbing the corner of the menu. 'Did you read that online?'

'Maybe.'

'I don't really drink because I choose not to. I guess that's not exciting enough for some people. Anything you don't eat?'

Madeline liked the way he was talking to her. It was *easy*, somehow. She wondered what he'd been like before fame...whether he was different now.

She thought about his question. 'Just coriander. I think you call it cilantro where you're from.'

He smiled. 'Can't stand it either. Tastes like old books.'

'I think it tastes like metal pipes.'

'You've licked a metal pipe?'

'Maybe.'

He was laughing now—she could see his shoulders shaking. 'Well, *there's* a way to start the memoir. *I don't like cilantro and I refuse to dine with people who do—especially if they lick metal pipes, too.*'

She shook her head, laughing with him. 'It has bestseller written all over it.'

They ordered a selection of dishes, and as they chatted idly she scribbled a few notes about his childhood, memories of the years he spent in Chicago looking up to his ambitious yet workaholic father.

'Do you have any siblings?' she asked.

His mouth twitched towards a smile. 'I thought all the basics were on the internet?'

'Some of them, yes, but I'd still prefer to hear it firsthand, from you,' she replied. 'As we've already discovered, people stretch the truth a lot.' She crossed her legs under the table. 'Have you ever looked yourself up on the internet?'

He nodded slowly. 'But it wasn't my smartest move.'

'Why not?'

He pulled a face, leaned back in his seat and turned his glass on the checked tablecloth. '"As we've already discovered, people stretch the truth a lot",' he mimicked. 'But some truths you read and you wish you hadn't.'

'Like messages from your boyfriend to his other woman,' Madeline followed, without even thinking.

She felt her cheeks flush instantly. *Stupid gin*.

When she looked up Ryan was looking at her, his

eyes dark now…in shadow. 'Sorry,' she said. 'Still raw, I suppose.'

'Were you together a long time?'

She couldn't look at him now. 'Four years. I thought he was about to propose.'

He exhaled through his nose. 'Damn.'

'To be honest, I haven't had time to think about him since I found out I was coming on this trip. I think I just need to keep busy.'

'Keeping busy helps.'

His tone made her lift her head. As he shifted in his chair she caught that look in his eyes again: a slow burning that unnerved her. Madeline wondered if she should just ask him outright whether he was ready to set the record straight about his team member Josephine McCarthy, but she was forced to close her mouth when the chirpy waitress tottered back over with the first few plates of tapas.

Ryan gestured for Madeline to serve herself a helping of *patatas bravas* and skilfully steered the conversation back to his siblings—one older brother called David, who'd moved to New York and married an art curator, and a younger sister called Monica, who was studying dentistry. Madeline had the feeling Ryan wouldn't be spilling any of his own secrets as quickly as *she'd* just done, even if she asked him outright. Especially not now.

She popped an olive into her mouth. No matter how difficult the mission ahead of her, she refused to be deterred. To think this time last week she'd been wondering how on earth she was going to raise the money she needed to re-do her bathroom. Who knew ghostwriting a book while in the Amazon would wind up paying more than she'd ever earned by putting her own book up on the *other* Amazon?

All she had to do was stay focussed.

CHAPTER FIVE

PILLAR-BOX-RED SUITED Madeline's nails, Ryan thought—although it was going to be pretty damn hard for her to keep any element of her beauty regime going once they got to camp. He'd never let on, but the shine of her hair was also likely to be dulled after a few days of washing it in murky pond water.

He'd felt for her when she'd mentioned her ex. While she amused him with her quirky comebacks, the stabs of pain he sensed in her with certain sentences had an effect on his heart. It seemed that for all of Madeline's bravado in public she was a tiny bit broken.

Not unlike me, he thought with a weary smile.

'So, when did you know you wanted to be a doctor?' she was asking him now.

He leaned further towards her, saw the candle flame between them flickering in her pupils. 'I think I was born knowing I would be.'

'Really? Care to elaborate?'

'Not much—but something tells me I'll have to.'

Madeline raised her eyebrows, putting her pen to her lips. Ryan replied to her questions in as much detail as he could, helping himself to more chorizo and making sure to keep Madeline's plate topped up with her share of the food as she made notes.

He wasn't entirely certain she had the right idea about the food they'd be getting once they reached camp; he didn't know if she had any clue that they'd be on rice, bananas and, if they were lucky, fish the entire time. Either way, he was determined to have them both eat as much as possible now.

He told her how his brother's love of art and the metaphysical had led *him* only to contemplate a career in the physical, and yet the same empathetic streak still rendered them closer to each other than either of them was with their sister.

He explained the cluttered corners of their large family home—the way his mother had diligently cleaned while silently resenting the fact that she had to before wealth arrived and saw to it that she could hire a cleaner—a dumpy, smiley Mexican lady called Rose, who had always jangled with keys and tiny candies for the kids wrapped in foil.

He told her how his mother hoarded books of every genre, and always had a jigsaw puzzle on the go.

'Hmm… I see… I think this would be good in more depth,' Madeline would mutter every now and then. 'Tell me more about your backyard? What trees and flowers grew there in summer? Did you spend much time outdoors?'

He talked and talked, encouraged by her encouragement, until the waitress brought a brand-new candle to replace the one that had sizzled right down to a waxed lump in its jar.

While Ryan was putting on what he thought looked like a pretty good show of wanting to get to work on the memoir, it was really just for Madeline. If Madeline Savoia had turned out to be the crinkly old cat lady of his imaginings he doubted he would have been so accommodating. He definitely wouldn't have been sitting here, opposite her, spilling his family history in a Rio restaurant.

He would have emailed his thoughts in a string of misspelled sentences, probably—last-minute musings thrown together after she had reminded him a hundred times that he was supposed to be helping her. He would have barely seen her, and she'd have sat alone in her room, or in the lobby, drinking coffee and working on her crochet, perhaps.

He'd been selfish with his admissions, with his heart, for years. To the world Ryan was a giving man, generous and kind, but inside he was a tangled mass of secrets that he'd do anything to protect. When they got to the jungle he knew he'd have to remember to keep her busy. He had a feeling she already knew that was his plan. Still, he wouldn't crack.

He wouldn't talk about Josephine.

When the dessert menu arrived she was asking him about his relationship with his mother.

'Mary Tobias, sixty-seven, now married to the ex-head of the Department of Genetic Research and Bioinformatics in Oslo. Is that right?'

'Correct.' He nodded, then ordered a cappuccino from the too-skinny waitress who'd been orbiting them like a satellite since the second they'd arrived.

Even before the television fame and camera crews he'd had no problem attracting attention from the opposite sex, but he'd learnt to be discerning over the years. There had been way too many photographs and way too many tweets.

'Coffee?' he asked Madeline, ignoring the way the waitress was hovering a little too close to him yet again, with her apron ties practically dangling over his shoulder.

'Flat white, please, no sugar,' Madeline said, still scribbling furiously. 'So she still lives in Norway?'

'They travel back and forth. She's good friends with my father, thank God,' he said. 'They're better apart—they were both so driven, so ambitious, they never managed to head anywhere in the same direction. You can write that down.'

'I am. Do you think you're more like your mother or your father?'

He contemplated this, amused at the way she bit her lip or frowned as the sentences took shape beneath her pretty fingers. She was a woman who took great care and interest in what she did—he could tell that already. He wondered if she'd been the same as a nurse and almost brought it up. He decided not to.

'I guess I have my father's drive to help others, and my mother's ambition to see the world,' he said thoughtfully. 'Thankfully I've forged a career that lets me do both.'

'A very successful one,' she followed up. 'Tell me more about your team. How do you choose who comes with you on your missions? Would you say you're as close in reality as you seem on screen?'

He reached out quickly, took the pen from her hand and placed it on top of her notebook. She looked up, surprised.

'I don't think we're there yet, are we?' He held her gaze. He couldn't help notice how she flinched.

'Sorry.'

'I thought we'd go over things in chronological order—my youth, my family, college... Don't you want to hear about my days in the acapella club?'

Her eyes narrowed in amusement. 'Seriously? *That's* not on your Wikipedia page.'

'Of course that's not online. If it was, everyone would be asking me to sing. My job is to save lives—not to kill people.'

She picked up her pen again. 'I'm sure you're not that bad.'

'Let's just say you can worm your way into a lot of things on looks alone. It was a pretty short-lived experience anyway. I only joined because I had it bad for one of the girls in the group.'

'So you were this handsome in college, too?'

She flushed as she said it, hiding her face behind her hair for a moment, and he did his best to hide his smile. He'd noticed the way she'd been sneaking glances at him, maybe a little starstruck herself. Although he had to admit she was a lot more subtle than a lot of people.

When their coffees arrived he sipped at the hot foam, breathing an internal sigh of relief that he'd diverted her most prying questions and potentially bought himself some time to decide exactly how he was going to keep diverting them once they came around to the elephant in the room. *Could* he get away with a memoir that didn't mention Josephine?

Of course he'd been anticipating questions about her, and he knew he couldn't stop this memoir being written altogether. He didn't have to bare his soul completely, though, did he? He'd kept things light—telling her all about the blonde-haired soprano he'd followed about campus like a puppy dog, before she'd hooked up with the tenor and broke his tone-deaf heart.

By the time they got back to the hotel it was gone eleven p.m., and thankfully Madeline seemed content that her writing was off to a good start. He walked her to her room. The door clicked open at the swipe of her key card and she turned to him.

'Thank you, Ryan, for tonight. It was…fun.'

He kept his hands in his pockets. In this light she looked *less* like Josephine. In fact, with her unique style, Madeline had been morphing since yesterday into her own skin right in front of him. It was getting easier to be around her in that respect…and when their conversation was under control she was easy to talk to, too. She was also incredibly, magnetically beautiful. It wouldn't have taken much to let all his professionalism fly out of the window.

Just for one night.

He cleared his throat. 'It was my pleasure. I doubt we'll get as much one-on-one time once we're at camp.'

He noticed she looked despondent.

'We'll get the job done,' he added, 'and who knows? Maybe you'll have the chance to dust off your nursing skills again.'

'I don't think that will be happening,' she said, clutching at the beads around her neck.

He saw a flicker of a warning in her green eyes—the kind he was already getting to know.

'I know you think it will, but it won't. I'm here solely for the memoir, OK?'

'OK.'

Madeline stepped into her room, turning to face him again in the doorway. He could see her bed, all made up behind her. He rooted his feet to the floor, dug his hands deeper into his pockets.

'Anyway,' she said, 'thank you for dinner.'

'You're more than welcome. It *was* fun. I have to say you make for excellent company, Maddy Savoia, even if you do ask a lot of questions.'

'There are a lot more I *could* ask,' she said, pursing

her glossed lips for a second. 'But I have a feeling you're going to make me work for it.'

'It's no fun otherwise.'

He leaned in to drop a kiss on her cheek. He was about to tuck a few stray strands of hair behind her ear when Madeline stepped back from him, putting the doorframe between them.

'Goodnight,' she said curtly, and shut the door.

CHAPTER SIX

THE JUNGLE STRETCHED below them like a deep green blanket and Madeline could imagine a million pairs of eyes on their helicopter—from monkeys to jaguars, bats, rats and snakes, all plotting to lure them in and keep them.

'How are you feeling?' Ryan asked from his seat next to hers.

She turned her head away from the window, her lips a thin line. He put a hand to her arm to reassure her, and she was grateful for his presence. He was dressed in a light blue shirt with the *Medical Extremes* logo on the right pocket and another pair of khakis. She was dressed the same, all the clothes given to her by the producer—only *her* shirt was a tight-fitting tank top.

'You're looking like part of the crew already,' Ryan said loudly over the whir of the blades. 'Are you ready for some flying doctor Amazon action?'

'I don't know how to answer that,' she said honestly, noting the way his hair was sticking out adorably from the sides of his baseball hat. She clutched hard at the notebook on her lap under her seatbelt. Her hair was a mess and she'd long since given up trying to tame the flyaway strands that kept escaping from her ponytail.

She assumed she should probably get used to looking dishevelled from this point on.

The flight from Rio to Saint Elena had been fine, but the helicopter now juddering towards the camp was an entirely different story. It was only the second time she'd ridden in one. Jason had taken her on a surprise flight over Manhattan the first time they'd been to New York together, complete with champagne.

Her fingers found the apple on its chain around her neck—a present from her ex on that trip. This helicopter had zero champagne. The box of ultrasound equipment sat strapped in place beside Ryan's feet, and various packages, bags and boxes took up every other inch of space. There was even a box or two of bananas and another labelled 'solar power'.

'Chargers—so we can do it nature's way,' Ryan explained, seeing her studying them. 'We use the sun instead of batteries for a lot of things now...except our phones. Like I said, not much signal out here. Did you make your last-minute calls?'

'A couple,' she said, remembering the one she'd had to make to her insurance company, and also the one she'd sneaked to Emma, during which she'd told her all about the pair of them out in Rio, eating olives and talking about the intricacies of Ryan's childhood.

Emma had squealed so loudly down the phone Madeline had been left with a partially deaf ear for ten minutes.

'But, Maddy, is he *single*?'

'I don't know,' she'd had to admit.

Madeline still felt weird around Ryan. He didn't seem as if he was in a relationship. There had been a moment just before she'd left him lingering in her doorway when she'd suddenly panicked that he was going to kiss her—

and not just on the cheek this time. She'd moved away from his face as if she'd been dodging a baseball. It made her hot, just remembering.

But even if they had been flirting a little over dinner there was no way in hell she was about to become another one of his adoring female fans and start looking at him the way that waitress had. Besides, she hadn't kissed anyone like that...like Ryan Tobias...ever.

'We don't just eat those—don't worry—but I'm afraid there won't be too many tapas restaurants...'

'What?' Madeline blinked.

Ryan was still talking. He leaned in closer...so close his nose almost brushed hers as she turned.

'The bananas. Sorry, it's tough to hear over the blades, right?'

'Oh, yeah, a bit. Don't you ever fly these things yourself? I thought I saw you in the pilot's seat in one episode.'

'Sometimes—for kicks,' he said, leaning his head back against the headrest. 'I have my licence, but I prefer to let the professionals do their thing while I do mine.'

'I see.'

'Have you ever flown a plane, Miss City Girl?' he asked, cocking an eyebrow.

'Lots of times! My brother had a radio controlled one. It worked pretty well until he crashed it into a tree in Hyde Park.'

He closed his eyes, faking disparagement. 'Crazy Brits,' he muttered.

But she didn't miss his smile, nor the dimples that had taken to appearing more each time they talked.

At first Madeline had felt like a celebrity, being ushered on board the flight with Ryan Tobias. The new cameraman she'd met at that first dinner at the hotel had followed them, watching every move Ryan made through his viewfinder, his eyes shielded by the rim of his own *Medical Extremes* baseball hat.

She still didn't know how she felt about appearing on camera throughout this mission, but the producer had assured her they wouldn't be making a feature of her. She wouldn't have to talk like the rest of the team, and if she appeared in the show at all she'd appear in the background. All of which went some way towards comforting her, she supposed.

'What do you think of the view from up here?' he asked her. 'Better than Hyde Park?'

A rush of wind ruffled the trees below them like a Mexican Wave as they watched the shadow of the helicopter move like a black eclipse on the canopy.

'It's amazing...' she breathed.

Madeline had seen the rainforest before—in Costa Rica. A very handsome man called Ricardo had dared to capture a poisonous red tree frog, which he'd located by following the sound of its distinct croak. He'd held it in his hands to demonstrate that such frogs were only poisonous at certain times of the year, when they'd eaten a toxic kind of ant.

She'd been fascinated as they'd walked on rope bridges, stretching into the air from lush tree to tree at howler monkey height. She'd felt relatively safe there, above the jungle floor with an experienced guide. Here, however, with an infinite ocean of green treetops disguising what she was sure were a thousand death traps, she was having trouble stopping her stomach from knotting—and they hadn't even landed yet.

'We're heading in, boss,' the pilot called over his shoulder after a few minutes, and when Madeline turned to the window at her side she could finally see a clearing.

They flew in closer. Ryan placed a foot on the box closest to him to stop it moving. Madeline could make out what looked like a thin, long pathway, and two long boats waiting on the murky brown coloured river nearby. The pilot was talking to someone on the ground on the radio, and as the sound of the blades increased her hair whipped up into what she knew with utter certainty would be a mass of unmanageable knots and tangles.

The landing strip was in clear sight now. Two men in knee-length shorts and sleeveless T-shirts were running towards them as Madeline held her hair back out of her face. Three minutes later they were bumping onto the ground in the clearing, gliding to a stop, and Ryan was leaning over her, impossibly close, undoing her seatbelt.

'Home sweet home,' he said.

She watched his big hands on her seatbelt. Her heart-rate spiked even further and she held her breath as her insides tangled like her hair.

One of the men on the ground helped her out of the helicopter with the backpack she'd been given for the trip. It held considerably less than her suitcase. The other man walked with her quickly across uneven ground covered in mud and grass towards the murky-looking water. The swish of the helicopter blades created a welcome fan, but already Madeline could feel the heat closing in on her.

'Sólo tiene que esperar aquí, por favor,' another guy said to her, helping her onto a small boat on the river.

A local, Madeline noted, seeing the black swirling tattoo which stretched all the way up the inside of one arm. He was looking up at the sky.

She replied that, yes, she would wait right there, but when she turned around on her seat she saw Ryan with the pilot, another cameraman she'd been introduced to as Jake and the other man who'd been waiting for them, all lifting each box from the helicopter through a haze of heat wafting up from the ground.

She stepped out of the boat again, walking back towards them. 'Here—I can take those,' she offered, and the pilot shrugged, handing her a box of bananas.

Back at the boat she apologised to the local man whose command she'd disregarded, placed the box carefully to the floor and held her arms out for another, and then another, ignoring the beads of sweat that had started to trickle from her temples.

She didn't miss the look of approval Ryan threw in her direction as he fastened a radio to his belt, but neither did she miss the mosquitoes that were gorging themselves on her blood already.

She put the last box of supplies inside the boat and slapped at the top of her arm as Ryan climbed in beside her.

'You might want to get the DEET out,' he said. 'I trust you've been taking the malaria pills you were given?'

'For three days already—yes, sir.' She reached for the pocket of her backpack. 'Need some?'

Ryan shook his head as she sprayed her arms. 'They don't touch me any more. My blood's not sweet enough.'

She raised her eyebrows. Ryan was sweating, too, but it made *him* look sexy. He lifted the hat he was wearing and swiped at his forehead before stepping to the front of the boat. She realised she'd always loved seeing him all sweaty on the show, and then rolled her eyes at herself. Behind her, the last of the other boxes was being piled into the second boat.

'How far is it to the camp?' she asked, spraying her legs, then shoving the DEET back into her backpack.

'Not far.'

Ryan climbed back over the bench seats to sit beside her. A guy with a long pole stepped on and pushed off from the riverbank with it, quickly leaving the helicopter behind. Madeline couldn't shake the growing sense of apprehension coiling around her like a python. They were literally in the middle of nowhere.

'We need to get to camp soon—that storm's coming fast,' Ryan said beside her.

He was looking at the sky. In the sunlight his eyes were shining under his *Medical Extremes* baseball hat, but she noticed a thick black cloud on the periphery of her vision that definitely hadn't been there when they'd landed.

'I hope the helicopter gets out in time.' He leaned back to rest his elbows on the bench behind them. 'Can you hear that?'

'Hear what?'

'The jungle talking. Gets louder when a storm's on the horizon—they sense it. The insects and the birds… the cicadas and the frogs. The usual volume is loud enough—it sends me to sleep like a lullaby—but I wouldn't trust any of it for a second. Remember what I told you before?'

'I remember. No wandering off on my own.'

'Not even when it looks and seems like the most idyllic place in the world. Promise me?'

She touched a hand lightly to his arm. 'Trust me, I don't want to get eaten by a snake any more than you do. I promise you.'

And then lightning struck somewhere inside her as he took her hand and squeezed her fingers.

'Good,' he said.

His radio made a sound. Madeline watched more insects swirling around them as he dropped her hand and pulled the radio from his belt.

Evan's voice sounded out in the boat. 'How close are you to our dock?'

'Five…ten minutes—what's going on?'

'Emergency—fast as you can. I've called the helicopter back,' came the reply.

CHAPTER SEVEN

THE DOCK WAS a flurry of action as it came into view through the trees. Ryan stood up as the boat drew closer and waved at Evan. He was standing on the edge of the water, supervising the scene. The sky was a dark chalky grey and the wind was raging. The weather could change in a heartbeat in the rainforest—he knew that well—but the timing of this particular storm was supremely unlucky.

'Will we be able to help her?' Madeline asked from behind him.

She'd obviously overheard what Evan had said about a local lady who'd been hurt. She'd been stepping into a boat with a heavy bag of fruit when she'd slipped and hit the metal stairs of the dock with such force that she could no longer move. She needed to be taken to a hospital.

'I hope so,' Ryan told her as their boat pulled up alongside the grassy bank and several guys from the village and the camp helped to pull them in. He felt the rain start to spit on his arms.

'She's still in a lot of pain,' Evan said as Ryan jumped onto the bank.

He ran to the next boat with him and stepped carefully down to go alongside the woman. She looked to be in her fifties, pale and trembling with pain. A man, possibly her husband, was holding her hand beside the makeshift stretcher, looking equally pale. Another of Ryan's volunteers was holding her head and neck in place.

'We've stabilised her. The helicopter can't get to us yet—the wind is too strong.' Evan crouched down beside him. 'We're hoping it's not a herniated disc.'

'Can she feel her legs?' Ryan reached for the woman's other hand. 'I'm here…you're going to be OK,' he told her, before remembering that she probably only understood Spanish. He said it again in broken Spanish and she nodded, then howled out in pain.

'She can feel them, but she says she feels tingling, which isn't good. We've given her some anti-inflammatories, but we don't have any ice.'

'She'll need an MRI,' Ryan said, as the wind screamed like a banshee in his ears.

He was already having flashbacks to what had happened in Patagonia, when the aircraft hadn't been able to take off or land in the storm. He knew Evan probably was, too.

Before he knew it Madeline was stepping down beside him, carrying something—a plastic sheet from their boat. She handed him one corner, motioning for him to make a cover with it to put over the woman.

'Thank you,' he said, moving fast to tie it up.

Madeline took the other end, just as a cameraman appeared from nowhere and started capturing their every move.

'This rain's going to get worse,' he said.

'Can I do anything else?' she asked, as he watched a huge raindrop cruise down her nose.

'You can round up all these spectators and get them out of here,' Evan replied, pointing at the crowd, still watching, all agog. 'We need everyone out of here so the helicopter can land.'

As he spoke, the wind picked up yet another notch and rocked the boat, but Madeline was already climbing back up to the riverbank, calling out in Spanish.

'Is there any language she can't speak?' Evan said to Ryan, half laughing in spite of the situation. Ryan shrugged, but inside he was reeling. So much for the nurse who didn't want to be a nurse.

Evan's radio buzzed again. Ryan glanced up at Madeline, now herding people out of the clearing. He could see some of his crew moving quickly to help her. She didn't seem particularly fazed that they'd only just arrived in the middle of nowhere and a first-class storm was building up strength around them.

'The helicopter's managed to take off,' Evan said in relief. 'We'll have to take her to Manaus—it's the closest.'

A tree creaked close by in the wind and Ryan felt the woman grabbing his hand even harder as she wailed again. She was in so much pain but there was nothing more they could do right now. She needed ice—which they didn't have—and it was important to keep her conscious, so she could recount what she was and wasn't feeling. He prayed to God it wasn't a herniated disc, or worse.

Eventually the helicopter whirred into sight, scattering the leaves on the ground around them. Thunder crashed in the distance, and then came even closer, almost drowning out the noise of the blades. Ryan looked on in dismay as he realised it might be too windy for it to land.

Madeline was running towards them again now and his heart lurched at the sight. 'Get out of the way!' he yelled at her, realising how unsteady in the sky the helicopter was.

But Madeline was still running—right underneath it. His heart almost stopped as the helicopter lurched and then lifted again. She reached them, panting. She was soaked through, but was holding some cushions from the camp. Ryan grabbed her arm, pulling her into the boat, under the plastic shelter they'd created.

'What were you *doing*?'

'She'll need these—there was nothing else around here that I could see…'

'I said don't do anything stupid—weren't you listening?' His hand was still around her arm as the helicopter finally descended in the clearing behind them.

Her eyes were wide, incredulous. 'It wasn't anywhere near me! The pilot saw me!'

'Goddammit, Maddy.'

'I'm *helping* you! I thought that was what you wanted?'

'She is helping us,' Evan confirmed, before motioning to the volunteer and Ryan to help him lift the stretcher carefully out from under the shelter.

It was very humid and the thunder crashed again, just after a bolt of lightning lit up the sky. The pilot turned off the engine.

Ryan dropped Madeline's arm. 'Let's go!' he yelled at Evan, and together they moved as quickly and smoothly as they could, while the woman continued to moan, wail and whimper.

Madeline was with them, speaking in quick Spanish, trying to comfort her, hurrying beside them in the rain.

They were all but drowned rats by the time they made it to the helicopter, but Ryan noticed Madeline didn't flinch or look away from the woman once. They loaded her and her husband into the back of the helicopter in the thrashing rain, taking one seat out in order to make the stretcher fit.

'Are you OK to go?' Ryan asked Evan.

He knew he would be of better use to the people at camp, and he realised that he didn't want to leave Madeline. God knew what else she might try and do.

'Of course, doc,' Evan said, climbing into the back with another cameraman.

The volunteer got into the front and Ryan pulled Madeline back against him as the engine started up again, her hair whipping his face.

'Wait—take these,' she said, breaking free and handing Evan the cushions.

He took them appreciatively and used them as padding around the woman's side, still being careful not to move her. Ryan knew she'd be moved anyway, thanks to the juddering of the helicopter in this weather. He wasn't entirely sure it was a good idea to fly, but some risks were worth taking. The heat and humidity in the jungle tended to accelerate people's injuries.

He guided Madeline away quickly by the elbow as the blades began to whir again. They turned around just in time to see the helicopter rise, then drop back onto the grass.

Madeline gasped.

'Damn,' Ryan cursed. 'They can't take off in this storm.'

'She needs a hospital,' Madeline said.

'I know, but we'll just have to wait it out. It won't last long—these storms never do. Where's our stuff?'

'My bags and yours? They were taken to the camp.' She brushed her wet hair back from her face with her hand.

'Go find them and get warm and dry—there's nothing else you can do.'

He wanted her safe. Not out here in the middle of

a storm. He was already viewing her as a liability. He knew it was unfair of him, but Madeline Savoia definitely had a stubborn streak. He watched as she turned and did as he'd ordered, albeit reluctantly, and felt some modicum of relief as one weight at least was lifted from his shoulders.

It took what felt like an eternity to get the helicopter off the ground, and when Ryan made it through to his team he was wet and shivering himself. The camp was a frenzy of action, and as he signed some documents on a clipboard thrust suddenly under his nose he noticed Madeline helping someone to move the boxes of bananas and the other stuff that had obviously been moved in from their boat.

'Ryan, how did it go?'

It was Mark Bailey—up in his face, forcing his eyes away from her. Mark was a young doctor who'd been with them for three seasons of *Medical Extremes*. He was well liked around the place—and even more so on Instagram.

'They're en route to the hospital—finally. Fingers crossed the storm doesn't start up again.'

'Looks like it's stopping,' Mark said.

'No other emergencies so far?'

Ryan adjusted his hat as he walked with him, trying not to look at Madeline again. He was surprised she was out of her tent. She was talking to people and he hadn't even made any introductions yet. Then again, she did seem to be a person who took the initiative. Sometimes too *much* initiative.

'A couple this morning—one sprained wrist and a spider bite. Steady trickles for general check-ups and queries all day. We know the other villagers are making their way over now word that we're here has spread up the river, so we're leaving Maria stationed for any strays tonight and planning on an early start tomorrow.'

'Good call.'

Ryan was glad for Mark's organisational skills, as well as everything else. He noticed that the producer was approaching Madeline, leading her away behind one of the stations.

The camp comprised four stations. One was simply a raised platform, on which stood three foldable tables. There his team doled out vitamins and basic medication, and assessed the symptoms of those seeking other medical attention. Everyone who needed care went there first. With the rain and the storm there were only three people in the line now, waiting to be seen.

The other three stations were for treatment, so they held a couple of beds and chairs, with boxes of fresh sheets, gauze and other equipment stacked in all corners.

Would Madeline know what to do with all this, from her nursing days? he wondered. He knew he had to think of more tasks for her. He'd witnessed her instinctual need to help on more than one occasion now, and all this might make her tired…perhaps too tired to ask for many details for that memoir…

He clenched his fists to his sides as Josephine's face flashed before his eyes.

Don't think about it.

In one of the stations one of his volunteers from Chicago—a fifty-something half-Japanese lady called Maria—was talking to two young children on a plastic sheet on the floor. The kids were young members of the local tribe, no older than seven years old. Often the kids in these remote places gathered around out of excitement at having new people to play with.

'Good to see you, Ryan,' Maria called out, and the barefoot children giggled and waved in their ragged, faded clothing.

He waved back. Then, content that his staff had everything under control, he turned in the direction of the sleeping quarters. The rain was only spitting now.

He found Madeline unpacking her bags, hunched over on the floor of her small green tent.

'Did you find the mini-bar OK?' he asked from the canvas doorway.

She turned around in surprise, still on all fours. The tent wasn't exactly big enough to stand up in.

A sheen of perspiration was causing her face to glisten and her long wet hair was stuck in strands to the side of her face. She obviously hadn't yet found time to get dried off. She got to her knees, swiped at her forehead and gestured around her.

'Five-star,' she said, smiling. Then her expression changed. 'How's that patient? Do you think she'll be OK?'

'They're on the way to the hospital—we'll know more once they do some tests,' he said. He cleared his throat. 'Thank you for your help. I'm sorry if I sounded a little harsh back there. You…you freaked me out for a second.'

'Why?'

'You can't just run under helicopters, Maddy. You're not Indiana Jones.'

She grimaced. 'Sorry, I didn't think. And, yes, the mini-bar is well stocked, thanks.' She reached for a bottle of water that was poking out of her backpack and held it up.

Her tent, which had been set up prior to her arrival,

complete with sleeping bag, blankets and a prized inflatable mattress, was luxurious compared to where most of the people in the tribe and surrounding villages slept.

'We have someone covering emergencies for now,' he told her, 'but with any luck things will be slow until the morning.'

'Great—well, maybe we can work on the memoir some more?' She stepped out of the open doorway and stood beside him. 'Where are you sleeping?'

He looked behind him. No one was around. 'Want to see?'

'OK.'

He led them past a line of tents—all for the crew—and past the makeshift fire they often gathered around in the evenings. The rain was less impactful there, thanks to the thickness of the leaves and branches overhead, but the wind was still muttering all around them. He put his pack on the mossy floor, crouched down and pulled out his prized possession. Holding it in his hands he stood and looked around, studying his surroundings.

'Where to go…? Where to go…?'

'Where to go with what?'

Madeline looked amused. She also looked sexy as hell, he realised with some annoyance, in her *Medical Extremes* tank top and no make-up. She wore rain pretty well, too, he decided, remembering when he'd first met her. It seemed like months ago already.

He walked to a nearby tree and patted it, then shook it a little. It didn't move. Perfect.

'Help me with this,' he said, holding out one end of his hammock.

Her eyebrows shot up to her hairline. 'You're not serious? You're *not* sleeping in a hammock out here in the rain?'

He wrapped one end of it expertly round the tree, motioning for her to walk with her end to the next one. 'Probably not in the rain, but I like to have my spot set up.'

'But you can't sleep out here anyway, can you? What about snakes?'

'Snakes like the ground.'

'Snakes like trees, too. You're going to wrestle one for bed space, are you, Indiana Jones?'

He grinned. 'I'll be careful.'

She rolled her eyes.

'I like a quiet place to read. I might even read one of your books. Feel free to use it, too, if you need to get away. I'm afraid there's no socket for your laptop, though.'

He finished attaching the hammock to the trees, stepped back and crossed his arms, admiring his handiwork.

'Looks good, if I do say so myself. It's the best you can get. We don't mess around out here.'

Madeline was still looking at him as if he was crazy, tapping on a fallen branch with her boot. She looked away for a second, then, 'You have one of my books?'

He nodded, walking back to the hammock and sitting in it, facing her. 'Your "geopolitical thriller". It sounded interesting, and I got a good deal for it on my e-reader.'

She was blushing now.

'What's wrong?' he asked. 'Don't you want me to read it?'

'No, it's not that…'

'I felt I should know some of your work, seeing as you're here to observe mine. Fair's fair.'

He stood up. A gust of wind threw itself at the hammock and caused it to turn over on itself. More raindrops started to splatter on their skin and Ryan quickly zipped his bag up and hoisted it back over his shoulder.

'We should go. Have you seen the dining hall yet?'

'No, I've not seen anything else. The producer got called away.'

'OK—well, in that case, let me be your jungle guide, Jane.'

With his hand on the warm small of her back, Ryan guided her towards camp. On the way he noted without saying a word that his tent had been set up just one along from Madeline's, with maybe three feet between them...

The dining hall was a basic set-up, beyond the tents and makeshift toilets, which looked a lot like a giant chicken coop for humans. A wooden platform was covered only by a roof thatched with palm fronds to stop the rain getting in. Mosquito mesh stretched between wooden posts on all sides, creating walls.

He opened the mesh door, letting her step through ahead of him as she brushed the rain off her arms with her hands. Several people waved at them as they entered, but Ryan steered Madeline to where a volunteer was serving portions of white rice and boiled vegetables onto plastic plates from a huge silver pot. The boxes of bananas she'd helped to carry were stacked at either side.

'Gourmet cuisine from now on,' he said, handing her a plate.

'I don't mind rice,' Madeline said, signalling for another scoop from the kindly lady behind the table.

'You won't be saying that in three weeks' time. Better get used to these, too.'

He picked up a banana and balanced it on the side of her plate beside the rice. She didn't object.

Ryan guided her to the end of one of the long communal tables, where piles of cutlery had been dropped haphazardly into a pile in the middle. He noted Pablo and Jake in the corner, filming them as they took a seat on the bench. The rain was hammering hard on the roof again now, making a racket on the mesh. The air smelled of DEET and damp foliage and the space was filled with quiet chatter and the clanging of cutlery.

Madeline picked up a fork opposite him, and he was about to take a bite out of a piece of boiled carrot when something large and brown landed on the table—right between their plates.

Madeline screamed and jumped up from the bench. Her plate of food went flying.

Ryan jumped up, too, as everyone else started scrambling backwards. 'Tarantula,' he said, trying to sound calm.

Madeline was beside him now, and her face was a shade of white he'd rarely seen. She had both hands over her mouth, as though to muffle more screams, and was trying her best to hide behind him.

'Make that two tarantulas,' he said, peering closer at the fuzzy ball that was now untangling itself right by the condiments basket.

He felt her hand on his shoulder, clenching on his shirt.

'They nest in the thatch,' he said, pointing upwards as Jake zoomed his camera in on the hairy spiders, sitting dazed on the table where they'd fallen. 'They must have been mating and forgotten how to hold on! I'm surprised they're still alive.'

'That's one hell of a fall from grace,' someone said, and people started twittering amongst themselves again.

Ryan noticed Madeline still wasn't laughing. He also

noticed tears in her eyes, and the way she was glancing at the camera, which was pointed straight at her.

'That's enough,' he said quickly, stepping forward and putting his palm over the lens.

Jake stepped backwards, his face popping out from behind the viewfinder. 'Ryan, that was *gold*!'

'She doesn't want to be on film. We discussed this, didn't we?'

'I was told to film everything.'

'Well, *I'm* telling you not to.'

He turned around, but Madeline was gone.

'Don't follow me,' he said gruffly to the cameraman. He nodded at the tarantulas, still stationary. 'And get rid of those…before their friends come looking for them.'

He marched out of the dining hall into the rain, spun around, but couldn't see her. Then he spotted a blur of white tank top heading towards her tent.

Pulling his shirt up over his head, he sprinted across the grass. The sound of frogs and cicadas was almost as loud as the rain. He watched her unzip the door hurriedly, getting it stuck halfway.

But before he could reach her he saw the two local kids who'd been sitting with Maria running up to her.

'Miss! Miss!' they were calling.

'Oh, hi,' he heard her say in surprise as he moved closer.

He watched her swiping at her face to clear away what was obviously embarrassment and tears as much as rain. One of the kids in a yellow shirt threw his arms around her waist and she stood there for a moment, seemingly unsure of what to do.

'Can we see?' he heard the boy ask, pointing to her tent.

'Curious, are you?' Ryan said, walking up to them.

The kids thought nothing of running around in the rain—they were used to it.

Madeline looked at him. The kids' arms were still locked around her.

'You can see inside,' she said kindly, untangling the arms from around her and finishing unzipping the door. 'Actually, I have something for you.'

Madeline got to her knees and crawled to her backpack. The kids followed after her.

'Room for one more?' Ryan asked, squeezing inside. He reached for one of the boys—the one in the yellow shirt—tickling his feet until he was giggling wildly.

Madeline handed them each a colouring book, and a set of pencils between them. They looked elated.

Ryan was touched. He leaned on one elbow on the groundsheet beside her. 'You OK?'

She lifted her swollen eyes to the canvas ceiling, let out a long sigh and watched the kids roll onto their tummies and start to colour. 'He got all that on camera. I almost made a tree fall down with that scream.'

'He won't use it.'

'How do you know?'

'I told him not to.'

She met his eyes, and mouthed *Thank you* over the kids' heads.

The little boy looked up. 'Why you cry, miss?' he asked.

Madeline put a hand out to touch his damp hair. 'I saw something scary,' she said.

'A tarantula,' Ryan followed up.

The boy beamed, showing gappy teeth. 'Tarantula not scary.'

'To me they are,' Madeline said. She looked at Ryan, 'Especially when they fall an inch from your dinner plate.'

The kid put his pencil down, got to his feet and pulled his friend up. *'Vamos!'*

'What?' Madeline laughed now.

'Vamos!'

She got to her feet, followed him outside, and Ryan went with them. The light was fading fast but he had a vague idea what the boys were going to show her.

They took her hands, one on either side of her, and led her to the same area where he'd strung up his hammock. The rain was still falling, but covered by the trees it was less noticeable.

They pulled Madeline to a thick tree trunk and dropped her hands, busying themselves walking around the tree, peering at it closely.

'Home!' one of them exclaimed after a moment. 'Look!'

Ryan put a hand to Madeline's elbow gently, throwing her a warning look. She frowned and turned to where they were pointing, then walked as close as she could to the tree and peered into a hole in the bark.

'Wow!' She stepped backwards, then seemed to compose herself.

The kids were giggling again, pointing to another hole in the bark. 'Spider house!' The youngest one giggled, tugging on her shirt.

Each hole in the tree was indeed a house. Ryan knew it well. Nestled inside each cosy mossy crevice was a giant tarantula, just waiting for nightfall.

'They come out when it's dark and hang out on the tree,' he explained.

Madeline scrunched her face up just long enough for him to note her disdain, but he admired how she tried to look excited for the boys.

'Wow, that's great,' she said.

'They're not so scary when you see them like this, are they?' Ryan replied.

He couldn't help the smile stretching out his face.

CHAPTER EIGHT

MADELINE DISAGREED. THEY were tarantulas. They were terrifying wherever they were—not that she wanted to make even more of a fool of herself than she already had. She half expected the kids to reach into the holes and grab a few, start stroking them like cuddly toys just to prove a point.

She backed away and was surprised when Ryan held his shirt above their heads to shelter them both as he led them back to their tents.

'Probably should have brought an umbrella,' he said, catching her glance.

She smiled at the gentleman emerging in him now, with the more time they spent together, and walked close to him, letting the kids back into her tent with her to collect their colouring books and promising she would see them again tomorrow. Then she watched them scurry off into the jungle as Ryan took their place in the tiny space.

'Amazing,' she said wistfully, aware that he was filling up pretty much every inch of spare room in her tent; it was a thin canvas bubble for the two of them. His shirt was wet, as was hers, and the sound of the rain on the canvas was louder now than ever. 'The kids, I mean.'

'They're pretty amazing, yes,' he said, leaning on one arm and stretching out.

His feet were almost touching the door. He looked as though he was making himself comfortable...as though he had no intention of leaving just yet. Madeline hadn't laid out her bed sheets yet—which she was now pretty glad about. Otherwise he would literally be lying on her bed alongside her. The thought made her nervous.

'Extremely resilient. They literally have no fear. Sometimes gets them in trouble, though.'

'I can imagine.' She swallowed.

'It was great of you to bring the colouring books. You're going to be pretty popular round here if you're planning on pulling moves like that.'

'I bought a few in Rio.' She reached for her pack and pulled out her notebook. She didn't want to admit— even to herself—how she'd frozen the moment that little kid's arms had wrapped around her. All she'd seen was Toby. But she couldn't think about Toby now. She couldn't think about his little arms around her on the ward at the hospital, his big brown eyes, the look on his mother's face when...

She took a deep breath. While Ryan was here she was determined to get some more answers from him. She was pretty up to speed on his youth now, but the closer they got to the present day, the more he seemed to skate awkwardly around her questions. She'd warm him up, she decided, by asking him something easy.

But he was looking at her quizzically. 'What's wrong?' he asked.

'Nothing,' she said, too quickly. I was just thinking... about the spiders. Being on camera looking like an idiot.'

'I told you—they won't use the footage. What else is on your mind?'

She looked at him and shrugged, flummoxed. How could he tell she had been thinking about more than the spiders? Was it because he could read the pain in her eyes the way she could sometimes read it in his?

'Nothing. So—I'm guessing you're a bit better prepared for this kind of adventure than me. What do you bring with you in your pack? Aside from the usual equipment and your hammock, I mean? You must need a different kit wherever you go…mountains, desert, jungle…'

She watched him stroke a hand across his chin, then take his hat off. He was literally three inches from her damp skin, and in the silence the symphony of crickets, frogs and raindrops seemed to rush through her like another pulse. Everything around them and between them was alive.

'You're right—it's different every time. But some things stay the same. I never go anywhere without my multi-tool.'

'What's that?' she asked, scribbling it down.

'Only the manliest tool in the world!' He reached into one of his pockets and pulled out something that looked like a penknife, flipped out one of the blades. 'It has a million features—the manufacturers sponsored Season Two of the show, didn't you see that?'

'I wasn't watching it for the sponsors.'

She could hear the smile in his voice when he carried on with his answer. 'And I carry anti-venom, of course.'

'Of course,' she said. 'Over one hundred thousand people die every year from snakebites. I saw that on one of your shows, I think.'

'Impressive memory. Wait one second.'

He crawled back out of the tent, and seconds later crawled back in again holding another fabric case. He opened it, revealing a vial and two long, plastic tubes.

'I always keep these around. Hope to God I never

need them, but you should know how to use this kit if you don't already.'

'That's OK. I'm sure plenty of people here know how to use it,' she said, eyeing the tubes warily.

'You're right, but still… We have anti-venom for most snakes out here. Simple to use—just get as much info as possible about what bit, then inject the right anti-venom into the elbow crease right here.'

He squeezed her in the spot he'd indicated, gently, making her pulse quicken again.

'You've done that before, I'm sure.'

'Yes, but like I've already said I'm not here to—'

'I'm sure you wouldn't worry too much about making excuses if someone urgently needed your help.' He put the vial and tubes down and rested on his elbow next to her. 'You haven't so far, at least.'

She bit her tongue.

'I also have a fire stick and a sharpener somewhere—oh, and we all get given a sat phone push-to-talk in case we ever get separated. I have a roll of gaffer tape, too—you never know when you'll need that—and a water purifier. Someone usually has rice and a stove in their pack in case we have to stray from camp—takes no time to use, plus it's light.'

'You're literally prepared for everything?'

He nodded. 'Have to be. Here in the jungle, though, a good knife and my British army boots are compulsory.' He motioned to the heavy black boots on his feet. 'These are something you Brits do very well. Oh, and my hammock. Naturally.'

'Everything but an umbrella,' she teased.

'And the kitchen sink.'

'Ryan…'

She put her pen down, sat cross-legged and faced him.

He was playing with his penknife now, flipping things open and closed absent-mindedly…the bottle-opener, the wire-cutter. She felt as if the tent was closing in—as though a flame had just been lit inside…one that could at any moment become a fire.

She took another breath. Then she let the question slide off her tongue. 'What's the most dangerous situation you've ever been in?'

She knew it was brave. Reckless, even. She just had to see what he'd say.

He flipped the knife blade out and in again, loudly, looking as though he was mulling the question over in his mind. 'Most dangerous?'

'Yes.'

He smirked. 'Being in the middle of the Amazon with amorous tarantulas falling from ceilings isn't dangerous enough for you?'

'I've seen you deal with worse,' she said, feeling her heart thumping against her damp clothes.

'Well, there was the pair of hikers we had to treat for hypothermia when they went off track in Iceland. Almost got screwed ourselves when the helicopter dropped us down on the winch and couldn't lift us out again because of the wind.'

'I saw that one,' she said. 'What about…?' She paused, wondering how best to phrase it—how far she could push it. She was treading on eggshells now. 'What about off-camera? Has there ever been anything so dangerous that you weren't allowed to broadcast it on television? Or talk about it afterwards?'

Ryan snapped the blade on his penknife closed one final time, then shoved it into his pocket. His icy eyes looked dark when he met hers.

He got to his knees. 'We show everything that happens, Madeline.'

'Except when *you* say not to, right?'

'What do you mean?'

'Like when women scream over falling spiders?'

He narrowed his eyes. 'The producers and editors have the final say.'

'Except when *you're* adamant that something isn't shown. Am I right?'

'I knew this was a mistake.'

He turned from her, started unzipping the tent, his fingers an angry blur. Madeline got on all fours and crawled closer to the door.

'Where are you going?'

'To my tent. We're done here.'

'What just happened?'

Ryan moved to step out, but turned at the last minute, bringing his face right up to hers. The trees were swaying behind him and the wind rushed in with the rain, making her shiver in spite of the heat.

'I told you we'd start at the beginning,' he growled.

'That's what we're *doing*!'

She'd blown it. She felt as if she was talking to a completely different person.

'I don't appreciate this hidden agenda. I know what you really want to ask me, Madeline, and I don't want to talk about it.'

Her insides were twisting more and more by the second at his anger and at his words, thick and cold like ancient lava.

She forced her face to stay neutral and mirrored his stance, sitting on her haunches. 'I'm sorry,' she said. 'But I'm writing your memoir, Ryan. You have to at least appreciate that your publishers are asking me questions about what happened that day…what you don't want anyone to know…'

'They're asking you to call me out. They want *you* to prove that the perfect, selfless hero you see on the television isn't real… They want it from the horse's mouth, don't they? So the world can get a kick out of how the mighty fall.'

Madeline was stunned. 'What? Why would anyone do that?'

'You tell me.'

'I would never write anything to hurt you or compromise your integrity.'

'We both know that's what they want so they can get more sales!'

'That doesn't mean we can't write it properly—say what *you* want to say…'

'Damn it, Maddy, I don't want to say anything at all!'

His hand was still on the tent's doorway and she watched helplessly as he unzipped the rest of it roughly and crawled out.

'Wait, Ryan—can we just talk about this?' she pleaded, sticking her head out into the rain after him.

But he was walking through the expanding puddles of mud, back towards the dining hall. She looked at the vial of anti-snake venom in its pack, still on the floor. Through the rain now striking viciously at everything in its path, Madeline could barely even see Ryan any more.

CHAPTER NINE

THE JUNGLE, RYAN thought from his place in the hammock, was merely a microcosm of the world in its entirety—a giant muddle of monsters trying not to look as if they'd eat you alive if they had to.

He sipped his coffee from the warm metal mug and thought that this might be something he'd tell Madeline for the memoir—after all, he'd seen a lot of the world, battled to save many of those harmed by the monsters in it.

But then he remembered with a small sigh that he was going to steer clear of Madeline for a while.

He'd seen her at breakfast, talking to Evan, who was just back from the hospital in Manaus with good news, thankfully. She'd glanced up and their eyes had met over the dining bench. He swore he'd seen her hand rise in cautious greeting, but he'd turned from her, grabbed his caffeine fix and some fruit and headed straight here.

He didn't want to make small talk and he damn well wasn't going to apologise to her either; he wasn't going to do *anything* with the cameras lurking like jaguars waiting to pounce.

'Ryan!'

A voice calling his name almost made him spill his

coffee. He sprung up from the hammock as Maria came into view, wearing her *Medical Extremes* uniform.

'Sorry to interrupt, but could we have your assistance?'

He was already walking towards her, annoyed with himself for hiding away too long. 'Of course, I was just finishing up. What's happened?'

'Skin condition and a fever with it. Evan and the other guys went back to the landing pad for the rest of the supplies.'

'I'm on it,' he said, walking faster with her towards the stations, kicking himself internally.

If he hadn't left the dining hall when discussions about fetching more supplies were underway he'd have known to be there already. Annoyance made his brow crease—Madeline was already affecting his work. All the more reason to stay away from her.

When they reached the medical stations bright sunlight was streaming into the clearing and a line of people had gathered, waiting to register. Three volunteers were taking their details, all of them in their trademark *Medical Extremes* T-shirts and hats. The rain had cleared in the night, and there were only a few fast-evaporating puddles to show for its appearance.

Madeline was talking to a small group of kids who'd gathered around her in a corner of the camp. Sunshine danced in her long hair. She was wearing a white tank and khaki shorts, exposing long, milky legs, and she was handing out the rest of the colouring books and pencils. Her eyes caught his as he passed her and he tried not to flinch visibly.

She was doing something good, of course, and having her do something practical around camp was better than her scribbling reams of notes about his shady past. But the sight of her caused something in his stomach to shift.

For a moment she looked as though she was going to say something, but he tore his eyes away before she had the chance, followed Maria into one of the medical stations and flipped the switch in his mind he always flipped when it came to focussing entirely on a patient in his care.

'What seems to be the problem here?' he asked as he approached a guy lying flat on one of the makeshift beds.

He was bare-chested, wearing faded red shorts down to his knees, probably in his mid to late thirties. His forehead was clammier than it should be, even in this thick heat, and several raised lesions on his legs and arms showed clear lines of demarcation at the edges.

Erysipelas lesions, he noted. It was a bacterial infection, common in these parts—simple to treat but dangerous if left too long.

He walked to the airtight container in the corner of the station, aware now of Jake in the other corner, filming him. He pulled out one of the kits inside as Maria translated the man's answers from his quick Spanish. He'd been feeling ill for two days, with headaches and vomiting, but had tried to push on without telling anyone. The muddy splashes on his legs showed he must have walked at least some way through thick jungle to get to them.

'We'll soon have this under control,' Ryan said, pulling on a pair of gloves and getting out the antihistamine. He'd have to be given prophylactic antibiotics, too.

He was explaining what his patient would have to do to ensure the lesions healed properly when a whirlwind seemed to sweep into the station. He turned and saw a little girl with braids in her long hair, no older than four or five, waving her arms around, bolting towards them.

'Daddy!' she shouted, reaching them in a flash and placing her little hands on the side of the bed.

Her cheeks were streaked with tears and her pale blue dress was covered in mud. His patient reached for her hand and started comforting her with soothing words in spite of his obvious torment. Ryan's heart broke a little.

Two seconds later someone else entered the station. Madeline.

'There you are,' she said to the little girl, walking over to her and placing a hand gently on her shoulder. 'Come on, they're treating your daddy and we have to let them work.'

She swept a hand through her own hair and Ryan was thrown for a moment—not least by the sight of her standing beside him. She switched to Spanish and, he assumed, repeated what she'd just said. The little girl gripped her hand.

This time he let his eyes linger on Madeline's as he pulled the packaging away from the hydrocortisone. He tried to ignore the rush of adrenaline he felt tearing through him as her sea-green gaze seemed to rip straight down the wall he'd been building around himself after their somewhat heated debate.

She stood there talking to the girl and ignoring *him* as he cleaned the man's wounds and bandaged the worst one, then made him promise to take it easy for a few days while the antibiotics did their work.

As he and Maria worked Ryan was aware of Madeline heading to the corner with the child, away from the camera, making her laugh, making her tears all but disappear. He wished he could hear and understand more of what she was saying.

By the time his patient was walking towards his daughter to receive a welcoming hug Madeline seemed to have become firm friends with her. Ryan tried not to give the impression that he'd noticed, but a part of him was more impressed with her than ever. What the hell had made her quit nursing? She obviously had a way with people—especially children. And hadn't she at one point during their extensive chats told him that she'd worked at St David's in London? The children's hospital? That must have been where she'd honed her skills at earning their trust.

He watched her step outside—saw the way she immediately became swarmed over by the kids. He was about to follow but another patient was being brought inside, this time by Mark. As the makeshift plastic sheet that served as a doorway fell down after him he heard her telling them all to follow her to the shade—that much he understood in Spanish.

'She's pretty good with those kids,' Mark said, sitting the patient—a lady in her mid-twenties—down on the chair beside the now empty bed.

'Who? Madeline?' Ryan said nonchalantly, stripping the paper from the bed and shoving it into a plastic bag.

'Yes, of *course* Madeline! She's got them all colouring under the trees out there like friggin' Mary Poppins. Usually they're running around under our feet by now and asking to wear the stethoscopes. Impressive Spanish, too. Did you know she was fluent in that as well as Portuguese? I think she said she lived in Colombia for a while.'

'Yes.'

Maria stifled a smile as she marked their last patient's notes on a clipboard.

'She's quite a hit out there,' Mark continued, oblivious

to Ryan's curt tone. 'I hope you don't mind, but I told her she could make a start on the dental hygiene project if she wanted something to do. Gave her the toothbrushes and worksheets. I figured Evan would have done the same thing. I know you guys are working on the memoir together, but—'

'The more hands on deck the better,' Ryan cut in, before the questions and the digging could start.

He had a feeling the team had all talked about the damn memoir behind his back already, and it made him uncomfortable to say the least. He caught Maria's sideways glance as he took his new patient's blood pressure.

'Everything OK?' she asked.

'Fine.'

He reached for a bottle of water. It was barely nine a.m. and already hotter than hell. The rain hadn't cooled things off for long, and there was undoubtedly more on the way. More patients, too.

It was several hours before he stuck his head outside into the sunshine. Evan and the others had fetched more antibiotics and yet more boxes of fruit. There was talk of a swim in the waterfall that he registered vaguely before Madeline caught his attention again.

He swigged from his water bottle, then stretched out his muscles, battling the urge to walk over to her. He'd been on form—performing routine duties one after the other, talking to the camera, trying not to let her creep into his thoughts. He was tired, he realised. And their argument was bothering him again.

From where he stood she seemed to be fully absorbed in what the children were doing, and he noticed that someone had stacked several cardboard boxes on the plastic sheets they were sitting on. She was laughing and smiling in the sunshine, her skin glistening with sunscreen and probably DEET. Maybe both.

He wandered over to her. Shutting her out was even more exhausting than letting her in.

'Colombia?' he said, clearing his throat, leaning on a nearby tree. 'You lived there for two years on and off? Is that right?'

The wind ruffled her loose hair, and from his stance looking down at her sitting cross-legged on the ground he could see her bra and the way it hugged her breasts beneath her tank top. He tried not to look as she fixed her gaze on him.

'Well remembered. Medellin, then Cartagena.'

A yellow and brown butterfly fluttered between them.

'I was writing a book.'

'Another geopolitical thriller?' he asked, folding his arms.

'A romance, actually.'

Her tone was blunt, and for the first time he considered that perhaps she was angry with him for what had happened yesterday. He *had* kind of turned on her out of the blue. Not that she hadn't deserved it after prying where she wasn't invited.

'It didn't really go anywhere. Guess I'm not too great with romance.'

He frowned, swallowed an apology before it bubbled out of him—she *had* to know there were lines she couldn't cross. And more that *he* couldn't cross, he added to himself.

'So, how do you feel about being involved in this?' he asked, gesturing to the dental hygiene boxes around them and the paper she had already handed out to the kids along with the colouring books.

'I think it's a great idea.' She got to her feet and faced him. 'Was it one of yours?'

'Actually, it was Maria's. It was kind of a joint wish for all of us to promote healthy eating, dental hygiene, basic first aid…all that as we go along. You start with the kids and it filters through to the elders, you know? How are those mosquito bites?'

He pointed to one on her arm—a small red welt. She covered it with her hand. 'I'll survive. Anyway, I think this is a good thing to be involved in. Teaching them basic health education while you're playing games—they think it's all fun.'

'Exactly. We wanted to focus first on helping them learn about brushing their teeth.'

Madeline nodded, looking at the fact sheets in Spanish about exactly that. Ryan noted one of the boxes was open, so she'd clearly seen the six hundred toothbrushes they'd brought with them.

'I've been colouring, then stopping to talk through the fact sheets, then colouring again…'

'Good start. And if you want to add songs at any point they love that.'

'Songs?'

'Evan plays guitar sometimes—makes up words. How are you at improvising?'

She shrugged. 'I guess I could give it a shot.'

Once again he was impressed. Having another pair of hands on the project would be a blessing. In other places where they'd tested the programme they had already seen an improvement in dental health and knowledge about how to prevent parasite infestation. It was one of their success stories, but they still had so much more to do.

Madeline shifted her weight from one foot to the other. 'Listen, Ryan, about last night...'

'It's forgotten,' he said quickly.

She let out a sigh. 'No, it's not, I can tell.'

He took her elbow, led her three steps away from the kids and lowered his voice. His hand tingled, just feeling her skin against his, and he withdrew it quickly, slightly shocked.

'Like I said, there are things I don't want to talk about, Madeline. *Ever*. I know you have a job to do, but if we could leave certain things out I'd appreciate it.'

'It's not going to work like that,' she said, frowning at him. 'You know the publishers will want answers about Josephine.'

A planet-sized rock shot up to his throat. Her name... *her* name...coming from Madeline's lips sent chills straight through him.

'We can write around it, but the stories...or the half-stories...are out there already.'

She reached for his arm. That spark again. He had to take a step back. His fists balled of their own accord.

'We can work this out,' she hurried on in a hushed tone, closing the gap again. 'You *have* to trust me, Ryan. Just trust me with the truth.'

Another butterfly caught on the wind beside her as he ran his eyes over her lips, her ears, the apple dangling on a chain around her neck. He wanted to trust her. He really did. She had some kind of strange effect on him... And maybe it was finally time for the truth.

He considered it for a second. Josephine and the real story behind that day had turned him into a walking wreck for the most part—shot a bullet through any real chance of a romance ever since. They'd all wanted to know what had happened and he'd flat out refused to say, building a wall up brick by damn brick till it was suffocating for all involved. Maybe it *was* time.

He opened his mouth, but one of the kids—a girl in a muddied shirt—jumped up and screeched with laughter, dragging a little boy with her over to Madeline. They both started talking to her excitedly in fast Spanish, pulling at her hands.

He closed his mouth.

'Sorry—you were saying?' Madeline said after a moment, breaking free.

The look of expectancy in her eyes tore him to pieces. He bit his cheeks. What the hell was he thinking? It wasn't time. It would never be time. He was letting his unnamed emotion and the heat interfere with his mental processes and it could never happen again.

'I don't trust anyone,' he said quickly, before his heart could hold him back.

He'd expected anger, and prepared himself to take the hit, but instead he watched confusion flood Madeline's eyes, then perhaps a hint of pity.

'That's a shame,' she replied softly. 'You must be really lonely.'

Then she sat down again with the kids, leaving him speechless.

CHAPTER TEN

MADELINE SAT ON the edge of the lake, drawing circles in the murky water with her bare feet. She clutched her coffee cup, turned the page of the book she was reading, but the words weren't sinking in.

She sighed, putting it down on the wooden deck, watching the dragonflies skimming the surface and leaving tiny ripples in their wake. One week in and she was growing to know each creature that dared to show itself around the camp—thanks to a book Maria had leant her.

She knew the iridescent *Rhetus periander* butterflies, with their vivid blue wings and red blotches, the black grasshoppers with their beady indigo eyes and bright yellow polka dots, the russet-coloured caterpillars which clung resiliently to leaves throughout every rainstorm and the sand flies that nibbled in invisible silence at her legs and feet, leaving marks she needed to remind herself constantly not to scratch.

Madeline knew a lot about her new surroundings already. But she still didn't know enough about Ryan.

Time passed slowly in the jungle. In seven days she hadn't once looked at herself in a mirror, but she could tell she'd lost weight. Her shorts were loose on her, as were her dresses. Even her bikini, which she was wearing now, wasn't as figure-hugging as it had been when she'd bought it. Rice and fruit were now the essentials to stop a rumbling stomach rather than something to enjoy.

Her phone had died three days ago. When Evan had offered her the solar charging kit she'd told him she didn't need it, instead charging her Dictaphone for yet another interview with Ryan that she knew wouldn't go anywhere.

In every awkward chat since that day under the tree he'd refused to step any closer towards the place she needed him to be—and that was the place where Josephine came into the picture.

She furrowed her brow at the shimmering water ahead. Madeline would only get paid if she delivered the kind of manuscript the editor had in mind. She was trying not to feel defeated but she couldn't really help it.

She couldn't help the chemistry still more than evident between her and Ryan either. Even thoughts of Jason were dwindling by the day. Their break-up had been a meteoric crash in her world, but she felt so far away from that now. Since coming out here she'd been swept into another existence entirely—one in which she was perpetually hot, sticky and dancing in dangerous circles around Ryan.

She shivered, even in the heat, remembering the night before.

Ryan had agreed to another interview on the condition that she accompany him fishing. Mark and Evan often went out on the river at night, and she'd been once, just for the boat ride and to clear her head. She'd never been off camp with Ryan. When he'd asked her to join him she'd been surprised, nervous and grateful all at the same time, because he'd chosen to spend most nights alone up till then, preparing equipment, stock-checking, talking to the camera or just hiding himself away in his tent.

She shivered again, twirling the water with her toes as her mind replayed what had happened in the boat.

'Ever tasted a piranha?' Ryan had asked, casting his line out into the blackness of the water.

The moon had been a bright yellow bulb above them, and with no other lights they'd been able to see a million stars. They'd also heard bats and monkeys in the treetops as they'd discussed his training days and a family vacation to the UK for the memoir.

Madeline had felt the Amazon closing in on them as he'd rowed them further away from camp. She'd sensed a thousand eyes and ears around them in the darkness—furry spies, she'd hoped, as opposed to any kind of drug runner.

She'd gripped the side of the small boat, watching his profile and keeping an eye out for caimans. 'Never,' she'd replied in answer to his question. 'What do they taste like?'

'A lot like sardines. They're pretty good when they're crunchy off the grill, but they're bony little things. Kind of a mission to get the meat off. Here—hold this.'

He'd thrust the fishing line at her then, and reached behind him to the small box he'd brought along and shone a flashlight into it. She'd seen raw chicken.

'They go crazy for this,' he'd told her, reaching for the line again.

His hand had brushed hers and he'd stood just an inch behind her, hooking tiny chunks of the white meat onto the end of the wire. She hadn't wanted to ask why *they* weren't being fed this luxury.

'Now, throw it in.'

'Me?' she'd asked, still processing the jolt she'd felt at his touch.

'This is a good spot. Don't panic—you'll be OK.'

He'd put the line back in her hands and moved up close behind her. Very close. So close that she'd felt his breath tingling over the nape of her neck below her ponytail. He'd put his hands over hers and lifted the line, helping her throw it into the water—hard.

Nothing.

Then everything.

The water had started moving around the end of the line.

'There they are!' Ryan had exclaimed excitedly, shining his light out ahead of them and putting a hand on her shoulder, over her clammy skin.

Madeline had gasped, feeling her face break out into a grin as a white-topped frenzy came into view. It had been as though someone had installed a tiny hot-tub in the middle of the river.

She'd felt the line tug as Ryan rested his flashlight on the bench, facing them.

'Don't let go—pull it in! Don't let the line go loose,' he'd urged as his hands moved to her quickly, gripping her waist over her thin blue dress to hold her steady.

'Don't let go of *me*—they'll eat me, too,' she'd said, leaning further into him.

'I won't. You've got it—you've got it...'

He'd been pressed against her in the boat. His head almost resting on her shoulder from behind as he'd helped her pull the fish in through the frenzy and over the side.

'Great job!' he'd cried, elated, holding up the line and moving away from her to reach for the flashlight again.

He'd shone it on their catch—a silvery fish about twice the size of a goldfish, with an orange tinge. It hadn't looked very scary, even as it wriggled and flapped. Madeline had reached for the line to get a closer look but Ryan had gripped her fingers and held them tight away from it.

'Not so fast!'

'Sorry.'

'You want to see what this thing will do if it gets a hold of your finger?'

His face had been so close to hers she'd practically been able to feel his stubble tickling her cheek. She'd smelled him: a raw, animal scent mixed with sunscreen that had made her a little wobbly on her feet. Luckily she'd been able to blame the boat for that.

He'd stuck a hand in his pocket, pulled out a thick green leaf. Holding the line with the fish still attached, he'd dangled the leaf in front of the piranha. Instantly the fish had opened its jaws, revealing an ominous row of razor-sharp teeth, and started chomping the leaf to pieces from bottom to top with ferocious zeal, as fast and as efficient as a chef's knife chopping a cucumber.

Madeline had watched with equal amazement and horror.

'Told you—you don't want to mess with these guys.'

Ryan had grinned, turned off the light and thrown what was left of the leaf overboard. His eyes had sparkled like ice cubes in the moonlight, and Madeline had sworn she'd never seen anyone so handsome in her entire life as Ryan when he was smiling, living in the *now*, not letting his past weigh him down like a hunk of lead.

'That's the most incredible thing I've ever seen,' she'd breathed, laughing with the sheer adrenaline of it.

She'd studied his lips, his mouth—so different from Jason's. She'd been so certain that she'd never even want to kiss someone else. But in that moment, awed by their primitive environment and slightly scared of the flesh-eating fish, she'd known she'd say *To hell with professionalism* and kiss Ryan Tobias if he'd initiated it.

As his eyes had raked over her lips under the infinite Milky Way she'd willed him to throw her down in that rickety boat and erase every last trace of her ex, and the others before him, from out of her for ever. At one point she'd been convinced he was going to—because Madeline had seen it in Ryan, too—looked it straight in the face.

That hunger. That unmistakable desire.

But he'd tossed the fish into the box under the chicken and rowed them back to camp in silence. Then, instead of sitting around the fire with her and the others, he'd given the piranha to Evan to roast, retreated to his tent alone and hadn't even said goodnight...

The trees shifted behind her, signalling that her time alone at the camp's only washing facility was almost up.

Madeline put her cup down by her book and jumped into the water with the small bar of organic soap she'd been given. It was one that left no trace of any chemicals behind. She swam for a few metres under the surface, popped her head up and looked back.

Her heart leapt like a rabbit as she saw Ryan standing on the deck, peeling off his shirt.

Had he seen her?

Her eyes glued themselves to his body. His muscles were rippling in the early-morning light; his unshaven face was shadowed around his jaw. He was fiddling with the button on his khaki trousers now, undoing it, sliding the trousers down his strong, lean legs and shrugging them off.

Madeline froze. If she moved he would see her. She considered closing her eyes, but it was too late. His boxers were already halfway down his legs and he was kicking them aside with his trousers and towel.

He was going for a swim. *Naked.*

Her breath caught in her throat. He lifted his arms and stretched up to the sun, as though expecting Mother Nature herself to stand and applaud her own fine work of art. Perhaps she was. The wind was riffling through the trees around the little lake, causing the cicadas to up the volume of their hum.

Madeline swallowed, digging her feet into the squelchy mud below her. She'd never seen a man with a body like his before. Ryan Tobias was pretty much perfect—the quintessential 'hot doc' calendar contender for the month of August, standing like some idolised enigma in shafts of yellow sunlight.

Bending over in the sunlight.

Pointing his hands at the water in the sunlight.

He dived in.

Madeline panicked.

She traced the line he was leaving on the surface with her eyes, as though he himself were a pack of piranhas. She considered swimming past him at full throttle and clambering out before he had the chance to see her. But, again, she was too late.

The water rippled out in front of her and his head appeared. Then his eyes sprang open, looking right into hers from less than a foot away.

'Hi,' she said, under her breath.

He shook his hair, sending a shower of droplets out around him. 'Good morning.'

'Didn't you see my book on the deck, with my cup?'

Her toes were still curling into the mud under the water. She couldn't see her feet, or anything else—a fact she was glad of as he stood there with a look of amusement spreading from his cool grey eyes down to his twitching lips.

He's naked, she couldn't help reminding herself, feeling the colour rise to her cheeks.

'Nope—didn't see. I was half asleep till I jumped in here. We had an emergency in the night so I didn't get much sleep.' He stepped closer to her, spreading his arms out on either side as though trying to gather the water between them. 'Nice surprise.'

Naked, naked, naked.

'What was the emergency?' she asked, stepping backwards slightly, aware that if she stayed where she was she might accidentally touch him with a very inappropriate part of her body.

'Poisonous caterpillar got to one of the kids and his finger swelled up so much the poor thing had a blue hand.'

He stopped right in front of her, his bare torso inches from her breasts in her purple bikini. She studied his face in the sun—the bronzed cheeks, the faint lines around his eyes—noticed how his eyelashes caught drops of water from his dripping hair before he blinked and set them on their downward path again.

Madeline felt as if she was under a searchlight all of a sudden, and another memory from the night before, of his hands on her waist in the boat, flooded her mind and her loins at the same time.

She turned onto her back in the water and felt his eyes on her breasts as they stuck above the surface like her toes. She studied the swaying branches overhead, and the darting dragonflies, reminding herself to breathe.

'Is the kid OK?' she asked without looking at him.

He floated on his back beside her. 'Yes, he's good now. Morphine always helps.'

'You must be exhausted.'

'All in a day's work. Or a night's. And I'm not the only one working hard—how's it going with your group of kids? You seem to really love them, and we can all see how much they love *you*.'

Madeline closed her eyes, swallowing as his fingers brushed hers under the water. She was still clutching her organic soap and he took it out of her hand gently, stood upright and then, to her surprise, took her left foot gently in his hands and ran the soap over it while she floated.

This was definitely not happening. Ryan was not going out of his way to touch her.

'I do,' she said in reply to his statement, though the words came out a little strangled. 'Love the kids, I mean.'

She tilted her head to look at him, but he seemed to be willing her not to say a word about what he was doing. In silence he trailed the soap between each and every one of her toes and massaged them with firm fingers… slowly, sensually.

Madeline's insides were on fire. Ryan wouldn't let her stand, though. He kept her feet against him, pulling her soles to his solid chest as he continued his massage, then worked the soap up her legs softly, firmly, then softer again.

If she hadn't been lying in a lake she'd be wet for other reasons by now, she realised, groaning inwardly.

'I don't know why you gave up nursing, Maddy,' he said softly, breaking into her thoughts.

He let her feet go but moved to her side, placing one hand under her back. He started to trail the soap softly in a circle around her navel.

'We've spoken about me a lot, but why don't we talk about *you*?'

Madeline was struggling to maintain an air of calm,

and she somehow levelled her voice, closed her eyes and allowed him to wash her. No one had ever done anything like this to her before.

'There's nothing to say. I'm happy to leave all that stuff to you guys while I write.'

He ran the soap between her ribs, up to the string at the front of her bikini. He pressed it against her flesh, released it and slowly ran the soapy trail up, up, *up* over her collarbone and neck. Then, with nimble fingers, he moved the hand that was beneath her in the water to the back of her bikini top and pulled it undone.

Every part of her was throbbing with desire.

'Is this what they call a medical extreme?' she whispered daringly as he pulled the flimsy fabric from her body, leaving her top half exposed to the sun and the sky.

She thought she caught a smile on his face. He trailed the soap over her nipples, taking his time, seemingly relishing the equal amounts of thrill and torture he was causing her. She could still sense his silent urging for her not to mention what was happening, just to let him continue. It was the most erotic situation she'd ever been a part of.

His body towered over hers, blocked the sun, and from behind her eyelids she could see him taking her in. She could feel his own longing mounting by the millisecond as he trailed the soap down over her midriff, down, down to her bikini bottoms.

'My God, you're beautiful,' she heard him say hoarsely.

She couldn't take it any more. She put her feet to the ground, moved her hand under the water to feel for what she had no doubt would be standing to attention like a soldier—but he grabbed her fingers, held them tight.

'Not yet.'

'Ryan...'

'Someone's coming.'

An enormous splash by the deck made her jump. She ducked under the water up to her shoulders and Ryan thrust her bikini top into her hands beneath the murky surface, sprang away from her side. Someone was swimming out in their direction, but she couldn't make out who it was.

With trembling fingers she rushed to tie her top up and noticed Ryan swimming four feet away from her, as if nothing had happened. As if they were just two strangers in a lake.

Her insides were doing cartwheels, and so were her thoughts. *Did that just happen?* What the hell were they thinking? They were here to work...not to romp about in the jungle like two wild animals. She wasn't another one of his lovesick fan girls—she was a professional writer on an assignment. And she was too heartbroken over her ex to notice anyone else anyway...*wasn't* she?

She rolled her eyes. She wasn't any more, and she knew it.

Whoever it was who'd come for a swim wasn't from the camp, she realised. The masculine figure swam right past her and carried on. She turned back to Ryan but he wasn't there. He was already swimming back to the deck.

He was climbing out, wrapping a towel around his waist, scooping up his clothes as if he'd already forgotten she'd ever been there. Then he walked quickly back the way he'd come through the trees, leaving her alone and still trembling.

CHAPTER ELEVEN

It wasn't as if he could have stopped himself, Ryan thought, buttoning up a fresh white shirt outside his tent and raking a hand through his hair as he walked quickly back towards the medical stations. His hands had moved before his head had even been able to begin to process what he was doing.

Madeline had been floating there next to him with the sun in her beautiful green eyes, wearing next to nothing, and he'd been completely naked. He was only human, for God's sake.

A stupid human.

He'd been careless, and that had been a close call.

'Ryan!'

It was Maria, calling him over to one of the stations. He strode across the grass towards her, past the line of people waiting to register for treatment. He kicked a football that flew at him from the group of children clearly waiting for Madeline and waved at them, putting on a happy face.

His heart was pounding harder by the second. What if one of the camera guys had caught sight of them just now, with a telescopic zoom and an eye for making some seriously dramatic television? Not that anyone *here* would do that, he realised thankfully, but still, nothing would stop them talking amongst themselves about him and Madeline.

He clenched his fists at his sides. He couldn't keep away from her. Even being angry with her didn't help. Madeline Savoia was a bomb threatening to detonate right in front of him, and she was all the more dangerous for the way she was sliding into his conscience, getting under his skin.

All he'd wanted to do last night in that boat was lay her down and feast on the look of wonder and excitement in her eyes as he showed her even *more* new things. Hell, the things he wanted to show her...

He loved how empathetic she was, how readily she'd adjusted to her new environment, never once complaining about how harsh and hard it was to be out here. The kids adored her and lined up for her in the mornings, bringing her fruit and flowers and any other present they could think of to make her smile. Maria was lending her books.

She was the saint of the whole damn camp already.

'Ryan,' Maria said, leading him inside. She looked agitated. 'We just had a radio call—there's a patient on the way from the village. Mark and one of the volunteers are bringing her in on the boat right now.'

'What's the problem?' he asked, glancing at another volunteer, who was wrapping a strip of gauze around a teenage boy's forearm in the chair beside him. The air was thick and hot and smelled of antiseptic spray and disinfectant. He scrubbed his hands at the basin of water.

'Seventeen-year-old girl, name Abigail, severe abdominal pains. Mark's already diagnosed her with an ectopic pregnancy, ruptured tube...'

'We have methotrexate close if we need it?' he asked,

drying off his hands on a paper sheet. It was the safest and quickest way to induce abortion.

'Already on it,' Maria said, doing up her scrubs as he prepared the laparoscope. 'This kid sounds like she's been through a lot already, from what Mark says. She's been hanging out here the past two days with her little brother and Madeline—she probably didn't even know she was pregnant.'

'Madeline?' Ryan turned around, pulling on a pair of surgical gloves.

As he spoke her name the plastic sheet over the door was swept aside and Madeline came rushing in, this time beside Mark and a volunteer, followed by Jake with his camera.

The canvas stretcher they were carrying held the pregnant girl in question, and he recognised her immediately from the village. Long-haired, chatty Abigail, lying on her back with her belly exposed, letting out the most horrific howls. It wasn't clear at all that she was pregnant, but the blood on her skirt made his heart sink.

Madeline was clutching the sweaty girl's hand, talking fast in Spanish. As they brought the stretcher up to the bed he didn't miss the tears in her eyes. Her hair was still wet, tied in a bun on her head and she met his glance for half a second—a glance that said nothing but, *Help this girl*.

Ryan could see that her nursing instincts were primed once again, probably pushing all thoughts about what had just happened at the lake completely out of the window.

He was already in action. As the camera circled he helped Mark and Maria get the sobbing Abigail gently off the stretcher and onto the table. Her skin was damp, and had a greyish tinge that concerned him. A crowd of people had gathered at the opening to the medical station, but Mark walked over and ushered them all away.

Madeline looked as though she was going to leave, too, but Abigail reached for her arm, clutched it and gripped on as if her hand was a metal vice.

'No quiero que te vayaso,' she was begging in Spanish. 'Don't go, please.'

'We'll have to do keyhole,' Ryan told Maria, who nodded in agreement.

'What? Here?' Madeline looked shocked.

The girl sobbed, gripping her even tighter.

'It's better than open surgery. Quicker recovery, less blood loss. Maria—general anaesthetic...'

'Yes, Doc.'

Maria turned around to the trolley that held the equipment she'd prepared the second the radio call had come in. They were lucky to have a laparoscope—a long fibre optic cable system which allowed them to see the area in question on a monitor connected to a generator, which they charged via solar power. It wouldn't cause the girl too much extra trauma.

Madeline appeared traumatised enough in this moment for everyone, but Abigail was still latching on to her like a leech.

'Crap!' Mark exclaimed from the doorway. 'Lady out here with a hip fracture—we need you, Maria.'

'Now?'

Jake was having a field-day, zooming in on their expressions, Ryan could tell.

'Evan's tied up...'

'It's urgent,' Mark told her. 'I'll meet you next door.'

'I can't!' Maria protested.

'You guys get on it. Madeline's here,' Ryan declared,

reaching behind him quickly and grabbing some scrubs from a box. He threw them at Madeline.

Her eyes widened in terror. 'Ryan... Ryan, listen... I really can't do this...'

'Yes, you can—you're just helping me. Wash your hands.'

'I can't *just help* you.'

'You're a trained nurse—of course you can. Wash your hands and put those scrubs on.'

He'd made the decision on the spot. He knew she could do it. Whatever fear she'd convinced herself she had about being in a set of scrubs around an emergency was all in her head; he was sure of it.

'I need you, Madeline,' he said calmly as he prepared the cannula and reached for the girl's hand. 'Abigail needs you.'

'I don't want to do this,' she protested again, panic causing her voice to shake. 'This isn't why I'm here. I've told you this. Stop trying to—'

'If she can't do it, Ryan, she can't do it,' Maria said, flustered. Beads of sweat were glistening on her forehead and she looked exhausted.

Ryan put the cannula down. 'Madeline is going to help me,' he said firmly, in a tone that made them both fall silent. He turned to her and fixed his eyes on hers. 'I have every faith in you. You're a nurse, Madeline. You know it and *I* know it.'

Her eyes narrowed in silent defeat. She did as she was told—scrubbed her hands, let Maria tie the scrubs at the back. Then Maria squeezed her shoulder and hurried out of the station quickly with Mark, leaving them alone with the camera.

'Trust yourself,' Ryan said, as soon as they were gone. He heard her take a deep breath, seemingly psyching herself up. He watched her place a hand on Abigail's forehead.

'I won't leave you. I'm here,' she said in Spanish, and Abigail looked relieved, smiling weakly and muttering her thanks before Ryan administered the anaesthetic into the back of her hand.

'Muscles are relaxed, breathing is depressed, eye movements slowing,' he told her after a moment, wheeling the laparoscope closer. 'I'm going to make the incision right here.' He pointed to a spot below Abigail's belly button. 'Once the tube's in you're going to pump the carbon dioxide in for me, OK? It's really simple. I'm setting it all up. You just move your hands, slow and steady, OK?'

Madeline nodded, but didn't make a sound.

He turned the monitor around and pulled his mask up over his mouth. Madeline did the same, leaving only her eyes visible. He tried not to register the fear he saw in the wide green pools—his job right now was to make her feel as much of an expert as he was, so they could help this girl as quickly as possible.

Forty-five minutes passed, with Ryan explaining everything he was doing to the camera and making his usual trademark comments—the ones that never ceased to win him thousands of tweets from touched and inspired fans, and from wannabe medical prodigies around the world.

He could almost see them already.

Who's the new staff member? New romance?
#DrRyan #MedicalExtremes.

He couldn't exactly tell them to edit this scene out as he had with the tumbling tarantulas. He blocked it from his mind. Having the camera lens on them meant he couldn't talk to Madeline either—not in the way he would have done without it—but slowly, as they worked together, he watched her fears seem to drain away, until all that was left was a determined young woman doing everything she was asked to do quickly, efficiently, in a way that made him proud.

Finally, after he'd closed the incisions with neat stitches, Madeline applied the dressing without flinching and by the time Abigail came round, groggy and confused, seemed completely calm.

Madeline pulled her mask down around her neck, stroked the girl's forehead again and held her hand, letting out a sigh.

'Ahora está OK,' she whispered. 'Dr Ryan fixed you up.'

'Nurse Maddy helped, too,' he added quickly, placing a hand on Madeline's arm.

Their eyes lingered on each other's perhaps a little too long, and when he turned to the camera he didn't miss the fact that it was directed straight at them.

Abigail was speaking now—softly, woozily. He could understand some but not all of what she said, and as she continued breathily Madeline's face was a picture of concern and fresh heartbreak.

She looked up at him, translating for his benefit. 'She says she got pregnant at fifteen, too. She went into labour for three days before coming for help, and then laboured for two more days before delivery.'

'What happened?' Ryan asked, remembering what Maria had said about Abigail's difficult past.

Madeline smudged a tear as it trickled down her cheek. 'She was induced, and then told that the baby had already passed away. A doctor from another village performed surgery, like you just did, but he wasn't a professional. So awful...'

A strange part of Ryan wanted to reach for Madeline suddenly, but he kept his hands firmly at his sides. He couldn't bear the misfortune this poor young woman had endured. Abigail was still a child herself.

'She couldn't walk for three months and was taken to the hospital in Saint Elena for physiotherapy,' Madeline said, still translating. 'She didn't know she was pregnant again, but she still wants a baby.'

Sympathy and despair for Abigail, and so many others like her, passed from Madeline to him like a secret note. Madeline's emotions were as tangible and hot as the jungle air. Her openness was rubbing off on him and she'd felt so good in his hands.

So good that in spite of being swept away again into another emergency, and trying his best to maintain focus, he still couldn't shift the image of her floating topless in the lake...of himself just moments away from making a mistake.

CHAPTER TWELVE

MADELINE HAD NEVER brushed her teeth so many times in one day. In the fading light, with her view polka-dotted by fireflies, she was sitting under the trees by the unlit fire, trying to demonstrate to the eight kids sitting around her how best to reach the backs of their mouths with their new 'toys'.

They seemed to think her sticking the toothbrush in her own mouth and making funny faces was the most hilarious thing they'd ever seen. It literally never got old. But they were learning fast, eager to impress her.

Truth be told, she was glad of the distraction, because every moment she wasn't busy she was back in that lake, being tenderly, sensually washed by Ryan.

Her cheeks flamed just at remembering, and she turned her attention back to helping the youngest child, a boy of just four, navigate his way around getting the paste out of a closed tube of toothpaste.

Her morning swim that had quickly turned into a semi-naked cleansing session at the hands of the infamous Ryan Tobias had been only marginally overshadowed by the surgery she'd helped him perform on Abigail.

Madeline was still shaking from it—picturing the blood, reliving the flashbacks that had struck like thunder as she'd pulled on those scrubs and put that mask over her face. How could she have stood there at that operating table and *not* remembered in vivid detail the last time she'd tried to help a child and failed?

She'd been so angry with Ryan that she'd almost stormed out, but the look in Abigail's eyes...it had been almost unbearable. That combined with the steel grip she'd had on her hand had given Madeline no other choice but to suck it up and follow his orders.

Ryan had forced her to face her pain today—even though he had no idea at all of what had caused it in the first place.

'Madeline, Madeline!'

One little girl called Alina was showing her a set of pearly white teeth and Madeline clapped her hands, then directed her to rinse her mouth out with bottled water and spit onto the grass.

She was annoyed with herself for being distracted. A small part of her was also annoyed at being putty in Ryan's hands after the way he'd handled her in the lake, but another part—a stronger part—was impressed that he'd called her out on her fears and, as a result, had shifted something inside her, somehow.

She smiled to herself as she watched a volunteer in knee-length denim shorts walk up with sticks and cardboard for the night's fire. Now she could think of Toby. Now she could compare the look of relief and thanks her young friend and patient had so often given her with the look of Abigail, a girl she'd been able to help. And now she could see that *both* times she'd done everything she possibly could have.

'Dinner!'

Someone called out the magic word from up at the camp, causing all the kids to start scrambling up, commencing their nightly routine of hugging her one by one, tightly. It was their cue to head back to their families and Madeline's to collect her boring rice and beans—not that she ever complained.

Seeing the way people lived in the Amazon, on whatever they could catch, or grow, or fetch in small supplies from towns after days of rowing upstream, was doing wonders for her gratitude levels in general.

'Night!' she said to the kids one by one, hugging them in return and watching them run off giggling into the twilight.

She was starting to forget she'd ever lived a life in which all thoughts of kids—of being around them, interacting with them—had been torture. Maybe she'd quit nursing too soon...

Ryan came in late to the dining room. Madeline was sitting beside Maria, finishing a second banana, when he walked in, grabbed a plate, filled it with food and walked back out again. He looked as though he was in a rush. Was there another emergency?

'Did he see another tarantula?' she joked with Maria, scanning the ceiling for a moment.

Maria smiled and shrugged, digging her fork into a boiled egg.

Disappointment, then annoyance swirled in Madeline's belly when she realised that Ryan might well be ignoring her after what had happened between them.

She couldn't help reliving the image of his well-endowed lower half, exposed to the sun on the deck right in front of her, the feel of his expert hands trailing the soap around her navel and down towards... Well... A mistake. Surely they both knew that?

She put down her banana peel, pictured having an early night—another torturous one with Ryan in a silent tent so close to hers—but to her surprise, when she walked outside through the usual flurry of buzzing insects trying to get to her flesh, she saw him sitting by the fire with Evan, unpacking what looked like a box.

Madeline stopped in her tracks, but Maria beckoned her forward. She was carrying two cups of tea for them in metal cups.

'Come on, honey—come and sit down. It's been a long day,' she said kindly.

Evan was playing the guitar that she remembered Ryan talking about. They each had a beer on the ground beside them.

Ryan stood up when he saw her, holding out another beer which he'd pulled from the box on the ground. 'For you,' he said, eyes twinkling.

He'd taken his hat off and his hair was sticking up crazily again, as though he'd wrestled with a bush. He looked as rugged and wild and ridiculously handsome as the first time she'd seen him on television—except that now, of course, she'd seen parts of him his regular audience never got to see.

'Thank you,' she said, taking the lukewarm bottle from him as Maria put her tea on the ground. 'I'll drink that after,' she told her, and Maria winked.

'We had it delivered especially,' said Ryan, offering Maria one. She declined. 'Figured we had a few things to celebrate.'

The light from the fire was playing in Ryan's hair, and although he looked tired he seemed relaxed, for once. He moved across the log he was sitting on so she could sit beside him.

'A *few* things to celebrate?' she said cryptically, and he raised an eyebrow in silent acknowledgement of their secret.

Madeline felt hot—and not just because of the fire Mark was now prodding with a long stick. She noticed Ryan's Boston Red Sox T-shirt, more casual than anything she'd ever seen him in, and his jeans as he stretched out his legs and feet towards the fire. He was still in his trusted British boots.

Others joined them as they trickled over from the dining hall. She felt Ryan's eyes on her every now and then, as hot as the sparks bouncing from the burning sticks, until eventually he leaned in to whisper in her ear.

'You did good today. You made me very proud.'

She turned to him. His face was so close she almost brushed his nose with hers, and the movement sent a familiar flight of butterflies coursing through her.

'What exactly are we talking about, here?'

He smiled, brushing her ear with his nose. 'You back in scrubs.'

She rolled her eyes, but he nudged her with his elbow.

'And out of them, of course.'

Madeline tried not to smirk as she took a sip of her drink. No one was looking at them, but she was more than aware of Jake, the camera guy, lurking not far away, no doubt waiting to catch anything juicy. She'd seen him zooming in on her before.

'That was a mistake,' she whispered, wishing she didn't have to say it.

'I know,' he said, brushing her ear again—with his lips this time.

She leaned away, her limbs growing weaker. 'I should thank you for what you had me do in surgery,' she managed after a moment.

Ryan took a swig from his bottle. Evan was strumming another song now and one of the volunteers, a lady in her thirties with straight red hair, had started to sing.

'I wouldn't have asked you to do what you did,' he said, 'if I hadn't thought all along that you could.'

'Well, you have more faith in me than I do,' she said, and sighed. 'But, seriously, you really helped me today, Ryan—more than you know. You've made me think about...things.'

'Like the thing that made you quit nursing?'

'Yes, I guess so.'

'Whatever it was, Madeline, you have to let it go. It's in the past.'

'You're right,' she said, nodding. 'Maybe *you* should remember that, too? Leave some things in the past?'

Ryan looked at the floor for a moment. A faint smile crossed his mouth as he shook his head. 'So what was it? *Who* was it that made you give up?'

'A boy called Toby,' she said, letting the words leave her mouth without giving them a chance to get stuck like they usually did.

She gripped her beer bottle in both hands, started picking at the label with her too-long nails.

'He was the first patient put in my care when I qualified—we got really close, you know? I would take him books and games, and I would tell him everything would be OK. Really, he was helping me as much as I was helping him. I was nervous, I was new, and he would say the right things... Like, "You're the best nurse, Madeline. I trust you, and I'm so glad you're here."'

'Sounds like a good kid,' Ryan said, putting his empty bottle down on the ground. 'What was wrong with him?'

'Leukaemia. Chronic lymphocytic leukaemia,' she said, feeling the familiar pang. 'He was strong for months, but one night on my shift he had sudden respiratory distress and I couldn't do anything...'

She trailed off, emotions rising.

'There was nothing I could do… He went into cardiac arrest and I couldn't even call his mother in time—'

'Of course you couldn't,' Ryan cut in, putting a big hand around her shoulder on impulse.

His voice was firm, as it had been in the medical station when he'd thrown her the scrubs. He pulled her in against him.

'You couldn't have done anything.' He shuffled closer to her on the log, moved his other hand to her knee. 'Toby never blamed you, Maddy—not for anything. And it wasn't your fault.'

'I know,' she said, putting a hand over his automatically in response. 'I know that now. But I didn't want to hear that for a really long time.'

'Because you missed him. And you felt like you'd failed him when you hadn't. You made his last few months so much better, and that was a parting gift he never would have had otherwise.'

Ryan's words were making her eyes turn to hot, wet pools again, and she blinked, not wanting to make a scene.

'Sometimes you *want* to feel the pain,' he whispered, 'because you don't believe you're entitled to feel anything else. Am I right?'

She could hear his voice crack just a little bit as he continued to hold her against him. He'd never touched her in public before. She was equally moved and afraid.

'You're so right,' she whispered back.

He looked down at his boots and after a while removed his arm from around her. She half expected him to stand up and walk away from his own feelings and the cameras yet again.

'Sometimes you think you'll just wallow in it for

ever, because you don't know how else to be any more,' she murmured.

He didn't get up. Instead he pressed his hot palm against her palm and laced his fingers through her own.

'God, Maddy,' he said on an exhale, 'I know exactly how *that* feels.'

CHAPTER THIRTEEN

HE DID KNOW. Ryan knew exactly how it felt to live under a blanket of insecurity and self-doubt. It was the exact opposite of the image he portrayed to the world.

He squeezed Madeline's hand, brought it onto his lap and looked down at their tangled fingers. The truth about Josephine seemed too big and too daunting to think about most days—even to himself. And he'd grown used to the ghosts that lived inside him...grown accustomed to the haunting taunts that had left him cold, even with a camera on his smiling face and four hundred thousand Twitter fans calling him 'hot'.

Madeline knew the bare bones of what was bothering him. He wanted to tell her everything—of course he did—because for the first time in a long time he realised he actually *needed* to talk about it.

He glanced at her profile, at the firelight bouncing in her eyes as she hummed along to Evan's music. He wanted to do so much more than talk with Madeline. She'd told him what had spawned *her* deepest insecurities. Couldn't he provide her with the same intimacy?

A frown creased his brow. Letting go of the past meant letting her in, and that was still a risk. Where would it end? Where would she stop with the information he offered her? How much would she put in a book to feed the vultures? She wasn't here to feed his ego, or his desires. She was here to write the book he'd been dreading and they both knew she couldn't give it less than her best.

'Mind if I play?'

Madeline's voice broke into his warring thoughts. She was talking to Evan. Everyone's eyes were on her so she dropped his hand back into the shadows. They'd probably seen anyway, he realised. After today, though, and the fears she'd faced in surgery, he had no doubt the producer would want to interview her about her back story, and him on why he'd been so insistent that she help him. Anything to make good TV.

At least he could pass their hand-holding off as affection between colleagues who'd saved a life.

With a slight look of surprise, Evan handed the guitar over to Madeline. He folded his arms across his chest as she pulled the instrument onto her lap.

'I only know a few songs,' she said a little shyly as she cast him a sideways glance.

Her fingers were already moving over the frets, though, creating a melody. Ryan noticed Mark and Evan grinning at each other like schoolboys, clearly impressed. Madeline had agreed to try improvising some songs for the kids, but she'd never admitted to being able to play like this. There was so much he still didn't know about this woman.

'Where did you learn to play?' he said into her ear.

'Colombia. I learned a lot there,' she replied.

Then she launched into a song he recognised immediately: *Moon River*.

Chills ran through his veins in spite of the humidity and the fire. He saw Maria's mouth fall open. Madeline could *really* sing. Her voice was like hot honey trickling over him, and he couldn't keep his eyes from her face. Her skin was glowing; her whole presence was pure light.

Ryan swore in that moment that he'd never seen or heard anything quite as exquisite as Madeline Savoia in his whole life.

When she wrapped up the final verse and chorus the circle broke out into rapturous applause—and *his* clapping, he realised, was the loudest. Evan shot him a knowing look, which he chose to ignore. For this one night, he decided, he was letting go. He was not going to give a damn what anyone thought.

'Can I keep this for tomorrow?' Madeline asked Evan, holding the guitar close against her. 'Ryan said the kids love to sing—we could probably do something fun around the dental hygiene stuff.'

'By all means, please do,' Evan said, holding his hands up. 'It sounds much better in your company than mine.'

Ryan smiled. 'I'm sure there's a tune in her about toothpaste.'

He heard Evan emit a snort—probably at the stupid words that had just slipped from his mouth. He stood up, rooted around in his pockets and pulled out his flashlight. Holding it up, he motioned for Madeline to hand him the guitar.

'I'll walk you back to the dining hall with that. No room in your tent, I'm guessing.'

She stood up herself and gave him the guitar. 'I was thinking of calling it a night anyway. It's been a long day, you know.'

'I know,' he said, feeling his pulse quicken suddenly.

He had no clue where this was leading, but he knew

he had to get them both away from the fire and all the prying eyes and ears.

They wished the group goodnight, and walked away into the shadows.

'You have quite a voice, you know,' he told her, shining his light into the dining room, opening the squeaky mesh door and resting the guitar on one of the benches before stepping out again and walking with Madeline towards the tents. 'I might have followed *you* around that university campus if you'd been there,' he said, 'instead of my acapella girl. She didn't even like me back.'

Madeline laughed, pushing her hands into her pockets as they walked across the grass and stopped outside her tent. 'How do you know *I* like you?'

The air was hot, even away from the fire, and Ryan couldn't help thinking that this would be the perfect night to be out on the river again. The fireflies were holding a glow-stick party in the trees around them and all he could think about was kissing her.

He turned off his flashlight, plunging them both into darkness.

'I know you like me,' he said in reply. 'You didn't exactly bat me off this morning.'

They were hovering outside her tent now. Her hands were still in her pockets. He stepped closer, reached for her arm and let his fingers slide slowly down from her elbow to the edge of one pocket till she was forced to set her hand free. He took it again in his, clasped his fingers around it, stepped even closer.

'This morning at the lake,' he said softly. 'I knew you were there the whole time.'

He could hear the smile in her voice when she responded. 'I thought about swimming past you and getting out, but I didn't.'

She was so close to him now. The crickets seemed to be serenading them. He reached for her other hand and she released it willingly, clasping it even tighter around his fingers. The tips of their shoes were touching.

Ryan leaned in closer. Their faces were an inch apart. He could feel her breath on his nose. Every bone in his body was weakening by the millisecond...except maybe one. He brushed her lips with just his shadow, but in a heartbeat Madeline was stepping backwards, swatting at something in the darkness and cursing.

'Are you OK? What happened?' He reached for her immediately in the darkness.

'Stupid mosquitoes. Just got me hard on the ankle.'

'Did you spray?'

'I forgot.'

Her hand was still in his as she scratched at her ankle with the other one, but the moment was gone—he knew it. He could feel it slipping further away into the trees.

He sighed to himself and shook his head. 'It's always the brightest lights that attract the most mosquitos,' he said, remembering a quote he'd read somewhere once.

'I'm not shining a light.' Madeline straightened up. 'And neither are you.'

He smiled. 'It's a metaphor. Your ex was a mosquito, drawn to your light. I was thinking about this earlier. Good thing you squished him.'

She stood still in the blackness. 'Very poetic. I should write that down. But he squished *me*, so to speak.'

'It's still a good thing that all the squishing went on... I think.'

'So do I. If I was still with Jason I wouldn't be here

now.' Madeline paused. 'Ryan, what's happening here?' Her question was cautious, but loaded.

'I have no clue,' he replied honestly, brushing his thumb against the side of her hand slowly.

He felt her shiver...practically felt her weaken alongside him as the moment they'd lost suddenly reappeared like a huge gaping window.

'I'm here to do a job,' she said softly, almost with regret. 'And I thought we agreed this morning was a mistake.'

He leaned forward so their foreheads were touching, feeling a zip through his insides at their closeness, at what they were surely about to do.

'Maybe it was. Maybe it wasn't. You're doing your job, Maddy, and more. So am I.'

'Not properly. I can't do it properly until you give me answers. Just now you told me you know how I've been feeling. What did you mean, exactly?'

He let out an anguished groan against her forehead. 'Why do you *do* this to me?'

'You know why. Ryan, I really don't think we should confuse this...'

'Screw thinking,' he growled.

Before she could say anything else he reached for the back of her head and pressed his lips to hers.

Madeline was almost flat against him in an instant, flowing into his arms like water as he bunched up her hair. She reached for his face, kissing him back just as hard. He felt his heart contracting and expanding in his chest as she flattened her hands against him, then clutched the material of his Boston Red Sox T-shirt as though she couldn't touch enough of him in one go. She tasted of beer and excitement, and somewhere at the back of his perpetually foggy mind he felt a cloud lifting.

Their tongues started a slow dance, then a faster tango as they kissed and kissed and kissed, and he found he was losing himself, losing his own tangled mind, for the first time in a really long time.

'We should move inside,' he whispered eventually against her lips, heart hammering, his flesh itching to touch more of hers.

Madeline's breaths were hot and heavy as her left hand reached for the button at the top of his jeans.

He motioned to the tent. 'Inside,' he said again, more urgently.

She turned around to unzip the tent, but a rustle behind them in the trees made them freeze. A flashlight appeared, pointing straight at them.

He stepped away from Madeline. 'Who's there?'

'Ryan? It's Mark. There's an emergency—we need you at the station.'

'Dammit,' he muttered, meeting Madeline's wide eyes in the flashlight as she stood up straighter. There was disappointment etched all over her face—and his, too, he was sure. Thank God Mark was standing too far away to see them clearly. 'Be right there!' he called, trying his best to sound as though he *hadn't* just spent the last five or ten minutes glued to Madeline's face.

Mark hurried off and Ryan closed the gap between them, snaking an arm around Madeline in the darkness. He kissed her again—hard and meaningfully.

'Duty calls,' he said with another groan. 'Get some sleep.'

'Will you wake me up later?' she asked suggestively.

She was sliding a hand down his chest to his jeans

again. He thanked the jungle for the darkness as something started standing to attention.

Pulling her hand away, he brought her fingers to his mouth and kissed them. 'Like you've woken *me* up?' he said gruffly. 'Madeline Savoia, you are officially killing me.'

CHAPTER FOURTEEN

With her hands against Ryan's firm torso, even with his T-shirt between her and his bare flesh, Madeline had felt rocket ships launch inside her.

She rolled over in her sleeping bag, listening to the bugs outside and the growing wind ruffling the trees. They were here to do a job, she reminded herself once again. She also had to keep reminding herself that she wasn't about to start leaning on any other man to help fill a void in her life. Even if that man *was* Ryan Tobias.

She wished she knew what time it was. Sleep had been eluding her for hours, and Ryan still hadn't come back. It crossed her mind that maybe he'd realised the error of his ways and retreated to his own tent after solving whatever emergency problem had come up, but her ego told her otherwise. He wanted her, no matter what. Right? *He'd* been the one who'd initiated everything. He'd approached her in the lake…held her hand by the fire. He'd kissed her.

She put a hand to her lips, swollen and plump from those kisses. Her chin was still tingling in the wake of his stubble.

She pulled the sleeping bag over her head. So much for her being a professional. She needed him next to her *now*. She needed to feel his skin on hers. She wanted him to make love to her so badly she didn't think she'd be able to function otherwise. But where the hell *was* he?

When dawn arrived and she still hadn't slept a wink, she grabbed her toothbrush and water, pulled the zipper up on her tent and crawled outside, yawning. The camp was eerily quiet. Usually there were one or two people milling about, cleaning their teeth outside their tents, doing star jumps to wake themselves up.

She wandered towards the medical stations. The sky wasn't as yellow as it usually was at this time of day. It was a deep, ominous grey, looming large against the treetops like the roof of another dark tent. Rain was on the way again, she thought as she spotted a howler monkey leap from one branch overhead to another.

She saw Maria, walking from one station to another. Madeline followed her, pushing back the plastic sheet over the door. 'Morning,' she said.

Maria spun around in surprise, her hands full of the gauzes she was relocating from a box to a table. 'Oh, Madeline, hi—you're up early.'

'I couldn't sleep. Where is…?' She paused, realising she probably shouldn't ask specifically about Ryan. 'Where is everyone?'

'It was kind of a crazy night,' Maria said, and for the first time Madeline noticed the dark circles under her eyes. 'Guy got attacked by a black caiman up the river; the crew left about an hour ago to see to him.'

'Attacked?' Madeline realised she was still holding her toothbrush. She slid it into the pocket of her denim shorts.

'Five metres long, it was—apparently. Guy got too close to her eggs, we're guessing.'

'Is he OK?'

'If you count being alive as "OK" he's OK. They flew

him to the hospital and now they're back at the village. The crew wanted to do some filming there, I think. They'll probably be gone awhile.'

Madeline couldn't help the disappointment settling in her stomach like a lead balloon. She felt for whoever had been chomped on by a caiman, of course, but she also felt selfishly resentful of being kept from Ryan even longer.

'Oh, the producer wants to talk to you,' Maria said, making Madeline's heart falter for a second.

'Really? What about?'

She started to pray internally. Had Mark said something about how close she and Ryan had been standing outside her tent when he'd sprung up on them? Were they all writing stories of their own already? Was the producer going to tell her to back off—to be professional or not be there at all?

'I think she wants an interview about the girl you helped yesterday, if that's OK?'

Madeline tried not to sigh out loud in relief. She was way too paranoid. 'I'm sure that will be fine,' she said.

She left Maria sorting her gauzes and made her way back towards her tent. But the heat was already making the air intolerably stuffy and she knew that in a canvas bubble she'd simply sweat and feel uncomfortable.

At the last minute Madeline turned, passed the ashes from the fire and followed the path towards the river. She sometimes liked to wander down and chat in Spanish to the local guys who hung out there, waiting to row people up and down from village to village. Besides, she needed to wake up before the kids started gathering around her for the day. She was so tired. Now that she thought about it, she was actually still in a dream.

'Madeline Savoia, you are officially killing me.'

The longing in his voice as he'd said those words had made a pinball machine of her body, sending hot white sparks zig-zagging downwards from her ears, to her nipples, to her toes.

She'd never been kissed like that before. It had been like something from a movie, she mused, the way he'd reached for her and yanked her forward, pressed his mouth to hers as if she was some kind of lifeline. Maybe she was.

So romantic.

She was halfway to the river when a voice in the trees, slightly in the distance, caught her attention. Stopping in her tracks and yawning sleepily again, she listened closer and heard it yet again. It was a man's voice and it sounded vaguely familiar. One of the crew?

They were probably filming just outside the village. Or maybe there was another emergency. She frowned to herself, feeling stupid. She should be helping them. After what had happened yesterday Madeline was starting to feel she should probably be doing a lot more around camp than simply writing and teaching the kids about cleaning their teeth—much as she loved them.

Maybe she should be assisting in every medical procedure she could, to build her confidence up. Maybe she should even go back to nursing when she returned to London…

Another voice, closer now, yanked her out of her thoughts. She turned towards it, started walking the other pathway towards the noise. As she did so a crash of thunder overhead made her jump. She noticed with dismay that the sky was even darker. She could hear the voices, still ahead of her, and she sped up, clutching her water bottle.

Raindrops started thudding onto the leaves and foliage above her, a few of them slipping through onto her skin. Rain always sounded so much louder in the jungle.

The path was thinning a little. Some way ahead she heard what sounded like the whole team having a heated conversation about something. The rain was too loud for her to make any of the words out, but Madeline was sure there must have been another emergency. She hoped she'd be able to help.

She pushed through a wall of vines and came to a small clearing with what looked like several paths of flattened grass leading away from it in different directions. At the sound of a male voice she carried onwards, and when she turned a small corner she saw them, gathered in a circle, looking down at something on the leaf-strewn ground.

Madeline was just about to call out when she froze in her tracks.

It wasn't the crew.

Her heart leapt straight into her windpipe as she took them in. A group of guys—maybe seven or eight—olive-skinned and covered in black tattoos, some in black shirts, some in white, all studying what she was pretty certain was a dead body. They were speaking quickly amongst themselves, loudly in Spanish, and they hadn't seen her.

Slowly, so as not to make a single branch or twig crack, she stepped backwards, never taking her eyes off them. That was when she saw a flash of metal: an AK-47 being brandished about wildly by a shirtless guy who looked and sounded angry about something.

Drug runners, she thought, trafficking between Colombia and Brazil, no doubt…or planning to. She was almost paralysed with fear. She couldn't be certain that was what they were, but she couldn't hang around to find out.

Somehow she forced herself to move, thankful for the rain now coming down even harder, silencing her footsteps. She found herself back in the clearing, but in a panic realised in horror that she couldn't remember which way she'd come.

She cursed under her breath, hearing movement behind her. The group was getting closer.

Had they heard her?

Which way was the right way?

Feeling nauseous, Madeline started to run. In her hurry she dropped her water bottle, found the path, then ran even faster till her lungs began to burn and the branches slashed at her limbs like an evil army.

As she gasped for air in the suffocating heat she couldn't for the life of her figure out where she was. The path looked the same as the one she'd walked in on, yet it was totally different. She was lost in the jungle.

Fear flooded her veins. The rain pummelled punishingly at her head, arms and legs. Thunder crashed above her and the bugs upped their symphony, as though trying to compete with the noise. She turned and ran back the way she'd come. At least she *thought* it was the way she'd come.

She couldn't hear the voices any more, but then she couldn't hear anything at all—nothing but the rain, and the wind, howling all around her like tortured spirits.

Tears of helplessness brimmed in her eyes. She heard Ryan's voice in her head—the way he'd sounded back when he'd warned her: *'The jungle has a way of luring people in and keeping them.'*

No. *No!* How could she have been so stupid? She had to get out. She had to get back to the camp.

She picked up her pace, but in another second her sandal caught on something long and sharp and she fell hard to the ground, smacking her head. She barely had time to yelp or blink before blackness consumed her.

CHAPTER FIFTEEN

'Where's Madeline?'

Ryan couldn't keep the question in any longer. He'd been back for over an hour and hadn't seen her playing with the kids under the tree or anywhere else, like she usually was. The guitar was still in the dining room where they'd left it, seemingly untouched, which he found odd because she'd seemed pretty excited about playing it and starting to make up songs.

He'd gone for a swim in the lake the moment the rain had eased off, hoping she might be there, but she wasn't.

'I haven't seen her since this morning,' Maria told him, taking the thermometer from the mouth of the kid who was sitting on the table in front of her.

'This morning?'

'First thing. She was up at dawn, before the storm rolled in. Is she not in her tent?'

Ryan's jaw started to pulse. He didn't want to seem overly concerned but something didn't feel right. He left the station and walked across the wet, muddy grass, sparkling with the remnants of the storm. It was gone four p.m. and it would be dark in a few short hours.

Reaching Madeline's tent, he rapped on the canvas door. No reply.

Without hesitation he unzipped it and looked inside.

Her sleeping bag was in a crumpled heap on the mattress. A can of DEET was resting beside it. He straightened up again, swiftly scanning the swaying treeline.

He saw Mark appearing from his own tent, and walked over. 'Have you seen Madeline?'

'No, sir, not since last night.'

'Call everyone into the dining room, now.' Ryan was already walking towards it quickly.

It didn't take long for word to spread and for everyone on camp to gather in the enclosed space. All wore looks of concern, which unnerved him further. Jake, who'd been following him all day as they'd fixed up the man who'd been mauled by a caiman, was still rolling the camera, obviously sensing excitement in the air.

Ryan took off his baseball hat, dashed his hand through his hair as he tried to force his voice to stay controlled. 'Has anyone here seen Madeline Savoia since this morning?' he asked.

Silence.

He could see people looking around them in confusion. The way Mark was looking at Evan almost made him snap. Others were shaking their heads, looking at the floor.

He turned to Maria. 'Maria, did she say anything about where she was going when she left you?'

Maria shrugged, looked helpless. 'Not a lot…but I was busy. I told her the producer wanted to talk to her and—'

'What did she say when you said that?' he asked, hoping to God Madeline hadn't freaked out and let any paranoia over their…*situation*…get the better of her.

'Nothing, really, just that she was fine with it. She sounded perfectly normal—a little tired, maybe…'

'Tired?'

'She said she didn't sleep much.'

Ryan rarely panicked, but he was panicking now. Madeline was exhausted and had obviously wandered off somewhere. That could only lead to bad things in the jungle. Maybe she'd been caught in the storm. Anything could have happened.

'We're splitting up and we're going to find her,' he said resolutely. 'Evan, Mark—go back to the village. Take the sat phones. Maria, go with Pablo to the river, get on the boat and keep your eyes peeled. Take your sat phone, too—everyone take your sat phones...keep in touch...'

Ryan doled out responsibilities, then watched his people hurrying off two by two until he was the only one left—just him and Jake with the camera.

He grabbed some bananas, raced to his tent and lifted his pack, slinging it over his shoulders. 'I'll be right out,' he called to Jake. 'Actually, can you grab some more water and meet me back here?'

'No problem.'

Jake turned back the way they'd come and Ryan took his moment to flee alone.

Anger, fear and dread propelled him forward as he set out on the path, fixing his phone to the belt of his khaki trousers. He'd been in this situation before, and he did *not* need a camera filming his every movement. He did *not* need anyone seeing anything they didn't need to see, if that was what this was going to come to.

He hoped to hell it wasn't.

Josephine's face flashed to the forefront of his mind, bright and smiling, then pale and cold. He bit down hard on the inside of his cheek, fought to keep his breathing steady and his feet treading safely, quickly on the path.

This day wouldn't end up like that one had—not if he

had anything to do with it. It *couldn't*. He couldn't handle it again. He'd barely handled it before. And even now, with the faint glimmer of sunshine that was Madeline on the horizon, those demons were still dancing around him in the darkness, willing him to slip up or break.

He called her name. The air was thick, hot, suffocating.

Keeping tabs on his own whereabouts, he crossed the clearing. His phone buzzed and squawked. He could hear people talking over the radio. His crew were all out there, spread like a spider's web between the trees. The village had their people out now, too, but no one had seen her yet.

He was just about to take another step when he paused in front of an object. He bent down, picked up a toothbrush. It was one of the same branded batch they'd brought with them for the kids. One that Madeline would have had. He shoved it into a pocket.

A shape up ahead caught his eye next. He stopped in his tracks, waiting for it to move.

'Madeline?'

He stepped closer cautiously, adrenaline pumping through him. It was a person—a woman, he realised with sudden nausea—lying still on the ground like a fallen log, rain-soaked and lifeless in an unnatural heap.

Ryan's heart plunged as he hurried to her side. She was facing away from him, and he saw with utter horror the pool of blood spreading like a crimson lake from her stomach out onto the muddy, mossy ground.

He fell to his knees as his very soul seemed to splinter around him.

'Madeline?' A whisper now. His voice barely audible.

Long dark hair was splayed across the woman's face, hiding her features, and he felt like throwing up. He put a hand to her cheek. Cold, clammy. She was gone. He swallowed the sob that rose in his throat. He hadn't deserved her. He knew it. He never had.

He pushed the hair back from her face, ready to haul her into his arms and let grief consume him, but shock froze him as her features came into view. The rounded nose, the plump lips, the thick, bushy eyebrows.

It wasn't Madeline.

This poor woman had been murdered. There was no doubt about that. But she wasn't Madeline.

Ryan stood up quickly and almost stumbled as he reached for his penknife and readied himself to wield it against an attacker. He swiped at his tears, spun around, half expecting a Colombian drug runner to lunge in his direction. But all he could hear was the wind and the birds and the distant howl of a monkey.

With his eyes on the treeline he pulled his sat phone from his belt, radioed in his grim discovery, reading out the GPS location so the crew could come back for her and carried on, on his way, hope his motivation.

The light was fading and the wind was picking up again—like the rain. He knew another shower was on its way and prayed it wouldn't be as bad as the last one. He'd changed course now and was only a few metres back from the river. This was far enough away so that Madeline would never be spotted by Maria and Pablo from the boat, but not so far... Madeline might have gone just a little off track and thought she was further away from camp than she really was.

He let out a silent prayer. The rain started pattering more heavily on his hat and Ryan struggled to keep it together.

'Any luck?' It was Mark on the radio.

'Not yet,' he replied, trying to sound optimistic. 'She can't have gone far.'

But he heard his own voice crack in despair.

It was happening all over again.

He was just about to sink to the ground when he saw her. He almost dropped his phone. She was huddled under a tree, arms wrapped around herself, her eyes closed.

'Madeline!'

He was in front of her in a heartbeat, kneeling on the ground, letting the rain slam into him as he pulled his pack from his back, dropping it next to her.

'Madeline, it's me—look at me.'

He reached his hands to her face, hoping her cheeks wouldn't be as cold as those of the lifeless lady he'd just touched. To his utter relief her eyes fluttered open just a little. There was blood on her head, trickling down her right cheek and onto his hands. She looked dazed.

'What happened?' he asked, scooting even closer to her, inspecting the damage. 'Can you talk? Are you in pain?'

'Ryan?' Recognition flickered in her eyes before they flooded with tears. She reached out to him and wrapped her arms around his shoulders.

She could move, thank God. Her arms were weak but that hug, along with the sound of her voice, was everything he needed in that moment. He held her tight against him for a minute, swallowed more tears in private against her soft neck, then untangled her from him.

'I don't know what the *hell* you were thinking,' he blurted, sweeping her matted hair behind her ears, scanning her eyes, hearing his own voice croak again. 'Didn't I tell you *never* to go anywhere alone out here? Maddy, you could've been *killed*! Didn't I tell you…? Weren't you listening?'

'I'm sorry… I'm so sorry…'

'I could have lost you, too.'

He held her face, pressed his lips to her forehead for a long moment, letting them burn into her skin, breathing in her life at the same time.

'I didn't know what I was going to find.'

'Drug runners,' she whispered, clutching his hand and wincing as she tried to move again. 'I saw them. I think they killed someone, Ryan.'

'I think you're right about that. Now we need to get you cleaned up.'

It looked as though she'd fallen and hit her head at some point. She was covered in mud, too, and had probably dragged herself to the tree after her fall. She was clearly disorientated, and likely dehydrated.

He reached for his pack, pulled out a bottle of water and held it to her mouth. 'You need to drink, Maddy,' he said. 'As much as you can.'

With her eyes closed she did as she was told. Remembering the sat phone, he announced that he'd found her, and told the crew his co-ordinates. As he was talking he noticed that the insect bites on her legs and arms had caused her limbs to swell. She'd obviously come out without DEET on again. Either that or it had been washed off.

He was amazed she wasn't more hurt.

The rain was coming down hard again and Ryan knew it was going to be hell, trying to make it back to camp with her like this. He reached into his pack and pulled out the thin plastic sheet, stood and shook it out. It took him less than two minutes to hang it between three surrounding branches, creating a makeshift shelter. He pulled another sheet out and laid it on the ground, helped her onto it and sat close beside her.

At least they were dry, for now.

'What's that?' she asked, watching him pull tincture from his pack, along with some swabs and gauze.

'Iodine,' he said, holding it up. 'Here, let me look at you. You're still bleeding.'

He placed two fingers under her chin and she balled his shirt in her fists against his chest as he swabbed at the cut on her head, then applied antiseptic.

She screwed up her face. 'Stings,' she said.

'I'm not surprised. Did you pass out?'

'For a bit, I think. I was trying to get away from them. I heard them behind me, then I got lost. I feel like such an idiot. I'm so sorry, Ryan.'

'Not as sorry as *I'd* have been if anything worse had happened to you. You must have lost them, but there's a dead woman not far from here. I think they left her there.'

He started to apply a patch to the wound, but Madeline pulled back, putting a hand over her mouth.

'So they *did* kill someone?'

He nodded grimly. 'I saw her. We're retrieving the body.'

Her eyes were wide. 'I saw them standing around her. I saw a gun.'

'She was stabbed,' he said, grateful again for the miraculous fact that the same fate hadn't befallen her. He pulled a banana out of his pack. 'Eat this—you must be starving.'

He swabbed at some of the blood on her arms and legs with a cloth. Thankfully most of it had come from her head and the rest of her was unharmed except for the bites.

'We'll wait the rain out, then we'll get you back. Why did you walk off on your own?'

'I thought I might be able to help with a case. I thought I heard you talking, but it wasn't you. I can't believe... That poor woman. Why would they do that?'

'Any number of reasons. They make up their own rules out here.'

He pulled her to his side, wrapped an arm around her shoulders protectively as she ate and drank slowly, both of them listening to the rain. As the crickets chirped and the bats started swooping he felt the frantic thudding of his heart finally begin to subside.

'What happened with the guy who got attacked by the caiman?' Madeline asked.

Ryan stretched his legs out on the sheet. 'He wasn't as lucky as you—lost most of one arm. Luckily he had a friend with him who was able to call for help when it happened.'

She grimaced.

'We're just skin and blood and bones in the jungle, I guess,' he said, resting a cheek against her hair. 'We're all the same. We're all just food in a chain. Moving targets.'

'Terrifying, isn't it?' she said softly.

'Terrifying.'

He tightened his arm around her small frame, banishing the thought from his mind that Madeline might have been the one mauled or eaten or shot.

Ryan hadn't even known it was within him to feel so responsible, to feel so...*anything* about anyone, until today. The depth of his feelings now—the way they'd sprung upon him around this woman—was as terrifying as the jungle. But it also made him feel incredibly alive. More alive, perhaps, than he'd felt in five whole years.

CHAPTER SIXTEEN

MADELINE WATCHED THEM bringing the body of the murdered woman into the camp from her place on the bench in the dining room. Through the mesh of the walls she could make out Ryan, Jake and the producer, plus two volunteers carrying the stretcher across the grass.

They'd been informed it was a lady from another village, probably employed to traffic drugs up the river. She tore her eyes away as tears blurred her vision, pulling the blanket around her for comfort. Shock was sinking in now that she was finally safe.

She also felt impossibly idiotic.

She'd never been more relieved to see anyone in her whole life than she had when Ryan had found her under that tree. He'd been angry at first—that much she understood. She could hardly blame him. She'd gone against everything he'd told her when she'd stepped off that path and followed what she'd thought were her instincts.

She knew half of his anger was coming from a place of fear, though: fear of her being hurt. He'd shown her nothing but kindness ever since.

The ibuprofen Ryan had given her had taken some of her aches away, and a soothing gel had stopped her bites from itching. She'd eaten what she could of a plate of white rice and vegetables, but thoughts of what might have happened to her out there kept careening through her mind like a crazy carousel, making her feel sick.

She put her fork down, pushed through the thin mesh door and walked outside to the fire, now blazing.

Maria held an arm out to her, beckoning her to sit next to her on the log. 'Did you eat?' she asked.

'I did, thank you.'

'How are you feeling now?'

'Stupid,' she answered honestly, staring at the flames.

Maria rested her head on her shoulder for a second, then smiled. 'Honey, we all make mistakes. We're just glad you're all right. It's a good thing Ryan sent the search party out when he did. It's just so crazy busy here that things can sometimes get overlooked...'

'It was *his* call to get everyone out looking for me?' she asked. She'd had no clue.

'He was the first to realise no one had seen you in a while.'

When Madeline turned towards Maria she noticed something in the older woman's tired eyes that she hadn't seen before. A slight twinkle.

'You're good for him,' Maria whispered, conspiratorially. 'Whatever it is you're doing, keep doing it.'

Madeline flushed, shook her head, but she didn't have time to respond before she felt a firm hand on her shoulder from behind. The next second Ryan was stepping over the log, crouching down in front of her, his handsome face in shadow, blocking the fire.

'Hey, how's your head now?'

He reached for the bandage over her wound to check it, and instinctively she brought her own up to cover his hand.

'I'll live,' she said, moving his hand down to her lap as he smiled in what looked like relief. Gratitude overwhelmed her. 'I can't thank you enough for coming to find me, Ryan—for sending everyone out to find me. Don't think I'll ever forget that.'

She reached out a hand to Maria, too, and as she looked between them she was flooded with warmth and the purest of appreciation for everything she had. Everything that the poor woman who'd lost her life out there would never have.

'I'm going to go back to nursing when I get home,' she announced. 'I want to finish what I started. For Toby.'

Maria squeezed her hand. Ryan raised his eyebrows as he sat on his haunches and tossed a stick into the fire. 'Good to hear it,' he said.

'You have no idea how inspiring you all are.'

'Well, thank you, honey,' Maria said, sounding pleased and a little embarrassed. 'Who's Toby?'

Madeline ran a hand through her tangled hair. It was weird, but she didn't feel as uncomfortable talking about him any more.

'Toby is the reason I'm here.'

As the words left her mouth she realised it was true. That little boy's death had forced her to run away from her duties...possibly even from her destiny.

She loved writing—she'd stumbled into it and had been blessed to have had adventures all around the world because of it—but it was still a means of escape. And in escaping she'd wound up here.

How strange.

She tilted her head up to the sky, to the stars. Had Toby planned this out? Anything was possible, she supposed. The longer she spent in the jungle, away from technology and crowds and confusing messages coming at her from every which way, the more she felt connected to the universe. The more she resonated with the truths she *couldn't* see.

The only things that were real, she decided, were the things she could hold in her heart.

Ryan was looking at her when she opened her eyes. He got to his feet, helping her to stand. 'You should rest,' he told her, his grey eyes full of concern.

'Goodnight—sleep tight,' Maria said, after giving her a hug, and Madeline didn't miss the surreptitious little wink she threw her in the firelight as Ryan led her away.

'I need a bath,' she said, halfway across the grass, pulling on his hand in the direction of the lake.

He looked back to camp—for the cameras, she assumed. Luckily there were none in sight.

'Come with me? I can't sleep like this.'

'I probably shouldn't,' he said, looking around them again warily.

But she was already guiding him down the path, through the trees and onto the deck. The moon was clear now the rain had gone, sending bright white beams across the black expanse of water so there was no need for a flashlight. The trees rustled overhead and the bats were swooping, catching flies. So peaceful.

She peeled off her shorts, then her muddied tank top, dropping them at her feet. Ryan was standing in front of her, watching her in what looked like wonder while taking off his boots. She smiled at him with newfound confidence, then stepped closer, reached for his shirt and motioned for him to lift his arms. With ease she pulled it over his head, shuddering as his hands landed on her waist and his lips grazed the top of her head.

'You're amazing—do you know that?' he whispered into her hair.

'So are you.'

'Infuriating...'

She grinned. 'So are you.'

'I kind of think I need you, though.'

His bare skin so close to hers sent shockwaves pulsing through Madeline's body. She pressed her hands to his chest, tilted her head up for his kiss, let her fingers trail down towards his khaki trousers and undid them quickly. He slid them off his legs, followed by his boxers. Then, when he'd swiftly undone her bra and tossed it to the side, he got to his knees, naked in front of her, dropped butterfly kisses around her belly button and slid her underwear down past her knees, over her feet and to the floor.

She gasped as he kissed his way back up, lingering on her inner thigh, running his hands up her legs as he did so.

'Let's get in,' he said, reaching for her hand.

They slid off the deck and into the water. Madeline was careful not to dunk her head, and to keep her bandage dry.

The water was a cool, blissful blanket, wrapping around her hot skin as Ryan reached for the bar of soap someone had left on the lakeside. He guided her out a little further, then pulled her back to his chest, kissing her neck from behind as he ran the soap over her chest. She held her arms out and he did the same to them.

The insect bites all over her skin were extra-sensitive, but strangely she found his gentle touch turned the irritation into something almost sensual. Madeline turned in his arms, returning his passionate kisses, and wrapped her legs around his middle. He held her up with ease, kissing her hungrily, and for a moment she wondered what they must look like from afar, chest to chest in the middle of a lake under the moon.

Take the drug runners and the dead body and the fact that she herself might have died today out of the equation and she couldn't help thinking that this was the greatest day of her whole life.

She grinned against his lips in spite of herself.

'What are you thinking?' he asked curiously, trailing the soap up and down her back.

'How life is pure magic,' she said.

He smiled into her eyes. 'That, right there, Madeline, is why I...like you.'

Madeline pressed her lips to his again, drawing him into another deep kiss, running her hands through his wet hair. He'd left a gap before saying 'like'. Had he been going to say something else?

Her heart thudded against his. It was trying its hardest to jump out of her skin. Of course he hadn't, she scolded herself.

She thought about the way she felt about him, the giddy smile he left on her face. She thought about the way he'd held her and helped her today, the way he'd all but forced her to face her fears about performing any kind of medical duty. Ryan had changed her life already...maybe even *saved* her life. And now they were kissing madly like teenagers in a lake, and there was nowhere else on earth she'd rather be...

They gathered up their clothes, and Ryan gave her his shirt to wear. Clutching the rest, they sneaked back the way they'd come, making absolutely certain not to be seen. There wasn't any discussion about where they'd be sleeping. Ryan simply looked around one more time outside his tent, unzipped the canvas door and motioned for her to crawl inside.

He crawled in after her, zipped up the door again behind them, and in a second it was just the two of them in the tiny enclosed space. Madeline's heart was doing back-flips.

He flattened out the sheets on his mattress accommodatingly, so she could lie down, then leaned over her on one arm and inspected her head. Just his palm against her cheek, then against the back of her head, had her breathing more heavily again in a second.

'We should change the dressing on that,' he said, reaching behind him for his bag.

She sat up and he pulled her legs around him so she was straddling him, and in the light of his flashlight he carefully reapplied the bandage over her cut with the skill she'd seen a hundred times on all those online videos.

Starstruck, she thought, *and at the mercy of his nimble fingers.* She *was* starstruck, but it was more than that now. He was a different person from the man she'd literally fallen into back in London. To her he was anyway.

When he was done he turned the light off, plunging them into darkness once again. Madeline reached her hands to his stubbled jaw, stroked his face and dropped kisses onto the edges of his mouth.

'Thank you,' she whispered.

Her legs wrapped more tightly around him of their own accord. In less than twenty seconds he somehow removed his shirt from her damp body, and everything from himself. Carefully he lowered her onto her back on the sheets, traced his fingers around her collarbone and down her stomach with a touch so light it left her skin a mass of tingles.

'How are you feeling now?' he asked, replacing his fingers with his lips and trailing kisses along her skin, back up to her mouth.

Madeline wrapped her arms around him from beneath, pulling him closer. 'Better, Doctor,' she breathed. 'A little bit better every second, actually.'

He continued his kissing trail, teasing her, driving her crazy. By the time he reached her inner thighs she was practically about to explode, but he stopped every now and then, found her lips again, and then let her flip him onto his back and sit astride him.

Madeline knew she had him in the palm of her hands...literally.

He groaned.

'Shh,' she teased, pulling away and flattening her hands against his chest, tracing his muscles, relishing every sinewy stretch of his amazing body. She was conscious suddenly that the wall separating their antics from the outside world was a millimetre thick and not exactly soundproof.

'It's pretty hard to be quiet when you're doing that,' he growled, and she pressed her lips to his again, silencing him.

The tent was hot, and already their bodies were melding together as one with perspiration. The bugs were still singing in the night outside. The wind whipped about the canvas every now and then like a jealous lover trying to get in. Her head was starting to hurt again, where she'd fallen, but when Ryan reached for his bag again and unwrapped a condom Madeline was beyond caring about *anything*.

'You carry these?' she asked in surprise, taking it from him and rolling it on.

He put his hands to her waist, lifted her with ease and flipped her onto her back again.

'Not for me,' he said in a low voice, resting on his hands either side of her and sucking on her lower lip for a second.

She moaned quietly as desire rocketed through her.

'Sometimes the crew need them. Sometimes we give them to the teenagers.'

'How generous,' she said, kissing him deeply as her legs encircled him from beneath once more.

She lost herself in their kiss again, in their twirling tongues and clashing teeth and soft moans and groans, until she gasped, biting on her own hand.

'Does it hurt?' he said softly, pausing, stroking her hair against the thin pillow.

'No, don't be silly. I just don't want to scream.'

'They'll just think you've seen a spider.'

'Very funny.'

'Seriously, Madeline, you feel incredible.'

Tears sprang to her eyes from out of nowhere and she wished it wasn't quite so dark. She was beyond exhausted and yet she was making love to Ryan Tobias—slowly, gently, beautifully in their own little bubble. There was so much admiration in his words and in his tone she felt it settle into her skin, deep into her bones.

He took his time, being careful not to hurt her any further after her ordeal, she was sure, but the result of his concern was something so passionate, so sensual she had literally never made love quite like it. Whatever he wasn't saying he was showing as he stroked and caressed her, kissed her everywhere he could reach over and over and over.

She reciprocated, of course, limited only by the space in the tent, and when Madeline woke up the next morning with his arms wrapped tightly around her she couldn't even remember when they'd finally stopped—or how, or why, or in which position. All she knew was that she'd never felt so worshipped in her whole life.

She also knew she was probably in deep trouble.

CHAPTER SEVENTEEN

RYAN WAS STANDING outside the medical station watching Madeline strumming the guitar under a tree. Her made-up songs were proving a hit. He couldn't be sure but he thought that right now she was singing something about cars on motorways, in Spanish. At any rate, the kids were squealing and singing along as if they'd never heard anything so fantastic.

He smiled, quashing the urge to walk over and join in. Of course hiding their relationship...or whatever it was that had blossomed between them since their first amazing night together in his tent...had not been easy.

Luckily they spent enough time together professionally to warrant her hanging out with him in the lake, and in his hammock, and in the boat on the river without too much need for explanation.

The boat had become a favourite of theirs. They liked to take a couple of blankets out with them, fish for piranhas and talk under the stars. Then they'd spend long hours making love to the sounds of the jungle, with the sighs of each other's pleasure mingling with the wind.

He pushed his hand into his pocket, remembering that first morning he'd woken up with his chest glued to her back with sweat. Instead of feeling panicked, he'd felt remarkably calm. Maddy had entered his life like a hurricane, but somehow settled like a soft blanket of snow, silencing everything, instilling peace amongst the chaos of his busy mind.

The short weeks since they'd been strangers were blurred in his head now; all he knew was the curve of her smile, the feel of her soft tongue dancing circles with his, the sound of her laugher.

'She adores them,' Maria said, appearing next to him from the tent and nudging his shoulder. 'She's going to find it hard to leave them, I'll bet.'

He straightened, sipped from his water bottle, suddenly aware that he'd been staring at Madeline—probably with a sappy look on his face.

'I'm sure she will,' he said, clearing his throat and screwing the bottle cap back on. 'She'll miss them a lot.'

'They're not the only ones, it seems,' she added, nudging him again, and then slipping back into the medical station with a new patient before he could respond.

He frowned to himself.

No one had asked any questions—although admittedly he hadn't missed the looks and the little comments thrown his way by Maria, Mark and Evan.

Aside from their affair, though, Ryan was rather enjoying watching a transformation occur in Madeline. She was more determined than ever to return to her position at St David's Hospital once she got home, so was spending even more time with the kids, helping them read in English and assisting in as many medical duties concerning them as possible. She was soaking it all up like a sponge.

And at night they soaked each other up, wherever and whenever they could, for as long as humanly possible, until they fell asleep exhausted.

Last night had been no exception. She'd found him in the hammock after dinner in the twilight.

'Are you really reading my book?' she'd asked, taking the e-reader from his hands.

Her hair had been damp from a previous swim—a swim he'd had to let her take alone, thanks to a visit from the wife of the man who'd been attacked by a caiman—she'd bought him a thank-you box of fruit. More bananas...

'Of course I'm reading it. I like it,' he'd told her truthfully. 'You have quite a way with words.'

'Well, I should hope so. I'm a writer,' she'd said, taking the Kindle from him and climbing into the hammock alongside him.

It had stretched almost to the floor with their weight, and she had smiled contentedly with her head against his chest.

'Lucky this is the king of all hammocks,' she'd said.

He'd laughed, peeling the strap of her tank top away from her shoulder and kissing her soft, warm flesh. When darkness had fallen they'd made love right there in the hammock—a feat he hadn't even known was entirely possible.

Ryan had never been so turned on in his life than he had been by the sight of Madeline, sliding her underwear off beneath her sundress, raising her arms above him to clutch at the mesh, and she'd relished every moan he'd let slip from his mouth as she worked him up and then slowed her pace again, then sped up, driving him crazy.

He'd almost forgotten to keep an eye on the treeline for the crew, and for Jake with his damn camera, but they'd grown good at multi-tasking by now—and besides, he was in too deep to care.

He watched her now, putting the guitar down on the

grass between the kids, strolling over towards him. His heart leapt and he rolled his eyes at himself.

Way too deep, he repeated internally. There was no way out either.

He was considering asking her to accompany him on another shoot...in a medical capacity, of course. They were headed for Peru in a couple of weeks, and after that to Bali. Maybe she could extend her deadline for the memoir.

The memoir she still hadn't finished because of him.

He silenced the thought.

'Hey,' she said, stopping in front of him.

Her hair was pulled back into a ponytail and he saw the faint red outline of the mark on her head from where she'd fallen. It had healed nicely in his care.

'Hey,' he said back, meeting her eyes and feeling that familiar rush of adrenaline shoot through his veins. He was still getting used to the feelings she stirred in him—a reawakening of sorts.

'We're wrapping up for the morning. Now I need another interview with you,' she said, biting on her lip.

He raised his eyebrows, appraising her in her green dress, seeing the way it was already sticking to her sexily in the heat.

'Do you think you'll have time for a quick one?'

He knew what *that* meant, and as usual he was a moth to her flame. 'Can we do it in the waterfall?' he asked, stifling a smile.

She was struggling to keep the laughter off her face, but it was shining in her eyes. 'I'd *love* to do it in the waterfall.'

'Great.' He called out to Maria. 'I'm taking a break!'

Luckily he'd put his board shorts on under his scrubs...

They walked a metre apart from one another across

camp, until they reached another clearing. One of the local guys had introduced them all to the secret waterfall just a ten-minute walk along a hidden path the last time they'd been here, and as soon as they were out of sight of anyone from camp he wrapped his arms around Madeline, picked her up and ran the rest of the way, jumping over the branches and piles of fallen leaves on the way.

She laughed as her arms latched around his neck. 'You just *love* to feel like Tarzan out here, don't you?'

'What makes you say that?' he said, putting her down on the grassy slope that led down to the pool and beating his chest as he faced the water.

He watched her peeling off the green dress, revealing her purple bikini as she waded into the cool, murky pool. She was being careful not to step on the sharp rocks, just as they'd been shown. The pool was only ten or so metres wide, but the water rolling dramatically off the high rocks above it was pretty much the perfect disguise for the sounds of mutual enjoyment.

He knew that *she* knew that was what he hoped was about to happen now. She was teasing him, though.

'I meant it when I said I needed another interview,' she said, turning back to him and observing him ditching his shorts.

Her eyes never left his naked body in the sunlight as he followed her into the water.

'I know you've been avoiding the subject—putting me to work on other things, thinking I'll forget what I really came here to do. It's what you've been doing all along.'

She pulled her long hair from its ponytail and ran her hands through it. Then she dipped into the water and floated on her back. *Damn*, she was sexy as hell.

'That's not entirely true,' he said, meeting her in the

middle and running a hand up her leg, letting his fingers brush the soft fabric of her bikini bottoms.

He'd tease her for a few minutes at least, he thought, before lifting her up onto one of the flat, long rocks behind the falls and using the rest of their 'break' in a very constructive fashion.

She didn't move—didn't respond to his touch in the way he'd been hoping she would. Instead she spun round and wrapped her legs around his stomach, pulling him in. He was trapped, completely in her control, and he liked it.

'You know, it won't be long before we leave this place,' she said, moving her arms around his neck.

'You want to talk about that? What happens next… away from the Amazon?' he asked, ignoring the caution in her voice and what he knew was inevitably coming.

He moved his hands to her bottom and pulled her even closer, dropped a lingering kiss on her lips.

'I've been thinking about it, Maddy. You and me. The future.'

'You have?'

'Of course I have. In case you hadn't noticed, I think you're kind of OK.'

She smiled playfully. 'I think *you're* kind of OK, too—in a weird, moody way. But that's not what we need to talk about right now and you know it.'

He sighed, trying not to show his frustration. Something was ready for action, and he wanted to make love to her right here and now, but he could see he'd have to earn that privilege.

'Talk to me, Ryan. Talk to me about Josephine.'

His chest tightened at the sound of her name. He swam with Madeline's legs and arms still around him over to the waterfall, dipped them both under the surface and brought them up again behind the falls.

'I told you—I don't want to talk about that.'

She let him go, put her feet to the ground and swept her mass of wet hair back over her shoulders. The water was rolling off her eyelashes, down her nose.

'Ryan, not telling me what happened with her feels the same as you lying to me, somehow.'

He pressed his back to the rocks. 'It's *not* the same, I haven't lied to you, Maddy—not once.'

'It *feels* like you have. Why can't you talk about Josephine? *Why?* This has been going on long enough.'

'Don't say her name—and don't write her name in this memoir, please,' he said, closing his eyes again and raking his hands through his wet hair.

'Forget the memoir.'

'What do you mean, forget the memoir?'

'Ryan, it's *me* you're talking to.'

He curled his fists to his sides, dunked down in the water to his neck as Madeline floated in front of him with the cascade of the waterfall behind her.

So many damn questions. Why the hell couldn't she just be a nurse...a normal goddamn nurse with no ulterior motives...a nurse he could hold flat against these rocks and lose himself in completely?

He opened his eyes as he felt her straddling him again, sitting across his lap under the water.

'Forget the book,' she said again, against his lips. 'I'm going back to nursing anyway.' She bunched tufts of his wet hair in her hands.

'I see. So I tell you all my secrets off the record, and then what? You write them down anyway?'

Madeline was silent.

'They're pretty juicy. We'd definitely get a bestseller you wouldn't be able to resist.'

He put his hands to her waist, but she shoved them away.

'Do you *really* think I would do that to you?' Her voice was furious now.

She started clambering off his lap but he pulled her back to him.

'Plenty would. Think of the money.'

'Seriously? Is *that* the kind of person you think I am? You think I'd get involved with you to get some *secret* out of you for my own benefit? Let me go!'

She went to clamber off him again, but he reached a hand to the back of her neck and pulled her head against his, pinning her in place.

'You're sexy when you're mad.'

'That's insulting. Get your hands *off* me!'

'You *like* my hands on you—remember?'

He pressed his lips to hers and she groaned, kissing him back for a moment, letting her arms move around his shoulder blades. But all too soon she pushed him away again, putting a hand to her mouth as if to block him from trying anything else.

She shook her head, her face still only an inch from his. 'No. I can't do this. Do you think because you're some kind of celebrity I'll just take whatever part of you I can get?'

'Of course I don't... Come on, I was kidding.'

'This is *serious*. I want to finish this memoir for *you*—so you can be *free*, Ryan! So you can put this whole thing to rest the way *you* want to by telling the story. I don't have to write it at all—we both know I don't!'

'Then don't.'

'Fine, I won't. But will you still tell me what happened with Josephine?'

'I...' He closed his mouth. He couldn't read her.

'Tell me right now. Tell me because you *trust* me, Ryan. And because you want a future with me. You just said that's what you want. And I'd rather have you than some book that's not even in my name!'

His head was spinning. Josephine's face was right in front of him now, in his mind, laughing, smiling. Then crying. Then cold and lifeless. His fault. *His fault.*

'If you can't trust me we can't be together. There is no future for us. We can't do...*this*!' She gestured around them.

Her face changed—hardened as if she was battling something internally.

'I'm going to ask them to fly me out of here early.'

A laugh spluttered out of him suddenly. 'Right!'

Her expression hardened further.

He stared at her for a second, feeling panic start to rise. 'You can't just leave,' he said, watching her push through the falls. He followed quickly.

'There's no point in me being here one second longer. You've been pushing me and pushing me, Ryan, but you won't give an inch yourself!'

'I've given you plenty of inches,' he said, too quickly, but she wasn't laughing at his jokes any more. 'Maddy, listen. I want to give you everything, I really do. You deserve that. But...'

'But—there's always a *but*. You won't let me in—you won't tell me anything that matters. I feel like you won't share the *real* you! You can't keep leading people on and then pushing them away when closeness gets inconvenient for you, Ryan.'

'I just… It will change the way you think of me.'

'No, it won't.'

'Yes, it will, Maddy…'

'Then don't try and stop me when I go.'

She turned again and he watched helplessly as she gathered up her clothes and hurried up the path. He floated onto his back, breathing deeply, anger pulsing through his body.

If he followed, he'd cause a scene on camp.

Was she testing him?

He counted to ten. Then twenty. Anger turned to apathy. Then confusion. Then back to anger and then fear. He counted to twenty all over again, floated there, festering in his own thoughts, for what felt like hours.

In reality it was probably only half an hour. Then, feeling like a total idiot, he swam so hard back through the water he practically dislocated his shoulders.

The second he pushed through the trees to camp a young volunteer with a name badge reading 'Raul' ran up to him, looking panicked and out of breath.

'There you are! Everyone's been looking for you.'

Crap.

'What's happened?' He was only wearing board shorts—suspiciously dry, he realised, after his 'swim'.

He started walking towards his tent with Raul scurrying at his side.

'Emergency up river. They think it's the drug runners again. We heard gunshots and everyone left…'

'What?' He stopped for a second. This was insane. 'Everyone's gone?'

'Pretty much,' Raul said. 'I was told to wait here for you. We need to set up in case they bring people back. They could only take limited supplies with them.'

Ryan reached his tent, unzipped the door and threw his shirt inside as dread settled around him, making his stomach sink. 'I'll meet you at the station.'

Raul sped off and Ryan bent to crawl inside. He stopped almost instantly. Madeline was emerging from her own tent, complete with her bags. She was fully dressed—boots and all.

Panic seized his heart. 'Madeline?'

She ignored him, started walking quickly across the grass towards the path to the river, swinging her heavy pack over her shoulder as she went.

He ran after her. 'Where are you going?'

'I've arranged for a boat to take me back to Saint Elena.' Her voice was steely, cold as ice.

'Now?' He was incredulous.

'Yes, now.'

'Do you know what has just *happened*?'

'I do, and I'm sorry, but I need to get out of here, Ryan.'

He caught her arm. He was still just in his board shorts, no shoes on his feet, no shirt. He felt powerless. 'Don't go, Maddy. Not now.'

'Don't make this any harder, please, Ryan.' Tears glistened in her eyes but she swiped them away defiantly. 'This is the best time for me to go. No cameras…no one asking questions.'

They were on the pathway now. He could see the river through the trees. The local guys she often talked with were sitting in the boat, laughing about something, waiting for her. What the hell was going on? His world had folded in on itself in a matter of seconds. She couldn't just leave everyone…she couldn't just leave *him*.

'Madeline—'

He shut his mouth the second he'd said her name, let

out a yelp, then an anguished cry. He staggered backwards, then pushed her away so hard she fell down, weighted by her pack.

'Don't move,' he managed, and looked back just in time to see the long, thick-scaled, stripy brown and black snake he'd stepped on slithering away into the undergrowth.

'Did it bite you?' Madeline was scrambling to her feet in the dirt. Her eyes were on the tail end of the snake. 'Oh, my God, did it get you?'

Her voice was shaky. She shook off her pack and was at his side in a second, hands on his shoulders as he sank to the ground.

'Ryan!'

'It got me,' he said, sucking in a breath. 'Surucucu. Madeline, I need the anti-venom.'

He doubled over for a second. The pain was shooting up his leg already. Madeline stood up quickly, calling to the guys near the boat.

'Help! Over here, please!'

'They won't be able to help me...you need to go back to the camp...find Raul.' The guys were already running from the river towards them. '*Go*, Madeline!'

'OK, hold on—OK.' She kissed him quickly on the mouth. 'I'm so sorry...just hold on. I'll be right back!'

She pushed her pack towards him so he could rest on it and sped off back down the path.

On the ground, Ryan grabbed his bare foot and studied the two fang marks just above his ankle. He winced in pain. Sweat had broken out all over his body. The Surucucu's venom took less than two hours to finish someone off. He'd seen it before—the after-effects on soft tissue at least. The venom was a powerful haemotoxin and, thanks to some of the longest fangs on any snake, it had been injected deep into his bloodstream.

He sucked in another breath, tried to focus.

But he knew in his gut that he was running out of time.

CHAPTER EIGHTEEN

'Help!' Madeline ran into the clearing. 'Raul! Anyone?'

She was panicked, desperate, but silence greeted her. Everyone was gone. Raul, too, it seemed. She spun around, calling out again, but clearly no one heard her because no one came.

Ryan's face flashed to the forefront of her mind. He'd turned ashen so quickly. The fang marks on his ankle had been deep and pronounced. It wasn't good and it was all *her* fault. She'd caused him to run after her barefoot, she'd been acting stupidly and melodramatically, and now... Now there was no one to help her or Ryan.

She called out again, shaking like a leaf.

Please, please, please...

Then she remembered something. Ryan had antivenom. He'd shown it to her the first night they'd got here. He'd even shown her how to apply it—not that she'd wanted to know.

She raced to his tent, pulled it open, threw herself inside and grabbed his bag.

Adrenaline propelled her forward, back the way she'd come.

'Hold on, hold on...' she said two minutes later, dropping to his side on the ground and resting her hand on his knee. He looked grey. He was leaning on her pack. 'Stay with me, Ryan! Can you hear me?'

Two guys from the river were sitting either side of him, holding his arms.

'We should not move him,' they told her in Spanish. 'We don't want the venom to spread.'

'OK, hold him steady.'

His eyes were heavy, drooping now. Sweat was glistening on his forehead and the snakebite was swollen, making his leg look twice its size. He clutched her hand for a second. He could barely speak, she could tell. She tried to stay calm, desperately channelling her inner nurse.

'I've got your bag,' she told him, pulling her hand away and opening it up in front of her. The contents spilled to the ground. 'Tell me how to help you, Ryan.'

'Anti-venom,' he mumbled. He was clearly struggling to keep his eyes open.

'I know, but which one?'

Madeline stared at the vials and tubes, the syringes and creams and containers. She recognised the anti-venoms, but there were several, all intended for different bites. She held one up to show him.

'This one?' she said.

He shook his head weakly, trying and failing to focus on the spread on the floor.

'This one?' she said, holding up another and reading from the label.

He shook his head yet again. The effort of not letting fear consume her was in itself threatening to make her crumble. He was deteriorating by the second.

'It's not there,' he managed slowly. He sucked in his breath, as if it pained him to speak.

'Then where *is* it?'

Madeline almost swore, but then realisation struck her like lightning. She cursed at herself. *She* had it—herself. She had put it in her pack that night to keep it safe, after he'd left it in her tent. She'd been intending to give it back to him but she'd forgotten. It was still in the pocket of her pack—which Ryan was now leaning on.

She reached behind him and motioned to the guys to keep him as still as possible while she pulled at the zippers on the pockets. Opening the one on the side, she pulled out the chain with the apple on it that Jason had given her. She'd forgotten to put it back on weeks ago. Then she found the vial she'd shoved in there that night and held it up to him, putting a hand to his clammy face.

'This one? Ryan, please tell me it's this one?'

'Yes,' he managed, wincing again. 'Do it.'

'Me? No, Ryan, you'll have to do it yourself.'

Madeline fumbled to unwrap a syringe. Her mind was screaming at her not to do this. What if it didn't work? What if she didn't do it properly and… God forbid…he died? He was semi-conscious, but *he* could do it. He knew how.

She pulled the top off the vial with trembling fingers and loaded the syringe. The guys were watching her with fear in their eyes.

Ryan reached for her hand. 'You have to do this, Maddy, Stick it right here.'

His breathing was laboured. His eyes kept closing as he held his arm out to her and pointed to a spot in the crease of his elbow. One of the guys held it in place.

'I trust you.'

She had no choice. He was growing greyer by the second.

Madeline took his arm, studied the place he was pointing at for the blue of a vein. 'OK, here goes.'

And before she could think any more about it she stuck the syringe into him and emptied the entire vial.

The next few minutes were a blur. The volunteer, Raul, appeared behind her, hot and flustered. He'd heard her calling, he said, but he'd had his hands full, shifting equipment around, and when he'd tried to find her she had disappeared. He radioed for help, explaining that they now had to get Ryan to the Cessna, which would be waiting for them on the runway when they got up river.

Along with the two local guys, Raul helped to carry Ryan to the boat. He'd passed out.

'Is he going to be OK?' Madeline asked, barely bothering to hide the devastation from her voice as she climbed in alongside them with her bag.

What if she'd got the anti-venom into him too late? What if he didn't make it? What if she lost him?

She couldn't bear it. This jungle was a nightmare— a total nightmare.

'He's just exhausted from trying to stay conscious,' Raul explained. 'We need to get him to the hospital. You probably saved his life, though.'

Tears of relief sprang to her eyes—but he wasn't out of the woods yet, she could tell.

Madeline clung to Ryan's hand as they laid him on the bottom of the boat. He looked like a shadow of his handsome self...so weak and vulnerable. 'I'm so sorry,' she whispered to him as her heart broke, and she crouched beside him, leaning over him, stroking his face.

Raul was frowning, looking at them as he spoke into his radio, and in the back of her mind Madeline knew she was raising suspicion—not that none had been raised concerning the two of them up to this point, she was sure.

She put a hand to his heart now, leant down and

kissed him. *Who cares? So what?* This was her fault. If anything worse happened to this man she knew without a doubt that she would never, ever forgive herself.

CHAPTER NINETEEN

PAIN. THAT WAS all he could feel. Pain and a tightness in his chest that felt a lot as if someone had stomped on him. A nurse was filling in some papers beside him when he opened his eyes, but a millisecond later he noticed someone else in the room, sitting on a plastic chair in the corner beneath the harsh, artificial light.

'Maddy,' he croaked.

He was weak. His leg and foot were bandaged, and he was wearing an ugly white gown, but he was alive. He had *her* to thank for that.

He saw her eyes flutter open, watched her rub them sleepily.

'She never left your side, Dr Ryan,' the elderly nurse said in a thick Portuguese accent, touching a hand to his shoulder as Madeline approached them. 'How do you feel?'

'Yes, how do you feel?' Madeline echoed, concern etched all over her features.

She was extraordinarily tanned, he realised now, in this brand-new setting away from the jungle. She was thinner, too, but so, so beautiful. He didn't deserve her.

'I'm OK,' he replied, looking into her sea-green eyes, feeling far from it.

Madeline reached for his hand and they both watched the nurse walk out of the room and shut the door.

'I owe you my life,' he said as soon as she was gone.

'Then I guess we're even.' She smiled, pulling his hand up to her mouth and kissing the back of it. 'I'm so glad you're OK.' Her eyes were tired and watery. Her hair was piled on the top of her head. 'You scared me, Ryan. I'm so sorry…if I hadn't been acting so crazy—'

'You had every right to act like that,' he interrupted, patting the bed at his side. 'I pushed you to it.'

She sat down. In the harsh light everything seemed clearer, somehow. His thoughts, her actions, the words he knew he had to say… She'd been right before. It had been going on long enough.

'Josephine was in love with me,' he said, before he could think any further.

Madeline's eyes widened, but she didn't let go of his hand. 'I had a feeling she might have been,' she whispered.

Ryan kept his voice steady and low, reliving the memories as he spoke and ploughing onwards anyway. 'But I didn't love *her*, Maddy, not in the same way.'

He moved his eyes to the spotless white ceiling as shame washed through him, as usual.

'We'd been dating in secret for a while—it was all kind of spontaneous and fun, you know? We argued about it…the fact that I could never admit we were a couple. We were arguing when she ran off…that's *why* she ran off.'

'What happened?'

Madeline's eyes were watery, he could see, but she wasn't clearing away her tears. Her fingers were gripping his like a vice.

'She ran into the damn jungle...got herself lost. We couldn't find her.'

'Oh, my God, Ryan...'

'It took four days. She didn't mean for it to happen... she was emotional and she got lost, ended up injuring herself, probably stumbling around in the maze of the jungle. By the time we found her there had been too much blood loss and no one could save her.'

He closed his eyes, feeling his hand grow hotter in hers. He couldn't even expand on the blood loss—it was still too raw.

'Mark and Even knew about us. They warned me to keep things quiet—they didn't want any extra attention from the media affecting the team—and of course I agreed with that. I didn't want the attention either. And then, when it happened...'

'I can imagine!'

'There were so many interviews, Maddy. Josephine didn't have any close family, or much of a life outside the crew, but obviously the world wanted to know what had happened to her. It was too late to tell the whole truth—that we'd been sleeping together and the reason she'd run away was because we'd been arguing about our relationship status, of all things... How could I admit that being with her in the first place had been a mistake on my part? I loved the fun we were having, but not enough to tell the world we were a couple. She thought we'd get married. But I was twenty-seven...she was twenty-eight.'

'Ryan, it's OK. I won't write any of this down, I swear.'

'I'm an asshole.'

'You're not—you were young. You just got carried away. You would have done the right thing in the end if you didn't want to marry her. You would have broken it off and gone your separate ways. Neither of you knew she was going to get lost, or what was going to happen in the jungle. People make mistakes. You have to forgive yourself. You *have* to let this go.'

'How can I?'

Madeline put a hand to his face, forced him to look at her. 'Just *choose* to, Ryan. Please. Just *choose* to forgive yourself. You get to start again. You get to be in love for *real*, if you want. You get to say I love you and mean it, and you get to hear it back. You don't have to deny yourself anything out of guilt or shame. I know that's what you've been doing.'

His heart lurched as she leaned in and kissed him softly on the lips, stroking his cheek and stubble. He leaned into her hand.

'I can imagine how awful that must have been for you,' she said. She touched her nose to his. 'It doesn't change the fact that I love you.'

He froze.

Madeline pulled back to meet his eyes as the silence stretched on and on and on. He watched her face change as the words played over and over in his head. Why couldn't he reply? Why couldn't he say anything?

He cleared his throat, searching her eyes. His head was spinning. 'Maddy, I...' He trailed off, letting the words hover in the space between them like heavy weights, waiting for someone to catch them.

And then he left those words to drop and burn themselves out as Evan and Mark entered the room with pretty much the entire crew of *Medical Extremes* and another cameraman.

They had balloons.

CHAPTER TWENTY

Three weeks later

MADELINE STARED OUT at the cold London rain. So different from the rain in the Amazon, she thought. The rain there had been harsh, but warm, and when it ended its assault it would trade places willingly with the sun, sending apologies down in hot white beams. Here it was just endless and mean, and the grey skies held no promise of swooping blue butterflies or lovemaking trysts with Ryan Tobias in waterfalls.

'Coffee?' the waitress asked, stopping at her table with a pot of sloshing brown liquid.

'Sure—thanks.' Madeline held out her cup.

Maybe coffee would cure her writer's block. She was stuck on how to end the memoir. She had over ninety thousand words already, and had thrown herself into writing pretty much the moment the plane had touched down in London. She'd had to—not least because Samantha was already on her back for the manuscript.

Typing about him every day, putting his history together like puzzle pieces on the page, was sheer torture. She missed him as she'd miss a vital organ—felt as if someone had amputated a limb. She couldn't get his face out of her head, nor his words when he'd finally opened up to her in that hospital room.

She remembered what he'd told her, word for haunting word, but knew she could never write it down. Of course she couldn't. Instead her mind played over the words she'd had to swallow when the team had walked in with their balloons.

Balloons. Ryan needed more than balloons to take his pain away. But he didn't *want* anyone to take his pain away—that was the problem. He thought he was destined to live out his days alone, racked with guilt about Josephine. He hadn't loved Josephine. And he'd refused to let anyone love *him* ever since.

Maybe he would never love anyone. Maybe he'd forgotten what love was.

She picked up her coffee, stared out at the honking traffic, thinking back over the flight she'd taken back home from Rio, knowing he was still there in that hospital the whole time. Knowing it was probably over between them. Knowing she was speeding further and further away from him in every sense.

Even so, she needed a better ending for him—something to inspire joy in other people the way he had in her.

Madeline had been accepted back at St David's and was already picking up where she'd left off. The same faces with the same smiles had been so understanding, so welcoming and helpful. She almost felt as though she'd never left.

Almost.

She put her cup down, sank back against the booth and let her eyes fall on the blank page on her screen. Her writing skills were all she had to give Ryan now, and she couldn't let them all be for nothing. She had no clue how she was going to finish the memoir, but she knew she had to find a way. She could write, and she could help others, and with more book deals at her fingertips—if she ever had time outside her nursing duties—she had the power to combine both.

She knew in her heart that she wasn't the same nurse who'd left St David's after Toby had died. An indelible line had been drawn between the old her and the new one. The new Madeline had taken risks and chances, had put herself in the line of fire and witnessed incredible things. The new Madeline had survived seemingly endless days on rice and fruit, learned how to trust in her own abilities and instincts, gained the respect of a tribe of children who sang from their hearts about the simplest of life's precious gifts, like butterflies and bananas and toothbrushes.

The new Madeline had felt love of the highest, most soul-splintering kind, spilling into her heart and filling the spaces there. She'd been lifted and bolstered by it—so much so that its absence hadn't killed her. She was still kind of floating. Perhaps a little bruised and unsure, but definitely grateful for a taste of what she now knew was out there.

Maybe she could find it again with someone else.

CHAPTER TWENTY-ONE

RYAN PUSHED THROUGH the door, feeling sweat break out on his forehead as soon as he stopped short under the bright, unforgiving lights. A woman in a tracksuit and neon pink sneakers seemed to recognise him instantly. Her eyes widened and she stopped in her tracks, looking as though she was about to race over to him in excitement.

Ryan held up his hand and hurried on past, pulling his baseball hat down further over his forehead.

He'd tossed and turned last night in his hotel room, debating whether or not to come, but Mark and Evan had finally sat him down at breakfast, shoved a black coffee under his nose and then given him another, perhaps even more effective wake-up call.

'She's the best thing that's ever happened to you!'

'With all due respect, Ryan, don't screw this up!'

'You *know*?' he'd said, feigning surprise.

You couldn't live that closely with people and not understand that they'd know when you were hiding something.

'It's been written all over your face ever since you first set eyes on each other. You're the smartest guy in the field, Ryan, but really you're an idiot.'

This room smelled of astringent fluids and the shiny

floor squeaked under his sneakers. Anxiety crept tighter around him like a rope. Seeing a reception desk, he made his way over. A girl of about twenty-one with a name badge reading 'Trudy' looked up, then did a double-take.

'Oh,' she said when he met her eyes. 'You.'

'I'm looking for Nurse Madeline Savoia. I was told she's here today?'

'Um…yeah…um…lemme just look that up…' Trudy trailed off, dropping a pen to the floor as she scrambled nervously for some papers.

Ryan tried not to smile and rested an arm on the counter. He was still getting used to people acting this way around him again. No one in the Amazon gave a toss who he was as long as he could help when someone needed him. If only the whole world cared more about those things…

He looked around him as a flummoxed Trudy scanned her computer screen. People in scrubs were walking alongside kids of all ages in gowns with dressings and gauzes. Parents and other relatives were milling about, lost in their phones and magazines. An elderly man was wiping up a coffee spillage by a vending machine. A young couple each holding a pile of kids' books looked at him with vague recollection, presumably trying to figure out where they'd seen him.

In his Red Sox shirt and jeans, Ryan looked like any other regular guy. Well, maybe an American. He wondered what people would do when they found out what he was planning—just as soon as he could locate Madeline.

'She's on Peter Pan Ward… No, sorry…they moved her group to Elephant and Giraffe today.' Trudy was beetroot-red now, fiddling with the braid that she'd pulled across her shoulder.

'Sorry?' he said. 'Elephant and Giraffe?'

Was this some kind of zoo?

'It's the haematology/oncology department.' She stood up, pointing a manicured finger down the hallway. 'She should still be there somewhere, if you go through those doors and take a right.'

'Right. Thank you.'

'Wait—Ryan, can you please sign this? I really love *Medical Extremes*…it's, like, my favourite show. And my mum's, too.' She pushed a piece of paper and a blue pen onto the desk, blushing even more.

'What's your mum's name?' he asked, taking the pen. He figured he needed all the good karma he could get.

'Sandy.'

He signed the paper—*To Sandy, love Ryan*—and added a heart, throwing Trudy a wink he knew would make her day.

Then, before anyone else could approach him, he walked quickly down the corridor and hurried through the double doors.

His thoughts were a washing machine on spin cycle as he walked the length of the ward, narrowly missing being struck by a toddler on a tiny tricycle. He'd never been this nervous in his life.

It had been the longest few weeks ever since she'd left him in that hospital in Rio. Her face had haunted him…that look in her eyes as he'd choked on his reply to her confession.

Fear had started rolling over him like waves from a tsunami the second she'd said what she had.

Did she *really* love him? Did he love *her*?

He'd watched her leave that hospital room, felt the ball of knots twist tighter in his stomach. Mark and Evan and everyone else had crowded around him with the balloons and he'd said nothing—just watched the back of her head and her hand sweep across her hidden face as she'd turned towards the door.

He'd needed to get his head around it. When they'd all gone, however, Ryan had felt as alone in that busy hospital as he had in the middle of the jungle at night. But in spite of the silence he had ached with the noises in his head.

He'd kept the truth locked inside some damn pointless Pandora's Box for so long that saying them hadn't felt real. Yet the words about Josephine had come out, no matter what Madeline chose to do with them. It hadn't been the thought of what she'd do with them that had plagued him, though. It had been the thought of losing her again.

All night he'd lain awake, his heart pounding as he'd healed. Visions of her smiling, laughing, floating in the lake had messed with his senses. He had almost smelled her, tasted her. Every movement she'd made in his arms, every molecule of Madeline, had seemed imprinted on his brain like a tattoo.

He'd wanted to get up and follow her, to catch her before she flew away, but as strong as his emotions were, and—dare he say it?—as strong as his love…his body was weak.

He loved Madeline, too. Of course he did. What was not to love? And who cared about a stupid memoir or what anyone else might think?

The people he was so concerned about were all just skin and blood and bones, living in the same jungle as him. He was just like everyone else in the world—doing his best to survive. Some survived longer than others, that was all. Josephine had run into trouble, but ultimately her death was not his fault—just as Toby's wasn't Madeline's.

He also knew he couldn't have forced love to exist where it hadn't back then. He'd been young and confused, of course, chasing adventure and fun. Josephine had made him happy in that moment—and perhaps he had been selfish. But what he'd felt for Josephine was nothing compared to what he'd grown to feel for Madeline.

Why should he deny himself happiness now? Why shouldn't he be allowed to say *I love you* to someone, and mean it?

He'd known even as he'd boarded the flight what he wanted to do.

Now minutes passed like hours as he searched the waiting room, the mini-cafeteria, the playroom.

Please, God, just don't let her tell me where to shove it.

Then...

It was the back of her head he saw first. He stopped and peeked through a window into the last in a long row of rooms leading off the corridor. He'd have recognised her anywhere. The soft slope of her shoulders in her blue scrubs...the knot of hair pinned to the top of her head.

He looked around him, then back into the room. There was one bed with a kid in it—no older than eleven or twelve. Madeline was talking to her, sitting on the bed, facing away from him. He could hear the TV on the wall, the faint, jovial preposterousness of a cartoon.

He put his hand on the door handle and before he could chicken out walked inside.

The little girl's head was bald, making her big blue eyes appear even wider as she gasped.

'Dr Ryan Tobias?' she exclaimed in disbelief.

Madeline froze. On the TV a cartoon mouse screamed with perfect timing.

'Is it really you?' the little girl asked, blinking and sitting up straighter in the bed.

He saw a card on the dresser that read *Get well soon, Camille.*

Madeline still didn't turn around.

His heart was thudding now. 'Yes, Camille, it's really me,' he said, letting his eyes fall on Madeline as he shut the door behind him.

'What are you doing here? Is this a dream?'

He smiled at her. Out of the corner of his eye he saw Madeline's face had turned pale, and she'd closed her eyes, lowered her head to her chest.

'It's not a dream,' he said softly, walking to the side of her bed. He was opposite Madeline now. 'I'm here to see your friend, and to tell her I've been really, really stupid.'

The girl giggled, seeming younger than eleven or twelve. 'You're not stupid! I've seen you on the telly!'

'Well, sometimes, Camille, I do stupid things that you don't see on the telly,' he said.

'Like what?'

He paused for a moment, then reached his hand across the bed to rest it on Madeline's shoulder. 'Like letting this amazing woman fly away on a plane without me.'

Madeline opened her eyes. She brought her hand up slowly to cover his and he swore he saw a tear trickle down her nose.

'Oh, my God, do you *love* Nurse Madeline?' Camille asked, eyes wide in excitement.

'Yes, I do,' he replied, conscious now of a group of people crowding at the window, looking at them from behind the glass. 'Very much. Nurse Madeline is a very special woman.'

'Yes, she is,' Camille replied quickly. 'But I can't believe it's really you.'

Madeline stood up and clocked all the people watching them. For a moment he wanted to yank the blind down, but then he figured, *What the hell?*

He met her at the end of the bed and took her hands. They were warm and slightly clammy. She had tears streaming down her cheeks now.

'What are you doing here?' she choked.

'Don't cry,' he whispered, wiping her tears away with his thumbs.

'I don't know what to say…'

'Don't say anything.'

He dropped to his knees, fumbling in his pocket on the way to the cold floor. He heard her gasp audibly. So did Camille, and the noise levels behind the window went up a notch.

'I love you, Madeline, that's all I came to say…and as well to ask you one important question.'

'Ryan, what are you…?'

'I knew I was in love with you the minute I almost lost you—when I thought that dead body was you. Probably even before that…'

'Ryan…'

'I can't live without you. I really can't. In fact, I refuse to. I want you to marry me. *Will* you marry me, Madeline Savoia?'

Madeline let out a sudden laugh as tears continued to stream down her face.

'Are you serious?'

He smiled up at her. 'Serious as a snakebite.'

'In that case I say yes!' She clutched at his hands holding hers. *'Yes!'*

He got up, took her hand in his, and she stared in disbelief at the ring he was sliding on her finger, its stunning diamond catching the light.

'Oh, my God—my friends will never believe this.' Camille was reaching for her phone, taking a photo.

Ryan didn't care. Let her Tweet about it.

'Ryan? Is this what you want?'

Madeline was looking from the ring to him, as if she might at any moment see a camera sweep in and pronounce her 'punked'.

He let out a laugh that felt like a dead weight falling from his shoulders and dropped another kiss on her lips—which she returned until they were kissing passionately in the middle of the room and everyone outside was whooping and cheering.

When he pulled away, holding a hand up at the window, he heard Camille clapping enthusiastically behind them.

'You know, I didn't exactly want to be in here,' she blurted from the bed, 'but I wouldn't have missed this moment for anything. So you're marrying *the* Dr Ryan Tobias, Nurse Madeline?'

Madeline shook her head for a second. 'I guess I am...' she said.

Ryan pulled her against him, once again breathing in the scent he'd missed. 'I hope that's true—because the second I walk out of this room I'll be mobbed, and I'll probably need my fiancée to save me.'

The words sounded strange coming from his mouth. He was planning a real future with Madeline and he was actually excited about it. There was so much he wanted to say, and even more he wanted to do... But not with Camille in the same room.

He cleared his throat. 'When do you finish your shift?'

'Not till seven...'

'Meet me at the Shangri La. We need to talk about things. We also need to talk about this memoir.'

'Ryan, I got pretty far, but then I stopped writing it…'

'Well, you need to start again,' he said, letting her go and putting his hand on the doorknob. He could hear more people outside gathering, talking, gossiping, gasping. 'I need you to get that story out there for the good of *both* of us. I'll call your editor and tell her why the manuscript is late. I'll explain that I wouldn't give you an ending, but now I'm going to write that part myself and send it to you. I want my memoir to have a *happy* ending—you hear?'

She shook her head, confused.

He kissed her lips, pressed his forehead to hers. 'I'm going to say that, thanks to an irritating, relentless but irresistible nurse, who saved his life in the Amazon, Ryan Tobias met the love of his life. And maybe a little bit more than that. But you can't edit that bit, OK?'

'OK…'

'Good. Now, I'm heading out there. If you hear a desperate scream it's just me.'

'I'll come and save you—I promise,' she said, smiling through her tears.

'That's what you do best,' he replied, and grinned.

EPILOGUE

Afterword from Flying High,
a memoir by Dr Ryan Tobias.

AS I TYPE my way towards the end of this book—a book I urge you to remember I didn't even want written—I'm feeling a sense of peace I never expected to feel.

I've thought a lot about why this is, and I think it's because when you acknowledge why you don't want to do something…when you really face that demon head on…you realise that what is really bothering you is yourself—and yourself is something you can change in a heartbeat.

You just have to want to.

I'm making some big changes in my life, and I'm not afraid to say that falling in love has helped me make them. The wonderful woman you've probably seen me out with has changed the way I see myself and consequently the way I see the world! There was a time when I didn't dare think I deserved such a love, or such a wedding, filled with so many friends, colleagues and people I love. Maybe you saw the photos? Then you'll know I'm a lucky man indeed.

Oh, and if you didn't think it was possible for this flying doctor's life to get any more adventurous, believe me, you're not alone. Let's just say we've been busy painting one of our rooms a lovely shade of blue, and my wife has recently commented that she can no longer fit into her favourite jeans.

It's a beautiful thing, knowing a whole new life is about to begin, and I sincerely hope you'll come along with us for the ride.

Till the next adventure!

Yours,

Ryan Tobias.

PS Please note: all proceeds from this book's sales are to be split between St David's Hospital Elephant and Giraffe Wards and the Ryan Tobias Foundation. Thank you for your support.

* * * * *

ONE PERFECT MOMENT

A.C. ARTHUR

Prologue

Staten Island, New York

"Just this one time," Ava Cannon whispered as his hands cupped her butt.

"Once is enough," Gage Taylor murmured while moving them farther into her trailer.

He kicked the door closed with his foot, pausing a second to reach back and lock it. Then his hands were on her once more, his mouth crashing down over hers. The kiss took her breath away, every stroke of his tongue sending searing bolts of desire through her system until her fingers were gripping his shirt. The feel of his strong biceps through the cotton material, coupled with the hardness of his body, now pressed closely against hers, caused Ava's knees to tremble.

This was what she'd been fighting for over the last couple of months. Each day she'd stepped onto the set of *Doctor's Orders*, knowing that he would be there. The strong hands that she'd seen holding her script as he'd checked the words she'd written, monitoring them for medical accuracy, now touched her body.

"It will be enough," Ava whispered when he tore his mouth away from hers and she could take a breath.

He tugged the hem of her shirt from her pants. She lifted her arms up over her head, and he pulled the shirt off. His hands immediately went around her to the clasp of her bra, which he quickly unhooked before removing and tossing it somewhere on the trailer floor.

"Enough," he mumbled as he dipped his head. "More than enough."

His lips were on her breast then, teeth holding a turgid nipple before he sucked her in deep. Ava arched her back, her hands going to his shoulders as she tried to hold on to him. When he moved to the other breast she let her head lull back, her eyes closing to the delicious sensations rippling throughout her body.

Dr. Gage Taylor was a brilliant obstetrician and researcher. He'd come highly recommended when she'd asked who in the New York area would be a good consultant for her show. And when he arrived in her office that first day, she'd been rewarded with how jaw-dropping handsome the guy was. Ava should have known then that she was in trouble.

Now, she was pulling at his shirt until the buttons popped off. He grunted and hurried to unsnap his pants while she did the same, toed off her flats and pushed her pants and panties down her legs. His shirt was on the floor, his pants undone, his hands moving quickly to pull a condom packet from his wallet. She pushed his pants and his boxers down as he ripped the condom packet open and then smoothed the latex over his length. He wore leather loafers that he kicked off his feet before stepping out of his pants.

Ava sat on the couch. She scooted back on the wide pillows and looked up at all of the heavenly goodness that was Gage Taylor. Six feet one inch of golden honey-hued skin, ripped abs, muscled limbs and a thick, long erection. She swallowed as her gaze rested there.

"Just this once," he said, his voice deep and husky in the confined space of the trailer.

Ava licked her lips and nodded. "Yes, just this once."

He was over her by then, his lips on hers, his knee spreading her legs apart. She opened her mouth to his persistence, clasped her hands to the back of his head to hold him there. He pushed them both back to a lying position on the couch, arranging himself between her legs. He said something, but Ava couldn't hear him over the pounding of her heart and the rush of desire.

Her legs were already trembling by the time the crest of his erection touched her entrance. He pressed harder.

She moaned deeper, and their "one time" began.

Chapter 1

New York City
Three Weeks Later

Gage stepped out onto the sidewalk on a warm September morning, three weeks after they'd wrapped up shooting on *Doctor's Orders*. Despite the strange hours he'd been keeping during the seven weeks he served as an on-site consultant for the network medical drama, this morning he was expected at the hospital by nine. That meant he was taking his usual four-block walk to the Nancy Links Medical Center, where he'd worked as an obstetrician for the last four years.

He held his briefcase in one hand, cell phone in the other as he walked away from the thirty-story condo building, his Italian leather dress shoes clicking on the sidewalk. This afternoon he was seeing patients, but this morning was relatively free, he noted as he looked at his mobile calendar.

Gage had discovered early in life that being organized was a necessity. Growing up in a household with five siblings meant he had to know what was his and where his personal belongings were at all times. He'd learned a lot growing up as one of the infamous Taylor sextuplets, enough to make not repeating past mistakes one of his main priorities in life.

He looked up in time to see the light changing and then crossed the street just before his phone rang.

"Dr. Taylor," he answered because he could see from the caller ID that it was the hospital calling.

"Good morning," his assistant, Carrie, replied.

Carrie had been with him for the last six months. For his first two years at the medical center he'd been in residency, and then his inaugural research paper on infertility and the strides that had been made in the field had been published. That had propelled his career forward, and Gage became a staff obstetrician as well as a grant recipient in the following weeks to continue his research. With those dual titles, he'd been given a corner office on the hospital's fourth floor, an administrative assistant and, just recently, a lab assistant. His first admin had gone on maternity leave just weeks before his father's death last September. Since then, he'd gone through three more assistants, who had been sent to him via an employment agency.

Who would have thought that after all this time out of the spotlight, there would still be someone—actually three someones, all female—who not only knew who he was, but were also ready to claim their place in the spotlight by either working for him, or possibly sleeping with him.

Gage blamed his father's death a year ago for the renewed interest in the first African American sextuplets to be born in Temptation, Virginia, thirty years ago. After leaving his wife and seven-year-old children, Theodor Taylor had gone on to become the CEO of Taylor Manufacturing, building an empire that designed engines for a Japanese automotive company. Stock in the company had soared at the time of Theodor's death, and when it was announced that the estate would be handled by the children, Gage recalled fielding calls from newspaper reporters to investors asking about their plans for the international company. That was until Gray, the oldest Taylor sextuplet, brokered a deal to sell Taylor Manufacturing and divided the proceeds evenly among the siblings.

"Dr. Gogenheim wants to see you as soon as you get in this morning," Carrie was saying as Gage shook his head to rid himself of the memories of his father.

"Really? I didn't see anything on my calendar," he replied. "I planned to reach out to that research facility in Paris before their offices close for the day when I get in."

"I recall you mentioning that yesterday when we spoke. However, Dr. Gogenheim's assistant just called to see if you were in yet. I told her you were on your way."

"I am," Gage said just before a driver slammed on

the brakes, subsequently causing the cars behind him to do the same.

Those were the glorious sounds of a morning during rush-hour traffic. When the noise subsided, he continued. "Fine, I'll go right up to his office, but please have the number and the name of a contact person at the facility in Paris on my desk for when I return."

"Yes, sir. I'll get that information now."

"Thank you, and, Carrie?"

"Yes, sir, I hadn't gone down to get your Caffè Americano yet. I'll wait about half an hour. It will be on your desk when you finish with Dr. Gogenheim."

Gage smiled. "Thanks, Carrie."

He'd never been a morning person. To survive undergrad, med school and residency required the strongest coffee possible. Luckily for him, there was a Starbucks on the ground floor of the medical center. Gage showed his appreciation for Carrie going the extra mile to get his coffee by opening a credit account with the barista and paying them monthly for all drinks and any other items that he and Carrie ordered.

After disconnecting the call, Gage scrolled through some of the emails he'd missed in the last couple of days because he'd spent the weekend at a colleague's house in the Hamptons. He had been attending, of all things, a baby shower.

Gage approached the hospital minutes later and walked through the revolving glass doors. His honey-colored burnished leather wingtip lace-up Tom Ford shoes clicked against the polished floors as he made his way through the lobby and down the hall toward the elevators that would lead to the obstetrics and gynecology floors. He slipped his phone into his suit jacket pocket just before stepping into the elevator. When he heard someone yelling, "Hold the elevator!" he extended his arm so that his briefcase kept the door from closing.

"Thanks," the woman, dressed in light blue scrubs, said as she made her way into the compartment and pressed the floor she needed.

"No problem," Gage said and returned the smile she was so eagerly offering.

As the elevator began to move, he thought of how pretty she was, with her dark brown hair pulled back from her face and green eyes twinkling each time she looked up at him. He could ask her out, but he'd decided a long time ago that the quick, no-commitment type of interaction he preferred to have with women didn't bode well in the workplace.

The elevator stopped on her floor, and before she stepped off, she turned back to look at him. "Have a great day, Dr. Taylor."

Her arm extended, and Gage looked down at the business card she held in her hand. He immediately accepted the card and wished her a great day, as well. When the doors closed and he was alone, Gage looked down at the card, a smile ghosting his face.

"Miranda," he said and continued to read the words on the card as the elevator moved again.

She was a radiologist on the third floor. And she was hot. He tucked the card into the side of his briefcase and stepped off the elevator when it opened on his floor. He wasn't going to call her, Gage told himself.

Regardless of how good she looked. He had rules, and he had learned the hard way that it was best to stick to them, always.

"Good morning, Dr. Taylor. Dr. Gogenheim is waiting for you," the receptionist said when he stopped in front of her. "Just go on back to his office."

"Thank you," Gage replied with a nod.

He was known throughout the hospital, a fact that should have bothered him considering he despised his family's notoriety. But this was different. Gage's recognition at the hospital came primarily from being a talented doctor who brought huge research grants to the facility and added to their already stellar reputation. The Taylors of Temptation, on the other hand, had commercialized a serious health condition for thousands of couples, and topped that off with a very public betrayal of marriage vows and desertion of a family. It had been the beginning of the worst years of Gage's life.

Thankfully, that was then and this was now.

He gave a quick knock and then entered the office. Mortimer Gogenheim sat behind his desk, his thinning black hair brushed neatly to one side of his head, thick framed glasses perched on his nose.

"Good morning, Gage. Take a seat," he said.

Gage nodded and moved to sit in one of the guest chairs across from the sleek, dark wood desk. "Good morning," Gage replied. "I was surprised you wanted to see me so early. I thought the board meeting was scheduled for this morning."

Which was why he hadn't scheduled anything on his personal or business calendar. Gage wanted to be available the moment the board of directors decided he would become the youngest chief of obstetrics at the medical center. With all the research work he'd done this year, coupled with the latest grant that would fund the department's research labs for the next three years, he was a shoo-in for the position. At least that's what Mortimer had told him a couple of months ago. After that conversation, Gage was elated that his dream was about to become a reality, much sooner than he had ever anticipated.

"We had the meeting last night over dinner. My son-in-law received a job offer in Europe, so my daughter announced two weeks ago that they were moving over there. My wife was beside herself with worry at not being able to see the grandkids. So I'm stepping down sooner than I'd planned because we're going to move over there with them," Mortimer said as he sat forward, letting his arms rest on the desk.

Gage nodded. "Family first," he said. "I understand."

He did understand that concept, even if he didn't have a wife and kids of his own. Outside of his job, Gage only had his family. His five siblings—Gray, Garrek, Gemma, Genevieve "Gen" and Gia—who lived in different areas of the United States. They'd grown up in a tight-knit household, and even though distance separated them, they'd tried to remain as close as their mother always wanted.

"Good," Mortimer told him with a nod. "So I'll get right to the point."

Gage sat up straighter in the chair and thought about how his sisters were going to react when they heard the news. His oldest brother, Gray, was an overachiever himself, becoming one of the first African American billionaires to own and operate his own electronics company before he turned thirty. And Garrek was an exceptional navy pilot who was steadily moving up in the ranks. They were both tenacious and goal-oriented, just like Gage. His sisters each had stellar careers, as well. Gemma owned an upscale beauty salon in Washington, DC, while Gen ran her own software development company, and Gia worked as an executive chef at one of Chicago's swankiest restaurants.

He'd call Gemma first, he decided as he nodded and stared expectantly at Mortimer. She would never let him live it down if he didn't.

"The chief position is going to Edgar Rodenstein. He's been in this field for more than thirty years, and he's worked with the medical director before. In fact, Bart was the one who recommended Edgar for the job. So we're confident that the transition will be smooth. You, on the other hand, well, we're extremely happy with the work you've been doing in infertility and multiple birth research. We'd like you to continue in that vein, and we will possibly entertain a chief researcher position for you in the future."

Gage was stunned. The calm and relaxed feeling he'd had only moments ago as he'd stepped off the elevator had dissipated. It was now replaced with a sick feeling that had him shaking his head.

"Bart—" he began and then corrected himself "—the medical director hand-selected who would work with him?" he asked, and then answered his own question. "Of course he did."

Because that's what men like Bart Thomas did when faced with a younger, smarter and more innovative candidate. He selected the guy he knew best, the one he could control under the guise of training, no doubt. Gage was livid.

"I guess that makes sense," he continued because he had no intention of showing Mortimer how truly upset he was about this development.

Mortimer nodded and cleared his throat. "It makes perfect sense. The board agreed. The transition will begin immediately. We'll need you to be on hand in case further press conferences or other media appearances are required."

"I'm not sure that will be possible, Mortimer," he said before he could completely work through his thoughts. "These past few months have been a little hectic with my research and patient list, combined with the work on the television show. I was actually considering taking some time off."

Mortimer sat back in his burgundy leather chair, setting his elbows on the arms and clasping his hands. "Really?" he asked and arched a bushy gray-haired brow.

"Yes," Gage replied, his tone smooth and even, as if this was what he'd planned to say from the moment he walked into the office. "My brother and his wife have just welcomed twins, and I've been meaning to get down to Virginia to see them."

"Well, the arrival of babies is always a festive occasion," Mortimer said. "Especially in our business."

Gage chuckled along with him. "Definitely. So I'll be completing the proper paperwork this morning and briefing the other doctors in my department on my patient statuses."

"How long do you plan to be away?" Mortimer asked. "The department agreed to work around the shooting schedule for that show because it was good exposure for us to have your name and the hospital's name running in the credits of a nationally viewed program every week. New-patient visits at the clinic have grown by thirty percent in that time."

Gage nodded. He didn't need Mortimer to tell him that he'd been an asset to the medical center. He already knew that. Which was why being passed over for this promotion was a bunch of good-ole-boy crap that Gage did not appreciate.

"I'm aware," he replied. "Which is why I believe that a three-week vacation is not only warranted, but justified."

While Gage had adjusted his hours at the medical center during the shooting of *Doctor's Orders*, he hadn't missed a beat with his own patients and had even been on call most of the time while on set, rushing to the medical center to deliver three babies for other doctors who were on vacation. He would wait to see if Mortimer pressed this issue to play that card.

Instead Mortimer nodded, his cool gaze resting on Gage. "You're right," he said. "I'd hoped, however, that you would be available to represent the hospital to the media."

"I'd rather stay out of the media, if at all possible,

Mortimer. I'm sure you understand my reasons," Gage told him.

While he'd been more than excited to have his research paper published and enjoyed the accolades that came his way in the medical industry, Gage did not do media. He never granted interviews and did not appear for photo opportunities or press conferences. Up until this point, Mortimer had been happy to stand with his chest poked out, speaking on behalf of their department.

This was why Gage had been more than surprised when a production assistant from the television network had contacted him with regard to working on a show they were developing. He'd immediately turned them down, thinking they were asking him to star in the show. Gage never wanted to be in front of a camera again. But when he found out the position was simply as a consultant where he could lend his expertise and still stay in the background, he'd agreed.

"Yes," Mortimer replied. "I do understand."

"Well, then," Gage said as he stood. "I'll head down to congratulate Ed and then take care of the arrangements for my vacation."

Mortimer stood. "How are you going to adjust for three weeks without being at the hospital?" he asked. "You are your career, Gage."

Gage nodded because just fifteen minutes ago he'd been telling himself that, as well.

"I'm going to be with my family, Mortimer," was all he said before walking out of the office.

Gage squared his shoulders and walked as proudly as if he'd just received the best news of his life, down the hall and back to the elevator. As far as his career went, he wasn't sure what his next step was going to be, but didn't doubt that he would figure it out. He always did. For now, Gage was going to see Gray and his new nieces and nephews. He was going back to family, the only people he could ever trust and depend on.

Los Angeles

Ava wanted to scream at her mother.

It wasn't the first time, and she was fairly certain it wouldn't be the last. But instead of screaming, she used the fact that she was running late for a meeting to get off the phone with Eleanor Cannon. That was only a temporary reprieve, but Ava would take what she could get.

Coffee spilled onto the marble floor as she stepped into the hallway of the Yearling Broadcast Network. Two years ago, when Ava was just twenty-five years old, she'd walked down this same hallway with her heart pounding wildly, her entire life bound in sixty-three typed pages. The TV script for *Doctor's Orders* was the result of a year and a half's work, researching and developing her idea for the new medical drama. She was young and unknown at that time, but had landed the face-to-face meeting with Carroll Fleming through the showrunner for another show where she'd worked as a staff writer. Now Carroll was her current executive at the network after helping her to develop and launch *Doctor's Orders*.

Today's meeting was with Carroll and Jenner Reisling, a development executive at the same network. Ava was going to pitch her new series idea to them and prayed that the success of *Doctor's Orders*, currently the network's number one show on Thursday nights, would add weight to the new pilot following the lives of African American law students navigating their way through school, the professional world and, of course, love.

She was only a few minutes late but hated that just the same. Ava prided herself on being professional at all times. She'd always had to be. As a woman in the television industry, she knew she had to be on her game, no matter what her credentials were.

"I apologize for being late," she said immediately upon entering the conference room. "I know your time is valuable, so I'm ready to get started."

Carroll, with his shiny bald head and long, bushy red beard, sat forward in the chair he'd been lounging in.

"Don't speak of it," he said, pulling some papers that had been spread across the conference room table into a neat pile. "We were just talking about the ratings for the season finale of *Doctor's Orders*."

"Phenomenal," Jenner, a slim man with dirty-blond hair and dark brown-framed glasses, said. "As a first year procedural in a really competitive time slot, you knocked it out of the box with this one."

Ava beamed. That was the praise she'd wanted to hear for the last year. Actually, the last five years, since she'd decided that writing was her niche. She didn't believe it was conceited at all to like hearing that she'd done a good—no, a *great*—job with her first network show. Especially after all the critical words she received from her mother in her lifetime. If she'd listened to anything Eleanor Cannon said, Ava doubted she'd be where she was today.

"I'm elated at the show's success," she said and pulled three copies of her newest screenplay out of her bag.

The bag was huge and just a little worn around the straps. It was her favorite because it easily accommodated all the necessities she carried with her daily. Today, in addition to the script, she'd added her handheld recorder so she would be sure not to miss anything that was said in this meeting, a second spiral notebook that would be solely dedicated to this screenplay and any additional work she needed to do on it, and her newest pair of reading glasses because she'd accidentally stepped on the old pair when they'd fallen off the desk in her apartment.

"We are, too," Carroll continued and folded his hands over his stack of papers.

Jenner sat right next to him, smiling across the table at Ava.

"Yes, that's great," she continued as she pushed copies of the bound pages toward each of them. When they were both looking down at the cover page, Ava took a deep breath and let it out slowly.

"That brings me to this new pitch. Two young African American women spend their weekdays attending competing law schools, drinking and partying on weekends and navigating the murky waters of dating 24/7. This new, vibrant, urban take on sex and young professionals in the city will cater to the twenty- to thirtysomething crowd. A prime time slot would be

Sunday evenings. This would be an hour-long show, with a huge draw to advertisers geared toward the female consumer."

Jenner flipped through the pages of the script and glanced down at them. Carroll did neither. Instead, Ava found him staring at her as he drummed his fingers over his stack of papers.

"We have another idea in mind," Carroll told her.

Ava was about to open her mouth to speak, but she thought better of it. She always tried to evaluate her words carefully. Something else she'd learned from her mother, or rather because of her mother. Eleanor Cannon said whatever she wanted to say, whenever she wanted to say it. Even if it ended with hurt feelings or offense. Her mother believed that because she was a millionaire, she was entitled to speak her mind and never apologized for doing so. But Ava believed in giving people respect and demanded the same in return.

"I don't understand," she replied finally.

"Not that this wouldn't be great," Jenner began. "You've already proven that you have your finger on the pulse of what viewers want. And your pitch was quite intriguing. But I'm looking for something specific to boost our reality television programming."

"I see," Ava said. "I don't write reality TV shows."

She rarely even watched them. While they were extremely profitable and most brought in huge ratings and large sums of advertising dollars, they didn't exhibit the creativity and originality Ava liked to pour into her shows.

"You haven't yet," Carroll said, his excited smile spreading widely across his face.

The last time Ava had seen that smile was the day he'd shown up in her trailer on the set in New York to tell her they'd been renewed for a second season. That had been just six hours before she'd returned to her trailer with another man—the man who continued to creep into her thoughts on a daily basis.

"These are notes on the previous show of this kind," Carroll continued. "We want you to look at these to get a feel for the subject matter."

"You'll still have creative freedom to work this out in the way you see fit, but we're really aiming for the family reunion angle. If you can have a preliminary outline of the show in three months, we'll be ready to shoot the first pilot right after the first of the year. We already have the time slot selected. It will air at eight o'clock Thursday evening, with its debut on Thanksgiving Day. This will give us time to put a vigorous promotional plan in effect," Jenner told her.

Carroll was nodding now as he pushed that pile of papers across the table to her.

"*Doctor's Orders* is number one in the Thursday at eight slot," she said slowly, not liking where she felt like this was going.

"We know! We know," Carroll continued with glee. "That's why this is so perfect. That's why you are the perfect one to write this new script."

"I thought reality shows were supposed to be unscripted," Ava told him. "If you already have the idea and time slot locked in, you don't need me."

Besides, Marcelle, her agent, hadn't said anything to her about the network wanting her to work on a different project. She'd spoken to her late last night, and they were both pumped about the new pilot idea. Ava wasn't interested in a reality television show.

"Oh, but we do need you," Jenner said. "I believe you can bring a fresh slant to this idea and the execution of the show."

Carroll nodded enthusiastically. "We both believe you can do this, Ava. Especially since you already have a foot in the door with one of the stars of the show," Carroll continued.

"What are you talking about?" Ava asked. "This is the first I've heard of this show at all. How do I know who is starring in it?"

Carroll rubbed his thick fingers together, and Ava could swear his cool gray eyes glowed with excitement.

"His name is Gage Taylor. He just worked on *Doctor's Orders* with you," Carroll said.

Gage Taylor, as in the gorgeous doctor whom she'd spent the last two and a half months acting as if she weren't attracted to? The man whom she'd finally decided to have once and for all as a celebratory prize for the second season renewal? The guy whom she hadn't seen since that night, yet had thought about at least once each day in the past two weeks?

"He's a doctor," she said after taking a deep breath and releasing it slowly. "Is this show about doctors? Because I really don't want to work in the same area. That's why my new show idea is so different from *Doc-*

tor's Orders. One is a procedural drama, while the other will be mostly drama, with lots of sex thrown in."

"No," Jenner replied. "This show is not about doctors. It has its own fantastic and totally original idea we're trying to bring across!" Jenner told her. "It's a reality television family coming back together thirty years after their original story aired. We're going to call it *The Taylors of Temptation: Remember the Times*."

Ava sat back in her chair and stared at them.

"Thirty years ago, Olivia and Theodor Taylor had the first sextuplets born in the town of Temptation, Virginia. The parents are dead now, but we want to bring the sextuplets together again, in Temptation, to see how their lives have changed," Jenner told her. "The network is already on board with the concept and you writing it. All you have to do is grab your computer and head out to Temptation to get started."

She had never heard of *The Taylors of Temptation*. Probably because she was only twenty-seven, and this show would have originally aired before she was born. Gage Taylor had come to her via recommendation from Daniel, her production assistant, whose wife, Leslie, was one of Gage's patients. Ava had known they'd need a consultant to make sure the story lines surrounding the doctors and the clinic where they worked was as authentic as possible. So she'd taken Daniel's and Leslie's word for how good Gage was and ended up enjoying working with him. A lot.

She folded her hands in her lap and shook her head once more. "I do not write reality television," she told them again.

This time Carroll's smile disappeared, and the cold edge of those gray eyes rested solely on her.

"Then you don't write another show for this network," he said with finality.

Ava couldn't breathe. She wanted to curse or kick something...possibly Carroll. Instead she kept her lips tightly clamped.

"Look, Ava, we like you," Jenner began. "*Doctor's Orders* is doing very well, and we'd love to continue working with you. To possibly develop other shows with you in the future. But for right now, this is the show we want. Do you understand?"

She absolutely did. They were giving her an ultimatum. One Ava didn't know if she could walk away from.

Chapter 2

Temptation, Virginia

One week after the tumultuous meeting at the network, Ava drove a rented fuel-efficient car into the town of Temptation, Virginia.

For the last thirty minutes, her speed had slowed. After passing the large heart-shaped sign with "Welcome to Temptation" written in bright turquoise letters, she'd felt a bit of calm take over. The drive from the airport took a few hours, and she'd hurried at first, driving as if she was on her way to an emergency. She wanted to get this over with.

Except Ava knew it wasn't going to be that easy. She hated that Jenner and Carroll had given her no choice in this matter. Or rather, she despised that their choice meant she would either have to shop her new idea to another network—and risk news traveling that she was difficult to work with—or do what she was told to do, something she'd sworn she was beyond doing.

Ava was not difficult to work with. Not on the set of the first network series she'd written for, or as the executive producer and writer of her own show. But that didn't mean Carroll wouldn't put that rumor out there, just to keep her from working anywhere else in television. That's how the industry worked. There were lots of intimidation tactics used by those in controlling positions, and Ava was glad that hers had, thankfully, only included a delayed green light of her new show idea. She knew of too many women who had suffered in other ways.

Ava was going to write the treatment for this show. Taking the next step in her career meant that much to her. And while she was sure she could use her family's influence to work with another network or even to produce her own movie if she wanted to, Ava chose not to do that. She wanted to do this on her own merit, and she would, even if it meant approaching a family who—she'd learned from the research she'd done in the last few days—had done all that they could to stay out of the spotlight.

Mature trees ushered her along the road, standing thick and tall on both sides. The sky was a perfect blue, accompanied by the fluffiest white clouds and shimmers of golden sunlight. She'd cut off the air-conditioning and rolled down the front windows, inhaling deeply the warm, fresh air. In the rearview mirror, looking as if they were somehow following her, were the peaks of the Blue Ridge Mountains. Ava figured they were just as majestic and beautiful up close as they were from this distance.

She wished this excursion would allow time for a hiking trip along some of the famous trails she'd read about during her research of the town. But she was on a tight schedule. Jenner wanted a thirteen-episode outline by Halloween—six weeks from now—and final consent contracts signed by each of the Taylor sextuplets no later than Thanksgiving. This would keep them on schedule for shooting to begin in January. Ava tightened her grip on the steering wheel and focused her mind once more on the plan she'd come up with.

Grayson Taylor was the CEO of Taylor Electronics and had recently returned to Temptation, found a wife with twins and renovated the old Victorian house where the original Taylor family had lived thirty years ago. Just three weeks ago, Grayson and his wife, Morgan, had welcomed a second set of twins, giving them a total of four children. Ava couldn't imagine taking care of anyone but herself—four kids would definitely be out of her league. Grayson and his family would be the key to getting all the siblings on board. She'd concluded that because, as the oldest, he also seemed to be the spokesperson for the Taylor sextuplets.

She made a right turn that landed her on a dirt road and was just about to check her GPS when her phone rang. It was on the console, connected to the charger, and she pressed the button to answer without looking at the screen. She was more concerned with whether or not she'd taken a wrong turn.

"You said you were going to call me back. You didn't. I despise lies, Ava. You know that."

Ava rolled her eyes and silently chastised herself for not checking her caller ID before answering.

"Hi, Mom. I'm in the car," Ava replied because she knew her mother hated her talking on the phone while driving—even if Ava used a Bluetooth.

"Then why are you answering the phone?" Eleanor immediately asked.

Ava smiled.

"I didn't want to ignore your call. Listen, I should be at the bed-and-breakfast in about twenty minutes. I'll give you a call as soon as I get settled in."

"Bed-and-breakfast? Where are you? And who stays in a bed-and-breakfast when there are perfectly acceptable hotels throughout the world?"

Not Eleanor Cannon, that was for sure. Her mother would only stay in the best hotels, drive the fanciest cars, pay a small fortune for the most stylish clothes, and buy whatever else her inherited fortune would allow. Everything her mother did was done with style and grace, while Ava had adopted a more frugal lifestyle that drove Eleanor insane.

"I'm on a research assignment. I'll give you a call with more details once I'm settled."

Her mother would want the name of the bed-and-breakfast and a landline number to reach Ava in case cell service suddenly went down worldwide. Being an only child hadn't been easy for Ava. In the past six years since Ava's father's unexpected death Eleanor had become even more overbearing.

"That will be fine. I'll wait for your call. Drive safely," Eleanor said before disconnecting.

Ava took that to mean she'd better call her mother back, or Eleanor might send out the cavalry to look for her.

Tossing the headset onto the seat, Ava returned her attention to the GPS. The directions took her down a long cobblestoned street. Hearty mums stuffed in big black pots circled each lamppost. Cute little storefronts had twinkle lights or harvest baskets, pumpkins and gourds decorating their slice of the sidewalk. People moved about, walking slowly and staring at the decorations or what the store had advertised in their front windows, Ava couldn't tell which. What she saw on their faces, however, was, without a doubt, contentment.

She drove the remaining ten minutes until making the final turn to her destination. The Sunnydale Bed-and-Breakfast was a stately white colonial house with black shutters, nestled in the center of a cul-de-sac and surrounded by a number of beautifully mature trees. It looked like something straight out of *Leave It to Beaver* or one of those other old black-and-white family shows. Ava favored nostalgic television over today's modern reality. But while recognizing the need to grow and accept change, she still tried to bring a sense of those old-time family values and simplicity into her writing. A fact, she hated to admit, that would come in handy for this project.

She parked the car and reached over to grab her

phone and purse before stepping out. She traveled light, with only one huge duffel bag and her laptop, which she retrieved from the back seat before locking the car and heading up the brick walkway toward the house.

The bed-and-breakfast looked exactly as it had in the brochure, including the chubby shrubs lined up along the perimeter with picture-perfect precision. Ava smiled at the pair of stone bulldog statues guarding the premises as she stepped up onto the porch. Opening the door, she walked inside and was further warmed by the historic charm that continued. Scuffed wood-planked floors, and emerald-green-and-white textured wallpaper stretched throughout the front foyer and along the wall next to a winding glossy cherrywood railing.

She liked it here. Liked the ambience and was glad she'd selected this brochure from the three Saraya, her assistant, had given her. The research trip had been quickly planned once she'd decided to go through with the project. And once that decision was made, Ava had known exactly how she wanted to approach it—straight through the heart.

The Taylors had loved this town and the people who lived here. If Ava were going to write this show, she had to get to know the people here. What they liked, how they lived, what they feared, all of it. Then she'd tackle the Taylor sextuplets.

"Well, hello, ma'am. Welcome to Sunnydale," an older gentleman said.

He stood behind the front desk—a continuation of the cherrywood, with a black marble top. There was a large fresh flower arrangement toward the end of the desk, closest to the wall, along with a shiny gold bell and a placard on the other end that explained all the forms of payment accepted.

"Hello," Ava replied. "I have a reservation. My name is Ava Cannon."

The man never even looked at the computer sitting on the part of the desk that faced a bay window. Instead he stood and came around until he was directly in front of her. He extended his hand and gave a toothy grin.

"I'm Otis," he said. "Welcome to Sunnydale and to Temptation."

"Ah, thank you," Ava said and shook his hand.

He was still holding her hand seconds later when a younger man entered the lobby area.

"The paint's still wet, but the job's done, Mr. Otis. I have to head back out to Harper's place, but just let Nana Lou know we'll be sending her an invoice in the mail," the second man said.

There was a big contrast between the two men, and Ava, always one to pay attention to the details, picked up on it immediately. The first man, the older one who had just been called Mr. Otis, wore dark gray pants that were baggy on his slim frame. Black suspenders helped to keep the pants from falling down, and his short-sleeved light blue dress shirt was wrinkled, with a floral trimmed handkerchief in his breast pocket. His skin was a very weathered almond complexion, and his hair—what was left of it—was short, gray and curled close to his scalp.

The second man was much younger, probably in his early to mid-twenties. He was at least six feet tall with a short bush of brown hair, and he wore faded jeans and a plaid shirt with drops of paint all over it.

"Pardon me," the younger guy said. "I didn't mean to interrupt your check-in."

They would know instantly that she wasn't from Temptation, and it had nothing to do with the cream-colored pantsuit she was wearing. Ava had left the jacket to the suit on the back seat of the rental car so that her arms were bare in the peach tank top she wore. Her shoes were comfortable leather flats, and the flashiest piece of jewelry she wore was the diamond tennis bracelet her father had given her as an eighteenth birthday present.

No, they knew she wasn't from here because they knew everybody in this town. She could see it by the way they were assessing her.

"Hi. I'm Ava Cannon," she said and was finally able to ease her hand away from Mr. Otis's grip. She extended it to the young man, who smiled as he shook it.

"I'm Craig Presley," he said. "Welcome to Temptation."

"Thank you," Ava said. Both of them were actually very welcoming and genuine.

"No thanks necessary. In fact, since you're new to town, I would like to personally offer my services to show you around," he said.

Craig Presley had a nice smile and warm, happy eyes. He was cute and friendly, but he wasn't her type. Nor was hooking up with a guy in this town on her agenda.

"Presley? Are you any relation to a Harper Presley?"

"Yes," Craig replied. "Harper's my cousin. Are you looking to have a house renovated or built? Presley Construction can definitely take care of that for you. We're the best in town. Here, let me get you a card."

He was digging into his back pocket now, pulling out his wallet as he hunted for a card.

Mr. Otis scratched the side of his head. "If you're thinking about planting roots here in Temptation, you should talk to Fred Randall about purchasing some land or a house. Then you get in contact with Harper. She's a wisp of a pretty gal, and she's mighty talented, too," Mr. Otis stated.

"I'm just visiting," Ava said and then thought quickly of something else. "But I like what I've seen of this town so far." She shrugged. "Would be nice to maybe have a vacation home here."

Craig handed her a card. "Then Presley Construction is definitely here to work with you. Phone numbers, email and address are on the card. Harper does all the intake for new clients. I can introduce you to her. I just need to make a quick trip back to the warehouse and clean up a bit. Then I would love to take you to dinner to tell you more about Temptation."

Ava looked down at the card and nodded. Harper may be the head of Presley Construction, but she was also the fiancée of Garrek Taylor, the navy pilot. How lucky was she to have made this connection to the Taylor family so quickly?

"Or she can just take a little walk down Sycamore Lane. Three blocks past the traffic light and to the left—

you'll probably bump right into Harper at Gray Taylor's house. They're having a barbecue tonight."

And the luck just continued to flow, Ava thought with a smile.

"Oh no, I wouldn't want to intrude on a family gathering. I can just call tomorrow to schedule an appointment."

"Nonsense," Mr. Otis said. "Nana Lou baked some cookies for Jack and Lily. I told her I'd run them over there, but you can deliver them in my place. Gives you the perfect opportunity to meet up with Harper."

It certainly did. Almost too perfect, but Ava decided she would take it. This wasn't LA or New York; people here were just friendly, she reminded herself. Nobody was going to be suspicious if a stranger just showed up with a plate of cookies. At least she hoped not.

"Tell Harper I sent you to her," Craig added. "I'll take a rain check for dinner."

Ava found herself liking Craig Presley because she could definitely relate to his tenacity.

"I sure will," she said. "Thanks, Craig, and you, too, Mr. Otis."

Craig headed out, leaving Ava and Otis alone.

"Like Craig said before, no thanks necessary, ma'am," Otis replied with a shake of his head. "I'll just run out to the kitchen to get those cookies for you. Then I'll take your bags up to your room."

"That would be great," Ava told him. "Oh, wait, don't you need to swipe my credit card, get my ID or have me sign something?"

Otis chuckled. "I can get all that when you come

back. If you're thinking of getting a place here, we definitely don't want to put that off."

No, Ava did not want to put off the beginning of her second phase of research. She smiled and thanked Otis once more. She hadn't been in Temptation for more than an hour, and already she was on her way to getting this story done.

Gage had been in Temptation for two days and he was already dressed down in basketball shorts, a T-shirt and tennis shoes. Garrek's fiancée, Harper, hit the volleyball with a force Gage wasn't expecting, and he ran backward in order to save the shot. He tripped over something and fell back instead.

And then she was there.

"Hello, Dr. Taylor," she said with that smile that never failed to take his breath away.

She stared down at him, dark hair framing her pretty face, a light pink gloss on her soft lips. And Gage thought he must be dreaming.

"Ava?"

He moved quickly, coming to stand in front of her.

"I think you were trying to catch this," she said and gave a light kick to the ball he'd been after.

Gage put his foot on the ball to stop it from rolling, but did not take his eyes off her. She looked amazing, her long legs clad in cream-colored pants, the formfitting peach blouse and all that thick hair hanging past her shoulders. He'd forgotten how sexy she was.

"Yeah, thanks," he said and then asked, "What are you doing here?"

"Delivering cookies," she replied and held up a plate covered in foil.

"All the way from New York or LA or wherever you live?" he asked.

It may have seemed like an odd statement since this was the last woman he'd had sex with. In a perfect world, he would have known more about her besides her last name and professional occupation. But in Gage's world, it was the norm. He didn't need to know much about the women he slept with, because he never intended there to be anything beyond the physical. It was easier that way.

"I'm ah...on a kind of retreat," she replied. "A writing retreat."

He nodded, noting the plausibility of her response, but still wondering how, of all the places in the world, Ava Cannon would turn up in Temptation.

"And a cookie delivery service?"

She looked down at the plate and then up to him again.

"They're from someone named Nana Lou. Mr. Otis at the B and B said she promised to make them for Jack and Lily."

Gage frowned. "Who?"

He'd come to Temptation to be with his family and so hadn't met many people living in the town.

"Nana Lou is like our grandmother, but not really. She bakes the best double chocolate chip cookies ever," Lily said.

The precocious seven-year-old girl appeared, leaning against Gage's leg.

"You're hogging the ball, Uncle Gage," she continued before bending down to take the ball he still had under his foot.

"You must be Lily," Ava said, her attention shifting to the little girl Gage had been thoroughly enchanted by in the last couple of days.

He'd come back to Temptation to meet Gray's new family and had been amazed at how much he adored the children. Sure, he delivered babies for a living, and he studied ways to help every woman wishing to have a baby fulfill her dream. But Gage didn't think of becoming a father himself. Still, not even the smiling faces of youth, or the pure sweetness of babies, had been able to erase the thoughts of his one night with Ava. In fact, it had been all those things combined that kept Gage from thinking about his career situation.

"I am Lily, and this is my Uncle Gage. I have another uncle—his name's Garrek—but he's away flying planes right now."

"Oh, that sounds cool. These cookies smell amazing, Lily. Do you think I could try one?" Ava asked.

"Sure. Mommy won't let me and Jack have more than one for dessert. But Jack doesn't like to share, so you should take yours now."

"Hey, guys, Morgan is calling us in for dinner," Harper said as she joined them. "Oh. Hi," she added to Ava.

"Hello," Ava replied. "I'm Ava Cannon. I'm in town for a writing retreat and was told to deliver these cookies."

"And she's Uncle Gage's friend," Lily added.

Gage didn't know what to say. Hence the reason he'd

been standing there watching the exchange between his niece and his ex-boss-slash-one-night-stand.

"Hi, Ava. I'm Harper Presley."

"Oh, it's a pleasure to meet you, Harper. I met your cousin Craig when I was checking in to the B and B. He gave me your card."

"Really?" Harper asked. "Do you have a house that needs to be renovated?"

"No," Gage replied quickly. "She's just here to write."

Harper, with her sandy-brown hair pulled back from her face, arched a brow as she looked at him.

"You two know each other?" she asked.

Before Gage could answer, his legs almost buckled once more as a laughing seven-year-old ran into him.

"Come on, Uncle Gage, you're gonna make us lose," Jack said.

"You already lost. He fell, and the lady got the ball. That means the girls win. Right, Aunt Harper?" Lily asked.

"I'm calling interference," Gage told Jack. "We'll need a rematch."

Lily pouted, and to Gage's chagrin, Ava knelt down until she was face-to-face with his niece.

"Boys always try to cheat. I think he fell on purpose so he could ask for a rematch," she said.

A mutinous Lily nodded her agreement. "I think so, too."

Harper chuckled. "Okay, we'll have a rematch, but Morgan has dinner ready. You two run along and wash your face and hands so we can eat."

Thankful to Harper for getting rid of the children,

Gage turned his attention back to Ava. It was close to six o'clock in the evening, and the sun was beginning to set; still, the last fading rays cast Ava's creamed-coffee-toned skin in a golden hue that looked surreal. Or maybe it was because this was the first time he'd seen her outside of the sultry dreams that plagued him each night in the last few weeks.

"Why don't you join us for dinner, Ava? Gray and Morgan always cook a ton, and since you're a friend of Gage's, you should definitely be here to help us celebrate his homecoming," Harper said.

The gratitude Gage had just felt toward his soon-to-be sister-in-law dissipated as he turned from Ava to look at Harper with a frown.

"I'd love to," Ava happily replied.

"Great, Gage will bring you up to the house," Harper said. "I'll just go and tell Gray and Morgan to set another place at the table."

When Harper was about to walk away, Ava spoke again. "I really appreciate the offer. I've been traveling all day, and I don't even know if my room at the bed-and-breakfast is ready yet. I just dropped my bags off and came straight here."

Gage touched her elbow to stop her from following behind Harper.

"Why would you come here? How did you know where here was?" he asked, because no matter how his body was reacting to seeing her again, his mind was still suspicious.

Old habits were hard to break.

A breeze swept by, and Ava eased her arm from his

grasp. She pushed her blowing hair behind her ears. And Gage thought he'd never seen anyone as pretty as she was at this moment.

"Small towns are great for writing retreats. Meeting Craig at the B and B and Mr. Otis having cookies that needed to be delivered were coincidences," she said.

Gage watched her lips moving as she spoke and listened to the slightly husky timbre of her voice. Not only did he listen, but he felt as if that voice, her words, somehow touched a part of him. It was ridiculous, he knew, yet…he decided to believe her. It wasn't that big of a deal. She could go wherever she wanted without needing his permission. Just because she ended up here, at the same time he was, didn't mean anything. He needed to stop being so suspicious all the time.

"I would have never expected you to be here," he replied.

"It's work," she said. "Everything I do is about my work."

Gage could definitely relate to that. In contrast to her writing retreat, however, he had been taking the last couple of days to think about things other than his career. She was one of those things, even though he'd called himself a thousand fools for thinking about a one-time fling weeks later.

"But I can go if it's weird for you," she continued.

Was it weird for him?

Considering he hadn't expected to see her again until it was time to start shooting the second season of the show, maybe. Realizing that his body had already begun reacting to seeing her—via the beginning of an erection as his gaze dipped from her big brown eyes to the unmistakable curve of her full breasts in that tight blouse—hell no, this wasn't weird at all.

"It's cool," he replied. "But we'd better get going. From what I understand, my sister-in-law, Morgan, does everything based on a schedule these days. Something about having a set of twins in elementary school in addition to a set of newborn twins and coveting any sleep she can get."

"Two sets of twins?" Ava asked with an incredulous look on her face.

Gage nodded and smiled. He ignored the burst of pride that spread throughout his chest as he looked toward the house and the back porch, where his family had begun to assemble at the table to eat the celebratory meal. Gage never talked about his family to anyone because he liked to believe they belonged to only him. Not a part of the world, the way his father had tried to make the sextuplets.

"Yes," he continued and began walking toward the house. "My older brother Gray is married to Morgan, an elementary school teacher. They have a boy and a girl, Jack and Lily, who you just met. Ryan and Emma are the new babies. Do you like babies, Ava?"

She shrugged as she walked beside him.

"I never thought about it," she said and then looked at him with a sinfully delicious smile. "I like how babies are made, though."

The semi-erection that Gage had been trying to ignore grew instantly as he recalled her smiling up at him that night he'd moved between her legs and thrust his length deep inside of her. She'd told him how much she liked it that night, and Gage would swear that the smile she was giving him now was meant as a reminder.

"Yeah," he said grinning back at her. "So do I."

Chapter 3

"Gage was working on a television show," Gray said for the second time as they all sat around the light oak dining table on the covered back porch.

His incredulous tone was not lost on Gage, or anyone else at the table, for that matter. Gage sat back in his chair trying not to address the unspoken questions that loomed over them.

"He was a great help to the show," Ava answered. "I'm certain we wouldn't have been renewed for a second season without his expertise. Comments about the show's authenticity were constantly in the reviews."

Gage hadn't read any of the reviews for the show. He enjoyed looking over the scripts and meeting with the writers—that part made him feel useful.

"I've seen the show," Morgan said as she returned to the table.

Ryan had been fussing while they ate dinner, so Morgan excused herself the minute Jack and Lily were finished. She took the older twins into the house with her while she tended to the new baby. In the days since he'd been here, Gage had concluded that Morgan was a good mother who adored her children. She also loved his brother, almost as much as Gage suspected Gray loved her. That realization had been a shock to Gage. His brother had found love and happiness, two things Gage knew would never surface in his own life.

"I love to watch procedurals," Morgan continued once she was seated. "And I thought the idea of one being set in an OB-GYN clinic on Staten Island was a fresh take compared to most of the drama series on television these days."

"I don't watch a lot of current television shows, but Corbin Yancy also has a show on the home improvement network. He and his wife are redecorating their house in Palm Beach," Harper added.

Ava nodded. She'd just finished taking a sip from her glass of lemonade. Gage watched her small hand with the neatly trimmed nails as it slipped from the glass and rested on the table.

"Corbin is great and his wife's a sweetheart," Ava told them. "He loves the show and worked really well with Gage to make the character he played come to life on screen."

"Wow," Morgan said. "So Corbin Yancy as Dr. Steven Renfield is actually Gage Taylor, my brother-in-law. I feel like I'm related to a celebrity now."

"I'm not a celebrity," Gage quickly replied.

The comment came in a sharper tone than he'd anticipated. The questioning and concerned looks coming from Harper and Morgan irritated him. For the two days that he'd been here, Gage had been successful in simply enjoying these new members of his family, and not thinking too much about the other family members who had let him down.

"I know some things that can help make the show work, but that's all I do," he said, trying for a lighter tone this time.

"Never thought my brother would be in show business," Gray said blandly.

Gage knew what Gray was thinking. From the moment he'd walked up onto the porch and introduced Ava, he'd been sure what Gray's reaction to who she was, and how Gage knew her, was going to be. Which was precisely why, when he'd first arrived in Temptation and Gray had asked what he'd been doing with himself, Gage had left out the part where he was working on a successful television show.

"Why is that? If you don't mind my asking," Ava said.

In addition to being a very good-looking woman, Ava Cannon was candid and real. Traits Gage hadn't thought Hollywood types could have. He'd watched her on the set with the crew and the cast, and each time he'd noted how sincere she was in whatever she was saying or doing. Whether correcting something in the script, or expressing her concerns to the director, or simply accepting a meal from one of the vendors, she always made eye contact and made everyone feel as if they were on the same level. Gage had admired that about her.

"Our family doesn't have a good history in the television business," Gray answered.

"But we don't need to talk about that right now," Morgan hurried to say. "It's just so nice to have Gage here visiting, and then for you to show up, too, Ava, is wonderful. I feel like we're celebrating so much these days."

"Almost too much," Gage said quietly.

When he looked up to see that Ava was now staring at him, Gage thought it was time to shift gears.

"So, Harper, when does Garrek think he'll be back for a visit?" he asked. "It would be great to see him while I'm here."

"Not until Christmas," Harper replied.

She was a nice woman—intelligent and talented, as he'd seen by the work she'd done on the old Victorian. She was not at all the type he'd thought Garrek would settle down with, but after talking to her and meeting her family, Gage could see the appeal. In fact, he was surprised at how it made him feel that his brothers had found really nice women. The Taylors didn't believe in happy-ever-after, because that wasn't how it had worked out for their family. All the happiness they'd once known had come crumbling down, and in the aftermath, each of the sextuplets had been left to figure out not only their place in the world, but what type of life they would have as a result.

Gage opted for work and family. Seeking emotional ties with anyone else was futile and doomed to end disastrously. It was that simple.

"That's too bad," Morgan replied with a frown.

"Still, it's enough time for you to visit the hospital with me to check on the progress of the new wing," Gray reminded Gage.

Gray was working on the Taylor Generational Wing at All Saints Hospital in Temptation. He wanted Gage's input on the obstetrics and gynecology department and research program that was set up in their mother's name. Even though he'd vowed not to think about work while he was here, there was no way Gage was going to refuse to help his brother.

"Absolutely," Gage replied to Gray. He needed to meet with both his brothers, but for now, Gray would have to do.

"How long are you planning to stay, Gage?" Morgan asked. "With the holidays coming up, I was hoping to get all the Taylors to come for dinner. I know it's been a long time since all of you were together, but that needs to change."

Morgan was petite, friendly and just a little bit bossy, which Gage concluded was exactly what Gray needed in a woman.

"That's a great idea," Harper added.

"I should have a few more rooms at the house completed by Thanksgiving, so whoever doesn't stay here can come out there with Garrek and me."

"Oh, a big family Christmas sounds amazing," Ava said.

She looked at Morgan and Harper with an expression that matched the women's excitement.

Unsure what to make of that, Gage replied, "I don't know if I'll be able to get away again that soon. And I only have three weeks to stay this time."

Silence fell around him, and Gage felt uncomfortable with the thought that he was spoiling their plans. He was even more uncomfortable about Ava being here, with his family, making plans for the holidays.

"Well, I think I should be going now," Ava said and pushed her chair back from the table. "I apologize for interrupting your family celebration. But I do thank you so much for your hospitality, Morgan and Gray."

"Don't mention it," Morgan said before leaning over to nudge her husband.

"Ah, she's right. It was a pleasure having you, Ava," Gray told her.

"We're all set for our meeting tomorrow," Harper added.

Ava nodded. "That's right, we are. I'm really looking forward to hearing your ideas about tiny homes. I've been thinking about having one built for a while, just haven't had the time."

"Well, you're in Temptation now," Morgan continued. "We take life at a slower pace here than in Los Angeles. I hope you get lots of writing done while you're here. And please feel free to stop by whenever you get tired of sitting at your computer. You're welcome here anytime."

Gage tried not to frown at that statement. He'd taken Harper's offer to stay at the house she was renovating for her and Garrek.

"Thanks. I'm just going to head back now. I'll be seeing you all soon, I suppose," Ava said as she stood this time.

Gage stood, too. He didn't know why, but he did.

"I'm going to head out, as well. I'll see Ava back to the B and B," he said.

"That's an excellent idea," Morgan added with a smile.

"I'll meet you for breakfast at the hospital in the morning," Gray said.

"I'll be there," he replied.

Gage moved around the table to hug and kiss Morgan and Harper good-night. He shook Gray's hand and then went to stand beside Ava. She was looking at him with a smile, and Gage wondered what she was thinking. He wondered what she'd thought about that night after they'd been together in her trailer. And he wondered if she'd thought about him at all since that time.

That thought stuck with him as he followed her back to the B and B in his car. And when he stepped onto the sidewalk and walked with her up to the front door, he continued to tell himself that the one night of great sex had been just that—one night.

Until now.

"Come inside with me," Ava said to him.

"Sure," he replied without hesitation.

***

"This isn't New York," Gage said after closing and locking the door to her room.

Otis hadn't been at the front desk when they'd walked into Sunnydale. A woman with long braids and a quick smile gave Ava the key and told her where her room was located. It had only taken Ava a couple seconds to realize the woman's quick smile was directed at Gage. That, for some insane reason, turned her on.

Gage Taylor turned her on. He had since the first day she'd watched him walk onto the set. Dressed in a black suit, white shirt and purple tie, he'd stolen the breath of every other female on the set. And he wasn't even a movie star. It was his swagger, Ava later surmised. The way his slightly bowed legs moved and the expertly cut suit hung on his broad shoulders. How his goatee was cut so precisely and his skin tone resembled the most decadent caramel. The husky and confident tone of his voice and the candid and intense way he had of looking a person straight in the eye when they talked. All of that combined with his quick wit and easy humor was nothing short of perfect. Perfectly, mouth-wateringly sexy. Period.

"No," she replied and turned to face him. "This is Temptation."

It was a place she'd arrived at only hours before. She'd come here to work on a project she wasn't one hundred percent on board with. She had not come here to have sex with Gage again. But she wanted to. There was no point denying that.

He crossed his arms over his chest. The chest she'd

known, from the way his dress shirts molded to him when they were on the set, would be deliciously muscled.

"That it is," he continued, his voice lowering slightly.

His gaze pinning her to where she stood.

"And I'm tempted," he said.

Ava tilted her head and once again replayed all the reasons why this was foolish. While they were currently in the off-season of *Doctor's Orders*, Gage had already signed a contract to work on the second season with her. Which made him an employee or coworker. In addition, he was one of the Taylors of Temptation, the family that her new project centered around. Her job here was to get each of the sextuplets to sign a contract that would allow cameras into their lives for three months. From her research, she had a feeling that wasn't going to be an easy feat.

So sleeping with Gage…again…wasn't a good idea.

"I am," she replied, "very tempted."

"I don't do relationships," he told her, but moved from where he stood, until he stopped only inches away from her.

"We've already had this conversation," she said and took the last step to close the distance between them. "You don't do relationships. You like your privacy. I'm focused on my career and will let nothing interfere with achieving my goals. You're attracted to me, and I'm attracted to you."

"For this one time," he said and used a finger to trace the line of her bottom lip.

Heat spread quickly throughout her body, her fingers clenching and releasing at her side as she tried to remain still for just a moment longer.

"Again," she whispered and gave in.

Coming up on the tip of her toes, Ava wrapped her arms around Gage's neck and pulled his head down so that her lips could touch his. That simple connection set off an explosion of heat that soared through her body. The memory of their night in the trailer had never dimmed in her mind; still, this touch sent her reeling in pleasure. He was a master at kissing, touching, seducing, and unlike in any other area of her life, Ava let go, let him take charge.

He slid his hand around her waist and down to grip her bottom. Ava sucked in a breath and moaned as he licked first her top and then her bottom lip. His fingers tightened on her, and in the next second he was lifting her off the floor. She wrapped her legs around him and eagerly delved back into the kiss.

"Bed," he mumbled between sucking on her tongue and gasping for air. "This time, the bed."

"Right," she replied as she realized he was carrying her to where he wanted her.

Ava couldn't think. She'd never been in this room before, so she wouldn't have been able to direct him to the bed anyway. Still, all her mind could absorb was the instant need that being near him sparked. She'd been afflicted with this situation for the past months as they'd worked closely together. And that night in her trailer, she'd perhaps foolishly thought that it would be cured. But it hadn't. She'd continued to want Gage long after that night. Only the thousands of miles that she'd put between them by returning to LA had kept her from showing up at his apartment and begging him to take her once more.

When he laid her down on the bed, Ava stared up into the face that had haunted her dreams too many times to count. He was possibly one of the most handsome men she'd ever seen. Certainly he was the best lover she'd ever had. But there was something else—she'd noticed it just now for the first time. Gage's dark brown eyes held a hint of wariness, even at this moment, a fact that shocked her.

"This is not why I came here," she said on impulse. "I didn't follow you so that we could do this again."

"Did you hear that?" he asked as he stared down at her.

"Hear what?"

"The sound of my ego deflating," he replied and then gave her that cocky grin she'd seen a few times before.

"I'm serious," she said, but found herself smiling, as well.

He shrugged and lifted the T-shirt he was wearing up and over his head. "I never pegged you for a stalker," he told her after tossing his shirt onto the floor.

She sat up on the bed and removed her shirt. "I definitely do not stalk," she said.

"But you stare," he added.

Ava's gaze snapped back to his face, as she'd been caught staring at his bare chest. He looked like he'd been sculpted instead of being a flesh-and-blood man. There was no other body like this, she was certain.

"Only when it's something I like," she admitted and kicked off the flats she'd been wearing.

Gage had removed more of his clothes during their banter, so that now he stood naked in front of her. She still had on her bra and panties, but he quickly rid her of them.

"So let's be clear," he said as he eased off the bed once more and found his wallet in the side pocket of his shorts.

"You're here to write and I'm on vacation."

Ava watched as he moved, loving the unfettered view of his butt and, when he turned toward her once more, his beautiful erection.

He handed her the condom packet and continued, "So this is just…"

She nodded as she ripped the foil and slid the latex out. "Is just one time. Right. Agreed."

Her hand moved slowly as she smoothed the condom over his thick length. She loved how he felt: hot, heavy, potent. She resisted the urge to moan, and he pushed her legs apart before coming over her on the bed.

"I'm going to enjoy this agreement," he whispered as he grinned down at her.

Biting on her bottom lip, Ava wrapped her arms around his shoulders and lifted her legs until they were around his waist. "Me, too," she said when the tip of his erection tapped her entrance, as if asking permission.

He rotated his hips. She lifted her bottom a bit off the bed until they were joined. He pushed inside her slowly. She dug her fingers into the skin of his back. He moaned until he was completely embedded inside her and her legs trembled. Tossing her head back against the bed, she gasped because there had never been a moment when she wanted anything as badly as she did right now. There'd never been another man to drive her to this point of desperation.

When he moved again it was to pull out of her slowly, and Ava thought she would scream. This was madness. It was torture. It was…intimate. It wasn't what she wanted, or rather, what she'd had in mind when she invited him up here. Her thought had been of him pounding into her with the same hungry ferocity that was roaring through her at this moment. She wanted to hear the sound of their bodies clapping together as they stroked and pushed to get to that delicious pinnacle. She did not want lovemaking because this had nothing to do with love.

As Ava had always done in her life, she took control. This way she was assured to get what she wanted. She moved quickly, catching him off guard and twisting their bodies until she came out on top. They both heaved out a breath as her hair draped down, the tips touching his cheeks as she grinned.

"I'll take it from here," she said and pushed back until she was straddled over him, his length still buried deep inside.

He gave her that smirk once more and lifted his arms so that his hands could cup her bare breasts.

"Do your thing," he replied.

And she did.

Ava rode him until they were both panting. His hands had gripped her hips, holding on to her tightly as she circled, lifted and sank down, taking everything he dished out and giving him all she had.

Minutes later, after they'd both moaned with their release, he wrapped his arms around her back, holding her against his chest. She felt his heart beating a quick rhythm, slowing only as time passed. She didn't move because she needed to catch her breath, as well. But the moment he lifted a hand and stroked the back of her head, once and then twice, as if he were enjoying the feel of her hair or something equally intimate, Ava pulled back.

"Bathroom," she whispered when he stared up at her, a quizzical look on his face.

He waited a beat before replying. "Yeah. Okay."

He released her, and Ava moved quickly, sliding off him and off the bed. "I have an early morning tomorrow," she began. "I want to get some work done before I'm scheduled to meet with Harper at her office. And I've been traveling all day so—"

He sat up, and Ava took another step back toward where she'd noticed a door, which she assumed led to the bathroom.

"Got it," he told her. "I'll get going."

"Ah, good night," she said and almost cringed at how crazy she must sound to him. *Good night. Thanks for the great sex. Now be gone.* Yes, definitely crazy.

Gage looked at her then, his gaze holding her to that spot. "A very good night, Ava."

When she couldn't decide whether he wanted her to say or do something else, or if she even wanted to say or do something else, Ave decided to cut her losses. She smiled and then turned before closing herself in the bathroom, leaving Gage—and the feeling that maybe they shouldn't have done this one more time—behind.

Chapter 4

"You're not listening."

"I am," Gage replied. He moved away from the windows where he'd been looking out at the town of Temptation.

He liked the view of thick trees, leaves already the rich orange, green and yellow of autumn and the rooftops of homes built in the colonial and Victorian style. Just beyond those homes was a field of grass that gave way to a thicker copse of trees. Farther east was the Lemil Mountain Lake, a popular tourist destination for Washington, DC, and Raleigh, North Carolina, residents, because of its less-than-five-hour drive. Feeding into the Potomac River, a tributary to the Chesapeake Bay, the lake area held fond memories for Gage.

Gray frowned before continuing. "This wing of the

hospital is dedicated to our mother. It's built to house the new obstetrics and gynecology department. As well as a spacious research facility to be dedicated to the study of—"

"Infertility and multiple births," Gage finished Gray's speech.

He turned away from the window to face his brother, who was standing a few feet away from him, dressed in black slacks, gray dress shirt and tie. Gage opted for a more casual look this morning, with jeans and a polo shirt. With one hand stuffed in his front pocket, he dragged the other down the back of his head.

"I'd like your hand in this," Gray said. "Dad wanted us to do this together."

Gage gave a wry laugh. "I'm still trying to wrap my head around you actually wanting to carry out Dad's wishes."

"We're not kids anymore, Gage," his brother told him.

Gray moved to stand closer to the alcove in the wall. Six feet tall, broad shouldered, intimidating glare—that was Grayson Taylor. He was always in control of his emotions, the situation around him, the people in his care, everything. Gray was born to be a leader. Gage, as the next youngest sextuplet, had always been carefree, fun-loving and easy to get along with. That's what Gemma would say. He wasn't the one in charge, nor was he the one the siblings thought would ever stay focused long enough to become successful. But he had, and now Gray was asking for his help. Pride swelled in Gage's chest at that thought, even though standing in this hospital talking about their father still managed to irritate him.

"I'm well aware of the fact that we're adults now. I mean, look at you with your lovely wife and four kids all settled in the house where we were born," he said.

Gray smiled. Happiness looked just as good on Gray as his expensive tailored suits.

"I love them more than I ever thought possible," Gray said.

Gage nodded.

"The way Mom loved us."

"Dad loved us, too," Gray said.

When Gage only raised a brow, Gray continued, "Look, I know about the past. We all know, Gage, we lived it. And we can't go back and change it. What we do now is what counts. It's the only thing we have control over, and it's all we have to leave our children."

"Unless you don't have children, like me," Gage countered as he fingered the keys in his pocket.

Touching that one key in particular had his mind circling back to the day he'd found out he didn't get the promotion. As disappointed as he'd been, Gage stayed at work that day. But instead of making the call to the foundation in Paris, he spent the day preparing for his time off. He drafted memos for Carrie to send to the other doctors in his department with notes about his patients with specific health concerns and tests that could not be rescheduled, and at the end of the day he returned to his apartment to pack for his trip.

The envelope that Gray had sent earlier this year was still unopened, sitting on the edge of Gage's desk in his home office. After their father's death, Gray had found envelopes marked for each of the sextuplets and a bank account under the name of Taylors of Temptation LLC. Each of the siblings were named as owners of the account holding a balance of 6.8 million dollars. In death, Theodor Taylor had been more than generous with the children he'd left for a production assistant all those years ago.

For endless moments Gage had simply stared at the envelope, knowing that now was the time. When he'd first received the envelope, he'd wanted to ignore it and whatever was inside of it, because it had come from his father. But since he was planning a return to his childhood home, Gage figured the time for ignoring the envelope had passed.

There were six sonogram pictures inside. They were lettered, so Gage put them in order from A to F. He was "Taylor Baby E" and he stared at that picture for some time before moving on to the only photograph from the envelope. It was of Theodor and Olivia holding their six little babies while sitting on the couch in the old Victorian house like one big happy family. On a ragged sigh, Gage had set all the pictures aside and checked the envelope one last time before tossing it into the trash. There was a key inside.

"Hey, you still with me?" Gray asked, interrupting Gage's memory.

Gage cleared his throat and pulled his hand out of his pocket.

"Ah, yeah. I'm good," Gage said. "It's cool. I'm on board. Do you have a plan for this wing? I mean, something in writing I can review and then add to if necessary?"

For a few seconds Gray just stared at Gage, then he took a few steps, his dress shoes quiet on the beige carpet.

"I do. They're in my home office. Is everything all right, Gage?"

"Of course everything's all right. Why would you ask me that?"

"Oh, because about five months ago Garrek suddenly appeared in town under the pretense of just stopping by for a visit. Turns out he had been reported as AWOL and needed an attorney to get his military career straight. So I'm asking you again, is everything all right?"

Gage had heard—via Gemma—of Garrek's troubles in the navy, and he'd reached out to his brother about six weeks ago to make sure that he was doing well in his new position.

"I should have come for a visit sooner," he told Gray. "I just didn't have time, or I didn't make time, if I listen to what Gemma has to say. I didn't get a promotion I was looking forward to at work, so I figured now was as good a time as any to take a step back and reevaluate things. And I opened that envelope you sent me."

Now Gray nodded. He folded his arms over his chest.

"What was in it?" Gray asked.

Gage shrugged. "Just some sonogram pictures of us and a picture of Mom and Dad."

"Speaking of that, we haven't had any success in figuring out who transferred that money into the Grand Cayman accounts."

"Garrek said they'd come from an address here in Temptation," Gage said.

"They did. But the house was used as a rehabilitation center at that time. There were at least twelve adults living there during the month the deposits were made."

Gage shook his head. "Is it really that important that we find out who put the money into those accounts? I mean, Dad is gone and whoever made the deposits is likely gone, too, so why shouldn't we just move on?"

"You don't want to know?"

"I don't want to live in the past," Gage told him. "My whole purpose in being here right now is to look forward to the future."

It had taken Gage a long time to be able to say that. He only wished that he totally meant it.

"And Ava Cannon is your future?"

Gage immediately tensed. He inhaled slowly, determined to keep his body and expressions as normal as possible.

"Ava Cannon is a television producer and writer. I have a professional relationship with her."

When Gray tossed his head back and laughed, Gage frowned.

His brother clapped a hand on his shoulder and said, "You keep telling yourself that."

Gage didn't reply to that comment because he hadn't come here to talk about Ava.

"Why don't you just tell me more about this facility?" he said instead.

And when Gray kindly obliged, Gage walked through the hallways of the hospital, listening to his brother talk about the town, the doctors and the additions he had made. He did not think about the vixen who had once again brought his body to a fierce release last night.

Or the fact that despite their declarations to the contrary, and what he knew he should do, Gage wanted her again.

Ava finished the last bite of the best meat lover's omelet she'd ever had while scrolling through pictures of tiny houses on her iPad.

"Presley Construction has never built a tiny house," Harper said from across the table where they sat in Ms. Pearl's Diner. "But one of my new interns is fascinated by them and has shown me some drafts she made of a couple. If you're really interested, I can set up a time for us to meet with Fred Randall. He's the best real estate agent in town. Actually, he's the only agent in town," she added with a chuckle.

Ava looked up as she reached for a napkin. Wiping her mouth, she chuckled, as well.

"Small town, I get it," she said. "I don't know if I'm ready for that step just yet. I only wanted to get your thoughts about the idea."

That was partially true. Looking at tiny houses had become one of Ava's guilty pleasures in the last couple of years. With work and warding off the blind dates her mother routinely sent her way occupying most of her time, there was rarely time to do the things she loved.

Harper sat back against the red vinyl-covered booth. Her sandy-brown hair was pulled back, hanging down in a straight ponytail. She had inquisitive brown eyes and a pretty freckled face.

"Are you sure you want to build a tiny house in Temptation? I mean, you're a producer and a writer. Why would you want to live here as opposed to in some luxury condo or mansion in LA?" Harper asked.

"I have a condo in LA. My mother is only twenty minutes away and drops by whenever she feels like it. My agent also drops by a lot instead of calling to discuss whatever business she has with me. So sometimes the condo can be a little too busy for writing. I'm always looking for a quiet place to get work done."

Harper chewed the last piece of her blueberry muffin. "I see. So this would be like a vacation home?"

"Something like that," Ava replied. "Your family has lived here for years, correct? Did the Presleys always know the Taylors?"

Ava had been up all night thinking of how she would start the conversation with Harper. She'd also been thinking about Gage and how they'd ended up in each other's arms once more. The last thought had given her much more trouble than the first.

"My father knew Theodor Taylor pretty well, and my grandfather knew Olivia Taylor's family. They both said the two seemed to be revitalized by the birth of the sextuplets. And there are people around here who still talk about having television crews here all the time, boosting revenue for local shops and B and Bs that housed them. It was a pretty exciting time."

"And now? I mean, in the years since they've been

gone, it seems like the town is still bustling without the added attention," Ava stated.

"You're right." Harper finished off her glass of water with lemon. "The town has come a long way and we've thrived over the years. But I have to admit that when Gray came back last year and saved the hospital and community center from going into a stranger's hands, the people here were relieved. It's like they've always wanted a Taylor to live here again."

Ava smiled as she digested that tidbit of hopeful information. "I'm sure you're happy they came back. Especially Garrek."

Harper's smile was quick and brilliant. It touched every part of her face from the rise of her high cheekbones to the little light that appeared in her eyes.

"I wasn't looking for love," she told Ava. "I was just trying to do a good job for Gray and Morgan, and then he appeared. It's been a roller-coaster ride, believe me, but one I'd take over and over again."

Ava tilted her head and resisted the urge to say, "Awww." She wasn't a romantic—far from it, if truth be told. Grand gestures like candlelit dinners, flowers and frilly words didn't mean much to her. Maybe because her parents didn't have that type of relationship. Or it could be that she'd watched too many girls in high school and college falling for one guy after another who gave them the words, the gestures, even the gifts, only to have the relationship ultimately break apart in the end. Either way, Ava had known all along that happy-ever-after was not for her. Tops on her agenda was professional success. After that, well, she'd settle at some point with a happy-for-now ending.

"I wish I could have met him," she said instead. "Gray seems like a nice man. He's definitely devoted to Morgan and the children."

"Oh, there's no doubt about that. They all have his heart and soul completely. I love being with them at the house because that love just radiates throughout the walls. And I'm glad that Gray's move back here seems to be bringing the other siblings back to Temptation one by one."

"Really? Do you expect the sisters to return to town soon?" Ava asked.

That would be perfect for her.

Harper had just begun to shake her head when her gaze drifted over Ava's shoulder and her smile spread once more.

"I'm not sure," she said. "Morgan's definitely trying for that big Christmas gathering. But for now, I think the whole town is just curious about his return," Harper said.

Before Ava could ask who she was referring to, or even turn to look in the direction of Harper's gaze, he was there. Standing at the table, staring down at them with dark brown eyes and that sexy-as-hell smile.

"Good morning, ladies," Gage said.

"Good morning," Harper said. "I thought you and Gray were having breakfast at the hospital this morning."

"We were," he answered. "But trust me, I've had

enough hospital cafeteria food. Thought I'd try to find some real sustenance here."

Harper and Ava both chuckled.

"Well, Ms. Pearl makes the best waffles. I can't eat them on mornings when I have to work because I get so full and they put me right to sleep. But you should definitely try them."

Gage was nodding his agreement when Harper began to stand.

"I have to get going to another site now, but, Ava, if you want to continue talking about the tiny house, just give me a call."

"I will," Ava answered while ignoring the questioning rise of Gage's brow. "Thanks so much for taking the time to talk to me about it."

"No problem. I'd love to work with you on the project. Just keep me posted. And, you, I guess I'll see around," Harper said to Gage. "Maybe tonight at the wine festival?"

"There's a wine festival tonight?" Ava asked.

Harper smiled as she moved out of the booth and Gage took her seat. "There's always a festival or celebration or some type of event going on in Temptation. We're heading into our fall festivities now. So tonight's the wine festival, and then in a few weeks we'll have the fall festival and pumpkin-carving contest. After that we're full swing into the holidays, and believe me you haven't seen anything until you've seen Temptation all lit up and ready to celebrate Thanksgiving and Christmas."

Again, Ava wanted to sigh with contentment. She'd

never lived in a small town and so had never experienced festivals or pumpkin-carving contests. Her childhood had consisted of boarding schools, summer camps, etiquette classes, ballet lessons and formal dinner parties.

"Well, I love wine, so I'm definitely there," she immediately replied.

"Then I guess I'm going, too," Gage said cheerfully.

"Great!" Harper said, excitement clear in her voice. "See you both later."

It was that excitement that put Ava on edge. Who was she kidding? Gage was putting her on edge. Again.

"So you love wine," Gage said immediately when they were alone.

Ava was saved from providing an answer when the waitress came over to ask what he wanted. He ordered the waffles and orange juice, and Ava thought the woman's face might actually crack, she was grinning at him so broadly. She shook her head at the obvious infatuation and wondered if Gage dealt with this all the time. And if he liked it.

"I need to get back to my writing," she said, suddenly irritated.

Gage reached a hand out quickly to touch her wrist. "Keep me company while I have breakfast," he said. "Otherwise that waitress is going to keep coming back, and I'm really not in the mood for that type of attention right now."

"So that not-so-subtle flirtation happens to you all the time?"

He shrugged. "Sometimes."

"And you normally like it, but not today. I see. Well, what makes today so different?"

Damn. She sounded testy and hated it.

Gage sat back, resting his hands in his lap now. "I don't know what's different," he told her. "I'm still trying to figure it out. But, maybe it's you."

No. It couldn't be her.

"That's ridiculous. We're not committed to each other in any way," she stated. But inside she wondered if that should actually be a question.

The thought was totally foolish. This was Gage Taylor, an employee and the subject of her new project.

"No. We're not," he told her. "But we are sleeping together."

"It was just for one ni—" she started to say.

Gage arched a brow again as her lips snapped shut.

"Look, I'm not in the market for a relationship any more than you are. But I like honesty. So I try to be as honest with myself as possible."

Ava tried to ignore the sting she felt when he said "honesty."

When he continued, she took a sip from her glass.

"We've been together twice now. That doesn't make us a couple, but it certainly classifies us as sleeping together."

She couldn't argue the logic.

He nodded and thanked the waitress when his food and juice were delivered.

The offer to get him anything he wanted and yet another bright smile had Ava's fingers fisting at her sides.

She forced herself to breathe and relax because she was being ridiculous.

"Well, I can work while you eat," she said and then looked down to her iPad once more.

"Or you can tell me why you're talking about building a house here in Temptation if you just came for a writing retreat," he said.

Right, Ava thought as she took another drink from her glass. She could tell Gage why she was lying about her real reason for being here. That was sure to go over well.

Chapter 5

"I'm still waiting for a call back on that rain check."

Ava turned at the statement and found herself staring up at Craig Presley.

It was a little after seven in the evening, and since daylight saving time hadn't occurred yet, the sun was just waning in preparation to set. The Fall Wine Festival was being held at Treetop Park, which was just down the street from Temptation's town hall.

After spending her day walking around the town and talking to the wide array of citizens, Ava had headed back to the B and B, where she'd showered, checked emails and dressed for the festival. When she'd stepped outside again, it was to learn that the evening weather had shifted to a more comfortable temperature than earlier, so her decision to wear the navy blue ankle pants and beige sleeveless blouse with nude-colored sandals was a smart one. She'd driven the fuel-efficient hybrid rental car and parked on the street across from the park. The one with all the colorful houses.

"Oh, hi, Craig. I'm sorry. I've just been busy writing and stuff."

He smiled, a really nice smile. Craig was a good-looking guy who probably had women smiling at him the same way Gage did. She shook her head in an attempt to get Gage out of her mind.

"It's cool," he said. "I understand. We just finished up a big project, so I'm glad to have the festival to unwind a little."

"It looks like a good crowd," she said turning her attention toward the stalls and tents where people were lined up.

"Come on, let's start tasting," Craig told her and took her hand before she could respond.

They walked past two stalls with super long lines and when Craig joked about people in Temptation not being afraid to get drunk in public, Ava laughed.

"What's so funny?" a woman who had just stepped in front of them asked.

She wore gray dress pants with a purple blouse. Her hair was feathered back from her carefully made-up face, and her lips pursed as her eyes assessed every part of Ava.

"Hi, Ms. Millie," Craig said, gripping Ava's hand a little tighter.

"Craig," the woman—Millie—replied. "You have

manners, son, I know your daddy taught them to you. So make the introductions."

Rude didn't quite seem to describe this woman.

"I'm Ava Cannon," she said because she was a grown woman and did not need Craig to make introductions for her. "I'm visiting Temptation on a writing retreat."

She was losing track of how many times she told that lie, but didn't want to think about that at the moment.

"Ava Cannon," Millie said and continued to look as if Ava had body odor or food stuck in her teeth.

"I'm Millie Randall. Chairperson of the chamber of commerce. We usually like to welcome the visitors to Temptation personally. But I didn't know you were here. Not until this morning at least when I saw you coming out of the diner with Gage Taylor."

"Yes. I had a breakfast meeting with Harper this morning, and then Gage showed up." For whatever reason, Ava felt like she needed to explain.

"And now you're here with Craig. Well, it seems you're certainly getting around. Are you writing about the men of Temptation?" Millie asked.

"I hope not," Gage said from behind Ava.

Her heart skipped a beat at the sound of his voice, but she did not turn to look at him. This situation had gone from strange to uncomfortable in record time.

"Hey, Gage," Craig said. "Glad you could make it to your first wine festival in Temptation."

Gage had come to stand next to Millie, across from Craig and Ava.

"I thought Ava and I would enjoy our first festival together," Gage said.

"Hmmmm." Millie made the sound and looked skeptically from Gage to Ava, letting her gaze linger there.

Ava wanted to scream. Or turn and run back to her car and drive all the way back to LA. Anything to not be in the middle of something she didn't even understand herself.

This was silly. She wasn't doing anything wrong. Gage had said so himself—they weren't a couple.

"I just got here and ran into Craig," she said.

"And then we ran into Ms. Millie," Craig said.

Millie nodded. "And now we're all here together."

Ava remained silent.

"Why don't you come with me, Craig? I have something in my car for your father. You can take it to him."

Craig looked at Ava.

"She'll be fine with me," Gage said in a stiff voice.

"Come, Craig," Millie commanded and turned around to start walking away.

With an audible sigh, Craig released Ava's hand. "I'll be back," he said to her.

"Oh, don't worry about it," she told him. "I'll probably leave in a few minutes anyway. I still have work to do."

He gave her a quick smile as he back-walked in the direction Millie was heading. "That's fine, but my rain check still holds."

Ava smiled. "No problem."

But there was a problem. When they were alone, Ava felt it. She couldn't explain it, but she felt it in the way Gage was staring at her.

"So," she said finally because she was tired of standing there feeling ridiculous. "I'm going to just grab one drink, and then I'll be going."

He wasn't frowning, but he didn't look happy either. "I think we both need a drink."

That was an understatement, and the first booth they made it to, Ava eagerly accepted one of the red wines they were offering. It went down smooth and had a sweet taste, so she took another. She didn't know if Gage was trying the white or the red wine, but she finished her second and was just swallowing the third, when he stopped her.

"Slow down there. You have to pace yourself when you come to these things. Otherwise I'll have to carry you back to the B and B."

Gage's voice was deep, and rubbed against all of her nerve endings with quick and potent efficiency. The fact that she was still undeniably attracted to him after their two hookups was not nearly as surprising as the low hum of guilt she'd been carrying with her since answering his question about her tiny house quest this morning.

"Oh, no worries about that," she replied. "I can hold my liquor."

"Really? Spending your evenings in bars putting back a few is how you roll?"

His tone was lighter than just moments ago, but Ava didn't feel like laughing.

She shrugged. "Boarding school wasn't nearly as prim and proper as my mother thought it would be."

He nodded. "So you were that girl, huh? Boarding schools, fancy cars, Ivy League college."

"You attended Columbia for undergrad and medical school," she said.

"Checked up on me, did you?"

"I did my research," she said. "As I do with all the people I work with."

"That makes sense," he replied.

He took the empty glass from her, their fingers brushing with the action. She was just about to pull her hand away when Gage reached for it.

"I'm not a holding-hand type of guy," he said, staring down at her fingers.

Ava was about to say that she wasn't either, but that would have been silly since Craig had been holding her hand when Gage joined them.

After a few seconds more, he released her hand and returned her cup to the stall.

Okay, she was being foolish, there was no reason this should feel awkward. She wasn't committed to Gage, and she hadn't been doing anything wrong with Craig.

So when Gage turned to her again she started to walk, and he joined her.

"I know this is your first wine tasting in Temptation, but have you been to one of these before?" she asked after they'd passed a few stalls decorated with plastic vines and grapes.

"I've been to wine and cheese receptions in the city, and I have a friend who lives in the Hamptons who has an annual get-together to showcase his family's vineyard, but this is different."

"I agree," Ava replied. "This is different."

He may have thought she was referring to the wine

festival, but she wasn't. Her thoughts were circling more around the fact that she was actually thinking about everything she'd said to Gage in the last two days, versus the two times they'd spent in each other's arms, and the truth of why she was here. It was complicated, and while she could simply tell him everything right here and right now, she didn't.

What Ava did do, however—and to her utter embarrassment—was trip over some power cords that had been stretched across the grass from one booth to another. With her arms flailing forward, she prayed she wouldn't fall flat on her face, but her feet were already doing some type of clumsy dance that almost assured that fate.

"Whoa, there," Gage said.

His arms went around her waist, and pulled her back against him as his words whispered into her ear.

A few choice curse words and a deep breath later, Ava's feet were once again solidly on the ground while her cheeks fused with heat. "These cords should probably be stretched behind the tents. Instead of across the path where people have to walk."

"That's very true," Gage replied.

His lips were close to her ear so that his words were warm and…oddly sexy. The arm he still had wrapped around her waist felt almost possessive, and her blouse rode up her back at their close proximity.

"I'm okay now," Ava said nervously and attempted to move out of his grasp. But he held on.

"You sure? How many glasses of wine did you have before I showed up?" he asked with a chuckle.

Ava managed a smile even though she was beginning to feel pretty warm in the cool autumn evening air.

"I'm not drunk, Gage. Just a little clumsy, I guess."

Even though she'd never been known to be clumsy before. Nor had she considered herself easily flustered by some guy.

Pulling down her shirt, she looked at Gage and tried to keep her smile in place. "The cords are a hazard and could incite a lawsuit."

"Say that a little louder, and I'm sure by night's end, everyone in town will fall over themselves trying to make your visit here as safe and enjoyable as possible. That's how threats tend to work here," Gage said.

"I didn't," she replied. "I mean, I wouldn't. I was just saying that someone else might. And how do you even know how people here would act? This is your first time back in Temptation since you were a kid."

For a few seconds Gage looked at her oddly, like maybe she shouldn't know that about him. Or maybe he just didn't like hearing that little bit of truth.

"And besides, different people have different reactions," she said after clearing her throat.

They were standing in the middle of the walking path and a woman bumped into Ava, mumbling a quick "excuse me" as she moved to another booth.

"Let's get out of the way," Gage said, touching her elbow.

They walked past the row of tents to an open area where lawn chairs and blankets were spread out around the gazebo.

"Morgan and Gray are trying to get a babysitter so

they can come out tonight. So I was sent down here early with blankets and instructions to get a good spot facing the stage."

"I didn't know there would be music," Ava said and turned to look at the men setting up instruments in the large gazebo.

This was a perfect location to view a concert. There were two large screens set up on either side of the gazebo for those in the back to see.

"Yeah, I hear they do this twice a year," he told her. "Have a seat."

Ava looked at Gage and then down to the blankets before taking him up on his offer and sitting down. He followed, but he leaned back so that he was propped up on one elbow right beside her. If she lowered her hand, she could touch the small mole just beneath his right eye.

She didn't, of course. That would have been... intimate.

"I don't remember anything like this when I lived here. I was only seven when we left, so most of my memories consist of riding bikes up and down our street and going to the lake for picnics," he said abruptly.

Ava waited a beat before following his lead.

"Did you like living here?" she asked.

He reached out and touched the tips of the belt knotted at her waist.

"It was a house in a town," he replied. "At the time, I didn't know anything else."

"But it must have been fun in that big house, and being celebrities." The last word was spoken quietly.

His fingers paused on the material as he slowly looked up at her.

"It wasn't a choice," he said. "We never had a choice in the matter."

This time they would, Ava thought. She would lay it all out for them, and she would offer them the opportunity to say what they would like their show to be.

"I know a few child stars, and they're ecstatic about being on television. Mostly they're happy when the workday is over for them and they can play with whatever new and not-yet-on-the-market toy their agent has acquired for them."

She chuckled lightly, but Gage did not crack a smile.

"When you build your tiny house, you should look for a space like this," he said after a brief pause. "A wide-open area with a killer view."

So they were back to her lie…or rather, her omission.

"A view of a stage?" she asked jokingly.

"No," he replied with a shake of his head. "Look beyond the stage, Ava. Look at what nature has for you."

She did as he said. She shouldn't have. The moment she saw the mountaintops pressing into the fading purple and blush sky, she sighed and silently agreed. This was a view she could wake up to each morning. If she were actually moving to Temptation.

"It's a great view," she said. "Do you recall waking up to it when you lived here?"

"As I said before, I left when I was seven," he replied. "My mother packed us up and moved us to Florida. We lived in a house on Pensacola Bay, so my view there was of the water. I've loved the water ever since."

"I don't know how to swim," she said absently. "I grew up in Beverly Hills. We had a pool, but I never learned how to swim."

It sounded strange. Everybody knew how to swim. Right? It wasn't her fault that she had piano lessons during summer camp when other children were swimming in lakes and sleeping in tents. And when her parents had pool parties, Ava wasn't invited. When her parents weren't having a pool party, the pool was gated off because Eleanor didn't want Ava to fall in and drown, since she didn't know how to swim.

"I can teach you," Gage stated evenly.

"What?"

"I can teach you how to swim," he repeated.

Ava looked down at him again, just as the music began. More people had joined them on the grass, some standing, others sitting on their own blankets. Gage pushed himself up to a sitting position and scooted closer to her. After the first few melodic strands were played by the jazz quartet, she replied, "I'd like that."

She'd always wanted to learn how to swim, and what better way to learn than in Gage Taylor's arms?

Gage had reserved the indoor pool at the community center for a few hours. He was going to teach Ava how to swim. And that was all. He could do that.

What he couldn't seem to do, to his dismay, was forget how he'd felt seeing her holding hands with Craig Presley. It didn't matter. Gage had spent the last two days telling himself that. Ava Cannon was not his to feel possessive over. Yet, he'd wanted to snatch her hand away from Craig's that night. He'd wanted to let Craig and any other guy in this town know that she was with him. But she wasn't, at least not in that way.

She was, however, walking toward him wearing a simple yellow bikini that looked like sunshine against her golden brown skin, beneath a sheer white shirt that brushed over her knees. Her hair was piled atop her head in a way that reminded him of how she looked in the moments after they'd both reached their climax. Her face was free of makeup and as lovely as he'd ever seen it.

"Hi," she said when they were standing just a few feet away from each other.

"Hi yourself," he said over a tongue that had grown thick with lust. "Glad you could join me."

Gage was lounging in the hot tub while he'd waited for her to arrive. The way his body instantly reacted to seeing her made him grateful for the warm rolling bubbles around him.

"Are we swimming or soaking?" she asked after a few seconds of silence.

"Swimming, of course." He resisted the urge to frown as he turned his back to her and walked up the three steps to exit the hot tub. His black swim trunks were baggy enough—he hoped—so that when he turned to face her, he didn't embarrass himself and possibly her at the same time.

"I did tell you that I've never had a swim lesson before," she was saying as she moved to one of the lounge chairs and dropped the large bag she'd been carrying. "Right?"

"You did. So we'll take this slow."

But the moment she grabbed the hem of that shirt and pulled it up over her head, all thoughts of slow vanished from his mind. He wanted to take her, hard and fast, right there on the lounge chair, or in the pool.

"Great," she said as she turned to him. "I appreciate you taking the time to do this."

Yeah, he was doing a great deed here. Teaching her how to swim. And thinking of how quickly he could get her out of that skimpy bikini and on top of him.

"It's no problem. Everyone should know how to swim."

Gage cleared his throat and mentally kicked himself for being a horny cad. She was serious about learning, so he needed to get serious about teaching. Which would probably involve touching.

With a shake of his head, he led them to the side of the pool that was five feet deep.

"Come on in," he told her after stepping into the chilly water. He immediately bent his knees so that he was submerged up to his neck, acclimating himself to the new temperature.

"Oh!" she said with a shiver after sitting on the side of the pool and putting her feet in first. "Cold."

"Yeah," he replied with a nod and a smile.

Gage walked over to where she sat, touching her ankles and then smoothing his hands up and down her legs, introducing the cold water to her skin.

"You have beautiful eyes," he said while his hands continued to move. "That's one of the first things I noticed about you."

"They're just brown," she said and tilted her head while staring at him.

"They're expressive," he replied. "Whatever you don't say with words is mirrored in your eyes."

She looked away, and Gage moved in closer until his shoulders were between her knees. He moved a hand from her leg and cupped her cheek, turning her gently until she faced him again.

"That's how I knew you wanted the same thing I did. In the studio, each time we looked at each other, I knew," he said, his voice gruff with growing arousal, and just a hint of something more.

"There's a professional code of conduct," she replied before her tongue snaked out to lick her bottom lip quickly. "I like to follow my own rules. Especially on set. And sleeping with my consultant wasn't a good idea."

His hand slipped down to the smooth column of her neck. "The idea may not have been good, at first," he said. "But damn if we weren't great together, Ava. Both times."

Gage watched as she tried to deny it. She opened her mouth, snapped her lips closed and thought about what to say. But her eyes were already telling him—and his body—what he wanted to know.

"I don't know how to explain it either," he said. "I'm not usually so taken by one woman."

She nodded. "Right. You're like the rolling stone," she said.

Gage froze, the lyrics to The Temptations' famous song playing in his mind. "No. That was my father."

"I—" Ava began, but Gage touched a finger to her lips.

"I can't think of anyone but you. Since the first day on set, it's been you in my mind day and night. I've given up trying to explain it," he told her.

In fact, he'd decided that maybe it was best not to overanalyze this. They were attracted to each other, and that was that.

"Besides," he said, bringing his other arm up to wrap around her waist, pulling her closer to the edge of the pool, "we're not technically working together right now. The second season doesn't start taping until next year."

The slight tilt of her lips had his chest tightening.

"You've thought of everything, haven't you?"

"No," Gage said. "I've only thought of you, Ava. Only you."

In the next instant Gage was pulling her into the water with him, wrapping her legs around his waist as his lips met hers. Her arms were twined around his neck, and their tongues joined together in a delicious duel.

That tightening in Gage's chest simmered to a warm glow that spread throughout his body, even as they stood in the cold pool water. Her breasts pressed into his bare chest as she licked hungrily over his lips. His fingers splayed over her back before moving down to grip the plump globes of her bottom. She tightened her legs around him, pressing her center into him. Gage groaned with the deep pangs of sexual hunger that pierced through him.

He moved his fingers down farther, beneath the rim

of her bikini bottom until he could feel the crease of her backside. *Farther*, Gage thought. He needed to go farther, to touch more, to feel... The second he pushed through the warm folds of her center, the pounding of his heart grew louder, echoing in his ears.

Ava arched her back, her hands moving to his shoulders, blunt-tipped nails digging into his skin. Through partially opened eyes, Gage watched as passion played over the delicate features of her face with his touch. Tracing his fingers back and forth through her arousal-coated folds had her eyes closing, lips parting as she moaned.

She felt like heaven, like the finest silk beneath his fingers. When she whispered his name and Gage pressed one finger deep inside her entrance, Ava bucked over him, and Gage eased in another finger. Her hips began to move, pumping against his fingers as he thrust them in and out of her. Water sloshed around them, creating a cool reprieve from the fiery passion rolling over them at this moment. She pulled her bottom lip between her teeth, in a look that was as enticing as any *Playboy* centerfold Gage had ever seen. Her head was tilted back, breasts cupped in the yellow material jutting forward. Her nipples were hard, and Gage ran his tongue over his bottom lip as he imagined taking them in his mouth.

Pumping furiously in and out of her now, he felt his arousal stretching to painful proportions behind the material of his trunks. Her arms had begun to shake; hair that had been pulled up into a messy bun had escaped and now flowed freely down her back. She moaned again, this time long and loud as her legs tightened around him and her nails pressed hard into the skin of his shoulders. Gage moved his fingers faster inside her, feeling her muscles tighten in an attempt to constrict the motion. Her release came strong and hot over his fingers as she moaned his name before leaning forward and dropping her forehead to his chest.

Seconds later and with his fingers still inside her, Gage heard her whisper, "If I'd known this was what a swim lesson consisted of, I may have signed up sooner."

Gage chuckled. He pulled his fingers from her and gripped her hips, letting her legs fall from his waist. When he was sure her feet touched the bottom of the pool, he looked down at her and then hugged her close on impulse.

"I would have offered sooner," he told her.

Much sooner. If he'd known what it would feel like to be with a woman more than once, Gage was certain he would have tried it.

But something told him that it wasn't the number of times that was making the difference. It was Ava.

Chapter 6

Ava felt both at home and out of place at the same time. Morgan's kitchen was homey and welcoming. The soft white cabinets and sage-green paint accented the stainless steel appliances. The countertop full of baby bottles, some empty and some full, a Batman thermos and four covered containers of different sizes kept the country chic design from looking staged.

"My granny loves to cook," Morgan said as she sat across the island from Ava. "The entire time I was pregnant, she talked about all the things she was going to make so that Gray and the kids would have good home-cooked meals while I was recuperating. Whereas my sister Wendy was all set to hit every fast-food and delivery spot in the vicinity to make sure we were fed. The babies are a month old now, and Granny's still sending food over here as if I'm bedridden."

She laughed and Ava smiled. Morgan Taylor was friendly and easy to talk to. She was also observant, Ava thought while finishing the last bite of the fresh-sliced country ham sandwich she'd had for lunch. The invitation from Morgan had come three days after her swim lesson with Gage, and the morning after her second run-in with Millie. The older woman had been with her girlfriends this time, coming out of the library as Morgan walked by. As Otis had already heard about the scene by the time she'd returned to the B and B, Ava figured the lunch invitation was for Morgan to find out firsthand what had happened.

"I never knew my grandparents," Ava replied and used a napkin to wipe her mouth and fingers. "My father's parents did not care for my mother, and by relation, never wanted to see me. And my mother's parents were deceased before I was born."

"Oh, that's sad. I'm sorry," Morgan said. She reached a hand across the table to touch Ava's.

The diamond ring on Morgan's left hand was more like a blinding rock of ice glittering up at her. It should have been too opulent for Morgan's small hand and wholesome personality, but it wasn't. Instead, Ava looked down at the ring and then up to Morgan and saw the love this woman had for her family. In turn, Gray Taylor had shown his love for his wife with this extravagant ring and the loving renovations to this house. It was sweet and on a level of emotion that Ava couldn't really understand.

"Thank you, but it worked out. I kind of liked being an only child, as well, and not having to attend any of the family functions my classmates always complained about," Ava told her.

There'd always been a fear of more people sharing her mother's thoughts and narrow-minded nature. With that in mind, Ava had been totally fine with not having any relatives to deal with.

"Well, we're all about functions here in Temptation. And everyone around town is just like family. Or they like to think they are," Morgan said.

"You're talking about what happened with me and Millie," Ava said when Morgan had pulled her hand away and settled back on the stool. "I'm not sure how all that came about."

Morgan waved a hand. "Millie planned it, that's how. That's what she does. You've been in town for two weeks and everyone's been buzzing about the TV producer who knows the Taylors. It's a wonder she hadn't gotten to you before now."

That made sense. When Millie had approached Ava at her car, it had been with a sugary sweet smile and wintry cool eyes.

"I did get the impression that she'd been waiting to speak to me again," Ava added. "The first words out of her mouth were 'So you're the one who works with Gage Taylor. What else are you two cooking up?' If I wasn't already used to dealing with the press on occasion, I might not have been prepared for the unannounced verbal assault."

Morgan chuckled. "I'm sure that's exactly what it

was, a verbal assault. Millie has a mouth on her, and she doesn't care what anyone else has to say, she's going to speak her piece every time."

"That's fine, but I hope she hears as well as she talks. I made it clear to her once more that Gage and I worked on *Doctor's Orders* together and that I was just here on a writing retreat."

"Oh, I'm sure you did," Morgan said. "That's just not what Millie wants to hear. But it seems like you have the right attitude where Millie's concerned."

"She can think what she wants," Ava told her. "People always do."

"That is certainly true."

Water boiled on the stove, and Morgan slipped off the stool to tend to it. Ava watched as she poured the boiled water into a plastic jug and then put those lidded containers into a shopping bag. Probably to go back to her Granny.

"I don't care what these new formulas call for, I still do it the old-fashioned way—boiling my water first." She smiled. "Never could manage breast-feeding, especially not with twins."

Ava smiled in return and continued to watch curiously until Morgan returned to her seat and picked up her glass.

"Does Gray want more children?"

Morgan choked on the water she'd just sipped.

"Not now," Ava said, reaching to hand Morgan a napkin. "I'm sorry, I should have been clearer. I just mean overall, does he want a big family like his parents had?"

"No," Morgan said, shaking her head. "Gray doesn't

want any of the things his parents had. Neither does Gage or their youngest sister, Gia. Garrek, Gemma and Gen think differently about what happened."

"That's Genevieve, right?"

Morgan nodded. "They used to call her Vivi when they were younger, but after their mother passed, Gray said she wanted to be called Gen. It was too hard to hear the nickname her mother had given her, I suppose."

From all her research, Ava had surmised that the Taylor children suffered traumatically from the early events of their lives. A part of her ached for them.

"When Theodor left, the siblings were emotionally split down the middle. Three of them sided with Olivia, while the other three held back from taking a side at all. Gage and Gia stuck close as the two youngest, but from what Gray has told me, they were adamant that their father never be forgiven for what he did to their family."

"That must have been hard," Ava said, thinking of Gage.

"You know about the Taylors of Temptation, don't you? You would have looked into Gage's past before you hired him. Isn't that how it works?"

Morgan was a schoolteacher, but she asked questions like a trained investigator. Not overtly like a police interrogation, but with an easy flow that garnered the information she wanted. Ava had only to decide whether Morgan's inquisitiveness meant she was a friend or foe in the quest to get the contract signed.

"I did," Ava replied. Again, she was telling a partial truth. She'd only looked into Gage's past a few weeks ago. "But nothing told of the emotion. I mean, there's the story of what happened and that's it. The allegiances, the toll this entire situation took on this family was not easily surmised in any of the stories I read."

"It can't be," Morgan said with a shake of her head. "Their grief is real and raw, and it lives inside them every day. Not just with the death of their parents, but also with reliving the demise of their family. That's what hurt them most. And at the same time, it's what holds them together."

"I understand," Ava said.

"Do you? Because if you do, you'll know that falling in love is not going to be easy for Gage. But when he does, he's going to fall with all his heart. Are you ready for that?"

"What? Why are you asking me that? I'm just here for a—"

"For a writing retreat, I know," Morgan said with a knowing look. "Of all the places in the world, you picked this town. And you picked it after you'd been working with Gage. I've seen how the two of you look at each other. At dinner on my deck that first night, and again at the wine festival when we finally showed up."

"Morgan, I think you're mistaken."

Morgan shook her head. "I don't think I am. But, to be fair, I hope you're getting lots of writing done while you're here."

The sound of crying poured into the room, and both women stared at the baby monitor sitting on the counter near the refrigerator.

"Duty calls," Morgan said cheerily. "I'll be right back."

Ava nodded, and the moment she was alone she let her head fall forward to rest on the cool surface of the island. She groaned with her eyes closed as she replayed the conversation. Morgan wasn't buying her being here for a writer's retreat. Was that good or bad? Was she going to tell Gray? And if she did, how was Gage going to react when he found out she'd been lying to him and his family?

"Well, look who stepped out of her writing lair."

Ava wanted to groan again. She wanted to slink out of this kitchen and take herself back to LA as quickly as possible.

"Hi!" she said instead, in a voice that was way too happy for the way she was actually feeling.

"Haven't seen you out and about in a few days," Gage said while walking farther into the kitchen.

"Ah, no. I mean, I've been out. Just trying to get some writing done. But I do come out and walk around town. I like seeing the sights and the people."

She was babbling, so she snapped her lips closed and stared at him instead. He looked good. Of course he did. Gage always looked good. Jeans and polo shirts had never actually appealed to her before, but on him, they were hot.

"That's great. I've been sort of busy, too."

"Oh, really?"

"Yes. Don't sound so surprised." He chuckled as he took a bottled water out of the refrigerator and opened it.

"Well, you are on vacation, right? And your fast *Playboy* car has been heard zooming on the streets around town. Otis told me that." Ava smiled at the recollection.

Otis had come to her room with a tray of lemonade and Nana Lou's sugar cookies that day. He made a point of visiting her while she was writing, always bringing snacks and tidbits of town gossip. He was a thoughtful but nosy man, and she liked him.

"Fast *Playboy* car, huh? For the record, it's a Jaguar XE, and she is pretty sweet when she gets going," he said before taking a drink.

Ava could watch him for days. Whether he was falling on his butt during a volleyball game, or lounging on a blanket in a park, he was very easy on the eyes. And she liked the way he looked back at her.

"You and your women," she said with a smirk.

"Hey, Gage," Morgan said, returning to the kitchen with an adorable bundle of baby wrapped in a blue Baby Mickey blanket. "Where's Gray? He said you two were meeting with a new doctor at the hospital and then he was coming home to relieve me."

Gage set the bottle on the counter and went to Morgan, gingerly taking the baby from her arms.

"That's why I'm here. To deliver a message. Gray's tied up with an overseas conference call. He'd planned to take it here at the house, but his assistant confused the times, and he had to get on the call in one of the offices at the hospital."

"But I have a meeting with Mrs. Camby about the Fall Festival. She's been the chair of this festival for the last fifty years and never leaves her house for a meeting. I don't really want to take the twins over there."

Gage had been smiling down at baby Ryan, rubbing a finger over the child's small hand. "JoEllen Camby?"

"Yes," Morgan replied. She picked her cell phone up off the counter and started scrolling on it. "Wendy's doing a double shift at the hospital today, and Granny has the food drive at the church. You remember Mrs. Camby?"

"Not really," Gage answered. "She and my mother kept in touch after we left. I remember seeing cards come in the mail from her."

"Oh," Morgan said. "Well, you two are in luck because I need a babysitter."

"A babysitter?" Ava asked.

Morgan nodded. "Yes. Two babies and two of you. I should only be gone an hour. Nana Lou is picking Jack and Lily up after school to take them to Movies and Games Day at the community center. So you won't have to worry about them."

Ava looked over at the baby Gage was holding. He looked pretty comfortable with the little boy in his arms. Ava, on the other hand, felt a wave of panic. "I've never watched a baby before."

She'd never even held one.

"I'll teach you." Gage winked at her.

Morgan looked from him to Ava with a raised brow. "Uh-huh, right. Okay. So it's time for them to be fed. Their next bottles are ready and on the counter over there. I'll finish the new formula when I get back. Ryan always wants to go first. I've already changed him. Emma's going to be up in a few minutes because she doesn't let Ryan get too much of a head start. When she wakes up, just change her diaper. Gage, give Ava my cell number. Call me if there's an emergency, and thank you both so much!"

Morgan was out of the kitchen in a blur of blue sweatpants and hoop earrings. Ava didn't know what to say.

Gage came to stand in front of her. He was so close she could smell the baby scent of Ryan, even though she resisted the urge to look down at what she knew was a bundle of cuteness.

"First things first," he said. "I don't have women. My car is *Jezebel*, and my yacht is *Seraphine*. Those are the only ladies in my life."

"Oh," was all Ava could manage as a reply.

Then her cell phone rang, and Emma's cry blasted through the intercom. Pulling the phone out of her back pants pocket, she frowned when she saw Jenner's name on the screen.

"Okay, well, I guess I'd better get…ah, both of these," she said and then repeated Morgan's previous quick exit.

She needed to get away from the extremely comfortable-looking scene of Gage holding a baby and still looking sexy. And also of Gage telling her that he didn't have a woman…so what was she?

Had she been jealous?

Gage walked to the counter and picked up one of the bottles. He removed the top and placed the nipple between Ryan's small lips. This was his nephew, a new generation of Taylor children. That made Gage smile.

Even while his mind circled back to the way Ava had said "you and your women."

He'd felt the need to clarify the women in his life, and in doing so he realized how lonely it sounded. So he didn't have a significant other. Was that such a big deal? She didn't either—or did she? It occurred to him that between their sexual tête-à-têtes and declaring that there was nothing serious between them, they had never verified that they were each available for such dalliances.

They were adults; that's what mattered. Any agreements they made were mature and thought out. There was nothing to regret.

Then why had he felt like a complete ass when she mentioned his women?

"What do I do now?" he asked, looking down into the innocent eyes of his nephew.

Of course Ryan didn't answer, and after a few seconds Gage wondered why he was even asking. Not his nephew, but himself. There was nothing between him and Ava that he should be wondering about. Hadn't he told himself that in the last few days when he'd been so immersed in the work at the hospital?

"What are you doing staying here so late? Shouldn't you be out with Ava?" Gray had asked last night when they'd both been working late.

"No. I'm not the married one, big brother," Gage had replied.

"Nope, your situation is worse," Gray had stated. "It's the dating phase. You have to work much harder on that part of a relationship."

Gage had shaken his head so hard, his neck had ached. "Not in a relationship either."

Gray's head had tilted back as he'd laughed. "Come on, Gage. You're smarter than that. Why else do you think she followed you here?"

"She didn't follow me and we're not dating," he'd replied.

"If you say so. But you've been seen at the wine festival together and then again at the community center. We can call those outings, but that's just a soft word for dates."

"She's...we...it's not serious." That was all that Gage had managed to come up with.

"Yet," Gray had stated. "And don't tell me you're not the marrying kind because I know better. There's no such thing. A man can commit when he wants to."

"I'm perfectly capable of committing, Gray. I've been committed to my career for the last ten years. That's not where Ava and I are headed," he'd said with finality because he desperately needed to believe it.

Now, Gage wasn't so sure.

When Ryan finished with his bottle and burped like a sixteen-year-old kid, Gage grabbed the second bottle and went upstairs to check on Ava.

Her cell phone was lying in the crib beside a pink Baby Minnie Mouse blanket that resembled the one wrapped around Ryan. She was leaning into the crib grumbling something as she pulled light green pants onto Emma. His niece gave a little cry, and Ava froze momentarily. He watched the rise and fall of her shoulders as she looked down at the baby and finally reached for the blanket. She wrapped her gently and then scooped her up into her arms.

"I don't know what I'm doing, so I'm gonna need you to take it easy on me," Ava whispered to Emma. "Now, we're gonna forget about the mean man on the phone and go downstairs to get your bottle. How do you like that?"

Emma made a gurgling sound and Ava chuckled. "I figured you'd agree with that part. Okay, let's go."

"Who was the mean man on the phone?" he asked before he could consider whether or not he should.

"Oh." She looked startled to see him.

She was holding Emma in one arm as she reached for the cell phone and slowly stuffed it into her back pocket.

"It was nobody," she said with a slight shake of her head. "I mean, nobody important. Just work."

Gage nodded, even while churning over the realization that he didn't like the thought of some guy being mean to her. Add that to his great dislike of other guys holding Ava's hand and Gage knew he was in trouble. He cleared his throat before speaking again.

"Well, I guess I won't have to teach you how to change a diaper after all."

"I figured it out," she told him with a slight chuckle.

Gage held up the bottle he was holding.

"You brought her bottle?" Ava asked.

"I did," he said. "Let's sit here."

The nursery was painted a very pale green with bold white stripes on one side, and pastel-colored balloons on the other. All the furniture in the room was white, including the matching gliders that faced a bay window, which opened to the front of the house.

He waited for Ava to sit before handing her the bottle. Then Gage took the seat next to her.

And there they sat for Gage didn't know how long, rocking the babies and looking out the window.

She didn't say a word and neither did he. Ryan was warm as Gage cuddled him in his arms. Beside him he could hear Ava making cooing sounds at Emma. It struck him then that this was a cozy scene. A scene he'd held in his mind for longer than he cared to admit.

His parents probably sat in this same room looking out the window all those years ago. And now, something clicked inside of Gage. It slipped into a place in his chest as if it had been the missing piece to a puzzle, and he almost sighed because it was finally where it belonged.

Just the way Theodor and Olivia probably had thirty years ago.

Chapter 7

"It's just a leave of absence, Mortimer," Gage said into the phone as he sat in the room he'd been occupying at Harper and Garrek's house. "I'll be back the first of the year."

"I thought this was just a three-week vacation," Mortimer Gogenheim replied. "What about your research? The grant?"

Gage had thought this all through after he'd left Gray's house last night and returned to this room. He'd stayed up half the night thinking of nothing else.

"I'll have weekly Skype calls with the research assistants. In addition, they'll send me weekly reports. I'll review everything, do my own analysis and decide what steps need to be taken next. We're not close to any clinical testing, so me being out of the lab for another two months isn't going to harm the research at all," Gage assured his boss.

"My last day is the end of this week," Mortimer said. "I believe Ed planned to meet with all department staff before then. I told him you would be back because that's what you told me when you left."

Gage kept his gaze on the huge trees swaying with the wind just a few feet away from the window. Leaves drifted in the air before circling down to rest on the grass.

"There have been some new developments." Gage cleared his throat. "Things relating to my father's estate. I have to take care of them before I can return. If it's necessary, I can call and speak with Rodenstein myself."

Mortimer didn't immediately respond.

"If there's something else going on, you can tell me, Gage. Is this about Ed getting the chief position instead of you?"

"I'm not that petty, Mortimer. I'm a professional, always. And I'm committed to my job. I have been for the last ten years. Which is why requesting a leave of absence to deal with my father's estate should not be an issue. But if it is, please let me know and I will deal with it accordingly."

"This just isn't like you," Mortimer said before agreeing to let Dr. Rodenstein and the rest of the staff know that Gage was officially taking a leave of absence.

For the next few hours, Gage thought about Mortimer's words. This *wasn't* like him. Since the day he'd decided to become a doctor, Gage had put nothing else before achieving that goal. And really, he told himself, he wasn't actually pushing his career aside this time. Designing and staffing the obstetrics and infertility research sections of the new Taylor Generational Wing at All Saints Hospital was an extension of his career. It was in his field and correlated perfectly with his work in New York. As such, in the last weeks, Gage had thrown himself wholeheartedly into the project.

He'd also spent more time with Ava Cannon than he had with any other woman, ever.

That thought reminded him of the text message he'd sent to her this morning, inviting her to dinner tonight. It also meant he had a lot to do before the time for said dinner arrived.

After packing the last of his clothes in the leather duffel bag he'd brought with him when he arrived in Temptation, Gage took the bag off the bed and stood in the room, looking around. It was a nice room in the old antebellum home that his father had left to Garrek, and that Harper was now restoring. The stately structure sat on multiple acres of luxurious land, and when finished, would be grand and gorgeous. Harper was really good at her job, even if Gage wasn't a fan of the ornate antique furniture in this particular room.

"Oh, are you leaving?" Harper asked when Gage was headed to the front door.

There was noise, as always here, with work being done on some part of the house every day. So he hadn't heard her approach.

"Hey, Harper. I thought you'd already be out on some other job by now," Gage said as he set his bag on the floor and faced his soon-to-be sister-in-law.

"I'm working here today," she told him. "Have to find some time to put into my own house. Especially if I want to have it finished by the time Garrek comes home."

"He's anxious to return," Gage said. He'd spoken to Garrek a couple days ago when his brother had called to ask why he was in Temptation.

His sisters had also called him because nothing was ever a secret between the Taylor siblings. What one knew, they all knew.

Harper beamed at his words. "But you're leaving? Your vacation is over."

"Actually, I'm not leaving Temptation just yet. I've decided to stay here awhile longer to help Gray at the hospital."

"Yes, with the generational wing. That's fabulous. So why are you packed like you're leaving town?"

"Since I drove my car down, I had to have my yacht shipped here. It's arrived, and I'm just going to stay there for the duration of the trip. As I'm sure you're aware, it gets kind of loud here sometimes, and it's easier for me to work where it's quiet."

Harper chuckled. "That's putting it politely. I know it's loud all the time, and I apologize."

"No need for an apology. It was generous of you to let me stay here, and this was better than intruding on Gray and Morgan with the kids and their schedules. I'll just be down at the dock, but still in town for family dinners and things like that."

"Good, I know that Gray seems really happy you're

here. And Garrek is, too. He only wishes he could be here with all of us."

Gage wished that, too. Quite a few times this week, he'd wondered how it would feel for all of them to be back here in Temptation.

"In due time," he told Harper. "We'll all be together in due time."

The words had reminded him of his mother. Once the siblings had entered high school, they'd often asked Olivia when she was going to do something for herself. They'd all agreed they wanted to see their mother happy, even if they couldn't agree on who or what would get her to that point. Olivia had only smiled and told them, "All in due time."

Now, hours later, Gage was on the luxury super yacht he was currently leasing. The *Seraphine* looked big and a bit ostentatious anchored along Temptation's weathered dock, but Gage didn't care. He loved nice things. They were the one indulgence he afforded himself as a reward for all his hard work. His condo, car and the yacht were like Gage's children, he thought dismally.

It was just about five thirty, and he'd already showered and changed into smoke-gray slacks and a lighter gray button-front shirt. He kept clothes on the yacht, so his decision to stay here longer wouldn't call for a trip to the mall.

"Helloooo down there! I say helloooo!"

Gage smiled at the sound of her voice. Ms. Pearl Brimley was a lovely woman with a wide, friendly smile and deep dimples in each mocha-hued cheek. Gage had stopped at Ms. Pearl's Diner on his way to the yacht and put in an order for dinner to be delivered here for tonight.

"Hellooooo!"

"Coming, Ms. Pearl," Gage answered as he stepped up onto the deck.

Ms. Pearl was standing on the dock, a large square-shaped warming bag in each hand. She wore a blue-and-white-striped skirt that stopped at her ankles and swayed in the breeze.

"Here, let me help you down," he told her as he went to the edge of the deck.

He unhitched the latch that kept the swinging door closed and reached up to take the bags from Ms. Pearl's hands.

"Gail and Meg are right behind me with the rest of the stuff. We'll get you all set up here," she said when Gage turned back to offer her a hand down.

"You said six o'clock, so we'll have to move quickly. But we'll get it all done."

In seconds Ms. Pearl's daughter, Gail, and her niece, Meg, came on board carrying more packages.

"This is so nice," Meg crooned. "I've never seen a boat like this before."

"That's because it's a yacht," Gail replied with a shake of her head.

"Just like the one in the pictures of Jay-Z and Beyoncé on vacation," Meg continued as she unpacked utensils and napkins from the bags she'd carried on deck.

Gage smiled and explained to Meg what type of yacht this was, and that, no, he was not as rich as Jay-Z and Beyoncé. Ms. Pearl beckoned them both back to work, and by five minutes to six, the three ladies were gone and the small bronze pedestal table at the far end of the boat was decorated beautifully.

At three minutes after six, Gage was standing at the door of the deck once more, smiling up at Ava as she stepped slowly onto the yacht.

"You look beautiful," he said, taking her hand to help her on board. "I'm so glad you're here."

And he was, Gage thought as he looked down into her deep brown eyes. He was glad to see her in the short blue dress that might have seemed plain on anyone else but her. She wore a blue-and-beige scarf draped around her neck and black boots to her calf. Her hair was free and flowing so that she had a fresh and innocently enticing look. Yes, he was glad she was here.

"I almost didn't come," she said and then shook her head as if trying to dismiss the words. "I meant to say, thank you. I'm looking forward to a great evening."

He heard the words and saw the small smile she offered, but Gage wasn't buying it. Her eyes and the slight slump in her shoulders said differently.

"Is something wrong, Ava? Did something happen to you today?"

"No," she said and waved her hand over her face like she needed to wipe away whatever was bothering her. "I'm fine. It's nothing. Let's just have dinner."

"Sure. Everything's ready," Gage told her.

He led her to the table and pulled out the matching bronzed iron chair, all the while thinking that she was a horrible liar. Something was definitely wrong with her, and he was determined to find out what.

So he could fix it. Gage knew in that instant that he would do anything to take that look off her face. Anything at all.

She was being ridiculous.

It was unlike her and she hated it.

No, it was just like her after speaking to her mother. That's what she hated more.

Ava took a deep breath, smelled the crisp evening air and looked out to the glistening surface of the water.

"It's nice here," she said quietly. "Who goes on vacation and has their yacht shipped to them?"

The last was said with a wry chuckle as she tried to shake the anger and sadness she'd carried with her for the last hour since her mother's call.

"I wanted to be comfortable since I plan to stay a little longer."

He had just slid onto the chair across from her. For too many torturous moments, he'd stood staring at her, waiting for her to tell him what was going on. Or waiting to figure it out for himself.

Ava turned slightly, hanging her purse on the side of the chair, and then turned back to face him. "How long are you staying now?"

"Through the holidays."

She folded her hands in her lap. "So you'll be here for Morgan's big Christmas dinner. Are the rest of your siblings coming?"

"Yes," he replied. "Morgan, apparently, is very persuasive."

"That should be nice. A family holiday." Ava couldn't help it.

She had decided that she wanted to be in Temptation for Christmas, as well. She wanted to attend the Harvest Brunch and then the Thanksgiving parade in November. And Morgan had told her about her annual class play at the community center. They hadn't chosen which Christmas story they would do this year yet, but Lily and Jack had been so animated last night, when they'd reenacted parts of last year's *A Christmas Carol*, that Ava knew she wanted to see anything those two acted in this year. And all of the Taylors had agreed to come back to Temptation for Christmas. Ava did not want to miss that.

She looked out to the water then and sighed heavily, recalling the earlier conversation with her mother.

"I mean, really, Ava, how long are you going to continue playing at this? May I remind you that you are not getting any younger? When I was your age, I was already married to your father and trying to get pregnant."

"I'm not thinking about marriage and children right now, Mother," she'd said through clenched teeth.

The fact that she'd thought of nothing else but the sweet smell of Emma and Ryan in her arms last night was something she'd keep to herself.

"That's my point exactly. You should be. It's time to stop wasting time with this writing thing and get on with your life."

"This writing thing has resulted in the number one

rated procedural drama last season. It's making a name for me within the industry and opening new doors for my career." At least she hoped what she was doing here in Temptation would do just that.

"Richard is preparing for a third run to keep his Senate seat. He needs your help on the campaign. Now, how soon can you get back to LA? I've already set up some meetings with my committees. They'll support as always, but I need you to get to the young people."

Richard McClain had been the Cannon family lawyer for as long as Ava could remember. Five years ago he had decided to run for Congress and had been elected in a surprise landslide. After Ava's father's death, Richard had been there offering his support to the family, which Ava had appreciated, so she did feel a bit of loyalty to him.

"I'm working and will not be finished with this until at least the first of the year," Ava had said.

"That's just not acceptable, Ava. Not at all. I want you to stop this foolishness right now. I've put too much time and energy into raising you right for you to wander off into some la-la land now."

Ava hadn't been aware that a successful producing career was considered la-la land.

"Look, Mom, I have to go. I have a da...I mean, a meeting tonight. So I'm going to have to call you in the morning."

"Ava, you will not keep putting me off. Now, I told Richard you would be back to help him, and I expect you to honor that agreement."

"I didn't agree to that," she'd replied.

"Do not disrespect me!" Eleanor had yelled.

The sound of her mother taking a deep breath and releasing it very slowly had echoed through the phone, and Ava rolled her eyes. Her mother had perfected the wounded woman act over the years, but this time Ava was prepared.

"I would never disrespect you, Mother. But I really do have to get to this meeting. We can talk more in the morning, I promise. Have a good night," she'd said before clicking off the call.

It wasn't hanging up if she said goodbye, or goodnight. Her father had told her that. It was a long time before Ava suspected it was because he'd hung up on Eleanor plenty of times in his life.

"Ava?"

It was his hand resting on her shoulder more so than the sound of his voice that jolted Ava from her memory and almost out of the chair.

"Are you all right?" Gage asked as he stooped down beside her.

He took her hands then, holding them between his as he stared up at her.

"Whatever it is, you can tell me, Ava. Tell me, so I can help."

She tilted her head, the corner of her mouth moving upward slightly. "You would try, wouldn't you? For as much as you like to give the impression that you're all about your professional life, there's a softer side to you, Gage. A side that wants to make things right for everybody."

"I just don't like the look in your eyes or the tone of your voice right now. Whatever I can do to help, I will."

"You came to work on the set of my show to help," she said. "Even when you wanted nothing more to do with TV networks. And you came back here to help your brother at the hospital. You're always helping."

"Fine. I'm always helping. So let me help you."

She shook her head. "It's nothing," Ava said.

"You're a terrible liar."

Those words were like icicles gliding over her skin. Gage had no idea how good a liar she actually was.

"It's childish and pointless," she said and then sighed because her head was starting to throb. "Just a silly argument with my mother. You know, like everyone has with their parents at some point."

His gaze remained steady. "Not me."

Great, now she really felt like an idiot. Here she was complaining about her mother when both Gage's parents were gone.

"I'm sorry. Let's just forget I even said anything." She tried for a genuine smile. "Guess I'm ruining our date. Is this a date?"

He grinned. "Let's dance."

"What? There's no music."

Gage was already tugging her from the chair. He slipped his arm around her waist and stepped closer, until their bodies were touching. Ava lifted her arms to lock around his neck and joined him when he began to sway. He smelled so good, like very expensive cologne and sexy man. And even though he wasn't holding her too tightly, she felt safe in his arms. Protected. Comforted.

Guilty.

"My mother used to say that dancing cures everything. The movement chases away old ghosts and prevents worries from piling up in your mind."

Ava sighed and let herself focus solely on moving.

"I'm just trying to do my job," she said softly. "All I've ever wanted to do is write. Not be some twenty-first-century debutante in search of a rich husband to continue some society circle nonsense."

His fingers splayed over her lower back, rubbing lightly as he stepped and moved, turning them in a small circle.

"She hates everything about me. Always has," Ava continued. She didn't know why. The words just tumbled free. "Nothing I've ever done has been good enough for her. Probably because I'm not like her. I prefer to drive an economical hybrid car instead of the expensive vehicles she travels in. I live in a reasonably priced condo and not a mansion, which, thanks to my inheritance from my father, I could absolutely afford. I'm not really into flashy things or people with titles and prestige. I just want to write my stories and live a normal life. Is that so much to ask?"

He kissed the top of her head and then waited until she lifted her chin to stare up at him.

"No. It's not," he told her. "You should be able to be whoever and whatever you want to be. That's what my mother used to tell us. It's why she wanted out of the television show. Because she thought it was creating a persona for us that we had no say in. We were stars before we even knew what that meant, or if it was something we wanted in our lives."

"You were doing what they wanted you to do because at the time you didn't have a choice," she said.

She wanted Gage and his siblings to have a choice this time. The same way she had made a choice to write instead of following her mother's plans for her life.

"Your mother did the right thing," she said.

"And your mother thinks she's doing the right thing, too," he replied. "You just have to stand your ground so that she knows her idea of what's right for you is not in your plan."

"I did," she told him. "I have so many times before. She just refuses to listen."

"Then that's her problem, Ava. It's not yours, so don't beat yourself up about it. You have a right to try this your way."

He looked so good staring back at her with his neatly trimmed goatee, thick brows and mesmerizing gaze. She couldn't have written a better scene where a declaration of love would come and happy-ever-after would ensue. Her heart tripped at the thought.

"If this were a date, I'd suggest we skip the meal and head straight to the bedroom," she said nervously.

Yes, she was nervous. Which was ridiculous, because she'd had sex with Gage before.

"Or it might be the part where I whisk you into my arms and carry you to the bed. I'd lay you down and peel your clothes from you slowly, taking the time to touch every part of your naked body, watching your reaction as I did."

She licked her lips and swallowed hard. "Oh, really? And then what would you do? If this were a date, I mean?"

They were still dancing, swaying in the cool evening breeze on the deck of his yacht. That's why she felt dizzy. No other reason.

"After touching every part of your body with my fingers, I would switch places. Using my tongue to taste you." His voice had lowered to a deep timbre.

"I would watch you ride high on the wave of pleasure, then crest and fall with your climax."

Her body tingled all over, her breasts swelling as she pressed closer to him. He was hard. She could feel his erection as surely as she felt the rise and fall of his chest.

"And…then," she whispered, the words trailing off as he'd begun to lower his face to hers.

"Then I would slip inside you, filling you, taking you," he said before brushing his lips over hers.

"Yes," she replied and kissed him back, dragging her tongue over his bottom lip.

Gage chuckled. "Yes what?"

She nipped his lip with her teeth and then sucked it into her mouth, before thrusting her tongue inside to dance along with his.

"Yes, this is a date," she said when they finally broke for air.

He nodded and then bent to pick her up. When she

was in his arms, Gage leaned in, brushing his lips over hers again. "Good. Because I'm ready for the touching and tasting to begin."

Chapter 8

He did just what he said he would, and Ava was profoundly grateful.

She was also more aroused than she'd ever been before.

Gage had carried her across the deck and down a spiral set of stairs. The bed was huge on this luxurious vessel. She hadn't expected anything less. From the moment she'd received his message to meet him at the docks and then stepped out of her car at the parking lot across the street, she'd known the *Seraphine* was going to be like nothing she'd ever experienced. She'd never been on a yacht before, the whole not-knowing-how-to-swim thing holding her back from cruises of any sort. Tonight, she was glad she'd pushed that anxiety aside.

He gently laid her on the king-size bed and first removed her boots. Propped up on her elbows now, Ava looked around briefly. The walls were dark, a mixture of blue and gray in a textured paper that reminded her of a deep blue sea. A crystal-covered lamp was on each nightstand, and beige carpet covered the floor. Gage's hands moved slowly up her bare calves and farther, until his fingers grazed the sensitive skin between her thighs.

Her attention solely on him now, she watched with anticipation as he pushed at the material of her tunic dress. He looked up at her and winked just before hooking his fingers in the band of her panties and tugging. Ava lifted her hips, allowing him to remove the white silk underwear she'd worn without question. Her scarf went next, and then he was pulling the dress up and over her head.

She was sitting up now, Gage kneeling with one knee between her spread legs, the other on the opposite side of her thigh. He leaned in, reached around her back and unsnapped her matching bra. Cool air hit her nipples, and they hardened seconds before his fingers brushed over them. She sucked in a breath and thought he may have done the same, before he pulled his hands away.

Backing off the bed now, Gage began to undress. She'd seen him naked before so that wasn't the reason for the immediate pounding of her heart. They'd had sex before, so the anticipation of that act was not making her anxious. It was the slowness with which he moved that had her skin tingling. Her eyes were riveted to his every move.

His long fingers moved precisely over each button on his shirt and continued to work steadily to undo his belt and then the snap and zipper of his pants. The shirt and the undershirt he'd worn beneath were removed first, so that when he bent down to tend to his shoes, Ava saw the muscles of his shoulders leading down to his back. He stood when his shoes were off and pushed his pants and boxer briefs down his muscled legs. Ava didn't move, even though a wicked storm of desire was brewing inside her.

"I want to touch you," Gage said as he kneeled on the bed once more. "Lie back and let me touch you, Ava."

She did as he said, hadn't even thought of not complying. His voice was low, so much so that she almost strained over the pounding of her heart to hear him.

He lifted each of her feet, kissing the arch and then the tips of her toes. He rubbed her calves once again, taking each leg in his hands and kissing behind her knee. Her fingers clenched the duvet beneath her as prickles of pleasure soared from each spot he touched throughout her body. When he came to her thighs, they'd begun to shake. She couldn't help the movement, nor could she contain the moan when his lips touched her inner thigh.

"So soft," he whispered.

Ava closed her eyes as her entire body began to tremble.

He kissed up the inside of one thigh, stopping just shy of her juncture before pulling away. She wanted to scream, but instead bit her bottom lip.

"Sexy Ava," he said as he went to the other thigh. "You've been tempting me since day one with your voice, your scent, your body."

She was going to explode. She wasn't going to be able to stop it. He was licking little circles over the skin of her inner thigh, moving upward once more until she wanted to lift her hips off the bed and offer herself to him.

"Gage," she whimpered, when he was just inches away from the plump folds of her center. "Please."

He did not oblige. Damn him.

Instead he blew his warm breath over her bare mound, causing her to shiver and groan.

"You're going to be sweet and warm," he grumbled. "I know it before I even taste you. My sweet and sexy Ava."

Oh no, this was taking too long. Ava released the duvet from her death grip and clapped her hands to the back of Gage's head.

He chuckled as he held back from her. "I'm hungry for you, too," he told her. "But we've got all night."

Ava didn't think she was going to last that long.

And she didn't.

The second Gage touched her tender folds, she almost bolted up off the bed. He placed one hand on her hip and used the other to spread her open before licking her up and down. Ava moaned deep and long, her thighs shaking around his head. Gage continued, licking, sucking and praising her sweetness until seconds later her release tore through her body like an earthquake, and she screamed his name.

He only gave her a minute to recuperate before he was moving upward, kissing her abdomen, licking up her torso and then covering one nipple with his mouth, holding the other breast in his hand. Ava arched her back and felt herself climbing steadily toward another climax.

The moment he pulled away to get a condom, she seriously considered screaming for him to come back immediately. That should have been the second clue that she was sinking fast where Gage Taylor was concerned. She never thought about dismissing safe sex.

Sheathed and coming over her like a gorgeous African god, Gage lifted Ava's legs, propped her ankles on his shoulders and speared into her with one swift motion. His name tumbled from her lips again and again as he moved expertly in and out of her. She felt like she was drowning. The pleasure was so deep, going far beyond anything in her wildest imagination, touching a part of her she'd thought did not exist.

"Look at me, Ava," he said.

She thought she'd opened her eyes, but he was asking her again, "Ava, sweetness, please look at me."

Her lids fluttered open. He released her legs, but stayed buried deep inside her, his elbows coming to rest on either side of her head as his thumbs caressed her cheeks.

"You are beautiful and you are enough," he whispered as he began to move inside her once more. "You are more than enough for me."

She wrapped her legs around his waist, her arms around his back, and moved with him.

"Gage," she whispered. "More. More than I ever expected."

"Yes," he replied. "So much more."

He was moving too slowly, going too deep, hitting her every spot just right and then some. He was too much. This was too much. But when they both trembled and fell together, Ava realized with startling clarity that it wasn't enough. Nothing she'd had with Gage so far was enough.

And wanting more was going to crush her.

"I didn't think I was going to like it here in Temptation," Gage told her as they lay in his bed once more.

After making love, they'd showered and had the dinner Ms. Pearl prepared for them while sitting in the center of the bed. It had felt like those nights when the boys and girls in his house would meet up in the kitchen for a late-night snack. Olivia did not like them eating upstairs in their room, so the siblings had to sneak and decided it was safer if they went into one room. Those were some of the best nights of Gage's life.

Now he could add tonight to that list.

"Then why'd you come back?" Ava asked.

They'd enjoyed the delicious, if a bit cold, food and cleaned up, only to lie back in the bed as if they did not have this spacious yacht to lounge upon.

"Responsibilities that I'd put off for way too long. And to see Gray and meet his new family," he said.

"Your brother has a beautiful family," she replied.

They were both lying on their sides, facing each other. Her arm was tucked under her head and her knees pulled up so that she looked almost like a child. Except Gage knew that beneath his New York Yankees T-shirt she now wore, Ava was all woman.

"I didn't think he would get that chance," Gage admitted. "Truth be told, I wasn't sure any of us would want to start a family after what we'd been through."

"Was it really that bad?" Ava asked. "I know your parents split up, but listening to you and Gray talk about your mother, it sounds like she loved each of you with all her heart. And that she gave you a good life."

"She was a great mother. A wonderful woman who deserved more than to end up raising six children on her own."

"Your father didn't help?"

"He sent money and gifts, if that's what you mean by help." Gage grit his teeth and then thought of his conversation with Gray at the hospital. He took a deep breath and released it. "I guess he did what he could. A person can only be who they are, not who or what someone else wants them to be."

She nodded at his words, and Gage hoped that she was retaining them for her own use, as well.

"My mother was the nurturer. She was meant to be a mother. Gemma is that way, too. I hope she finds love and builds a family of her own one day. Gen is tough, so for any man to crack her shell he might need to be a magician." He chuckled at the thought of his older sister.

"Gia has a soft heart. She trusts and sees the best in everyone. Too soon and usually to her detriment, but I think she'll be a great mother one day, too."

"What about you?"

"What about me?"

"Will you be a good father one day?"

Gage let the uneasy feeling that immediately filled his chest settle before replying.

"My father left his children everything he had. His company, real estate and money. I wasn't shocked by how much his estate had been worth or how quickly Gray managed to divide everything up equally amongst us. Gray has always been a good leader. The other money that Gray found did surprise me a bit, and then the pictures. I'm still trying to figure out why he left them for me."

When he caught her looking a little confused, Gage realized what he'd just told her. He couldn't take it back, and he didn't really want to. He hadn't planned on sharing his thoughts and feelings about his father with anyone, but he had. With Ava.

She reached her free hand across the bed to take his. "What were the pictures of?"

"Us," he replied after lacing his fingers through hers. "A four-month sonogram photo of each of us, and one of us after we were born with my parents."

"Maybe he wanted to show you that he'd always loved you. Regardless of what happened, he'd never stopped loving his children or his wife."

"He cheated on her," Gage snapped. "He had an affair with a production assistant and then decided he'd rather be with her than with his family."

His words were cold and stung as he spoke them. He hadn't realized how much animosity he still held inside because of them.

"My father didn't leave us for another woman. He drank," Ava said. "So much that sometimes I don't even think he saw me. He was a partner at a prestigious law firm in LA. He represented so many stars, and sometimes a studio would call on him for contractual work. He had money, houses, cars, everything, and he drank so much that one day he drove his car right off a cliff and into the ocean."

"Dammit, Ava. I'm sorry," Gage said, immediately feeling like scum as he complained about his father.

She smiled. "Don't be. He lived the life he wanted to live, and he drank because of some problem he couldn't figure out how to solve. I wish he had been able to overcome his issues, but I don't hate him for how it ended. And you shouldn't hate your father for things that, in the end, he could not change."

She was right. Gage knew that. And so did Gray. It was time to move past all that hurt he'd clung to, which was why he'd told Gray he didn't think they should continue to pay those investigators to try to figure out where the Grand Cayman money had come from. The money was divided between the children just like everything else Theodor Taylor owned, and that was that.

"Thank you for saying that," he told her. "And for joining me tonight. I know you came here to write. That's why I try not to bother you every second of every day."

But he'd wanted to. He could admit that to himself. During the hours he spent at the hospital, or when he was walking through town or having dinner at some restaurant, he thought about her.

"Oh, it wouldn't be a bother," she said. "I write better in the early-morning hours anyway. By midday I'm already beginning to fade, unless it's crunch time."

"So you're writing new scripts for the next season of the show?"

"Actually, no, I'm writing something new and totally different."

He brought her hand up to his lips and kissed her fingers. "Well, it'll be great whatever it is."

"Yes," she said after a few minutes. "I think it will be great. But right now—"

She paused and leaned over until she could reach the nightstand drawer. She'd seen him retrieve a condom from there earlier, and she pulled a packet from the box now. When she returned to him, it was to push him over onto his back.

"Now it's my turn to touch and taste," she told him as she grabbed his shirt and lifted it up and over his head.

When Gage lay back on the pillow, she straddled him. And when her warm tongue touched his pectoral muscle, he groaned.

She could take her turn…as many times as she wanted.

"Is that how you Hollywood people do the walk of shame?" Millie said the moment Ava stepped off the dock and onto the cement walkway.

The sun was barely up, shimmering over the water in hazy orange-and-red rays when she'd crept off the yacht. Seagulls flew low, bellowing a choking call to whoever else was up this early.

"Good morning, Ms. Millie," she said in as cheerful a voice as she could muster.

The woman had stepped right up to her so that Ava struggled to keep from telling her that she was invading her personal space. Millie's hair was perfectly styled as it had been on each occasion that Ava had seen her. Her makeup was likewise flawless, Millie's red-painted lips drawn in a thin line.

"I was coming to tell Gage Taylor he needs to take this monstrosity back to wherever it was before now. It's bringing unwanted attention down here to the docks where simple folk are trying to make a living."

Ava looked around, even though she was certain there was no one out here right now but her and Millie. To the woman's credit, there were a couple of smaller boats already out to sail not too far from the dock with what Ava guessed were fishermen on board.

"I don't think the yacht is a disturbance," Ava said, taking a chance at responding. "It seems the people who need to go to work are doing just that."

Except for busybody Millie, that was.

"Don't get sassy with me. You're not in California with your snooty friends," Millie snapped.

Ava was certain she didn't have snooty friends. In fact, she could count on one hand how many actual friends she had.

"Well, it was nice seeing you, Ms. Millie, but I have to get going."

"Where to at this time of morning? Because I know you didn't spend the evening on that boat with Gage Taylor writing. I want to know why you're really here,

Ms. Cannon. If it has something to do with this town, I have a right to know."

"My work is my business," Ava said, squaring her shoulders. She had been trying to be polite, but she wasn't going to be bullied by this woman a second time.

"Not if it's taking place in my town. I don't believe for one minute you're just on a writing retreat. Seems too fishy that you and Gage show up at the same time. And you're in the TV business, too. Oh, no, too suspicious." Millie was shaking her head.

Ava smiled. "Ma'am, you can make what you want out of it, but I've told you all that I plan to. Now, you can have a nice day."

Ava skirted around the primly dressed woman and did everything short of breaking out into a run to get to her car. Once behind the wheel and pulling out of the parking lot, Ava thought the first call she was going to make when she returned to the B and B was to Jenner.

The Taylor Reunion reality show was not going to come to fruition, at least not the way he wanted it to.

Chapter 9

Two weeks later
Santa Monica, California

Were they really ready for this?

As the limo rode through the streets, taking them to this year's location for the Critics' Choice Awards, Ava thought over the last six weeks of her life. She was in a different place now, somewhere she'd never thought she would be.

"Nervous?" Gage asked.

He was sitting beside her, holding her hand. Dressed in a black Tom Ford suit, his shirt and pocket square crisp white, and sporting shined Ferragamo oxford cap-toe shoes, he looked stylish and delicious even without the help of a stylist. But when they'd arrived at her

LA condo two days ago, Saraya had already called on Ava's friend Landry Norris to get her and Gage ready for the awards show. Now married to the Crown Prince Kristian DeSaunters of Grand Serenity Island, Landry's family still lived in California, and she frequently came home for visits.

"A little," Ava admitted to Gage.

She tightened her fingers around his, seeking and receiving the comfort she'd become slightly addicted to in the past weeks. He was like the rock she hadn't realized she needed in her life. After all these years of depending on herself, relying on her own instincts and discipline to get where she was in life, Ava had never imagined being able to lean on anyone else. Which made what she planned to do in the coming days so much harder.

"Don't be," he told her. "You look stunning and smell amazing. And regardless of what happens tonight, you'll still be the youngest African American writer and producer with a number one rated show on network television right now. Nothing else matters."

Ava inhaled deeply and felt the breath releasing slowly, calmly as she looked into his deep brown eyes. He'd commented on the scent of her perfume the second he'd entered the bedroom after he'd finished dressing. Landry had still been putting finishing touches on Ava—diamond stud earrings and matching cuff bracelet. The Tony Chaaya mermaid-cut black gown Ava wore was gorgeous and made her feel sexy and confident. The messy bun with loose curls around her face was elegant, her makeup flawless, and still her stomach would not settle.

"Thank you," she whispered. "For saying that and agreeing to come here with me. I know you've been really busy with your work at the hospital, and this was sort of last-minute."

He shrugged and smiled. "My schedule's a little flexible at the moment. Besides, this is an important moment for you. I'm honored that you asked me to share it with you."

She had asked him as they'd sat on the steps at Harper's father's farm after a seafood feast. Her agent, Marcelle, had called her that morning to tell her that she'd been nominated. Since she'd been in Temptation, Ava had been basically off the grid, so the news of the nominations hadn't immediately gotten to her.

Now, the night was here and she was nervous about possibly winning in the Best Drama Series category. Corbin Yancy and Miranda Martinez were also nominated in the Best Actor and Best Actress in a Drama Series categories. That gave *Doctor's Orders* a total of three nominations for their first season. It was an amazing accomplishment, one that Ava did not take lightly.

"I especially want to thank you because I know you do not like being in the spotlight," she told him as the car had begun to slow down. "I want you to know that I do respect your feelings about things that happened in your past. I was just thinking that having the experience as an adult may be totally different. But I would have understood if you'd turned me down."

He leaned in and kissed her lips quickly. Just a peck because Landry had warned him about messing up her makeup when they were at the hotel and she'd mentioned how Gage was staring hungrily at Ava.

"I'm here because I want to be here with you. That's it. We're not bringing anything else into this. Got it?"

Ava smiled because if she'd had any doubts or reservations before, she knew now with absolute certainty that she was in danger of falling in love with Gage Taylor. And that was not a good thing; at least it wouldn't be if she continued to put off telling him the truth.

"Got it," she replied just as the car stopped.

They would be walking the red carpet, posing for pictures and talking to reporters. She was ready for this. It was her dream, right? Yes, it was, and she had the best guy here with her, to share her perfect moment. She could do this. She was ready to do this.

And apparently, so was Gage.

He was magnificent, holding her hand as they first stepped onto the red carpet, smiling and posing when cameras were aimed at them. Joking and being cordial with reporters who tossed out questions like, "How long have you two been dating?" and, "Are there wedding bells in the future?" Ava had no idea how they'd even known who Gage was, but when the first reporter had approached them asking, "Mr. Taylor, how does it feel to return to the spotlight after your family's retreat thirty years ago?" Ava had thought Gage would turn back and go to the limo. But he hadn't. He'd answered every question with brutal honesty, cutting the reporters short when their questions became too pushy with a stern, but polite, reply. He was perfect.

And later that evening when they opened the envelope and called Ava's name, her perfect guy had stood and hugged her, whispering, "I am so proud of you," in her ear.

Following the show, they headed to one of the two after-parties Ava was scheduled to attend. Saraya had handled everything from securing their tickets, arranging transportation and even sending Ava and Gage the entire night's itinerary in a detailed text. The first party was at the Viceroy, where Ava and Gage mingled with guests and posed for yet more pictures. Her cheeks had already grown sore from smiling, but adrenaline continued to rush through her each time she was approached by someone else.

Until those someones were Jenner and Carroll, both beaming as they strode toward her. Gage had stepped away to find them something to drink. There was no shortage of champagne and other mixed drinks being floated around by resort staff, but they both wanted water, which was obviously too simple a drink to be offered to guests at this party. She immediately clutched her purse tightly in her hands and straightened her back. There was no doubt Jenner would want to talk to her about their last phone conversation. He hadn't been thrilled with Ava's progress, and she hadn't cared. That bravado seemed a bit easier over the phone; still she was determined not to falter.

"Congratulations, Ava! We did it!" Carroll said before pulling her into a tight hug.

"Yes, we did!" she replied and genuinely returned

his hug because Carroll had taken a chance on her, and she respected and appreciated him for that.

Jenner's hug and congratulations were just a little less exuberant.

"With this feather in our cap, our new project is guaranteed to be a hit," Jenner immediately said.

Carroll was nodding so intently that his jowls shook with the motion. "And you brought him with you. That was a great PR idea! Wish we had come up with it."

Jenner clapped his hands together and smiled gleefully. "It's perfect! The press is loving it. Sending your itinerary for the night and the name of your date to a few key members of the press was a brilliant idea. The buzz is already starting about the Taylors. So we'll be all set to announce the show just before Christmas."

Ava shook her head. "You sent my itinerary to reporters?" she asked. "Are you crazy?"

"No," Jenner said, sobering just a bit. "On the contrary, I count myself as being quite smart. I knew you'd be great for this project."

"I told you it wasn't going to go down the way you planned," Ava said through clenched teeth. They were in a crowded room full of people either trying to get the next big Hollywood scoop, or trying to get a part in the next winning movie or show. None of whom she wanted to overhear this conversation.

"My proposal is going to outline the show, leaving lots of leeway for the siblings to determine the content. My pitch to them is contingent upon their having control over how their lives are presented to the world," she told Jenner. "We discussed this already."

"And I told you we would see about that. As for now, we're starting the beginning publicity rounds. You and Gage embracing when you won that award only adds another layer to the project. We'll get to cover the love interest of one of the siblings, with our very own producer. It'll be like déjà vu," Jenner said, his eyes gleaming with his excitement.

Ava couldn't believe it—he was actually becoming happy about exploiting Theodor Taylor's infidelity, thirty years later, on television.

"That's not the outline I'm going to write," she said adamantly.

Jenner took a step closer to her then, taking her arm and pulling her to him. "You are going to do what I tell you to do. I got stiffed once by Theodor Taylor dying after he'd already signed on for this show, and dammit, I won't get shafted again. Now, you have that proposal to me next week or your career will spiral to an end as quickly as you've soared to the top."

"Is there a problem here?" Gage asked as he joined them.

He was holding two water bottles, but he stuck them in his jacket pockets as he placed a hand on Jenner's shoulder, pushing him away from Ava. He reached behind with his other hand and found Ava's, twining his fingers tightly with hers.

She cleared her throat and made the introductions, to which Gage remained unfazed.

"It's a pleasure to meet you, Dr. Taylor," Jenner said, his boisterous smile in place once again.

Jenner extended his hand to Gage, but Gage made no move to return the shake.

"Yes, it is," Carroll chimed in. "We hope you're enjoying your stay here in Santa Monica. If there's anything we can get you, please do not hesitate to let us know."

"I don't need anything," Gage told them and then looked to Ava. "Are you ready to go?"

"Yes," she replied immediately, not bothering to look at Jenner or Carroll again before walking away.

Gage thought he'd been doing well. But five hours into this glamorous evening full of celebrities, producers, agents and groupies, he'd started to reach his limits. The final push could have been when he'd been in search of their drinks and he'd bumped into a familiar face.

"Dr. Gage Taylor, what a surprise it is to see you out here," Miranda Martinez had said as she'd stepped right up to him.

Her long red-painted nails were a bright contrast to his dark suit jacket as she rubbed her hand down the lapel. Lips painted the same vibrant glossy hue and hair black as night falling in fluffy curls past her shoulders weren't as alluring as they should have been for some reason. She wore a purple gown that left more of her skin exposed than was necessary, and her perfume stung Gage's nostrils.

"Hello, Miranda," he'd said reluctantly. "Congratulations on your nomination."

She pouted, an effort that came across as foolish and almost cartoonish, with her full red lips.

"What do the critics know anyway?" she said. "I mean, they did say we were the best drama series, but that's only because of me."

Right. Gage stepped away from her. "Well, if you'll excuse me—"

She'd cut him off by lifting her hand to cup the back of his neck. "Not so fast. We hardly ever had a chance to really talk while on set. And now you're here. How about we ditch this party and go somewhere a little quieter?"

"No," had been Gage's immediate response. And since she didn't take the response to mean he didn't want her touching him, Gage clasped her wrist and eased her hand away. "I'm going to get Ava something to drink."

"Oh, she looks like she's well taken care of at the moment," Miranda had said before nodding her head in the direction across the room.

That's when Gage had seen the two men boxing Ava in. He'd been instantly irritated. He'd abandoned plans of searching for the water and moved in that direction. One of the staffers stopped him before he could get there, thrusting two water bottles and another beaming smile his way. With a curt "thank you," Gage had taken the water and then went directly to Ava. It was as he'd come closer that he'd seen the man's hand on Ava's arm. Rage as he'd never experienced boiled inside of him, and he'd gone into action.

Now he was holding her hand tightly, moving them

through the crowd as quickly as possible. He wanted to get out of here, away from all these unscrupulous and mean-spirited people. So being stopped again irritated the hell out of him; still, for Ava's sake, he managed another smile.

"Ava Cannon," the man, wearing a navy blue jacket and wide smile standing in front of them, stated.

He was quickly joined by another man of the same stature, but dressed in a dove-gray suit.

"Yes," Ava said, bringing back the smile she'd also kept close this evening. "Hello."

"Hello," the man continued and extended his hand to her. "My name is Parker Donovan, from Donovan Network Television. Let me congratulate you on the big win for *Doctor's Orders* tonight."

"Oh, well, thank you, Mr. Donovan," she replied and eased her hand out of Gage's to shake Parker Donovan's.

"This is my brother, Savian," Parker said, signaling the man beside him.

"Congratulations," Savian said. "My wife watches your show faithfully."

"Oh really? Well, tell her I said thank you."

"I will. She's a lawyer and says it's easier to sit back and watch a show about another profession and their drama than her own," Savian continued with a chuckle.

"Well, my wife might be reading for a spot on your show soon, she's such a fan," Parker added.

"Your wife…wait a minute, Adriana Bennett-Donovan? Is she your wife?" Ava asked. "I've seen her work. She's very talented."

"She is on both counts," Parker replied with a smile

that could only come from a man who really loved his woman.

Gage relaxed at that thought and extended his hand to them. "Hello, I'm Dr. Gage Taylor."

Parker and Savian shook his hand and spoke with a genuine sincerity that Gage hadn't seen much of tonight.

"Were you heading out?" Savian asked.

Ava looked to Gage. He didn't speak, but let her make the decision on her own. This was her night, after all.

"Ah, yes, we are. But I'm so glad we met up with you before doing so," she said warmly.

"I am, too," Parker told her.

"We won't hold you up," Savian said. "But we would be interested in meeting with you."

"Definitely," Parker added. "We're always interested in adding new and innovative shows to our schedule, and you definitely have your finger on the pulse of what viewers want."

Gage saw the surprise on Ava's face and once again took her hand in his, pride swelling in his chest.

"I...I would love the chance to talk further with you," she said. "Ah, I'm heading back to Virginia tomorrow morning, but if you get in contact with my agent, we can definitely set up a mutually convenient time to chat."

Parker nodded. "We'll do that very soon," he said. "Now, you two have a good night."

"Thanks," Gage said with a nod to both men.

"Take care, Ava," Savian said. "We'll speak soon."

"Thank you both. Good night."

They were in the limo when Gage finally pulled

those bottles of water out of his pockets and set them on the bar.

"Well," he said when he sat back against the seat. "You've had a pretty cool night."

"Yeah," she said, still smiling. "I have. And you know what?"

"What?" he asked.

She lifted her hands to cup his face. "It's all because of you."

He tried to shake his head. "No. This has been all about you. I didn't do a thing."

"You were here when I needed you. I'll never forget that, Gage," she said, her voice soft.

He brushed a hand over her hair and leaned in closer. "There's no place I'd rather have been, Ava."

When his lips touched hers, Gage realized how much he meant those words. He wanted to be with Ava. In the morning, on his yacht, in Gray's backyard, on the set in New York and the red carpet in California.

He wanted to be with her. It was that simple and that terrifying at the same time.

Chapter 10

Temptation, Virginia

Four days later, Ava had just finished her final draft of the outline for *The Taylors of Temptation: A Whole New World*. She'd renamed the show and changed it from a full season to a two-hour feature with a focus on each sibling and their reflection on how the original show shaped their current lives.

She'd read it over twice, making sure that she hit each emotional beat possible. In her mind, and after being in Temptation for almost two months now, this was the key to this family. While she hadn't spoken to Gen, Gemma and Gia personally, she'd learned a lot from talking with Morgan and Harper about the sisters. Gray and Gage spent a lot of time at the hospital, but on the nights she was with Gage on the yacht, his memories of his sisters and all the torturous things the brothers did to them during their years in Pensacola were unforgettable. They were the years that the Taylor sextuplets formed their bond. The bond that remained steadfast and unbreakable now, all these years later. That's what she wanted the world to see and to remember this town and these people by.

And she hoped with everything in her that the Taylor sextuplets would go along with her plan. It was the twenty-ninth of October. The Fall Festival was tomorrow. She and Gage were slated to judge the pumpkin-carving contest, and Craig—who insisted that Ava had broken his heart—had selected a perfectly gruesome movie for everyone to watch on the night before Halloween. It was going to be a great time. So she would wait until the family dinner scheduled for the day after the festival at Morgan and Gray's to propose her idea to them. Their agreement was important to her, regardless of what Jenner said. If he wanted the Taylors on television as badly as he said he did, then he would accept any changes the sextuplets wanted to make. And if not...

A brisk knock on her door had Ava almost jumping off the bed where she'd been sitting cross-legged staring at her laptop. She wasn't expecting anyone, and as such, was dressed in old gray leggings and a peach tank top that had certainly seen better days. Before she could get to the door, there was another knock and then a familiar voice.

"Ava Marie Cannon, if you do not open this door

right now, I'll have this man break it down. Although I'm not sure he could as he looks a bit frail."

Ava groaned as she reached for the knob and pulled the door open.

"What are you doing here, Mother?"

"Yes, hello to you, too," Eleanor said.

She'd been holding a handkerchief that she now placed in the palm of her hand. She then used that palm to push the door open farther and enter the room.

Ava sighed and tried counting to ten. Otis stood in the hallway, his baseball cap balled up in one hand, while the other hand scratched the tight graying curls on his head.

"You can go now," Eleanor said to him from behind Ava. "Close the door, Ava."

Ava felt awful. "I'm sorry," she said to Otis.

The man simply shook his head, his leathery almond-toned skin lifting on one cheek as he resisted a smile. "No problem. Was nice meeting you, Mizzus Eleanor Cannon," Otis said as he looked past Ava to her mother.

Ava looked back to find her mother had gone deeper into the room and was now running her handkerchief-covered finger over the top of the dark oak armoire.

"You let me know if you need anything, Miss Ava. I'll be right downstairs," Otis said with a nod to her.

"Thanks, Otis. We should be fine. Have a good night," she told him and waited while he waved and attempted to look farther inside the room once more before closing the door.

Flattening her back against the door, Ava glared at where her mother now stood near the bed.

"Does this place really not have any good hotels? I mean, this is ridiculous, Ava," Eleanor said. But before Ava could answer, she continued. "Well, I guess it is what it is. And that means it's a good thing I'm here. Let's get you packed. I have a driver waiting downstairs to take us to the nearest city with suitable accommodations. Then we can fly out of here as soon as possible."

"I'm not leaving," Ava said almost to herself.

"Where are your suitcases? Come, Ava, don't procrastinate." Eleanor continued to move throughout the room, stopping at the floral-printed couch in the sitting area of the room and scrunching her twenty-five-thousand-dollar nose at it.

"I don't need a suitcase, Mother," Ava said, pushing herself away from the door and walking toward Eleanor. "Because I'm not ready to leave Temptation."

"Well, I certainly am," Eleanor told her as she set her large Givenchy Atigona tote on the coffee table.

For a moment Ava could only stare at the woman who had not only raised her, but had also given birth to her. How could they have been any more different? Was it truly possible that people who shared the same DNA could be any less alike? The answer to that was obvious as she watched Eleanor Germaine Stanley Cannon smooth down the skirt of her winter-white Chanel suit and sit ever so gingerly on the edge of the couch. She was a very fair-skinned woman with auburn-colored hair that dared not ever show a speck of gray, or she would personally choke her hair stylist. Diamonds glittered from the ring fingers on both hands, at her ears and in the choker at her neck. Her pumps were Louboutin, her nails long and perfectly manicured, makeup light but efficient. She was beautiful and cold and the only family Ava had.

"When my work is finished I'll return to LA, then probably back to New York for site-scouting on the show."

"Nonsense, you pay people for that, and I told you Richard is expecting you."

Counting hadn't worked, and deep breaths weren't helping. Words were failing miserably. So that was three for three. Maybe food and a public place would be better.

"I'm hungry," Ava said quickly. "How about we go get dinner and discuss something else. Like, I don't know, maybe how I just received a prestigious award for my show almost a week ago."

She didn't wait for Eleanor's answer, but walked back toward the bed and slipped her feet into the flats she had there. She grabbed a jacket and her purse from the chair on her way to the door, and then turned back to see her mother still sitting with her hands folded primly in her lap.

"Are you coming, or do you want to stay here and have dinner with Mr. Otis?"

"I don't see why we couldn't have the driver bring us," Eleanor complained when she climbed out of the passenger side of the hybrid vehicle. "This…car, or whatever, is horrible. And where are we? Does this place even serve Troubadour Pinot Noir? I need a drink and a medium rare steak."

And Ava needed a tranquilizer and a six-pack. Or maybe a one-way ticket to Budapest, a place she was almost positive her mother wouldn't follow her to.

"It's a nice Italian restaurant, Mother. They have wine and pasta. You like pasta," she said as they walked up to the doors of the Temptation Trattoria.

"Well, hello, Ava. Nice seeing you this evening. I heard about your award. You go, girl!" Niecy Monroe, a tall, slim nineteen-year-old saving money to move to Hollywood to chase her own dreams, worked as a hostess at the restaurant. She and Ava had become fast friends since Niecy admired everything about Ava's life—except Eleanor, Ava was certain.

"Thanks, Niecy. Can we get a booth in the back, please?"

"Sure, sure," Niecy replied and then leaned over the podium and iPad they used to keep their seating chart to whisper, "Is she an exec from Hollywood?"

Ava almost laughed. "No. This is my mother, Eleanor Cannon."

"Oh my, well, hello Mrs. Cannon," Niecy said as she grabbed two menus and led the way to their booth.

"I'll bet you're brimming with pride for Ava. She's so talented and nice. I heard stories about those Hollywood producers being stuck up or mean. Ava's nice and friendly. She's fit right in here in Temptation. Almost like she was born here," Niecy continued as they walked through to the back of the restaurant.

"Well, she was not born here, thank the heavens," Eleanor snapped.

"Oh, well," Niecy said when they were both seated and she attempted to hand Eleanor the laminated menu.

When Eleanor only looked at the girl with a weary expression, Ava accepted the menus, and gave Niecy an apologetic smile.

"Right, so Raquel's your waitress, and she'll be over soon to take your drink order."

"Please tell her that I'd like a glass of Troubadour Pinot Noir. As a matter of fact, just bring us the bottle. We can take it back to that shack where my daughter is staying," Eleanor said without bothering to look at Niecy, who was now frowning.

"Thanks, Niecy," Ava said and waited until the girl was gone before chastising her mother.

"You really don't have to treat them like this. They're nice people here."

Eleanor sighed and reluctantly sat back against the seat. "I'm sure they are, Ava. But this is not what I'm used to. It's not what you were raised to accept. Why you refuse to take advantage of all the things available to you, I have no idea."

"I like doing things my way, Mother. It has nothing to do with you."

"That's what I'm sensing," her mother replied. "That you don't want to have anything to do with me."

"That's not what I meant," Ava said. "I'm just tired of trying to make you see me for who I am. I am not, nor will I ever be, the daughter you planned for. I'm me, and I love and respect you as my mother, but if you don't stop criticizing me and ignoring my accomplishments, our relationship is going to take a bad turn."

There. She'd said it. She'd kept her cool, and she'd maintained a respectful tone, all while telling her mother in no uncertain terms to cut this crap out.

"Well," Eleanor said before clapping her thin lips shut.

She blinked at her daughter as if just seeing her for the first time in forever, and then shook her head.

"I don't know where I went wrong—" she started and then held up a hand when Ava would have said something else. "But you are my only child, and I love you. So I guess we'll work this out. But if you think I'm going to eat from Styrofoam containers, as you just said, our relationship is going to take a bad turn."

Ava grinned. "They have real dishes here, Mother."

Working things out still meant that Eleanor had definite opinions about Ava's life and her career, and it was going to take a little more than delicious lasagna, buttery garlic bread and a great red wine to change that.

"You can still afford a better car than this." Eleanor was fussing as they drove onto the road heading back to the B and B.

The trattoria was located about twenty minutes outside the main part of town, but Ava loved their food, so she made the drive frequently. Only, her trips were usually during daylight hours. As it was a little before nine, it had grown pretty dark, and there weren't any streetlights on dirt roads. She switched on her high beams and tried to tune her mother out.

"And why television? If you're going to be in entertainment, why not go for movies? You'll certainly make more money there. I believe there was a studio executive who hired your father's firm at one point. I can probably look him up when I get home to civilization," Eleanor was saying.

"I don't need you to help me get into movies, Mother. I'm doing exactly what I want to do right now."

If that included holding the steering wheel with a death grip as a crack of thunder sounded and the skies opened up, dropping buckets of rain down around them, then so be it.

"Crap!" she said and switched the windshield wipers on.

"It's awfully dark out here, Ava. I don't like it."

"I know you don't like it, Mother. You've spent the three hours you've been in town telling me how much you don't like it here."

"Well, I don't. And that rude woman who came over to our table. What was her name? Millie something? I mean, really, who names their child Millie, nowadays? And she had on too much lipstick, looking at me as if I had offended her in some way," Eleanor continued.

Her mother had definitely offended Millie, considering she'd told her that she could purchase better wigs at professional salons instead of online. In response, Millie had run her fingers through her natural, but permed, hair as she stood over Eleanor and made a snide remark about Ava and Eleanor being suspicious characters in town. After that, and considering the other times Millie had pushed Ava's buttons, Ava hadn't even bothered to apologize for Eleanor's comments.

"Millie Randall is a special character," Ava was saying before something hit the car's fender.

She kept her grip on the steering wheel, but the car had already spun around and was now going down a slight embankment.

Eleanor screamed from the passenger seat, holding her chest and mumbling something about a heart attack, while Ava tried desperately to press on the brakes and keep them from crashing into the trees ahead. The sounds of her heart thumping wildly and her mother's screeching didn't help, so when the car slammed into something hard and the airbags exploded, knocking Ava back against the seat, she sank blissfully into the darkness.

Gage laughed like he hadn't since he was younger. Since he and his siblings were all together in Pensacola.

They were seated in the room that, according to Harper, would eventually become their formal living room. Right now there were two couches and two recliners positioned on an Aubusson rug around a long coffee table that Harper's cousin Craig had made.

Gray and Morgan sat on one couch, while Gage and Harper had pulled the recliners close to each side of the couch. Gray held his phone out with Gen on FaceTime. Gage had his phone with Gia, Harper had hers with Garrek, and Morgan, who had become fast friends with Gemma, had hers out, as well. This was how they'd had a family get-together after dinner.

"I'd forgotten all about that," Gage said after he'd laughed until his sides hurt.

"Well, I didn't," Gia replied. "All of our dolls were floating in the ocean after you and Garrek decided they could take a cruise on the raft you'd built out of branches and old shoeboxes."

"Gia cried for days," Gemma recalled with a chuckle.

"And Mom punished us for a week because we didn't ask permission to use your dolls on the virgin voyage," Garrek added.

Gray laughed. "I warned you two not to go in their bedroom, but you wouldn't listen."

"Gage was a master manipulator back then," Gen said. "He'd convince you that anything was a good idea. Remember he got Mom to let us open a gift not only on Christmas Eve, but on the day before Christmas Eve, too. Telling her it was a shame that only those two days out of the month got all the attention."

"And I used to cry about being an only child," Harper said, shaking her head.

"Those were good times," Gemma said. "I miss us all being together."

"I've missed it, too," Gage admitted. "But Gray's kids have reminded me of all that."

"Oh yes, I'm sure Jack and Lily have reminded you of how much mischief youngsters can get into," Morgan chimed in.

"More like reminding all of us how important family is," Gray said soberly.

"Speaking of which," Garrek announced and cleared his throat. "The last time we all met, Gray informed us that he'd narrowed down where the money that was deposited into the Grand Cayman account had come from."

"Someone who lived in a group home on Broad Street," Gage added.

He didn't really want to talk about this, but figured it was probably best for them all to decide to leave it alone.

"I've driven past there a few times, and I have to say, I really don't care who lived in that house or who followed Dad's instructions and deposited that money in the account. I've decided to use some of my share to start my own research foundation," Gage said.

He hadn't planned to announce this just yet, but since they were all here—so to speak—now was as good a time as any.

"Really?" Gray asked. "When did you decide this?"

"I've been thinking about it since I arrived in Temptation. My career didn't exactly work out the way I had planned, so I figured it was time for me to regroup and start again," he told them.

He left out the part that included Ava being a big influence on his decision. She'd always known what she wanted to do in life, and she'd even gone against her mother's wishes to achieve her goals. Gage had even told her she was doing the right thing, that she had a right to live the life she wanted. Well, he was making plans to live the life he wanted, with or without Mortimer Gogenheim and the chief of obstetrics position at Nancy Links Medical Center.

"I'm going to use my money to open my own restaurant," Gia announced.

"And I've been thinking about teaching and expanding my company to offer design grants in some of the colleges," Gen added.

"Onward and upward," Gemma told them. "Just like Daddy used to say."

There was a moment of silence, and then Gray spoke.

"I'll dismiss the private investigators, and we'll all accept that Dad left us this additional money because he loved us."

Morgan touched her husband's knee and smiled up at him.

"I agree," Garrek said. "We'll finally begin to focus on our future instead of being bogged down by our past."

"That's a great idea," Harper told her fiancé.

The Taylor sextuplets agreed.

"Now, with that said," Garrek began again, "I hear Gage is settling in to Temptation with a certain young lady who's been visiting, as well."

Oh no, Gage thought as all eyes, even the ones via FaceTime, zeroed in on him.

"Yes!" Morgan exclaimed. "You should see them together. They're so cute. Especially when they babysit the babies. I've used them as sitters twice now, and I would definitely recommend them."

His sister-in-law happily grinned at him, and Gage could only shake his head. He'd grown to love her and the stability and happiness she'd provided for his older brother.

"Ooooh, tell us more," Gia prodded.

Gage dragged his free hand down his face and groaned. "It's no big deal. Her name's Ava, and we worked together on her television show earlier this year. She's in Temptation for a writing retreat."

"Uh-huh, during the same time that Gage decided to come back for a visit and has since decided to stay on longer," Harper added.

"Yes, I came back to see Gray and his family. And I started working on the project Dad wanted at the hospital, so I don't want to leave until it's up and running smoothly," Gage said.

"And she just showed up? At the same time?" Gen asked. "Hmm."

"Right. Hmm," Morgan added.

"It was a coincidence," Gage said, but had to admit the words didn't sound accurate even to his mind.

"A coincidence that one of the famous Taylor sextuplets would be selected to work on another television show. And then that the producer from that show would arrive in our hometown at the exact same time that you did?" Gen asked.

"That's a pretty big coincidence," Gray said.

"Ava didn't know I was coming here," Gage replied calmly. But he was feeling anything but calm at the moment.

Why had they brought this up, and why were they questioning what had been just a chance happening? He had nothing to do with Ava showing up here and neither did his family.

Another phone ringing interrupted the conference, and Harper handed Morgan her cell phone as she stood and crossed the room to answer the landline.

"Morgan, it's Wendy for you," Harper said.

Morgan gave her cell phone to Gray and took the cordless phone from Harper.

"So we're all set for Christmas?" Gemma asked. "Everyone's coming back to Temptation for dinner in the Victorian on Peach Tree Lane?"

She sounded wistful as she smiled, and Gage wanted nothing more than to reach out and hug her. Gemma was the closest to their mother, and Olivia's love and caring nature radiated through his sister. He hadn't realized how much he missed being close to her until this very moment.

"Ava's been in an accident," Morgan said, her words effectively ending the good mood of their family conference.

"What?" Gage asked as he stood, immediately dropping his phone onto the couch.

"Wendy's on duty tonight, and she said they were just brought in by ambulance. A trucker was driving down Chambray Road and saw her car in a ditch," Morgan announced.

"I'm going now," Gage announced and had taken only a couple of steps toward the door before Gray came up behind him.

"I'll go with you. Here, take this," he said and handed Gage his phone that he'd dropped.

Gage didn't know when his other siblings were disconnected from their call, but he was on his way out the door in the next few seconds and heading to his car. All he could think about was Ava at this moment. Was she hurt? What had happened? Would he ever see her again?

Chapter 11

"Is there a possibility that you could be pregnant?"

Gage felt the world around him shift as he paused outside the curtain in the emergency room. It was only partially closed, and he'd been directed this way after he'd asked for Ava. He could see her lying on the bed, the doctor who had just asked the question holding her hand, checking her pulse.

"No," she replied. "I'm on birth control."

And he'd used protection. Each and every time they were together, Gage had dutifully donned a condom. So why had his heart rate significantly increased the moment he heard that question? More importantly, why was he feeling a sting of disappointment at her answer?

"Okay, good. We'll note that on your chart in case

we need to send you for an MRI or CT scan," the doctor continued.

He reached forward and grabbed an otoscope from the shelf on the wall, then proceeded to check Ava's eyes. When he was finished, he used his fingers to check down her neck and her limbs. She lay on the bed, staring up at the ceiling as the exam continued, and Gage resisted the urge to immediately go to her. As a doctor, he knew it was imperative for this physical exam to occur without interruption or distraction. So he remained where he stood, watching every part of the exam and breathing a sigh of relief when the doctor finally said, "I think you have a mild concussion."

"That means I can go home, right?" Ava asked. "I mean, I don't have to be admitted?"

"No. But I'd like someone to be there for you in case your symptoms change. You're just visiting us in Temptation, is that correct?"

"Yes. I'm staying at the Sunnydale Bed-and-Breakfast."

The doctor nodded. "Louisa Reed's place. She's a great innkeeper and would probably watch after you, but I don't think she lives on the property anymore. Moved into a smaller house near her daughter after her son, Harry, went to jail."

"She can come home with me," Gage said, finally entering the room completely. "I'll be able to keep a close eye on her in case her symptoms worsen."

"And you are?" the doctor asked when he spun around to see Gage approaching.

Gage extended his hand and said, "Dr. Gage Taylor."

With a smile and a curt nod, the doctor shook Gage's

hand. "Yes. Talk around the hospital is you were here and taking charge of the new wing your brother just finished building."

"That's correct. I'm in obstetrics and gynecology," Gage told him. "I'll take Ava home when you discharge her."

She'd started to sit up then, and Gage moved closer to the bed, taking her hand.

"And you're staying in that nice pretty yacht down at the dock. She's a beauty. I'm Dr. Ralston Hackney. My wife owns the ice-cream parlor at the end of the dock. She can't stop talking about that yacht. Think I may have to look into buying a boat or something just to keep her quiet."

Gage smiled. "Let me know when you're ready, I've got a great agent who can work wonders with the financing."

"I'll keep that in mind."

"Um, excuse me? Can I go now? I'd like to check on my mother."

"Oh, yes, Ms. Cannon. Sorry about that. I'll get started on your discharge papers. Dr. Taylor here will know what to watch for, but the nurse will go over everything when she comes in with the paperwork. Also, your mother's been taken down to X-ray. Dr. Leon Schilling in orthopedics examined her and thinks she broke her ankle. He's not talking about surgery, so she may be put in a cast and ready to leave in a few hours."

Ava sighed. "Just great."

"You're both very lucky the airbags deployed, Ms. Cannon. From what the paramedics said when they brought you in, that little compact car of yours is a total loss," Dr. Hackney said.

"It was a rental," Ava said and closed her eyes.

"Well, then, that's the rental company's problem," Dr. Hackney continued with a grin. "I'll go get your paperwork started. Take care of her, Dr. Taylor."

"Please, call me Gage, and yes, I will take care of her," Gage said and waited until Hackney was out of the room before he turned his attention back to Ava.

Her hair was splayed over the pillow behind her. The T-shirt she wore was wrinkled but not torn or splotched with any blood. Her legs looked good, ankles straight, feet still wearing flat shoes. Everything looked just fine, he concluded after he completed his own visual assessment. Everything except her eyes were closed tight and her fingers trembled in his.

For the first time since Morgan told him about the accident, Gage breathed in slow, measured intervals. Relief eased over him, and he leaned down, kissing Ava's forehead.

"You scared the life out of me," he whispered. "I didn't know what I was going to find once I got here. And I'm pretty sure at least six people are going to report me to the sheriff for speeding through town."

"It was a deer," she said quietly, her eyes opening as he pulled back slightly. "It was so dark and then it started to rain. My mother was complaining, and I just wanted to hurry up and get back to the B and B so I could get her a room of her own and I could find some peace and quiet."

Her voice cracked at the end.

"I wanted her to shut up. She hates it here, and Millie didn't make that situation any better. But I just wanted her to be quiet, or to not be here and now…" Her words trailed off.

"Now, she's going to get her ankle fixed up and spend a few more days here with you," he said and squeezed her hand. "She's fine, Ava. She's going to recover just like you will."

"The car."

"It's a rental. They're insured. And if they're not, I'll pay for the damn car," he said.

She started to shake her head, and Gage saw the moment pain radiated through her with the action.

"Shhhh, baby. Don't move. Don't think about any of this right now. I'm gonna take you home and get you into bed. You'll feel better after you get some rest."

"Home," she said when she opened her eyes again and stared up at him. "Everybody keeps saying 'when I go home.' But I live in LA."

"Logistics," Gage said. "I own a condo in New York, so that's technically my home. But for the last couple of weeks, since we've been staying on my yacht, that's felt more like a home to me than any place I've been since I was a child."

It was true, as the warmth spreading throughout his body and the intense weight he felt in his chest at this very moment indicated. Gage lifted her hand up to his lips and kissed her fingers. He closed his eyes, and words he'd been thinking the last couple of days came tumbling out.

"I haven't trusted any relationship since I was kid,

Ava. Once my dad left, I started to feel like a relationship between a man and woman could never work. Someone was bound to stop caring, or loving enough, and then it would be over."

He stared down at her, into her brown eyes. With his free hand he traced the line of her jaw, before brushing his knuckles over her cheek.

"Then when I was in the sixth grade and had just started middle school, I met these two guys, Fredro and Kelvin." He gave a wry chuckle. "I thought I was finally going to have friends who weren't my brothers. Gray was on the basketball team and Garrek had joined the Boy Scouts. I hadn't yet found my niche, that's what my mom said. Fredro and Kelvin just seemed to have so much fun. Laughing and joking all the time in the cafeteria, in class and on the bus. So when they invited me to go to the park with them one day I thought, This is great! I'll be doing something without my siblings. Because, you know it's hard sometimes being part of a group."

Gage took another deep breath.

"It was a cool friendship for about a week, and then Fredro asked if they could come to my house. I asked my mom and she said it was fine. That Saturday afternoon they came over. The next thing I know they're in my room, going through my stuff saying what they'd like to have. Fredro wanted my baseball bat and glove because it was signed by Eddie Murray. My dad had given it to me for my last birthday. Kelvin wanted the Lakers jersey my mom had given me for Christmas. I told them they couldn't have it. And Fredro looked me right in the eye and said, 'You think you're too good to share your stuff. Just because your family's famous doesn't make you better than us.' I couldn't believe it."

"Gage," she whispered.

He shook his head.

"I told them to put my stuff down and leave, but Fredro refused. So I punched him, and when he fell back on the bed, I took my stuff from him. He charged me and we fought. Kelvin would have jumped in, but Gray heard the noise and he came into the room. Kelvin didn't move and Gray let us fight. At least until my mom came in. Fredro's and Kelvin's mothers called our house later that day, and I heard my mother telling them to teach their kids some manners and they wouldn't end up in fights. Gray and Garrek told me not to worry about it. And on Monday when I went to school, I was prepared for round two. What I wasn't prepared for was the way everybody stared at me in class that day. Nobody talked to me or even wanted to look at me. Not that day or the days that followed. I was an outcast, again. Just because I was born a Taylor sextuplet.

"I vowed to never trust any type of relationship—"

Gage paused, trying to process the things going through his mind at this moment, the memories and the pain.

He lowered his forehead to rest on hers and closed his eyes. "I could have lost you tonight."

"I'm fine, Gage. Really I am," she whispered.

"But it could have been different. Without those airbags...if you hadn't been able to slow your descent...it could have ended differently."

She'd lifted her other hand to rub down the back of his head. "But it didn't and I'm going to be fine. I'm still right here with you."

His eyes opened at her words, and he pulled back just a little until he could hold her gaze once more.

"With me," he said. "That's where I want you to be. Stay on the yacht with me."

Gage didn't know what he expected, but tears definitely weren't on the list. Of course, he'd never done this before, but he didn't think that asking a woman that he was sleeping with to stay with him on his yacht, instead of at a B and B, was such a bad idea.

"What's the matter, sweetness? Are you in pain?"

She shook her head quickly, an act that Gage knew had to cause her some pain, if she wasn't already experiencing it. He immediately cupped her face with his hands to keep her still, the warmth of her tears touching his palms.

"No. I mean, a little. But I just… I should say so many things to you first, Gage."

"Nonsense," he said. "All you need to say is yes, and I'll take care of everything else."

She waited for what felt like the longest moment in his life before blinking more tears, and replying, "Yes."

"This isn't a hotel, but the decor is impeccable," Eleanor said after Morgan and Harper had gotten her situated on the half tester bed.

"Thank you so much for letting her stay here," Ava said as she came to stand beside Harper. "I'll hire a full-time nurse to look after her until she's well enough to travel. And I'll come by every day to make sure she's not harassing you or any of your staff."

Harper touched Ava's shoulder. "It's fine, Ava. Dr. Schilling gave us plenty of pain meds. Not that we plan to overdose her or anything."

Ava shook her head and managed a smile. "Believe me, you're gonna want to."

"We'll all pitch in and help keep watch over her. They said it was a clean break, but Wendy said with her age, any number of complications could arise if she doesn't heal properly," Morgan told her.

Ava sighed. "I don't know how to thank you two. I mean, you hardly know me and you all showed up at the hospital, and you're so willing to help."

"That's what families do," Morgan said as she moved to put an arm around Ava's shoulders.

"She's right," Harper added. "Now, you should really get some rest yourself. A mild concussion is nothing to play with."

Ava did have a headache, but she feared it had nothing to do with the car accident. She wasn't in a hurry to go back to the yacht with Gage. He was going to undress her and put her to bed, and then he was going to lie beside her and cuddle her in his arms.

And while all that sounded just fine, the real reason for her headache was because she was a big liar, and she had been deceiving him and his family for two months.

"Yes," she admitted. "I am really tired."

They left her alone with her mother, who was already dozing off as a result of the strong pain medication Dr. Schilling had prescribed for her. Ava took a moment to look down at her mother and then to think on everything Gage had said to her just a few hours ago.

It was time to stop letting the past dictate her future. If her mother couldn't do that, it was her decision. Ava was only going to focus on moving forward.

"Good night, Mother," Ava said as she leaned over and kissed Eleanor's cheek. "I'll see you in the morning."

With that she left the room, walking down the grand staircase in Harper's gorgeous home. It was another one of those movie-like romance scenes as she descended the stairs and Gage stood at the bottom looking up at her, waiting for her.

Each step Ava took grew heavier as she realized what she now stood to lose because of the sacrifice she'd decided to make for her career.

"Ready to go?" Gage asked her.

Ava nodded, words clogged in her throat because she knew which ones she needed to speak, but couldn't bring herself to do it. Not yet. Not tonight. Her head was still throbbing, and her body had begun to ache. Gage had asked her to stay with him, which was a huge step for both of them. It had been an eventful enough night. Waiting a few more hours to tell Gage about her plans wasn't too much to ask.

Still, by the time they'd arrived at the yacht, the weight on her chest had become too much to bear, and as soon as they'd entered his bedroom she opened her mouth to speak. Gage, however, lifted a finger to touch her lips.

"A warm shower, a pain pill and rest. That's what I'm prescribing for you," he said.

"Gage, I need to tell you—" she tried to say.

"Not tonight," he interrupted. "Let me just take care of you tonight."

It was so easy to give him what he wanted. So blissfully intimate standing in the shower stall while Gage lathered the sponge and bathed her. So peaceful lying in the bed cuddled in his arms.

"I can't wait for you to meet my sisters," he whispered as Ava began to doze off. "I hope you'll be able to arrange your schedule to be here for Christmas."

"I want to be here for Christmas," Ava said, her eyelids too heavy to hold open any longer.

She'd been chilly once she stepped out of the shower, but now, with his arm wrapped around her and his body cocooning hers, she felt warm and safe. And loved. She really liked those feelings.

"And I've decided to resign from the hospital in New York. I'm going to open my own clinic and research foundation. All Saints cannot provide funding for parents who cannot afford fertility treatments, or certain aspects of taking care of multiple infants. I want to start some programs that will help," he was saying.

Ava's lips lifted in a smile. Gage had stopped her from talking, but he clearly had lots to say tonight. She snuggled closer to him, loving the sound of his voice and thinking of how it would be to do this every night with him. To lie in bed and discuss their goals and dreams, the future they would share. She wanted that. Ava wanted it so very much.

So before she drifted off and while Gage was still talking, she said a little prayer, asking a big favor.
Please let him understand.

Chapter 12

Ava rolled over and reached for him, but felt the cool sheets instead. Cracking an eye open, she saw the pillows still indented from where he'd laid his head throughout the night. She rolled over again, this time plopping onto her back and then groaning at the slight thumping in her temples.

Dropping an arm over her forehead, she sighed and thought about Gage holding her in his arms last night. It was a magical feeling, one she knew now that she wanted to feel every night of her life. With that thought, Ava sat up slowly. There was no nausea and no dizziness, just the mild headache. Encouraged by the minimal symptoms, she got out of the bed and headed toward the bathroom. The note was taped to the door, and she smiled as she read his words.

I knew you wouldn't stay in bed as per doctor's orders. Gray needed my help with festival setup so Morgan's taking the morning shift with you while Harper stays with your mom. In the afternoon, Harper's going to come over. If you're doing well, Harper will bring you to the festival in time for the pumpkin-carving contest. If you have any symptoms you are to stay in bed, or at the very least, on the yacht and I'll hurry with the contest and come back to you. Gage

After a warm shower, Ava dressed in jeans and a button-front plaid shirt and slipped her feet into slippers that she knew had been at the B and B. Someone must have gone there and brought her things here because as she looked around the room, she also saw her bag, laptop and the toiletries she'd had on the dresser there, now sitting on top of the second dresser here.

It was different seeing her perfume bottles sitting next to Gage's cologne, her laptop on the table near the door with his right across from it. She turned back and looked again at the rumpled bed where they'd slept and sighed. If she wanted this lovely scene to be a part of her future, she had to set things in motion.

Morgan was on morning duty, so that meant she was probably above deck in one of the lavish rooms up there, waiting for Ava to emerge. Finding her phone on the charger sitting on the nightstand, she picked it up and moved to the table. Taking a seat, she booted up her laptop and called Marcelle.

"Hi there! I know it's early, but I really need to talk

to you about something," Ava began the moment she heard the groggy "hello" on the other end.

Marcelle was not a morning person, so calling her at seven thirty LA time would normally be a no-no. In this case, it was urgent, so Ava ignored the time.

"This better be good, Ava," Marcelle replied.

"I think it is," she said. "I'm sending you an email right now. I need you to review the two attachments. There's a synopsis of the two-night miniseries featuring the Taylors of Temptation and notes on how this deal has to be brokered."

"Has to be?" Marcelle asked, her voice a little clearer now.

Ava had known that business would wake Marcelle up completely. It always did.

"Yes," Ava told her. "Because this is how I'm going to pitch the story to the Taylors, and I'm pretty certain if I pitch it this way, and they agree, they're not going to take kindly to any abrupt changes."

"I take it this is different from what Jenner and Carroll told me about when they called me last week."

Ava's fingers stilled over the keyboard, and she had to readjust the phone she'd tucked between her ear and shoulder. She probably should have hunted through her purse to find her Bluetooth, but she hadn't wanted to waste any more time.

"They called you? Why?" she asked Marcelle.

There was some rattling in the phone's background, and Ava figured Marcelle had climbed out of bed and was now heading toward her home office so she could boot up her computer and read the email while they talked.

"They were pretty excited about this show and wanted to get started on getting you signed on officially."

"Well, you might want to hold off on that," Ava told her. "Because if they don't agree, I'm walking."

"Really?" Marcelle asked, her voice clear and questioning. "What about your new show idea?"

"I'm not going to be bullied by them," Ava said, wondering why she hadn't taken this stance from the start.

Fear. That was the clear-cut reason. She was afraid that going against top network executives would get her blackballed in the industry. And there was still a chance of that happening. Only now, she didn't give a damn. If she had to use her trust fund money to make her own movies, or buy a network where she could decide which shows would make it and which ones wouldn't, that's what she planned to do. Asking for and waiting for permission or validation from pompous men in this industry was over.

Gage had told her that. He'd said she shouldn't apologize for who and what she was to her mother and that she was enough on her own. Ava believed him because he believed in her.

Marcelle gave a whoop and said, "That's what I've been waiting to hear from you. Okay, let me look at the notes first because I already know your pitch is awesome."

"I don't want their lives intruded upon for months on end. The four-hour series can be taped in a month, edited the next month, advertised and shown in the same timespan they already have mapped out. But making this a full thirteen-week series is out of the question. They have lives and families and it's just too much to ask them to go through all of this again," Ava said.

"Okay, this all looks good. I'll work on your numbers. You're doing them a huge favor, and in return they're going to pay you a big damn chunk of money. And I want a clause in this contract that guarantees your next two shows. And…hmm, wait a minute," Marcelle said.

Ava was going through her email inbox seeing what she needed to read and what could be trashed, so she didn't speak while Marcelle paused.

"Well, this is very interesting indeed," Marcelle said after another minute or so.

"What's that?" Ava asked, just as she was about to close her email in-box. She needed to get topside to let Morgan know she was all right; otherwise Morgan might come down to check on her. Ava didn't want to be seen working when she was supposed to be recuperating.

"Apparently I need to check my office voice mail quicker. Parker Donovan sent an email to follow up to the message he left for me yesterday. He's very interested in meeting with you and discussing creative opportunities for you at Donovan Network Television," Marcelle told her.

Ava sat back in the chair and smiled. She couldn't help it—a fist bump in the air also came as she did everything she could to withhold the squeal of excitement that bubbled inside her.

"Yes!" she exclaimed. "So Jenner and Carroll can definitely take this deal for the Taylors or kick rocks!"

"You're damn right!" Marcelle yipped, excitement clear in her voice, as well. "Okay, since they're on the East Coast like you right now, I'll give them a call to let them know that I've received the message and I'm checking your availability. I'll also get a preliminary idea of what these Donovans are possibly talking about offering you to come to their network."

"Great. Keep me posted," Ava said. "Now, I've gotta go. Today's the Fall Festival."

Marcelle chuckled. "You're really settling into that little town, aren't you?"

Ava shrugged even though she knew Marcelle couldn't see her. "It happened so naturally. I mean, one minute I'll be sitting in my room writing and the next Otis is knocking on my door with the best homemade lemonade I've ever had and some sort of snack. While I eat, he tells me whatever is going on in town for that day. Then I go outside and people stop me on the street to talk about this or that. And the Taylors, they're super nice and very involved and—I guess I am getting caught up, huh?"

Marcelle chuckled. "Definitely. But Gage Taylor is scrumptious enough to have any woman moving to a small town and going to fall festivals, whatever those are."

Ava agreed and ended the call with Marcelle. She had just stood from the desk when she heard the door to the room open and Morgan come down. Just in time, she thought and then fixed a smile on her face to greet one of the nicest women she'd ever known. A woman who she could easily picture as a sister-in-law someday.

Gage could not ignore the instant swell of happiness that spread throughout his chest the moment he saw Ava come through the double doors of the old Hatlenbinger horse barn. It was chilly today, so she wore jeans, those sexy brown boots that tied up the back of her legs and a brown leather jacket. Her hair was styled in two braids, each hanging over one shoulder so that she looked younger and prettier. She stood still for a few moments, looking around the large structure similar to the way Gage had when he'd first entered a few hours ago to help Gray and the others set up.

The barn used to house Hatlenbinger's prized stallions and foaling mares when Gage had been younger. But, as told to him earlier by Fred Randall, Tom Hatlenbinger died of a massive heart attack ten years ago. After an argument with his two daughters prior to his death, he'd left everything he had to his second wife, who in turn sold the horses within the same month that Tom had passed away. The land had been bought by the town for taxes a few years prior to Tom's death, so his wife couldn't sell that, and the town decided to use the barn space to host the weekly farmer's market. The house had been renovated and was being used as a horse museum thanks to one of Hatlenbinger's daughters, who had returned to town.

Today it was filled with booths showcasing homemade items for sale. They had everything from jams to baskets to knitted sweaters. There were also tables crowded with cakes and pies, cookies and smoked meats for tasting and sale. In one of the far corners were bales of hay and a tractor for picture-taking and playing, as some children were already doing. Next to that section were five tables and an insane amount of pumpkins all ready for the contest.

"You just gonna stare at her for the rest of the day?" Gray asked.

Gage hadn't heard his brother approach and didn't bother to look over at him because he knew the smirk that would be on his face.

"She's mingling," he replied.

Two women Gage did not know had just stopped to speak to Ava, and he watched the exchange in awe of how quickly she'd made friends in this town.

"And you're ogling," Gray said. "You're so pitiful."

"Hey," Gage replied and then tore his gaze away from Ava long enough to glare at Gray. "No name-calling is allowed when you came here to sell three pieces of property and ended up marrying a woman, getting her pregnant and adopting her children."

Gray didn't look the least bit bothered by Gage's words, but instead shook his head. "You're not me," he said with a slow grin.

"Whatever, man. I'm not ashamed to admit that I came here for a visit and ended up falling in love."

"That's cool, because denying it would have been foolish. It's written all over your face," Gray said. "And truthfully, it looks good on you. I'm happy for you, especially considering how you both came to be here."

Gage did not want to hear about that coincidence again. He'd been thinking about it off and on since his siblings brought it up last night. It wasn't on purpose, he'd told himself finally, and that was that.

"To be fair, we hooked up after the end of shooting the first season of the show," he told Gray.

It wasn't something Gage would have normally told anyone, but he was tired of them acting as if he and Ava were only connected because they ended up in Temptation together.

"Really? Sleeping with the boss?" Gray said and folded his arms over his chest.

"Nah, it wasn't like that. There was this chemistry between us from day one. We fought it the whole time we were working, but then once the shooting was over, I guess we just figured it was fair to proceed." Gage thought back fondly on that night in Ava's trailer. "It was only supposed to be one time."

"But then she showed up here," Gray said.

Gage nodded. "And we were at it again. But this time it was different. I knew one more time wasn't going to be enough."

"It never is when you find the one." Gray clapped Gage on the shoulder. "Like I said, I'm happy for you. Ava's a good woman. Morgan and Harper love her, so all you have to do is get Gen's, Gemma's and Gia's approval, and you can go ahead and propose to her."

"Propose? I don't know if I'm ready to start thinking about marriage."

Gray chuckled. "Yeah, you keep right on telling yourself that."

"Really, I wasn't."

"Uh-huh. Well, if you aren't thinking about putting a ring on it, you probably should," Gray told him and then pointed toward the door once more.

Gage followed his brother's direction and saw Ava laughing at something Craig Presley was saying. More importantly, he saw how close Ava and Craig were standing to each other and how Ava easily rested her hand on Craig's arm.

He took a step in their direction and heard Gray laugh.

"Yeah, that's what I thought," his brother was saying, but Gage kept walking, until he came up behind Ava and Craig.

It was just in time to hear Ava say, "I'm sorry I never followed through on the rain check for dinner. I had work and then things just started happening."

Craig smiled down at her. "Yeah, things like you and Gage hooking up. I get it, and there are no worries. I was just offering to show you around."

"And I appreciate it," Ava said. "You were very friendly and helpful when I first arrived."

"Hey there," Gage said when he finally stepped up to them. "You look like you're feeling better."

"Hey. I am," she said and then looked up at him as if nobody else in that barn even existed.

"How's it going, Craig?" Gage spoke and extended his hand to shake the younger man's.

"Hey, Gage. Going great. Been pretty busy with projects, but Harper said we'll slow down for the holidays. We're still waiting on Ava to decide when and where she wants to build her tiny house, though," Craig said.

"I haven't even had a moment to think about that lately," Ava said.

"Well, you should," Craig continued. "Temptation's a great place to have a small getaway home."

Gage agreed. "You don't have much time to think about it now either. We're up," he told her. "The contest is about to start."

"Oh, right. See ya later, Craig," Ava said as Gage took her hand.

"What do you mean, 'see ya later'? I'm entered in the contest, so be prepared to be wowed by my creation!"

As they walked across the barn to the area set up for the contest, Gage couldn't help but think about Craig's words to Ava. Temptation was a great place to build a house. But what else? A family? A home?

An hour and a half later, Ava hugged Craig and placed the goofy jack-o'-lantern sponge hat on his head. He was the winner of the pumpkin-carving contest, and as such had won the lovely hat and a fifty-dollar coupon to O'Reiley's Pumpkin Patch. His pumpkin-turned-Darth-Vader was the best carving Ava and Gage had ever seen.

Gray, Jack and Lily came in second place and had posed happily with their creation—a crooked but valiant attempt at the Grinch. The contest had been a blast. The hot cider and sugar cookies being passed around were even better. But overall, it was just the people,

Ava thought, that made this a fantastic event. She'd been to who knew how many Hollywood parties and corporate functions with her mother, but none of them compared to this.

"It's movie time!" Jack yelled excitedly.

Morgan was there shaking her head. "I don't know. I heard Craig telling Harper that he picked something extra scary for tonight's movie. I don't think you and your sister will be able to watch."

Harper waved a hand. "My aunt Laura quickly put the kibosh on that," she said. "We're watching *It's The Great Pumpkin, Charlie Brown* first, and then Craig's allowed to show *Poltergeist*, but not the other horribly gruesome movie he was planning on."

"Charlie Brown! I love Charlie Brown!" Lily announced.

"Okay, then let's head on out so we can get a good seat in front of the screen," Morgan told them.

"We're just going to clean up here a little. Save us a seat," Ava told Morgan and Gray.

"Oh no, you're not," Gage warned. "You're going to go on and sit down. I'll clean up, and then I'll join you. So you can save me a seat."

When Ava opened her mouth to argue, Wendy, Morgan's sister, touched her shoulder. "Don't even bother. Take the offer of help 'cause who knows when you'll get another one."

Ava liked Wendy because she reminded her so much of Marcelle. She agreed with her, and they all walked outside to where chairs had been set up in rows on the grass like they were at a real movie theatre. A large screen had been rented and placed up front for the movie viewing. They found seats in the fourth row, and Ava eased down the aisle to sit alongside the Taylor family.

It felt perfect sitting here, waiting for the movie to begin, talking to Lily, stopping Jack from climbing over the chairs in the next row and laughing with Wendy and Harper. She'd never had moments like this with her mother, or even with both her parents when her father was alive. This was what it was like to belong to a real family. She smiled to herself and thanked every deity possible for her good fortune.

"Attention! Attention!" A woman stood in front of the screen with a microphone.

Ava recalled meeting her before. She was one of the women who had been with Millie the second time the brash woman had approached her. Her name was Shirley Hampstead, and she was the town comptroller. Ava loved putting names with faces and job titles. It was a lot better than putting names with the last movie someone had done, or the last scandal they'd been involved in. She put a finger up to her lips and gave Jack a stern look before returning her attention to Shirley.

"We'd like to thank everyone for coming out to this year's festival. It's been a wonderful day, and we owe it all to the Magnolia Guild for their fund-raisers throughout the year that help us pay for events like this." Shirley gave a nod to someone in the audience, and there was applause.

"Also, on behalf of Mayor Pullum, who's still recovering from knee surgery, we want to thank all of this year's volunteers. Without you we wouldn't have been set up on time." With that, Shirley and a few other people in the audience laughed and clapped.

"As always, a very special thanks goes to JoEllen Camby for planning this function—from her house—every single year. JoEllen does a magnificent job," Shirley told the crowd, who clapped in response.

Wendy leaned over to whisper to Ava. "And that, my dear, is how you serve sarcasm here in Temptation."

Ava laughed and shook her head.

Then her smile faltered slightly as a familiar face joined Shirley. Millie wore a burnt-orange pantsuit with a white blouse and a large pumpkin pendant on the lapel of her jacket.

"Now, I've saved the best for last," Shirley said. "I'm so excited about this announcement, I could just bust."

Shirley did a little shake that may have been meant to accompany her words about busting, but actually made her look a little insane, as she wore a tight green dress that surely would not support her body parts in the event any busting were to actually take place. Millie snatched the microphone from Shirley before anything like that could happen.

"As the chairperson of Temptation's chamber of commerce, I'll be making the next announcement," Millie started to say.

Ava looked around for Gage at that moment because she really didn't want to hear anything that Millie had to say. The woman was a troublemaker, and she was rude and annoying.

"This time last year, we welcomed back to town a

member of one of our most esteemed families. I'd like to ask Grayson Taylor and his wife and children to stand," Millie said.

Harper leaned over in her seat, looking past Ava to where Wendy sat. Wendy shrugged and Harper shook her head. Ava watched as Gray stood with Jack on his shoulders and Morgan stood with Lily standing in the seat beside her. The audience clapped once again.

"Yes, welcome back to the Taylors," Millie continued. "I'm saying that with a plural because Garrek Taylor was back with us for a few months this year. Just long enough to snag the heart of our very own Harper Presley. Harper, you come on and stand, too."

Harper groaned as she got to her feet, and Ava gave her a conciliatory pat on her back when she sat down again.

"It seems like all the Taylors are coming home," Millie went on to say. "And with that comes our big announcement. As you all know, once upon a time *The Taylors of Temptation* was a reality show. And this show brought lots of revenue to our fair town. Now, thirty years later when reality television is still going strong, the Taylors are going to help our town out once again by filming an all-new reality show."

Ava's heart sank, and her throat went dry as whispers began to sound in the audience.

"That's right, the new show is going to be called *The Taylors of Temptation: Remember the Times*. And it's all set to air this time next year. Filming will start soon after the first of the year, so in addition to welcoming the rest of the Taylor sextuplets home, we'll also be preparing for visitors. The crew and all those Hollywood folk will be staying here in town and eating and shopping. We'll make enough money to fix the bridge down by the stream and make necessary improvements to the dock, as well as help some of the local businesses refresh their storefronts. We want to look our best, of course."

All of a sudden Ava didn't know what to do with her hands. They'd been resting in her lap, but now she was wringing them, and when she realized what she was doing she hurriedly dropped them to her sides. She didn't want to look to her left or to her right, because Wendy and Harper were most likely staring at her in question. Instead she looked over the heads of the audience toward the barn, where Gage now stood, his gaze zeroing in on her.

"So let's give a great big round of applause to the Hollywood producer Ava Cannon, who has been staying with us these past couple of months. Ava's been here scouting locations and getting the Taylor family ready to be in the spotlight once again. Come on and stand up so we can all see you, Ava."

Ava didn't stand. She didn't need to. All eyes were immediately on her. But the only ones she gave a damn about were his.

Chapter 13

Gage gripped the steering wheel as he drove them toward the dock. So many things had been flowing through his mind since they'd left the festival, but he knew he'd needed to take a moment to get his thoughts together.

"Is that what this has been about?" Gage asked when he stopped his car.

After Millie's announcement he'd stood still, unable to move a muscle as he watched Ava moving through the crowd toward him. She was trying to get out of the row where she'd been sitting, but people kept congratulating her, or simply standing just to shake her hand. To shake the hand of the producer of the new Taylors of Temptation reality show.

"No," she immediately replied. "We… What we have is separate."

"Separate from you brokering a deal for a show that was never going to happen," he replied.

His hands slipped slowly off the steering wheel to rest in his lap. He felt calm, dangerously so.

"The deal happened before us, or rather, before this 'us' began," she said and then turned sideways in the seat to look at him. "Let me just explain from the beginning."

Gage shook his head. "You followed me here and weaseled your way into my family, so that you could film us again. You knew how I felt about that show and being in the spotlight from day one, and you stayed, you continued. You lied to me. You used me and my family."

"That's not entirely true," she continued. "When I was approached about this deal, all I knew was that your family had stayed out of the limelight for the last thirty years. I didn't know why."

"And you didn't bother to ask," he responded and felt his entire body begin to shake.

"I wanted a chance to get to know you and the family first, and then I was going to—"

"You were going to what, Ava? Would you have married me if I asked? Had my kids maybe? All to get your precious show. What's the matter, one successful show wasn't enough? Or was it that you couldn't stand your own dysfunctional family so you decided to squirm your way into another one to see if you could destroy it, too?"

She jerked as if he'd physically assaulted her, and Gage frowned.

"I can explain," she said slowly. "I can tell you exactly how this came about and the terms I've requested for you and your family."

"I don't give a damn about any terms," he said, this time through clenched teeth because the calm he'd possessed was slowly slipping. "I don't care about your explanations. This business ruined my family once, there's no way I'm going to let that happen again."

"Gage—" she started.

"No!" he yelled. "I drove you back here so you can get your things. I'll call you a cab while you pack."

He opened the door and stepped out of the car. He closed the door but still stood beside it waiting...for what, he had no idea. To wake up possibly, from this horrid dream. For her to tell him that Millie had lied and none of this was happening. That the woman he'd fallen in love with hadn't screwed him just to see her name roll in the credits of another television show.

He heard the passenger side door open and close softly.

"I apologize for not telling you sooner," she said. "I should have. I knew it all along, and I didn't say anything. I guess I didn't want to destroy the perfect moments we were having."

"They weren't perfect," he replied and gazed at her over the top of the car. "They were lies. All of this was a lie. Just like the show that was on television thirty years ago. We were never that happy family enjoying the limelight. My father was never the happily married man madly in love with his wife. We're not on television right now, so if in your mind this was going to end with a big wedding, a house and kids, you were wrong."

"If you would just let me explain," she tried once more.

"Explain what? That you were just fine sleeping with me and dragging me to parties, but when it really came down to it, you didn't give a damn about me or my feelings."

He took a breath, but more words came, and Gage was helpless to stop them.

"You want to explain why you lay in bed with me every night and never once bothered to tell me you were having my baby? Why did I have to find out the day after you aborted my child when the clinic called to check on you because your blood pressure was running high when you were discharged? Why are you constantly lying and deceiving me when I've told you how hard it was for me to trust anyone?"

Silence fell between them after those last words. Ava stared at him with tears and confusion in her eyes.

Gage cursed.

He ran his hands down his face and cursed again.

"Gage," she gasped.

"No," he said. "Just no. It's enough."

"I didn't know. I'm not like whoever she was. Let me—"

"No!" he yelled. And then sighed. "Just stay the hell away from me."

When she didn't move or speak, he walked around the car to stand directly in front of her.

"I mean it. Get yourself another consultant for your

show and find another family to exploit, because it won't be me or the Taylors. Stay away from me and my family."

He walked away then, letting himself onto the yacht but going straight back to the lounge room, where there was a bar. He needed a drink. And he needed her off his boat and out of his life...before he could deal with the fact that his heart was breaking once again—and this time it had nothing to do with a television show.

It was her fault.

She shouldn't be irritated as hell with Gage. But she was.

How dare he order her to get her stuff off his yacht and then call her a cab to get her away from him as fast as possible? And on top of all that, he'd warned her to stay away from him and his family, as if she had no choice but to listen to him on this matter. There were five other adults involved in this situation—whether she'd talked to all of them directly or not—and they each deserved the opportunity to listen to her proposal and provide an answer. She should just set up a meeting with them and see what happened.

But doing so would hurt him more.

More than what this woman had apparently done to him. He'd had a child, and she took it from him without even telling him. It was no wonder Gage didn't trust people. And Ava had lied to him, as well. She couldn't deny that fact.

Pressing this issue, forcing his family into the spotlight—with or without him—would seal Gage's distrust box closed tightly forever. And even if he couldn't bring himself to stay with her, he deserved love and happiness with someone.

By the time Ava climbed out of the cab, it was almost midnight.

She walked around to the trunk, where the driver was removing her bags. "Here you go." She extended the twenty dollars to him and bent down to pick up the duffel bag he'd placed on the curb.

"Fare's already taken care of," he told her. "I'll carry these others to the door for you."

Ava frowned. What kind of guy put a woman out and paid for her cab fare?

The kind she was desperately in love with.

She knocked on the door, the last bits of her pride in her back pocket, and waited. Harper opened the door and offered her a small smile. A genuine smile.

Once she and all her stuff were in Harper's foyer, Ava cleared her throat and said, "I apologize. I should have been up-front with everyone the moment I interrupted the volleyball game that day."

"You could have done that," Harper said as she folded her arms over her chest. "But then you wouldn't have learned all you did about the Taylor family, and you wouldn't have had the chance to fall in love with Temptation and Gage."

Ava ran her hands through her hair and sighed. "I don't know how any of that happened. I was just trying to do my job."

"But something else occurred," Harper said with a nod. "Been there. Done that."

"You deceived and alienated a family that you not only needed for work, but loved and admired, as well?" Ava asked and chuckled to keep from crying.

"Not exactly," Harper replied. "But it took me a minute to accept the love that had blossomed because of my independence and everything I'd built my life to be."

"There's nothing to accept now," Ava said quietly. "Absolutely nothing."

She walked away from Harper and up that gorgeous romantic stairway with heavy steps. It was all over. Tomorrow she would arrange for her and her mother to go back to LA.

"Oh, Ava. Darling, I wasn't expecting you," Eleanor said and then giggled.

Yes, Ava thought with a start as her eyes widened and her mouth gaped, her mother was giggling. And she was sitting up in the bed accepting grapes from Otis, who sat on the side of the bed, also giggling.

"Ah, hiya, Miss Ava," Otis said before popping another fat grape into her mother's mouth.

"What. Is. Going on here?" Ava asked. She couldn't stop her feet from leading her deeper into the room. Even though her eyes were burning at the sight of her mother in such an—for lack of a better word—intimate position with a man.

"Otis took off work today. He's been here taking care of me since this afternoon when Harper left to go see about you," Eleanor said. "Did you have fun at the festival?"

"No," Ava replied instantly. "That's what I came to talk to you about."

"Well, go ahead and talk," Eleanor told her. "Otis has been such a doll, making sure I had everything I need while recuperating."

"Right," Otis said. He looked from Ava to Eleanor and then back to Ava. "But I think I'll be going now."

"Thank you," Ava said. Since her mother apparently wasn't getting the hint that she needed to talk.

"I'll come check on you tomorrow," Otis said as he stood. He set the bowl of grapes on the nightstand and was about to walk away when Eleanor reached for his hand.

"That's very nice of you, Otis."

"We won't be here tomorrow," Ava said. "I mean, I'll be making arrangements for us to fly out tomorrow."

"We are?" Eleanor asked, the surprised look on her face real and perplexing.

"Oh. Well, yeah, I'll just be going. I, um, guess I'll give you a call or something sometime, Ellie."

Ellie?

Otis touched her mother's hand, and the two shared a look. It wasn't a look that Ava wanted to explore, and so she glanced away from them. Seconds later Otis was touching her shoulder lightly as he walked past.

"It was a pleasure, Miss Ava," he mumbled before leaving the room.

Once the door was closed, Ava moved closer to the bed. "What was that?"

"That was me having the most fun I've had in the last ten years," Eleanor quipped.

Her words, in addition to the situation, once again startled Ava, who sighed and sat on the end of the bed.

"Well, I messed up big-time. So the fun for both of us is over," she said.

"You? The one who has her life together, who knows what she wants and is going to go get it with or without her mother's approval. *You* messed up?"

Her mother was a lot of things, and condescending was one of her specialties. Ava very rarely admitted that Eleanor was right.

"I thought I was doing the right thing," Ava said after recounting the whole story for her mother. "I figured if I could just rework the deal, the Taylors would definitely go for it. And I was going to tell them everything tomorrow night at dinner. I had it all planned out."

"Yes, you seem to plan things out very well," Eleanor said. "The problem is, you don't account for life happening throughout your plan."

Ava kicked off her shoes and turned around, pulling her legs up onto the bed. "What are you talking about?"

Eleanor waved her hand and then fluffed the pillows behind her before settling back again. "Life, Ava. It happens to all of us. Do you think I wanted my successful and handsome husband to turn into an alcoholic? Did I want to have the managing partner of the firm call me and tell me that if my husband didn't get himself together, he would be fired and we would be thrust into the poorhouse?"

The last was a bit dramatic considering Eleanor and Ava had huge trust funds courtesy of Eleanor's godfather, who died six months after Ava was born. In addition, Ava's father had made millions at the firm. He was a shrewd investor and doubled his yearly earnings consistently. So when he died he left a pretty hefty estate, with enough to take care of his wife and daughter comfortably for the rest of their lives.

"I wanted my fairy tale," Eleanor continued. "I'd fallen madly in love with Haywood Cannon, and on our first date had pictured our lavish lives together. We would have a magnificent house full of beautiful children and want for absolutely nothing. I had to have an emergency hysterectomy after giving birth to you. Fifteen years later Haywood found out he was adopted. His birth brother killed four people before taking his own life. And when Haywood traced the rest of his family, he found out his parents were also criminals and had died in jail.

"He was devastated, and a glass of wine in the evenings turned into a bottle of scotch hidden in his office drawer, our bathroom and his home office. I thought if I continued on with our lives, proving to Haywood that I would stand by him no matter what his birthright, that things would eventually return to normal. The phone call in the middle of the night informing me that my husband was dead was a cruel wake-up call."

Eleanor blinked. Her eyes shone with tears. Ava couldn't speak—she didn't know what to say because she'd never heard this story before.

"Life happens, Ava. There's no way to plan for it, and no amount of running away from it will fix problems. It just happens."

"I could have told him," Ava said quietly and looked down at her hands. "I could have just told Gage the truth."

"And I could have insisted your father get help."

"It's not the same," Ava argued.

"The circumstances aren't, no. But the concept is. Look at me, Ava."

At the sharp tone, Ava's head shot up, and she stared back at her mother to see tears streaming down Eleanor's face.

"If I had told Haywood to get help, if I had insisted and then worked with him to get through the disillusionment he'd suffered, maybe he wouldn't have thought driving off that cliff was the only answer. I had the love of my life, and I didn't do enough to hold on to it."

When Ava opened her mouth to speak, her mother held up one elegant hand.

"If you had told Gage about the show for his family from day one, he might have said no and sent you away. Or he might have listened to you and let you speak to his family, and they might have all made a decision. But that time has passed. You cannot determine what the outcome would have been at this point any more than I can. But you still have the opportunity that I missed."

Ava shook her head. "I don't know what to do now. I mean, I do. I should just go. I betrayed him, all of them."

"You were doing your job and you fell in love. That's life. But you are no quitter," Eleanor told her. "You're not like me. Don't miss the opportunity to say something, do something, that might change the course of these events. If you really love this man, you need to grab hold of that love and don't let go."

She heard what her mother was saying, and she knew what she meant, but Ava was tired, and she was certain that she never wanted to see Gage looking at her the way he had just a short while ago again. Her heart couldn't take it.

"We're going home tomorrow, Mother," Ava said and crawled to the head of the bed to sit next to her mother. She took her hand and laid her head on Eleanor's shoulder. "Thank you for talking to me about Dad and what really happened. I'm sorry it didn't turn out better."

"Not as sorry as I am, my baby. Every day I wonder and I hurt. Well, every day until I met Otis."

That made Ava smile. "Wow. You and Otis."

Eleanor chuckled. "I know. There's just something about this town."

That was something else Ava and Eleanor could agree on. There was something about Temptation and the people here. Especially the Taylors. But that something would soon be in Ava's past. It had to be.

Chapter 14

Two weeks later

Gemma Taylor sat at the head of the formal dining room table in Gray's house. She was a tall woman, at five feet ten inches, with a heavily creamed coffee complexion and ink-black hair that fell in perfect soft waves past her shoulders. She sat with her shoulders squared, brown eyes searching and assessing everyone in the room with her. She looked, to Gage, just like their mother.

"This is ridiculous," Gage said. "There's nothing to discuss."

"That's not your call," Gemma told him calmly. "This involved all of us, so we should have all been consulted."

"I agree," Gray, who was sitting across the table from Gage, said. "This is how it should have happened from the start. All of us here, listening to what the network has to say and then deciding how to proceed."

"I don't want to be on a television show," Gage insisted.

"And neither do I," Garrek chimed in from the Skype call he'd been connected through. "But I don't think I can make that call for anyone else."

"He can't," Gia replied.

She and Gen had once again been connected to the meeting via FaceTime calls, with Harper and Morgan sitting at the table holding the phones.

"And you're certain Ava never mentioned this to you, Gage?" Gemma asked. "You could have simply dismissed it because you're so firm in your answer."

Gage stared at her blankly for a moment, and then he fumed. This was all Ava's fault. Now she was pitting them against each other.

"I definitely would have remembered her telling me that she was here to spy on my family for the sake of a new show," he said.

"It could have been after those steamy bouts of sex on your lovely yacht," Morgan said and then looked across the room as if she hadn't just aimed those words at him.

The doorbell rang, and Harper set her phone on the table, saying, "I'll get it."

Gage could have sworn he heard her chuckle as she walked out of the room and headed to the door. He wisely remained silent and sat back in the chair. He rested his hands on his thighs and decided to play this as cool as he possibly could. It wasn't going to be easy. Not like handing in his resignation to the hospital and packing up his condo had been. That was a surprise to him, because he'd spent his entire life striving to get to those places. It shouldn't have been so easy to walk away. But he hadn't wanted to examine the reasons for that. He'd just wanted to get back to Temptation and to get started on his new dream, even if a huge part of it had fallen through.

"Everyone, this is Ava Cannon. She's here on behalf of Donovan Network Television and would like to present a business opportunity to the family," Harper said.

Gage heard his siblings speaking to Ava and thanking her for coming. He did not turn around to look at her, nor did he say a word to her. He couldn't. There were no words to describe what these last two weeks had been like for him. And heaven help him, he couldn't figure out the words to make things better.

"Thank you for inviting me," Ava said.

From the sound of her voice, and because he could see her movement out of his peripheral vision, he could tell she'd entered the dining room and followed Harper to stand at the other end of the table.

"It's a pleasure to meet you all. I've heard a lot about you from…your family, and then I've done some research," Ava said.

"You should probably focus more on what the family says," Gemma joked. "Even though they can embellish a bit, too."

Everyone around the table laughed. Except Gage.

"Well, I'll get right to it," Ava said. She pulled out a laptop and placed it on the table. After tapping some keys, she turned it to face everyone.

Gage couldn't help but look. On the screen was a purple-and-gold logo that read The Taylors of Temptation. In seconds, that screen dissolved and in its place was Lemil Mountain Lake, the words "A Whole New World" appearing in shimmering letters over the water.

"Awww, it's the lake," Gia said. "You remember playing softball there, Gage? You were always begging Mom and Dad to take us there on pretty summer days."

"I hated swimming," Gen said. "But Gage loved the water."

"He still does," Gray said frankly.

Ava cleared her throat.

"I was first approached by producers at my former network to create a show surrounding the Taylors. It would have been a thirteen-episode reality show following each of you and your new life around Temptation. Marketing and scheduling were already in place. I didn't ask why in the beginning, but I should have. As it turns out, the producers had already worked out a deal for this show with Theodor Taylor. They'd even paid him an advance in the amount of seven million dollars."

Silence filled the room.

"I've since gathered additional information," Ava continued. "The advance money was wired to an account in the name of S. Frank Brewster. He was a carpenter who worked on the houses on Bond Street. S. Frank Brewster died last month, and his son, Tobias Brewster, has a Christmas tree farm just south of Temptation.

Tobias was kind enough to let me go through some of his father's papers, and I found email receipts of when Frank set up an account in Grand Cayman Island with 6.8 million dollars. The remaining money was reported as a fee to Frank from Theodor, and Tobias inherited it upon his father's death."

"I'll be damned," Gemma said, resting her elbows on the table and staring at the laptop screen.

"So Dad decided we were doing this show without conferring with us either," Gia said. "Ain't that something."

Gray shook his head. "It's something, all right."

Gage remained speechless. He'd said he didn't care about where the money had come from, but it was nice to finally hear about the money trail and receive the full story.

"When the executives came to me about the show, it was because upon Theodor's death, the signed contract they had became null and void. But they were out seven million dollars," Ava told them.

"So they needed you to come here and make it happen. They needed you to get the show on air because you'd done such a great job with *Doctor's Orders*," Morgan stated.

"And they knew that Gage had been working on the show with me," Ava said.

This time her voice—which Gage had been trying to convince himself he hadn't missed hearing—cracked a bit, and guilt settled into his chest like a pile of hot rocks.

"All of this was happening in LA," Harper said. "How did Millie find out?"

"I can explain that, too," Ava said. "My agent found out that Miranda Martinez, one of the actresses from *Doctor's Orders*, was sleeping with one of the execs at the network. She wanted to be involved in the reality show as a possible love interest."

Gage frowned at those words. He recalled Miranda's not-so-subtle advances when they'd been at the awards show.

Ava continued. "When they turned her down, Miranda threatened to leak the show idea to another network. To counter her threat, the execs hurried to release a preliminary announcement about the show to a few key press contacts. We assume someone from the press contacted Millie in the hopes of a background story about the town."

Gemma shook her head. "This is unbelievable," she said. "The things that go on in the world of television and celebrities."

Which was exactly why Gage had wanted nothing to do with this world. But hadn't he already been involved in the world? He was working on a television show, even as a consultant, and he'd been sleeping with a writer/producer.

"So what happens now?" Gen asked.

"I am no longer working with that network," Ava told them. "Their idea for the show and what I was willing to present to you were different. They weren't open to a compromise, and neither was I."

Gemma leaned over and pinched Gage's knee.

"Soon after I severed ties with the station, I went to Miami and met with Parker and Savian Donovan from Donovan Network Television. They asked about you, Gage," she said.

When all eyes fell on him, Gage looked down the table to Ava. She looked amazing in a black pantsuit and teal blouse. Her hair was pulled over to rest on one shoulder, and that spot he loved to kiss—the hollow of her neck—beckoned him. He cleared his throat.

"Why would they ask about me?"

"You met them when we were at the awards show, and they remembered," she replied.

"Oh, yeah. Right," Gage said, and after a pause continued. "What happened at the meeting?"

"I'm not sure if any of you have heard of them, but the Donovans are a very large and prestigious African American family. They have their hand in just about everything, from oil to television to casinos. Anyway, the Donovans are all about family first. So when Parker and Savian asked about Gage, I took that as a sign, and I pitched my revised idea for the Taylors of Temptation show. And they loved it!"

Gia squealed. "What's the revised idea?"

Ava explained the four-hour, two-night special and that they could decide which siblings appeared and how their story would be told. She talked about payment and contracts and negotiable points. She suggested, if they were considering it, that they should each get an agent or a lawyer to look over their contracts and advise them further of their rights before they commit.

And then she said, "I never meant to exploit any of

you, or what your parents went through. I was reluctant about even taking the job at first. But then I came to Temptation, and I saw Gray and Morgan and the kids. I met Harper and I listened to how she talked about Garrek and falling in love with him. I listened to Gage talk about your childhood and the things you lost because of the show. And I changed my mind. I didn't want to do anything that would hurt any of you. I should have told you all from the start, but I didn't know how."

She shook her head. "No. That's not true. I didn't want to. I didn't want my time with this family and with…" She paused, her gaze resting on Gage. "I didn't want any of it to end. So I pushed it off, and I worked on an idea that I thought would suit you better. But believe me, I understand completely if you don't want to take it. If you want to remain a family outside of the spotlight, I get it. I do, and I envy you for it."

"I'm in!" Gia yelled. "It'll be great exposure for my new restaurant."

"I think you're right," Gen added. "We could get some great advertising for our businesses out of this."

"I'm not sure what my schedule will be like," Garrek said. "But if you want to get in on the advertising possibilities, Harper, I'm okay with it."

Gage looked across the table to see Gray staring at him.

"Morgan and I have to talk about this," Gray said. "We're the only ones who have children involved, and I don't want to risk them in any way," he said.

Morgan reached out to take his hand. "We'll talk about it and figure out what works best for us."

Gemma smiled. "Well, I don't know. I've got a lot going on right now and…I just don't know."

Gage looked at his sister. He'd been wondering why she'd shown up in Temptation six weeks before their scheduled Christmas dinner, but he hadn't found a moment to ask her about it.

Conversation about the show and questions for Ava continued, but Gage didn't want to hear any of it. He'd heard enough and now…well, now he was right back to being unsure of what he should do or say. So he opted to leave instead.

He couldn't help it; he looked at Ava as he stood. She was in her element, talking about shows and episodes and advertising blocks. She was great at her job; that had never been a question to him. It was everything else. How she felt in his arms. How it felt to have her sleeping next to him, writhing beneath him, laughing beside him. All of that had been amazing and he'd fallen for it. Hard.

Now, he needed to figure out how to pick himself up again.

An hour later, Gage stepped out of the First Unity of Temptation Bank and looked up to the sky. That's where his mother was, and he wondered if she were looking down on him, curious as to what his next step would be. And if his father were in heaven, too, was he standing beside his wife—the woman Gage had once heard Theodor say was the love of his life—watching to see what their fifth-born child would do about his future at this moment?

Gage held the key his father had left for him in one hand, his cell phone in the other, and stood in the middle of the sidewalk on Crane Street for another few minutes. He looked up and down the street to the people moving about. The two male tourists who walked hand in hand looking into the window of a gift shop specializing in Lemil Mountain Lake memorabilia, and the grandfather across the street holding his young granddaughter's hand while they waited for the traffic light to change. Cars drove past, at a much slower speed than they traveled in New York, and the coffee shop just a few blocks down served coffee, sticky buns and much better conversation than the coffee place on the main level of Nancy Links Medical Center.

He smiled as he turned to walk toward where his car was parked, because in this moment Gage knew that he'd made the right decision. Although none of this had been part of his original plan, he felt with every fiber of his being that this was what his life was meant to be.

He drove for almost half an hour before parking his car on a grassy spot. He reached into his back pocket and pulled out the papers he'd retrieved from the safe-deposit box in the bank—the one that his special key had opened. He checked the address on the papers and then looked at his GPS. He had arrived at his destination, but there was nothing here.

Gage stepped out of the car and stuffed his keys into his pocket. He kept the papers in his hand, but rolled them up as he walked across the grass. There were acres of grass to one side, and to his delight, mountains on the other side. He continued to walk because he heard a familiar sound—the rustling of water over rocks and sand. The lake was about twenty miles ahead. Folding his arms over his chest, Gage stood and simply stared, enjoying the sight before him.

"Patsy and Jebediah Johnson built a house here sixty-two years ago," a woman said from behind.

Gage turned abruptly to see her standing there, wearing a long purple dress fringed in lace that looked as old as the years of which she'd spoken. Her gray hair was pulled up in a neat stack, pearl earrings at her ears that perfectly matched the color of the wool coat she wore. Her gloved hands were clasped in front of her while gray eyes stared directly at him.

"You don't remember me," she continued. "I'm JoEllen Camby, and I remember you very well. Patsy was beside herself with joy the moment she found out her daughter, Olivia, was pregnant. Teddy and Olivia had tried for so long, Jeb had begun to believe he'd never get grandchildren. But Patsy, oh, she was a praying woman. Yes indeed. She and I used to stay at the church long after Sunday service was over, and we'd go down to the altar and get on our knees. We prayed until times got better, yes, we did."

The woman talked with the old lyrical voice of someone who had seen and experienced a myriad of events, and nothing but her faith had brought her through. Her honey-brown skin was wrinkled and sagged a bit at the cheeks, but she stood straight and strong. She sounded wise and knowledgeable, and Gage was instantly captivated by her words.

"You and my grandmother prayed for the in vitro treatments to work," he stated.

"Yes, we sure did. Some silly folk in the church thought it wasn't godly, but we knew that the good Lord made a way for his faithful children. And if the only way Olivia and Teddy were going to have a baby was with the help of science, then so be it," Mrs. Camby said with a swift nod. "And, oh, when Teddy announced it at the town council meeting he was attending one night, we all cheered. We couldn't wait until the babies were born. Then those TV people came, and the devil went to work."

She shook her head then. "Olivia was unhappy after the first two years of the show. She wanted desperately to have her husband and her babies to herself. She cried to Patsy many a day, and Patsy walked up on my back porch or we came right out here to look at the water and talk about how such a happy time had gone sour so quickly. I thank the good Lord for taking Patsy and Jeb away from here in that fire, three years before their only daughter packed up her children and left town. But I still come out here from time to time."

Gage remembered his mother telling them about her parents and how they'd died. He also remembered talk of his great-grandfather, Patsy's father, who had offered his vacation home in Pensacola to Olivia and the children when she'd left. He'd lived until Gage and his siblings were fifteen.

"This is the land their house was on," he said after thinking on Mrs. Camby's words for a few seconds.

She nodded. "Yes. Right here. It was a great big ol'

house because Patsy had wanted more children, but that wasn't meant to be. The remnants of the house and the land fell to your mother after her parents died. So she could have repaired the house and moved you children here after what Teddy did to her. But I understand why she had to get away. Gossip can be unrelenting, especially in a town like Temptation."

"People have a hard time minding their own business," Gage said, thinking about Miranda and Millie.

"Ain't that the truth," Mrs. Camby said with a smile. "But this is your mother's land, free and clear."

Gage shook his head. "It's my land now," he said with a glib smile. "My mother apparently missed a tax payment at some point, and when the town would have foreclosed on it, my father bought it. And when he died," Gage said, holding up the hand with the rolled-up papers in it, "he left the land to me."

Mrs. Camby nodded and smiled. "Teddy loved himself some Olivia. I never believed he stopped loving her or his children."

"He just couldn't do right by her or us," Gage said drily.

"Every man can't make the right decision all the time. It's not natural," she told Gage. "You should know that for yourself. But if it's your land, you do with it as you please. Just don't forget the love that was here. That's what happens too many times to count—people forget about the love."

Gage didn't. He couldn't. And that's why he'd sent the text message to Ava before he'd left the bank.

For what seemed like a long stretch of time after Mrs.

Camby left him alone on the property, Gage heard a car stop and park. He looked out at the water, holding his breath and rehearsing the words in his head. He needed them to come out right, and he needed her to listen and to accept his apology, his heart and his soul.

Ava stepped out of the rental car and looked straight ahead to where Gage stood. His back was to her, but she had a feeling he knew she was there. Of course he should, since his text message had said for her to meet him here. She had only planned to stay in Temptation overnight, making herself available in case the Taylors had immediate questions about her offer. But she hadn't wanted to chance being here any longer because the memories were just too tough to ignore.

In the two weeks they'd been apart, Ava had used every ounce of strength she had to hold her head up and forge forward with her work. But there wasn't a moment in each day that she didn't think about him, about the brief time she'd been allowed the dream of what they could be together.

Seeing Gage earlier today had proven to her that the dream had fizzled and burned. He hadn't even wanted to look at her as she'd stood in his brother's house, and a part of her couldn't blame him. Another part was pissed with him for not at least hearing her out and then making an informed decision. And for not telling her about the woman who had broken his heart and his spirit. But that was beyond her control.

Walking toward him now was a bad idea—she sensed it, and yet she didn't pause.

"Thank you for coming," he said, when she finally stopped and stood silently beside him.

"You asked me to come because you had something to say. I wanted to give you the chance, even though you denied me the same," she said in a tone that she knew was frosty, but she couldn't help it.

He surprised her by replying, "I know. That's what I wanted to tell you, that I was an idiot."

"Oh," was all she could manage to say. "Well. Okay. Then I guess I'll get going."

Ava didn't know why exactly, but she hurriedly turned away to leave. Gage's hand on her arm stopped her.

"Don't," he said.

She glanced down to his hand and then up to him. He looked as good as she recalled. Not that it was logical to think that in fourteen days he would age fifty years, grow a potbelly and regret ever letting her go. That had been one of her thoughts when she was lying awake at night, cursing him for making her fall in love with him.

"Do you have something else to say?"

"I do," he told her. "But first, I've been thinking about this for the past two weeks."

"Thinking about wh—"

Her words were cut off when Gage pulled her to him, wrapping an arm tightly around her back to hold her there, and his lips crashed down over hers. The kiss was hot and rough, rugged and delicious. His tongue worked masterfully over hers, his hands moving over her back, down her arms and to cup her hips. She wrapped her arms around his neck because there was nothing else she'd rather do with them. Her palms flattened on the back of his head as she leaned into him and they took the kiss deeper.

"One perfect moment," Gage whispered when they finally broke apart.

He was breathing fast, and so was she.

"What?"

"This was the one perfect moment. Right here, in this place and at this time. It was the perfect moment to kiss you and to tell you that I'm madly in love with you. I want to spend the rest of my life with you," he said.

He was staring down at her so intently, and Ava was still trying to catch her breath. "Wait a minute. You told me to stay away from you and your family."

"And you didn't listen," he replied.

She nodded. "Yes. But you acted as if you wanted nothing else to do with me. And I kind of understood, because I lied."

"You should have trusted me enough to tell me what you were doing," he said.

She opened her mouth to speak again, but Gage kissed her once more. A slower kiss, but potent nonetheless.

"And I should have trusted you enough not to accuse you of being like Bethany. She's the woman I was involved with for two months, three years ago. I let her in and she lied and betrayed me. She killed my child, and while I get that it was her body and her decision, it was my child. I deserved to know."

"Yes," she said, her heart breaking at the memory of seeing him with Ryan, Emma, Jack and Lily. He was going to be a terrific father.

"You deserved to know," she continued.

"But you're nothing like her. And I should have trusted you enough to at least let you explain why you did what you did."

He took a breath and let it out quickly. "But it was easier and more familiar not to believe there was something good between us."

Ava sighed, because all the wind had been taken out of her sail. All the life that she'd thought she'd had in her had been washed away by this new feeling, this new opportunity for a life with Gage.

"I meant what I said, Gage. I never meant to hurt your or your family. I was just so focused on my work and proving myself to everyone. I love you and your family too much to ever intentionally hurt any of you," she said.

"Me," he said, lifting his fingers to run along the line of her jaw. "Right now, I just need you to say that you love me."

Her heart was thumping wildly in her chest. "I love you, Gage."

His smile and the warm hug that followed brought tears to her eyes as she thought about the fact that she never imagined she'd get to say those words to him.

"I want to build your tiny home right here in this spot so that when we're in Temptation we can look out at the lake, just like my grandparents used to do," he was saying.

Ava had pulled away from him and was now looking at him through eyes swimming in tears. "What did you just say?"

"We can set up a time to meet with Harper and her crew in the next few days, but I want to get started on the house relatively soon. And I want to marry you, Ava," Gage said.

"Wait, you're talking too fast and I can't keep up."

He chuckled. "Well, get out your notepad so you can take notes. I want to marry you. Not next year, but next month. All my family will be here for Christmas. What better time to start a new life with my beautiful new wife?"

"I don't know what to say," Ava managed as she used her hand to wipe away the tears.

Happy tears that she felt deep down in her soul. Tears that she shed for the love her parents had lost somewhere along the way, and for Theodor and Olivia Taylor, who had gotten swept away in the limelight and forfeited their love as a result. Between her and Gage, she felt all that love, all that hope, and wanted to reach out and grab it and hold on tight, just as her mother had advised.

"Say yes," he told her. "Say you'll marry me and we'll build this house and we'll live happily ever after, no matter what."

She was shaking her head as she cupped his face in her hands. "No matter what, Gage," she whispered. "I will love you and I will marry you and we will be happy together, no matter what."

* * * * *

THE PREGNANCY PROJECT

KAT CANTRELL

One

In one of life's great ironies, Dr. Dante Gates, PhD, had a chemistry problem he couldn't solve.

Not one single data point from his doctoral thesis had provided clues to this puzzle. Nothing he'd researched in the name of his hit TV show, *The Science of Seduction,* had revealed even a hint of an answer. Even the work he'd done on proving the effectiveness of quantum chemical models for protein analysis—which had nearly landed him a Nobel Prize—hadn't helped. And Dante was beyond frustrated by the lack of progress in unraveling this chemistry problem named Dr. Harper Livingston.

Dante and Harper had been friends for a decade. She was the standard by which he judged all other women. Which meant Dante spent a lot of energy being irritated that he could never find a woman as beautiful or as smart as Harper. She did it for him, in all the right ways.

Or *wrong* ways, more like. Because they were *friends*.

His relationship with Harper was the one constant in his life, the only thing he could count on. They had a sacred bond he valued, one he refused to disrupt.

Dante had pretty much convinced himself the only reason he had such a thing for Harper lay solely in her unavailability. Surely if they tried taking their relationship to the next level, it would be a dismal failure. Once he had a taste of that forbidden fruit, Harper would instantly lose her attractiveness. He'd never think of her *that way* again.

The problem was that once he'd started imagining just how delicious that fruit would be, he couldn't stop.

This morning, Harper had called to say she was at the Dallas airport, about to get on a plane and would be at his doorstep in two hours. She hadn't come to visit him in Los Angeles in the three years since he'd moved here. Something big was up. Seemed like the opportune time to solve his chemistry problem, one way or the other.

LAX was one screaming baby short of hell. Like always. Only Harper could drag him to the airport when he had no plans to fly. Dante checked his Breva watch, which featured an anemometer that he'd geeked out over even though he didn't sail. Harper's plane had landed ten minutes ago but no passengers had disembarked yet.

Finally, a stream of people carrying backpacks, pillows and water bottles burst through the gate. Dante leaned against the nearest post, arms crossed, to wait for the woman he'd come to collect.

Harper wasn't hard to spot. Her flame-red hair stood out from the crowd, and she carried herself differently from everyone else, barreling ahead with no fear. In Harper's world, hesitation was for losers. It was his favorite of her qualities.

She caught sight of him and instantly lit up with a

whole-face smile that whacked him in the gut with unexpected heat. Before he could process that, she dropped her bags and flung herself into his arms. Automatically, he balanced his weight to take on hers, snuggling her deep in his embrace, because holy God she felt good.

"Hey," he murmured into her hair, breathing it in.

Harper's perfume wound through his senses, infusing his blood with her essence. Which was not how perfume worked. At best, the scent should remind him of food and thus something his body needed to survive. It was supposed to smell nice, not make him want to kiss her until she couldn't breathe.

He ignored the heat. It wasn't easy, but he did have a lot of practice.

Harper—mercifully—pulled back enough that Dante didn't have to worry about her noticing the inappropriate stuff going on down below.

"What are you doing here?" she exclaimed as she drank him in with her bright gaze. "No one has picked me up at the gate since 9/11. I forgot how nice it is. How did you get past security without a plane ticket?"

He chuckled. "Simple. I bought one. Surprise."

Dante traveled so often for his job as a TV show host that he could always change the ticket later when he planned to actually use it. Or if not, so what? Harper was worth blowing a few hundred bucks over.

She socked him on the arm. "You didn't have to do that. But I love that you did. I thought you were filming today. I was totally expecting to take a cab."

And if she'd been anyone else, he'd have sent a car. Shrugging, he picked up her carry-on bag and shouldered it. "We finished early and now I'm off for two weeks, which I plan to spend with you. Perfect timing for an impromptu visit."

Perfect timing to figure out how to kill his attraction to her. Surely it would only take a kiss. One simple kiss, it would be weird and he'd be done. Back to being friends.

"Your girlfriend won't expect to spend time with you? The supermodel. What's her name?" Harper snapped her fingers a couple of times as if to jog her memory.

"Selena," he supplied. "Actually, we're not really an item anymore."

He'd lost interest in Selena as soon as he'd started seeing her, what, like six months ago? But it was good for his career to be photographed with her, and the sex wasn't terrible, so he'd held on much longer than he should have. She was a sweet girl in a long line of sweet girls who developed instant Vacant Eye when Dante dared throw X-ray crystallography or self-synthesizing materials into conversation. Harper was the only woman he'd ever been able to talk to about anything and everything.

"That's too bad. I'm sorry. But I'm sure it's for the best since there's no way she was good enough for you." Harper grinned. "Oh, I forgot to tell you. Cass is pregnant."

"That's fantastic," he said and meant it. Babies were great. For other people.

Harper and Cass had been friends a long time, since college, when they'd devised a plan to open a company together, along with two other friends, Alex and Trinity. Fyra Cosmetics had thus been born and Harper had made a place for herself as the chief science officer. He was so proud of what she'd accomplished since getting her doctorate in analytical chemistry. Dante had known all four ladies for a decade, but as he had the most in common with Harper he'd naturally become closest to the redhead.

"Gage is making a big deal out of it." Harper sighed dramatically and rolled her eyes. "As husbands go, he's perfect for Cass. But I would shoot him if he treated me the way he does her. 'You're working too much,' he says. 'Let me take care of you.' And my favorite, 'You might be craving potato chips, but you need to crave vegetables.' Men. Like they know anything about pregnancy."

Dante couldn't imagine a woman as fierce as Cass letting Gage railroad her. "His heart is in the right place. How is Alex doing, speaking of pregnancy?"

"Much better now that she's further into her second trimester. No more morning sickness."

He hadn't realized so much of what was happening with Harper's friends revolved around babies. The whole subject made him vaguely uncomfortable, no doubt because of his own history. Sure, people started out wanting kids, but no one could know that they'd still want one next year, or the year after that. After being shuttled from home to home as a foster kid, Dante knew that fickleness firsthand.

Dante guided Harper toward baggage claim. She laced her fingers with his and held his hand as they walked, chatting about her friends and business partners.

It was companionable. Or at least that was probably how *she* viewed it.

Dante had a burning awareness of her that was only heightened by the glow radiating from Harper's face. That glow was new. Where had that come from? He adjusted his trademark horn-rimmed glasses with his other hand, but the corona didn't fade. Why the hell was she so much more beautiful today, of all days?

He might have to get to that kiss sooner rather than later, or this whole trip would slide into disaster.

"Did you have a good flight?" he asked.

Harper pushed her soft, red curls behind her shoulders and nodded. "Not bad. But the vending machine by my gate at DFW didn't have any Reese's Peanut Butter Cups and that's the only thing I want. I'm starving."

"Come on." He pulled her into a newsstand shop and scouted until he found the candy in question, picked up the entire box from the shelf and handed it to the clerk along with his American Express.

"Dante!" Harper laughed. "I just wanted one, not twenty. You'll have me looking like a blimp if you keep that up."

The cashier did a double take as she zeroed in on Dante's face, then she glanced at the credit card, her eyes rounding. "Dr. Gates! I'm a huge fan of your show. Please, can I get a picture with you?"

She held out her phone, because of course the answer was yes. Fans were part of the gig, and as the producers of *The Science of Seduction* funneled millions of dollars into Dante's bank account to host it, he couldn't really complain. But secretly, he hated nearly everything about the show.

Money was nice, he could not deny it, but he missed *real* science. The kind that made a difference in the way people understood the known universe. Helping a guy hook up didn't amount to a whole lot in the grand scheme of things, no matter how good Dante was at his job. Science had long been his refuge when the rest of the world didn't care, yet he'd abandoned his roots for sensationalism.

He let the cashier fawn over him as much as she wanted because fans had made him a celebrity, and he did not take that for granted. Harper watched with no small amount of amusement.

Finally, he extracted himself from the cashier and the newsstand, handing Harper the bag of candy. "Sorry about that. Comes with the territory."

With a snort, Harper grinned. "Are you kidding? That was awesome. I rarely get a chance to see you being Dr. Sexy. Due compensation for losing your attention."

He matched her grin. "I have to live up to my tag line."

Dr. Dante Gates Brings Sexy To Science. That line had graced magazine covers, promo for his show, you name it. Never in a million years would Dante have assumed that agreeing to host a show about how to use science to attract a lover would mean he'd become the poster boy. Of course, he *had* positioned himself as an expert in the subject. He should have realized women would come out of the woodwork to beg him to test his theories on them.

The attention flattered him. At first. He was only human. The field research alone made the women worth his time, and he'd long ago acknowledged that being abandoned by his birth mom to foster care had created a craving for acceptance and connection. It wasn't a crime. The real travesty was that not one of the truly inventive and quite beautiful women had eclipsed his attraction to Harper.

Because she was the only one he couldn't have. Probably.

Harper rolled her eyes as they arrived at the baggage claim area for her flight. "You don't need to appear shirtless in a dish soap commercial to be sexy, silly. Your brain is the most attractive thing about you."

Something about her smile caught him sideways and he nearly did a double take. He'd let her reference to Dr.

Sexy roll off because…well, that was part of his TV persona. But now this. Was she *flirting* with him?

Interesting. Had these nuances been there before and had he missed them in his struggle to keep his thoughts about Harper in the friend zone?

After all, she'd just admitted she found him attractive, which he liked far more than he should. What if she'd been shooting him subtle signals this whole time, hoping he'd make a move? She probably thought he was blind. This impromptu trip to LA might have been solely designed to correct his vision.

With that in mind, he guided her to a secluded spot in the very back of baggage claim, between two dark, locked offices. The milling people around them were focused on the stationary carousel, which meant he had Harper all to himself for a few minutes. At least until luggage started arriving.

"Hey, in case you've forgotten, scientists are not known for their six-packs," he murmured and leaned in, eliminating the space between them. "I worked hard to put on muscle after spending so many years hunched over pages of equations. If someone wants to pay me to take my shirt off, I'm not going to say no."

All this talk of shedding clothes had set off serious sparks. Did she feel them, too?

She blinked as she looked up at him, her smile slipping a touch. Her tongue darted out to drag across her lips and he followed it pointedly with his gaze, then shifted back to her eyes. The heat in her cheeks mirrored the flare in his gut as he let the moment drag out.

Would wonders never cease? She *was* feeling it.

Maybe she'd clued in that he was a hot property. Not that he'd let any of his press go to his head. But come on. Women flocked to him. Empirical evidence suggested there was something about his spiky brown hair, horn-rimmed glasses and fit body that they liked.

It was way past time to get his inconvenient attraction to Harper worked out. If he'd read her wrong, they'd laugh about it and go on. He'd prove there was nothing here other than a healthy appreciation for a great woman. The electricity in the atmosphere and the heightened sense of anticipation was nothing more than the product of his imagination.

Without taking his gaze from hers, he reached out and traced the line of her jaw. Not as a friend. Not companionably. But with intent.

"What are you doing?" she asked as a line appeared between her brows. "This isn't... I mean—we're not..."

"Haven't you ever been curious?" he interjected smoothly. "About what it would be like between us?"

"Be like? What *what* would be like?" Her eyes widened as his meaning must have registered.

There was still time to backpedal if taking things up a notch ended up being the worst idea ever conceived, but that window of opportunity rapidly shrank the longer they stood here in this blanket of awareness.

"I've thought about it. A lot," he continued, since she hadn't pulled away and hadn't fled in horror. "No time like the present to find out."

Before logic could kick in and remind him of all the reasons this could go south, he sank his hands into Harper's soft red curls, spread his fingers across the back of her head and tipped it up. Slowly—because he wanted to give his body plenty of time to soak in the lesson to be learned here—he lowered his lips to Harper's and claimed them in a sweet kiss.

Which instantly caught fire. Heat erupted where

they'd joined, sensitizing him, claiming him. Harper flowed through him, waking up his blood.

And that's when he realized his mistake—one kiss and all he'd proven was that he was *not* done. Not even close.

Dante was kissing her.

Shock opened Harper's mouth without her permission and he took it as an invitation, swirling his tongue forward to find hers and *oh, my God*.

The sensations overwhelmed her and all she could do was cling to his shoulders. She'd meant to push him away. She didn't do this, not with Dante, not with any man. And then she wasn't pushing him away because *wow*.

The chemical reactions firing off inside her body were fascinating, amazing. Unprecedented. She wanted more. That was the most shocking thing of all because normally she avoided this sort of contact.

Her lips tingled as he reshaped them. Little pulls in her abdomen increased the urgency and she leaned into him, her hands drifting from his shoulders to his back. Hard. Strong. He felt good under her palms and she dipped lower, eliciting a groan from deep in his chest. It vibrated her own, teasing her breasts, and that's when she realized their torsos were touching.

That sculpted chest was pressed up against hers. Dante was kissing her and she was kissing him. *In the airport.* Oh, God. This was all wrong. What was she doing?

She sprang back, wrenching away, and he followed for a half second until he realized she'd stopped. Hugging the wall behind her and legs shaking, she stared at the man who had been her best friend for a decade. "I'm sorry."

His big brown eyes watched her from behind his horn-rimmed glasses, which sat slightly askew. Her fingers flexed to fix them automatically, as she'd done a hundred times. But she didn't.

"For what? I'm the one who kissed you."

Yes, he had. For God's sake, why?

Some better questions were why she'd kissed him back. Why it hadn't felt weird. Why her body felt like it had been twisted in a knot and dipped in a volcano. Why of all men, Dante had jump-started her sex drive.

The problem was, Harper knew exactly why. How was she supposed to explain that she'd completely overreacted due to an influx of hormones that her body didn't know what to do with? That she'd hopped on a plane to share the most exciting news of her life with her friend?

Somehow, she hadn't envisioned blurting out *I'm pregnant* in response to being kissed by the man she'd come to for support.

"I'm the one who didn't stop you," she said instead.

"No. You didn't."

When he didn't ask how come she hadn't, the swirl of uncertainty under her skin pulled the response from her throat anyway. "I was…curious. But please, don't take that the wrong way."

He already had, she could tell. Dante wasn't inexperienced, not like she was, and he'd noted how much she'd liked kissing him. It was a surprise to her, too—she hadn't been kissed in years and even then, it had been a horrible experience, never to be repeated.

This kiss…it had been the stuff of teenage dreams and an R-rated movie all rolled up in one. Because Dr. Harper Livingston's body reacted to conception by suddenly craving the touch of a man. Apparently. What was she supposed to do with that—ask him to kiss her again?

"How could I possibly take that the wrong way?" he asked.

She was botching this and if she didn't fix it, she'd lose everything important to her. "It can't happen again. Dante, I need you. As a friend. Please don't change anything."

God, this was all backward. The results of the four positive pregnancy tests she'd taken that morning weren't the only reason she'd hopped on a plane to LA. Her career had imploded over Fyra's decision to develop a product that required FDA approval, and she really wished she'd known that snafu was coming *before* she'd visited a fertility clinic.

On the brink of both professional and personal disaster, she'd run to the one person who had always been there for her, who was one-hundred percent on her side... only to smack headlong into something she had no context for.

A foreign expression popped onto his face. "Harper. I wanted to kiss you. Surely you realize there's something new happening between us—"

"No!" Her lungs hitched and somehow, a lone tear squeezed out before she could catch it. "Nothing new. I need everything to be exactly the same as it's been. You're so important to me. As a *friend*."

Friends had each other's backs. Friends were there through thick and thin and she needed the promise of knowing she had that in him. That he'd be the way she'd thought of him every day for the last ten years. Until this one. She'd responded so readily to his experimental kiss that he'd gotten the wrong message.

His eyes narrowed behind his glasses. She knew that look. He was about to argue with her and she could not do this right now.

With a strained smile, she touched his arm, like she'd done for years and years, before thinking better of it. "Let's just forget about it for now. Would you mind getting my bags?"

Ever the gentleman despite the tense circumstances, Dante firmed his mouth and did as she asked, then ushered her into a sleek, red Ferrari. The silence laced with weirdness settled heavily in the car, nearly choking her, as they hurtled down the freeway toward his home in the Hollywood Hills. She scarcely enjoyed the unfolding LA scenery, but what could she say to get everything back to where it was supposed to be?

Dante rolled the Ferrari to a stop at a gated drive, then pointed a clicker at the black wrought-iron gate. It opened, allowing him to drive onto his lush, expansive property, where he parked on the circular drive in front of the sprawling Spanish villa. All without uttering a word.

Which lasted only until they cleared the doorstep. He dropped her bags on the Mexican tile under their feet in the spacious foyer and faced her, brows lowered. "We've been friends a long time. Why would that change just because we're exploring what else might work between us?"

"Because I don't want to do anything more," she burst out. "All of this scares me."

How could she get through the problems at Fyra, pregnancy, birth—good grief, the next eighteen years with a kid—if she didn't have the friendship that had carried her through the last ten years?

"Come here."

Before she could blink, he whirled her into a deep hug, the kind she'd welcomed so many times in the past, but it was different now as his strong body aligned with hers.

So different. The tease of his torso against hers set off tingles in places that shouldn't be *tingling* over Dante. She tore away, devastated that she couldn't stay in the circle of his embrace, devastated that things had already changed without her consent.

Hurt sprang into his big brown eyes but he banked it and crossed his arms. "So now I can't hug you?"

"Sure you can, if you drop twenty pounds of muscle," she shot back before realizing how that sounded. Quickly, she amended, "I want things like they were before you turned into Dr. Sexy."

And that wasn't much better as explanations went. He'd been Dr. Sexy for a long time—what she really meant was before she'd become aware of it. But he had her all flustered.

A brief smile lifted his lips. "I thought you liked that side of me."

She did. That was the problem.

Dante was one of the few friends she had left who was still the same as he'd always been—she'd *thought*. She didn't make friends easily. Cass and Alex, two of the three women she'd built Fyra Cosmetics with, had moved on to new phases in their lives, marrying great men and starting families. Which was amazing, and she didn't begrudge them their happiness. But Harper felt… left behind.

Which was why she'd decided to have a baby of her own. But minus the husband, who would expect things of Harper she couldn't fathom giving. Intimacy. Control. A promise of everlasting romantic love that no one could guarantee because it was nothing more than a series of confusing chemical signals in the brain.

Men complicated everything.

"How many friends do I have, Dante? Should be easy for you to count them. No advanced degree required to get to four." She ticked them off on her fingers. "Cass. Alex. Trinity. You. Now imagine that two of those friends have recently gotten married and started families. Everything's changing around me and I can't stop it. I need you to stay the same."

Because she was the one who had already changed things, the one who had gone off and gotten pregnant, and by default, Dante had to be the constant in this equation.

Understanding dawned in his eyes. "You're scared of things changing."

"I'm pretty sure that's what I just said."

Instead of backing off, he leaned in and captured her arms, holding her in place. "You did. I'm just catching up. So it's not that you mind the idea of me kissing you. You're just scared of losing our relationship. But I don't want to lose it, either."

Those melty chocolate eyes speared hers, and all at once, she didn't like the way he was looking at her, as if she held the secrets to his universe. Except he'd always looked at her like that and she'd explained it away as affection between friends. But now that he'd veered completely off the friendship track, it made her uncomfortably aware that he'd just had his mouth on her in a very non-friendly way.

"You're practicing selective hearing." She shook her head and tried to back up a step so she could breathe. And pick up her luggage, so she could…do something with it. "I do mind the idea of kissing. And everything that goes along with it. Or comes after it."

"Everything?" he murmured and somehow she was still in his arms. "You mean sex?"

Heat leaped into his expression and that was so much worse than the melty eyes because her body flared to life at the promise of feeling the way it had when he'd kissed her. *More. Now.*

"Yes." She squeezed her eyes shut, groaning. "I mean, *no*. No sex. Geez, what is this conversation we're having? I came here to visit my *friend*. How did we start talking about sex?"

"You brought it up," he reminded her needlessly. "I was just trying to clarify."

"Sex is not a part of this conversation."

"What if I want it to be?" he countered softly and his fingers slid up her arms to grasp her shoulders. "Your hearing is bordering on selective too if you can so easily ignore what I've been trying to tell you."

Caught, she stared at him, taking in his familiar horn-rimmed glasses and spiky hair, desperate to get back to a place where she could be secure in her relationship with him. "What are you trying to tell me?"

"Our friendship is the most important thing in my life. That's why I'm trying to save it. I can't unkiss you. There's something here that isn't going away until we explore it. Harper…" He drew out her name reverently and the sound sang through her suddenly taut body. "Kiss me again. Think of it as an experiment. Let's see how far this thing goes, so we can deal with it, once and for all."

Her eyelids slammed shut because *holy mother of God*. "That's a hell of gauntlet to throw down."

"Tell me no and I'll step away."

"No." Instantly, his hands moved from her arms and his heat vanished. She opened her eyes to see him standing a few feet away, his expression hooded and implacable.

"Can I at least know what your major objections are? In case there's something—"

"I'm pregnant, Dante." She didn't know whether to laugh or cry. "And that's only the first in a long line of objections."

Two

All of the blood in Dante's brain drained out. "You're... what?" he whispered.

"Pregnant," she repeated and the word still sounded like *pregnant*.

"With a baby?"

"Science has not yet successfully crossed human DNA with any other species, so yeah," she confirmed darkly. "I didn't want to tell you this way but you gave me no choice."

Blindly, he stuck out a hand and sought the nearest hard surface to sink onto. Happened to be an end table in the adjacent living area but so what? His knees wouldn't have held up much longer.

"I don't understand how this happened. Are you seeing someone?"

There was no way. Not as eagerly as she'd responded to his touch. Not as close as he'd have sworn they were. She'd have said something about a man in her life.

Wouldn't she? He thought back to the last time she'd mentioned a guy—all the way back in college.

She shook her head. "No. Artificial insemination."

"Why in the world would you do something like that?" He bit off the syllables, not bothering to temper the harshness.

Babies needed a family. A father. She'd deliberately set herself up to be a single parent. It was inexcusable.

Her face froze as she took in his expression. "I wasn't interested in sharing parenting duties with anyone long-term. So a donor who was willing to sign away his rights seemed ideal."

This got better and better. Or worse and worse, more likely. He laughed without humor. "Most people have a life partner they decide to have kids with. Because they're in love and want to raise a family together. Did that ever enter your thought process?"

"Not once." She tossed her red hair. "A romantic relationship would only complicate everything."

"A baby needs a male influence," he insisted. "That's not an opinion. Study after study shows—"

"I know that, Dante!" Hands on her hips, she towered over him as he perched on the end table. "Why do you think I said I needed you, you big moron? That's why I'm here. I want *you* to be the male influence. Dummy me, I thought our friendship was strong enough to add a baby and then you had to go and kiss me."

Dumbfounded, he blinked. "Did you think to ask me about this before you got pregnant?"

Because he would have talked her out of it if she had. This was the most ridiculous idea she'd ever heard.

"It's my life and my body," she announced as guilt flashed through her expression.

She must have guessed he might react like this, because she knew his history, knew how he felt about kids. And had done it anyway. "You know anonymous donors don't always tell the truth about their medical history on those questionnaires. There's no telling what kind of genetic mess you've created in there."

He jerked his head toward her abdomen. She had a baby in her womb and it was suddenly a sacred place, not available for desecrating with the kind of activities he'd had in mind mere minutes ago.

He'd actually been strategizing on how to get her back into his arms so they could finish that kiss. How else would he exorcise his attraction to her? What small taste of her he'd been granted had thus far only whetted his appetite for the main course. Hers, too, obviously, despite her denial.

Dante was an expert after all. She wanted him as much as the reverse was true.

But she was already shaking her head. "That's why the donor wasn't anonymous. I did a lot of research into this before I made my decision and I carefully selected my baby's father. Dr. Cardoza is the perfect—"

"Dr. Cardoza? Dr. Tomas Cardoza is your baby's father?" Red stained Dante's vision, his hands curling and uncurling as he fought to keep from unleashing his frustration on the drywall.

"He's a renowned chemist," she explained as if he might be confused about Cardoza's contribution to the planet.

"I know," Dante somehow got out through clenched teeth. "If you recall, he's the reason I didn't win the Nobel."

Harper's eyes widened. "Well, yeah. But that was ages ago. Surely you're over that, especially given that you've moved into another field."

He couldn't help it. The laugh bubbled out and he pinched off his glasses to wipe his eyes. Of all the people she could have fathered a baby with, she'd picked Cardoza, the sorriest excuse for a human being that ever walked the earth, and that included Dante's parents, whoever they were.

No. He wasn't *over it*. Cardoza was the reason Dante had been forced into TV. If Cardoza hadn't cheated on his methodology, he'd never have won the Nobel and Dante would have at least had a fair shot. After Cardoza had won, all the interest in Dante's research had dried up, leaving him lab-less, fundless and desperate for someone to give him a new opportunity.

The Science of Seduction had been born.

Of course, it had been lucrative beyond his wildest fantasies. But a nine-figure bank account didn't make up for having his long-held scientific goals stolen out from under him.

"Just out of curiosity," he said once he thought he could talk without betraying the wash of emotion beating at his breastbone. "How did you manage to pick Cardoza?"

Of all freaking people.

"Oh. I ran into Tomas at a convention recently. The thing I told you about in St. Louis? He was presenting a paper and I loved his conclusions. When I saw him later in the hotel lobby, I introduced myself and we got to talking."

"Got chummy, did you?" Dante practically sneered. *Tomas.* Like they were all friends here.

"Sure, he's a brilliant man. Great cheekbones. His genetics were the main reason I became interested in him."

Something black bloomed in Dante's chest. "He hit on you."

"What? No. Well, okay, yeah, I guess if you count the fact that he asked if I'd consider getting pregnant the old-fashioned way 'hitting on me.'" she accompanied her words with air quotes, oblivious to the way Dante's stomach had lost its lining. "Then I guess he did."

Dante massaged the ice pick that had formed between his eyes. "Please, for the love of God, tell me you said no."

She scowled. "Of course I said no. I have no interest in that kind of relationship with any man."

Relief flooded his chest so fast, he almost saw stars. The thought of Cardoza putting his filthy paws on Harper—he swallowed the bile. Thankfully, she'd handed the horrible man his hat.

With anyone else, this would be the point when he'd ask if she meant that she preferred women. But he'd felt her reaction when he'd held her in his arms.

She was straight, 100 percent. "No interest in any man except me, you mean."

"Uh, no. Not with you, either," she corrected. "Haven't you been listening?"

Oh, he'd heard every word, much to his chagrin. "You're interested, Harper. You're so interested you can't stand it."

The way she'd curled into him when he'd kissed her, the thrill of her eagerly offered tongue against his—he'd be reliving that in need-soaked dreams tonight. She was interested. And not happy about it, clearly, as her reaction to the kiss had prompted this little game of true confessions.

Pregnant. As mood killers went, that one took the cake.

"I don't know when you developed that industrial-sized ego," she said primly. "But it can go anytime."

"Please." He snorted. "Lie to yourself, but you can't lie to me. Not when my mouth was on yours. I could feel your interest clear to my bones."

Not ego talking. Okay, maybe a little, because it did warm him up plenty, even now, to recall how fervently she'd responded. She'd thrown herself into the kiss, no holds barred, like she did everything, practically climbing into his pants while he kissed her, and he'd have let her.

The attraction between them was mutual. Whether she liked it or not.

A blush worked its way across her cheeks. "That's just hormones."

That got a chuckle out of him. "Yeah. That is generally the way it works, or have you forgotten everything you learned in college?"

To his surprise, she sank onto the couch and buried her head in her hands. Her shoulders started shaking and that's when his bad mood vanished in favor of the mood he should have had all along—concern for the woman he cared about.

He wedged in next to her on the couch and gathered her into his arms, holding her without a word because what would he say? He'd already ruined her big announcement, one she'd only made under duress because he'd been pushing her past her comfort zone.

In another shocker, she relaxed into his embrace and it almost felt like normal. Sure, the smell of her hair crossed his eyes like it always did, but he'd been ignoring the physical pull of Harper for a long time. He could buck up for his friend, who'd spelled out her need for him in no uncertain terms.

"I'm sorry," he murmured into her hair and she nodded. "I just don't understand. Why a baby? And via artificial insemination to boot?"

"I told you," she mumbled against his shirt. "Romance is not my thing. It's all a bunch of chemical reactions that people mistake as an emotion greeting card companies tell you is love. Then those reactions stop and what are you left with? My way is so much easier."

The arguments against all the mistakes in her theory bubbled to the surface and he almost started firing back facts from the hours and hours of research he'd done into the chemistry between people, but he cut it off at the last second. She didn't need his opinion, professional or personal. Not right this moment. Not when she'd already made the decision.

"Congrats, regardless." He bit back the rest of that, too. Foster care had colored his view of people who had children and the various ways they ended up making the kid's life hell. Until he could be objective about Harper's baby, he'd shut up. "For the record, those chemical reactions come with a hell of a kick."

"I wouldn't know," she said, her voice so muffled he almost didn't hear her.

All at once, the subtext whacked him over the head and he realized she wasn't talking solely about love. "You're still a virgin?"

Pieces of this puzzle started falling into place at a rapid clip. She'd confessed as much one night back in college, but he'd assumed that somewhere along the way she'd—but then, she'd probably have told him if she had. Idiot.

She froze. "I've been busy getting a doctorate and then building Fyra's product line from the ground up. Who had time?"

His head fell back against the couch and he stared at

the ceiling. Some doctor of seduction he was. He'd totally missed the most important aspect of the dynamic at work here.

Harper was scared of what he'd made her feel. He'd tied up a normally fearless woman in knots because she'd never been properly introduced to the pleasures between a man and a woman. That was a travesty of the highest order.

And a blessing. His resolve solidified. Dante had been gifted an amazing opportunity to be her first. Then he'd finally have one up on Cardoza, that was for sure, and he wasn't going to apologize for being smug over it. He and Harper could burn off their attraction, get back to being friends, and go on. Win-win in his book.

"It doesn't change anything," she said defensively. "I'm still pregnant and I still need your support, regardless of your opinions about my choice of donor or methods of impregnation. I can't do this alone. Can I count on you to be my *friend*? To be there for me?"

The realities of the situation crashed down on him. His best friend was pregnant with the offspring of his most hated rival and all he could think about was claiming Harper in some kind of testosterone-filled territory grab.

She knew him well enough to hone in on his biggest conflicts, but naming it and claiming it didn't change his views on babies. If he said he supported her, he had to do it. Keeping his word meant something to him. This friendship meant something to him. He had to put his money where his mouth was.

"Of course you can count on me."

And she could. But he wasn't going to back away from the attraction between them. Instead of scaring him off, she'd inexplicably created a challenge he couldn't ignore.

He wanted her. Perhaps even more now than he had before, thanks to her confessions.

New plan. Nothing but a full-bore seduction would do, and he had an undeniable urge to put every ounce of his energy into verifying the strategies he promoted on his TV show actually worked. Even on a woman who'd never had a lover before. Even on a friend. A *pregnant* friend. Was he an expert or not?

Dante had the next two weeks to find out.

Dante's sprawling home in the Hollywood Hills had enormous charm and Harper loved it. A housekeeper showed her to the guest suite, pointing out the kitchen, the dining room, the back terrace with the multilevel swimming pool on the way.

Wow. Harper craned her neck as the housekeeper breezed past the triple set of French doors overlooking the pool. Cerulean water rippled in the sunlight, and beyond the bougainvillea and palmetto palms camouflaging the wrought-iron fence around Dante's property, Los Angeles unfurled at the base of the hills, urban and busy, but stunning despite the layer of smog.

Dr. Gates had done very well for himself.

Heavy exposed beams stained the color of triple-strength espresso held up the high ceiling in the breezeway to the back of the house. The housekeeper opened one of the doors and stepped back. Harper blinked at the lavish sitting area off to one side, complete with a flat-screen TV. A large mission-style bed had been placed opposite the sitting area. What a beautiful room.

"The bathroom is through those doors," the housekeeper pointed with a polite smile. "You need anything, you let me know. I'm Mrs. Ortiz, and my daughter, Ana Sophia, cooks for Mr. Dante. No request too small or too big. We live in the old coach house near the gate, and Juan, my husband, keeps the grounds."

"Oh, okay." Dante had servants. More than one. Had any of them overheard the conversation in the foyer earlier? Harper shut her eyes for a beat. Too late now. Would have been nice for Dante to warn her that they weren't necessarily alone as she went around blabbing about personal stuff.

But then, he'd apparently decided to make blindsiding her a habit. She didn't especially care for it.

"Thanks, Mrs. Ortiz," Harper said as graciously as she could. It wasn't this nice lady's fault her boss had gone slightly off the deep end.

The housekeeper nodded and closed the door behind her as she left. Harper spent a few minutes unpacking but it didn't take nearly long enough to settle her trembling insides.

After that fiasco of a kiss had forced her to drop the pregnancy bomb, Dante had melted away, presumably to give her time to settle in, but probably more to give them both breathing room. Or was she the only who'd needed it?

Before she'd gotten on a plane to LA, her relationship with Dante had made sense. Her feelings for him were uncomplicated, easy and eternal, unlike what would inevitably happen in a romantic relationship. That was why she'd never entertained the slightest notion of having one with any man, let alone one she liked as much as Dante. Friendship had so much to recommend itself.

Until Dante had flipped everything upside down by kissing her.

What could she do to get back to the place where she had her friend by her side, holding her hand through this new adventure?

Because she needed him. Badly.

Pregnancy was freaking her out.

She was scared she'd made the wrong decision. Scared that she'd picked the wrong time, given that her career might be in the toilet. Scared that she'd failed to cross some *T* when dealing with the legal aspects of using a donor. She'd never second-guessed a decision like this and the only thing she wanted to do was crawl under a blanket, let Dante stroke her hair and tell her everything was going to be okay.

That was all wrong. She'd wanted pregnancy to be a happy experience. One that would create a new bond with Alex and Cass, who were also new mothers or soon-to-be, and strengthen the bond she had with Dante because of course he would be her baby's favorite…uncle-like person.

She hoped.

The look on his face when she'd said, *I'm pregnant…* she never wanted to see that again. But the shock coloring his expression replayed in her mind on an endless loop. Apparently she'd miscalculated how he'd feel about it, but she couldn't figure out if he was upset because she hadn't consulted him or because he still had residual bitterness over losing the Nobel Prize. Or both.

There was every possibility that despite claiming he'd be there for her, Dante might change his mind. He might end up not wanting anything to do with her baby. That would be devastating.

Angst was killing her. What had happened to her usual logic and reason? *Poof.* Add a baby and suddenly she was a mess.

She changed out of her plane suit and slipped on an unstructured sundress with spaghetti straps that she'd bought in anticipation of an expanding waistline. Wishful thinking, since she hadn't confirmed her pregnancy until this morning.

None of this heated introspection would resolve the open issue—how to get back to normal. Harper worked best with absolutes and only Dante could give her those.

Get the data, formulate the problem and then solve it.

Her relationship with Dante was going to be the same today as it was yesterday, or she'd die trying to keep it that way. She refused to let either the baby or the kiss put a wedge between them, not when so many other things were out of her control. The FDA rejection being exhibit A.

Determined, she wandered through the open floor plan toward the kitchen in hopes of finding Dante and a cup of hot tea, and not necessarily in that order.

"Called it in one," she murmured as she caught sight of his dark head bent over something.

She walked in and skirted the island. Dante glanced up.

His gaze softened behind his lenses, instantly turning his gorgeous eyes the color of melted chocolate. If he looked at other women like that, it was no wonder they were tripping over themselves to get to him.

Which was a totally uncomfortable thought, all at once. *Did* he look at other women like that, with that same blend of concern and affection? And why would she care? She didn't. Dante was her friend and he could look at a woman any way he chose.

Except her. Definitely he could not look at her like that.

"I was just about to make a pot of tea," he said as if nothing had changed.

Nothing *had* changed, she reminded herself sternly. He'd kissed her in some sort of misguided notion that there was something between them. She'd disabused him of that notion, and it was over. "That would be great."

She cleared the squawk from her throat and wished the tension could be so easily dispelled.

Tea was one of their shared passions, one she cherished. When Dante came to Dallas, he always picked up a fresh bag of Gyokuro Imperial Green Tea—her favorite—from the Teavana shop at DFW airport and they drank it on the patio of her condo, which overlooked Victory Park. She loved their ritual more for the conversation and easiness than the tea, though it only took the barest whiff of the scent to make her mouth water.

He handed her a press pot and nodded to the loose-leaf tea in a container printed with Chinese symbols, which sat on the counter near his elbow. "I'll boil the water if you scoop the tea."

The familiar rhythm soothed her, and she moved around both the kitchen and the man with more ease than she would have expected. Maybe the weirdness was all on her. If she acted like everything was cool, it would be.

Tea made, they took their mugs onto the lanai that overlooked the lush pool and outdoor kitchen. Dante settled onto a cozy love seat and patted the next cushion, which she gratefully sank onto.

"Your house is beautiful," she commented. "Why did it take me so long to visit?"

"A fair question." He nodded once. "And the answer is?"

"Busy." Her gaze drifted back to the landscape as she searched for the truth. "Fyra's been a mess lately and Cass and Alex have had personal things going on. Leaves me and Trinity to hold the seams together."

Regardless, Dante had always made time to come visit her. She'd written it off as a function of his insane travel schedule; of course it was easier for him to pop into Dallas. It was one of the major US airport hubs.

In that moment, with every nook and cranny of their relationship under a microscope, it felt…wrong. Unbalanced.

"Why did you come this time?" he asked quietly, and it was the opening she'd been looking for.

"I took my first pregnancy test this morning," she admitted and forced herself to go on, no matter how uncomfortable the subject. Because regardless of what he'd said earlier, it still felt like an elephant in the room that they had to work through. "And then I took the next three."

Surprisingly, he flashed a smile. "Because four gives you better odds of getting an accurate result."

"You know me so well," she joked automatically, but when his jaw tightened, she wished she hadn't said it.

"I'm hoping to learn more," he returned cryptically. "How did it feel? When you saw that it was positive?"

So many things had flooded her chest in that instant. How did she catalogue them for someone else—and a man at that? "The clearest sense of awe. Glee. Accomplishment."

She'd picked the right donor, clearly, since the procedure had worked the first time. Of course she had. She'd done extensive research into genetics, legalities, odds—and Dr. Tomas Cardoza had been the obvious choice. Tomas had two doctorates, impressive Spanish ancestry and dark skin that would hopefully guarantee her child wouldn't have to slather on as much sunscreen as its Irish mother. He'd agreed to be her donor, including signing away any paternal rights, and that was that.

Somehow, she didn't think Dante would appreciate those details.

"I hate this." She set her mug down and swiveled to

face him, one leg bent underneath her. "I feel like I'm walking on eggshells, like I have to watch what I say or it'll start another fight."

He cocked his head. "*Another* fight? We're not fighting. Are we?"

"Well…yeah. Earlier. When I told you I was pregnant. That was a fight." Wasn't it? He'd been so angry and disappointed in her.

"It was a conversation," he corrected and set his own mug down in favor of taking her hand, holding it tight as he caught her gaze. "About something going on in your life. I didn't handle it well. You surprised me, that's all. But I care about you and want to know everything. It's not okay that you think you have to hold one single thing back."

Warmth spread across her palm, feathering outward. She stared at Dante and all at once, he morphed back into the man she'd loved for ten years. And then the warmth climbed into her chest as he smiled at her. It was so normal—and such a relief—she nearly wept.

Except she was changing things. That was really her biggest fear, that she'd irrevocably damaged their relationship by getting pregnant. She and Dante told each other chemistry jokes and talked about quantum mechanics, not diapers and breastfeeding.

She centered herself with a string of biofeedback techniques. Everything was going to be okay.

"Then I want to start over. Dante, I'm pregnant."

His eyebrows shot up in mock surprise, bless him. "That's fantastic news. Congratulations. I can't wait to meet the little version of you swimming around in there."

And that, against all odds, made the whole thing *real*.

She had a life growing in her womb. A baby. One that would be hers and hers alone, who would be a brilliant addition to the world of science from an early age. She would raise him or her with all the best educational opportunities and be this baby's everything, since she'd be a single parent.

That was when the panic started.

It was a baby. A helpless tiny thing who couldn't communicate its needs. She'd have to figure it out. By herself. The flutter behind her breastbone grew nearly audible. And then she realized that was the sound of her heightened pulse thundering in her ears.

Breathe. And again. She'd wanted it this way. Love between mother and child was absolute. Preordained. There was no potential for error, like there was when romance entered the picture, confusing everything with signals her brain couldn't interpret. Thus, this baby would fill a need in her life that no man could ever hope to. She'd never be lonely again, yearning for something she couldn't quite put a name to.

Plus, it would solidify her place among her business partners who valued the institution of motherhood. Or at least Alex and Cass did. Trinity had and always would march to the beat of her own drum, but regardless, she and Harper had long agreed about the value of a permanent man in their lives—zero.

Except this one. She squeezed Dante's hand and swallowed. "I'm scared."

"What? Why?" Clearly puzzled, he tucked a lock of hair behind her ear and smoothed it back, exactly as she'd envisioned he would when she admitted her fears. "You're the most capable woman I've ever met. You've got this, hands down."

"There's some…other stuff going on. Fyra is in trouble."

"What's going on?" he asked softly. "Whatever it is, we'll deal with it."

The thick bands around her chest loosened. She'd come to LA precisely because Dante was the one person in her life she could turn to. If she could just talk about it, maybe a plan would come to her, some way to haul herself out of the professional hole she'd fallen into. Then the pregnancy decision wouldn't seem so…ill-timed.

"Something happened with Fyra's FDA approval for Formula-47," she blurted out. A sudden burning behind her eyes mortified her. She never cried. Was this how it was going to be then? Emotions out the wazoo around the clock?

"What? Tell me," he demanded instantly.

Formula-47 had been her first baby, conceived and crafted in her lab with one sole purpose—to heal scars and wrinkles better than plastic surgery because it used revolutionary nanotechnology that she'd developed. It was brilliant. And it might never see the light of day.

No. She would fix it.

She took a deep breath. "Phillip—Senator Edgewood—you know how I told you he was helping us grease the FDA wheels in Washington?"

"Sure, because you're releasing your first product that requires FDA approval. I remember."

"The committee suspended the request."

It was nearly the worst moment of her life to hear those words come out of Phillip's mouth. The process should have been easy. Submit an application for approval for Formula-47, which she'd poured two years of her life into perfecting, give the committee a tour of the lab, explain her formulary methodology, send samples and research. Done. Approval to sell the formula as a product would be in the bag.

Nothing had gone according to plan.

"What?" Dante's expression mirrored the righteous

indignation of his tone. "Why would they suspend the request?"

"They had questions about my samples. And my lab."

The expletive Dante muttered made her smile.

"Your methods are beyond reproach," he groused. "How dare they question anything about your lab."

She couldn't help but revel in his unconditional support, which was precisely what she'd come for. None of her partners really understood what the allegations had meant to her professionally. Personally.

Dante got it. Understood instantly why the whole thing felt like someone had driven a railroad spike through her gut.

"There's more. I think the questions cropped up because someone deliberately sabotaged the samples." Even uttering that heinous suspicion aloud nearly caused her stomach to revolt.

Because that was the bottom line. She had a traitor in her lab. *Her lab*. Her sanctuary.

Until she got that sorted out, she was afraid she'd never fully embrace or enjoy the next nine months.

Three

Dante smoothed Harper's hair back again because she was still trembling and that needed to stop. She didn't have to know that her hair felt like satin under his fingertips and thus the soothing motion benefited them both.

"Sabotage," he repeated and scowled. "That's not cool. Who do you think it is?"

"I don't know."

She shook her head against his palm and he feathered a thumb across her temple, which shouldn't feel so intimate, not in the midst of her crisis. But he couldn't help the fact that step one in his seduction plan included getting Harper relaxed with him again.

She was upset. She needed him. Which naturally led to him comforting her and *voila*. Here they were, holding hands on a small love seat. His fingers toyed with her hair. They were a couple of millimeters shy of an embrace. One small sway forward and he'd have easy access to her lush mouth.

But he didn't move. Not yet. Step one wasn't complete. He couldn't execute step two until he got her good and over her freak-out from the first time he'd kissed her. His mistake had been assuming one kiss was all it would take, and then they'd go back to normal, with his attraction to Harper easily handled and resolved.

Episode twenty-six of his show had been dedicated to that exact phenomenon. The mind played tricks on you sometimes, leading you to believe you had chemistry with a person, when in fact, the moment you locked lips, it became apparent there was nothing there. That's why he'd thought it was best to get that part established immediately, especially since he'd been seventy-five percent sure the attraction between them only existed because of another very well-documented phenomenon—the allure of look-but-you-can't-touch.

Hadn't worked anything close to how he'd hypothesized.

And the whole game had changed with the addition of Cardoza, Harper's pregnancy and her virgin state. A mere kiss wasn't going to cut it. He wanted it all. And had no issue whatsoever with working for it.

They could go back to being just friends later. After he'd introduced her to the pleasures to be had when a man took his time with a proper seduction. After they'd burned out this spark. After he'd had the opportunity to revel in the fact that he might not have bested Cardoza at winning the Nobel, but he'd sure as hell beaten him in all the ways that counted.

"This FDA mess sucks," he said simply. "What can I do?"

"You're already doing it."

She sighed with a little smile, oblivious to the way her chest rose and fell under her dress. She'd changed into a flirty number that dipped between her breasts, cradling them provocatively. It wasn't even all that low-cut, but it didn't matter. On her, it was sexy.

Off her, it would be epic.

"How about if I do something that actually solves the problem?" he growled because he couldn't keep the awareness from his voice. "I'll come with you back to Dallas and we'll tackle this together."

It was perfect. So much so that he couldn't quite believe this opportunity had fallen into his lap. He'd have every excuse to spend night and day by her side, just the two of them in a place that turned them both on—a chemistry lab—and then he'd swoop in at the eleventh hour to solve all her problems. He'd be the hero, short only of the white horse as he rode to her rescue.

Harper was both a virgin and a scientist. He couldn't use run-of-the-mill strategies to get her into his bed and have any hope of success. As seduction plans went, this one was killer.

Harper's eyes widened. "I can't ask you to do that."

"You didn't. I volunteered. I have two weeks off from filming and nothing planned. Do you have the option to give the FDA new samples?"

Nodding, she bit her lip, her sharp mind clearly working through the idea. "But it's a lot of work and my job, not yours. I have to fix this."

She wasn't connecting the dots fast enough. The idea of getting his hands on a real test tube made him nearly giddy. When was the last time he'd gotten dirty with the periodic table? Ages.

Harper and chemistry at the same time? He could not think of anything he'd enjoy more unless it involved her spread naked on the lab worktable, beakers shoved aside and forgotten, as he pleasured her with his mouth until she screamed his name.

Okay, that image had to go or he'd blow this carefully planned seduction.

"You're pregnant, scared and said you needed my support," he pointed out. "What better way can I support you than this? Let me help you create the new samples. I want to. It'll be fun, not work."

In response, she closed the gap between them, throwing herself deep into his arms in enthusiastic agreement.

His body reacted instantly, hardening in places she would surely notice in about two seconds since she'd nearly climbed into his lap. An erection the size of Minneapolis was impossible to hide.

"I thought I wasn't allowed to hug you anymore," he muttered darkly.

She stiffened and pulled back. *Idiot.* That's what he got for opening his big mouth, but holy God, what was he supposed to do when she was clinging to him like Saran Wrap and smelled like something he wanted to take a bite out of?

"Sorry, I got carried away in my gratitude."

Cursing inwardly, he willed back the rush of heat and grimaced. With any luck, it might look like a smile if she squinted. "I like hugging you. I was just—"

Enormously turned on. Gauging whether I could actually feel your nipples through your dress. Thinking about how seriously hot that kiss was.

He should quit while he was behind. Step one in his seduction plan did not include alienating Harper, confusing her or making a move too soon. She needed time and space to acclimate to him again or step two would die a nasty death.

Seduction was a science, not an art. There was no room for missteps.

Dante cleared his throat. "I'll call my assistant in the morning to book me on your return flight. No arguments. We're in this together."

Her tremulous smile went a long way toward smoothing over his blunder.

"Thanks. You have no idea what this means to me. I finally feel like I'm back on track."

That made one of them. But the genuine relief radiating from her expression warmed him. Not as well as her body had mere moments ago. But nicely enough. Because he did care about her and wanted to help. It was just a really awesome coincidence that the problems in her lab so neatly coincided with his agenda.

"I'm excited." She clapped like a five-year-old presented with a birthday cake. "We haven't spent two whole weeks together in…forever."

"Not since college." And even then, they hadn't been under the same roof. Living in the same dorm, sure. But the dynamic had been completely different back then. He'd attended college on an academic scholarship and every grade counted. The hours he'd spent with Harper had most often happened at the library or in the computer lab. Studying.

"Ooooh, we'll get to relive our glory days. It'll be just like it was back then."

"You mean when we had to exist on ramen noodles and four hours of sleep a night?" He grinned, only half kidding. "Speak for yourself, but I much prefer being able to afford a steak anytime I want it."

And this time around, he had a much better idea how to get this woman into his bed. He'd had his share of girlfriends in college, mostly due to simple things he'd never have dreamed would be such chick magnets: manners, an old-fashioned insistence that a man should pay for dinner and zero interest in sports.

Harper had always eluded him, though he'd felt a buzz the very first time he'd laid eyes on her.

"I *loved* college. Remember the spring break when neither of us could go home because we'd grossly underestimated the reaction of that substrate to the graphene?" She touched his arm enthusiastically, lost in her story. "We had to do the whole experiment over again and the project was due in like a week and a half. I was so panicked but you were Mr. Calm."

"I remember," he murmured, but not the same way she did, obviously.

Dante hadn't gone home for spring break ever. Or Christmas, summer break, random weekends. Because his foster home hadn't been a *home*, it had merely been where the people who'd agreed to raise him lived, and when he walked out the door at eighteen, he'd never returned. He'd loved college, too, but only because it gave him somewhere to go, somewhere to succeed. A place to belong.

A friend in Harper Livingston.

"Those were the days. We didn't have much, but we had each other." She smiled fondly, and his own return smile bloomed automatically.

Harper had been the first person in his life to really care about him, what he thought, whether he was eating well. He'd conveniently forgotten all of that in the heat of the moment, focusing so hard on how to get to the next step with her that he'd lost sight of why Harper had stayed so firmly in the friend zone all these years.

He needed her, too, as the one stable relationship he'd ever had. The only person who had ever demonstrated what it meant to value one another. It was the closest thing to love he'd ever felt.

Was he confusing that with attraction?

Guilt and agitation squeezed his chest and he didn't like it. There was a reason they called him Dr. Sexy instead of Dr. Emotional Expert. Physical chemistry he understood, very well. The psychology of the unquantifiable feelings between people, not so much.

If he succeeded with seducing Harper and got her naked and breathless, would that screw up their bond?

No, surely not. They were both adults and neither of them had much use for the emotional part. It was one of the many reasons they were still friends after all these years. They had a lot in common. The squiggle in his chest was nothing more than a reminder that he had a stake in ensuring nothing ever affected their friendship, even sex. Especially not sex. He'd keep one hand on the ripcord and shut down his seduction campaign if even a hint of a complication reared its ugly head.

Harper slid a cool hand up his arm to squeeze his shoulder, leaning in to kiss his cheek. Somehow, he managed to mask the sound of his lungs strangling over a breath as he fought to keep from turning his head to capture her lips with his.

"I'm so glad I jumped on a plane," she said brightly, thankfully clueless to the mayhem happening on his side of the wicker love seat.

He should be thrilled. Clearly, she was back to being relaxed around him. Step one could be labeled a rousing victory, *rousing* being the operative word. Unfortunately, step two promised to be more of the same since the goal would be to make her aware of the spark between them. So she could act on it when *she* was ready.

"Let me take you to dinner," he returned hoarsely.

He had to get some traction on step two before he lost the lone speck of sanity he had left.

Harper spent an inordinate amount of time dressing for dinner, taking a hot shower to wash the airport from her skin, then using the enormous three-way mirror to carefully apply a spate of cosmetics that she'd personally had a hand in developing. A swipe of Prague Sunset lipstick finished off the look.

The results sang, if she did say so herself.

She stepped into a dress the shade of cotton candy, which should have competed with her hair, but didn't because Harper had a near-savant ability to mix color. It was what made her exceptional at her job.

She had a healthy appreciation for how chemistry improved a woman's natural assets. She'd built a career on it. Only to see the culmination of her dreams screech to a halt due to tainted lab samples. And for the first time in a month, she finally felt hopeful about the future of Fyra. Dante was going to help her fix the problems and the FDA would approve the new samples. Simple.

That more than anything had dissolved the weird tension between her and Dante. He'd brightened at the thought of helping her and honestly, it sounded like fun to her, too.

Her stomach rumbled. She hadn't eaten lunch and after the…fiasco at baggage claim, the Reese's Peanut Butter Cups had lost their appeal. Dinner sounded like exactly what the doctor ordered.

She went in search of Dante through the labyrinth of halls in his enormous home, wandering toward the sound of running water. Being unfamiliar with Dante's house, she didn't realize it emanated from his shower until she was already in the doorway of his bedroom.

She raised a hand to knock just as he strode from the adjoining bathroom, bare chested, towel draped over his lower half. The terry cloth had settled low on his lean hips, almost to the point of indecency. But the uncovered part was enough to set off all sorts of bells and whistles in her head.

And other places.

A brilliant green dragon tattoo spread over his left shoulder, spiraling down around his upper bicep, accentuating sinewy muscles that she'd never seen before, but had certainly felt. His torso had turned sleek and brown, as if he'd spent time in the sun, and crisp hair lay against his chest in a trail leading to the stuff underneath the towel.

Her mouth went dry and her legs locked. Her brain might have melted, too. Or she wouldn't have stood there staring as he caught sight of her and grinned, totally unaffected by his state of undress.

"Hey," he said and casually pushed his glasses higher on his nose, as if she'd seen him wearing nothing but a towel a dozen or more times.

Because she had, especially in college when they'd lived in the same dorm with a communal bathroom. But that was before he'd filled out so much. Before he'd decorated his skin with something as…*sexy* as a tattoo. Before she'd deliberately introduced a plethora of hormones to her body that obviously rendered her stupid and prone to being affected by the sight of Dante's bare chest.

Before he'd kissed her and she'd felt all those muscles pressed up against her.

A blush prickled her cheeks and she spun, turning her back to the half-naked man that she couldn't reconcile with the one she'd known for years and years. Things were supposed to be back to normal. The *same*. What had happened to her sweet, slightly banal feelings toward her friend?

God, she'd always thought of Dante as sexy in a sort of detached way because of course he was good-looking. *Sexy.* It was just a word, but all at once, the root of the meaning became painfully clear because there was nothing *detached* about what was happening to her body.

"Harper. Are you okay?"

His voice washed across her skin as he called out from behind her. He'd said her name before. Lots of times. Using that same voice he'd always had. And yet it was not the same *at all*.

It was deeper, with more color. Was he also remembering that kiss that should be forgotten but clearly couldn't be removed from her memory? Was *he* thinking about how it would feel to try that kiss again while he wore nothing but a towel?

Oh, God. He was wearing nothing but a towel. Awareness raised goose bumps on her bare arms and sent a sharp pull through her abdomen. What the hell?

She'd hunted him down. Served her right for coming upon him in his bedroom going about his business. Naked.

"What's the matter?" He'd come up behind her and settled one hand on her shoulder.

She nearly yelped as his palm burned her skin. Why had she picked a strapless dress?

If she stepped away, wiggled out from under his touch, did anything other than stand there, she'd tip him off that she was midfantasy about turning around so she could get evidence about whether the second kiss would feel like the first.

Because protesting about wanting things between them to stay the same wasn't necessarily the same as protesting the kiss itself. Though she might have presented it that way. It was entirely too...*wrong* to be thinking about kissing him.

Didn't make the image fade.

"Nothing. I just...um, didn't know you were, ah..." *Naked. In your bedroom. Tattooed.* "Sorry. Your door was open and—"

Her throat seized. What was wrong with her? This was *Dante*. They'd gotten back to normal. No more crazy talk about "something between them," which she planned to deny had a grain of truth.

Hormones, hormones, hormones. She was stronger than her body's chemicals.

"Yeah. If I had anything to hide, I would have closed the door." He sounded amused. At her. Because she was being silly by refusing to look at him, like that would change the hyperawareness of his state, so of course he'd gotten a good laugh out of it.

"You should. Close the door," she amended lamely. "Now that you look like that."

"Like what?"

Oh, God. Somehow she was supposed to explain that he'd gotten her all flustered and confused, and then come right out and admit that he'd elicited a physical reaction from her? She barely understood it herself. There was no way she could explain it to him, not even with a dictionary and a copy of *Human Sexual Response* with notes in the margin written by Masters and Johnson themselves.

"Like *that*."

Twirling her fingers in the air didn't knock loose any good phrases from her brain to describe the sight of a man any other woman would have called hot, gorgeous or delicious. But not her. Because it was Dante. They were buds, intellectual equals, platonic. She shouldn't think of him as someone to be ogled. *Shouldn't*. But that didn't make it stop. He was a finely built man aesthetically speaking, and no one could possibly argue with that.

Could he tell? She shut her eyes as her mortification grew. Did he at this very moment realize that she'd developed an awareness of how sexy he was? This could *not* be happening.

"You, um…have a tattoo now," she explained.

Yes. Stick with the facts. Do not mention the riot of hormones that had exploded all over their friendship. *How* would she brazen this out with someone who knew her so well he could practically read her mind?

"I got it a few months ago. I generally try to keep it covered because it's mostly for me, not public consumption. Do you hate it?" His voice rumbled in her ear as he stuck his arm out, presumably so she could review it again before answering. "They edited it out of the dish soap commercial because they said it was too fierce for their target demographic."

She eyed the dragon from her peripheral vision. Wrong. The tattoo added to his appeal, but she'd take that notion to the grave, especially since any further discussion of that subject would mean she'd have to come clean about how she'd never watched his shirtless commercial. It seemed silly to objectify a man to sell dish soap, but now that she'd gotten an eyeful of the goods, it was a wonder the company hadn't developed an instant shortage of the product.

"I don't hate it," she mumbled.

"Then what's up?"

She needed space. Air. Distance. Before she uttered another word, she had to get back on an even keel or she'd ruin everything by admitting he might have a point about dealing with this…whatever it was between them that had cropped up out of nowhere.

She didn't want to deal with it. She wanted it to go away so she could work with him in her lab and not be constantly reminded of how his mouth felt on hers.

And that was only in the next two weeks. What about all the weeks after that, when she panicked about the baby, or being a mother, or some other unknown? Dante was her center, her constant, and there was nothing about this situation that felt the slightest bit *centered*.

"Nothing," she squawked. "Jet lag maybe. I probably need to go to bed. By *myself*. I mean, not that you were thinking I meant with you—"

Oh, God. *Shut up*.

"Dinner," she corrected hastily. "I need dinner. Let me know when you're not naked."

She fled. Pregnancy had completely and thoroughly scrambled her genius-IQ brain.

Four

The first thing Harper did when she got back to work on Monday was call an emergency meeting with Fyra's C-suite. And then she spent twenty minutes in the bathroom of the company she'd helped build from scratch puking her guts out.

Seemed as if her body had finally figured out she was pregnant. Better it happen here than at Dante's den of temptation. Of course the flight back to Dallas hadn't been much of a reprieve, either. The wide first-class seat should have been comfortable enough for her to relax, allowing her to catch up on some much-needed sleep, but the stewardess had recognized Dante zero-point-four seconds after takeoff.

Honestly, Harper had been shocked the woman's shameless giggle hadn't jump-started a precursor to the yak-fest currently going on. Dante had been just as shameless, flirting outrageously and calling her Candy like they were…intimate.

To be fair, the stewardess's name tag had prominently displayed her name. But Dante didn't have to say it with that hint of wicked in his voice, like he wanted to lick her in order to find out if she tasted as sweet as her name.

It didn't matter. Or rather it *shouldn't* matter. The fact that it bothered her—then and now—was yet another problem Harper did not want to deal with.

Finally, she got her faculties somewhat stable and freshened her makeup while sucking on a peppermint that succeeded in settling her stomach quite well. No mystery. It was a time-honored remedy for pregnant women. Harper had done extensive research on all the stages of pregnancy so she would have a handle on what to expect.

Unlike the suspension of Fyra's FDA approval for Formula-47. That was not something she could quantify or gather enough data to explain. Her business partners needed to know that Harper had it under control. That she had a plan and had brought in expert reinforcements to help.

She left Dante in her office with a terse, "Be right back," and pretended like it was easy to keep her mind off the image of what he looked like naked.

She ducked out of her office before he could comment, and hightailed it through the beautifully appointed halls of Fyra. Purple, the company's signature color, graced nearly every surface and matched their packaging perfectly. Fyra, the Swedish word for four, had been a dream for so long…and someone wanted to undermine all their hard work. That wasn't going to happen.

When Harper arrived in the conference room, Cass Branson, the chic-as-hell CEO of Fyra, already had a virtual meeting session up and running on the large flat-screen TV. The face of Fyra's CFO, Alex Edgewood—beautiful even in a T-shirt and wearing no makeup—filled the screen and she smiled as Harper came in view of the webcam. Alex lived in Washington, DC, with her husband, a US senator, and only came into the office a few days a month.

A second later, Fyra's chief marketing officer, Trinity Forrester, rushed into the room, a volcano in Versace who couldn't spell the word tranquil with a dictionary.

"Am I late?" she asked breathlessly, though it was clear they hadn't started yet. "I was on a call with our Facebook rep, hashing out some ad placement."

"No problem." Since she'd called everyone here and the next steps in the FDA approval process belonged to her, Harper should be the one to lead the meeting.

Except all at once, as Harper glanced around the table at her three friends, her throat closed and right on schedule, her eyes turned into faucets.

"What's wrong?" Cass rounded the table instead of taking a seat at the head like she always did.

"Sorry," Harper gasped and fumbled for a tissue from the box in the center of the table. "I don't know what's wrong with me."

"You're stressed about the FDA fiasco?" Trinity suggested mildly. "You're working too many hours a week in compensation? Jet lag? Take your pick."

Harper pressed the tissue to her eyes, thankful at least that the smudge-proof mascara she'd developed as part of Fyra's premiere product line allowed her to cry without fear of looking like a raccoon. Small victories.

"I don't think so." Alex, sharp and analytical even from over a thousand miles away, zeroed in on Harper's face. "Do you have something you'd like to tell us?"

Oh, God. Really? Was the fact that Dante had kissed her bleeding out of her pores or something? Could everyone tell that she had a near-constant hyperawareness of the man who had been her friend for a decade? Her brain was officially fried.

Mortified, Harper sank down in her swivel chair a quarter of an inch and blurted out the first distraction she could think of. "I'm pregnant."

"I knew it!" Alex exclaimed over the sounds of Cass and Trinity absorbing that news with their own comments. "I couldn't figure out why you'd suddenly developed an interest in taking me to the doctor, asking all those questions about what it felt like to be pregnant. Congratulations."

Cass hugged Harper and then pulled back to peer into her eyes, warmth in her gaze. "How far along are you? If you need a rec for an obstetrician, mine is wonderful. I'm seeing Alex's doctor, Dr. Dean. I'll text you her number."

"Not far enough along to have a doctor picked out," Harper returned, absurdly grateful no one had jumped on the third-degree bandwagon, like Dante had. She had a list of doctors a mile long, of course, but why spend a few hours sorting through all that data when she could trust Cass's recommendation?

Trinity raised a brow. "Is no one else's jaw on the floor besides mine? Come on, ladies. This is huge news. Who did you finally do the deed with, honey? Because if you say anyone other than Dante, I'm going to be really disappointed."

Harper blinked. It sounded an awful lot like Trinity had expected Harper to confess not only that she'd lost her virginity, but that Dante had fathered her baby.

"What are you babbling about? Dante and I are *friends*," Harper stressed vehemently. "I got a sperm donor."

Trinity shot back a mock gag that set her dark angular bob in motion. "Are you kidding me? The only fun part about getting pregnant is sex and you denied yourself that? You're certifiable. Especially when you've got a man who looks like Dr. Gates at your disposal."

"Thanks for the support." Harper scowled. Dante was not at her disposal. "Some of us don't think of sex as a recreational sport, and I would never compromise my friendship with Dante to that degree."

That was a mantra she should stick to. If she repeated it a thousand more times, maybe her stupid hormones would finally get the message that Dante was off-limits.

How dare he put her in this position with that stupid kiss. This was all his fault.

"Too bad." Trinity waggled her brows. "I bet Dr. Sexy has some smooth moves. If I had to pick someone to be my first all over again, that man would be at the top of the list."

"Can we stop talking about my sex life?" Or lack thereof, which her friends well knew was by design. Harper appealed to Cass with a pointed plea. "We have much more important things to discuss."

"Like why Dr. Gates is hanging out in your office, maybe?" Cass suggested brightly. "I wasn't expecting you to bring him home with you when you announced last week that you were taking a personal day to fly to LA."

"Yes, exactly." Relieved to be back on track, Harper cleared her throat. "When I told him I suspected sabotage, he volunteered to help me create new samples. Really, it's a great plan. We don't know how the original samples were tainted, but odds are good our culprit is in the lab."

It still baffled her. The lab was sacred, the place where

the magic happened. Who hated her enough to desecrate the samples designed to take Fyra to the next level?

"So Dr. Gates will act as an expert consultant," Alex supplied and Harper nodded gratefully. "I'm in favor of having an independent third party involved. I'll run it by Phillip, but I think the FDA committee will view it as a good step toward resolving the issues with our lab."

Issues with our lab. The very concept threatened to bring on another round of toilet-hugging. But in reality, harsh or not, the FDA committee didn't care if the original samples weren't the ones Harper had intended to submit, that someone had switched them, or tampered with them. All they knew was that Fyra had presented the samples as products of Harper's lab and they were not acceptable. So there must be a problem with Harper. As she held the title of chief science officer, they were right.

Everyone looked at Cass. The four women shared equal stake in Fyra, but as the CEO, Cass had the final say. She nodded. "Let us know if Phillip has a problem with Dr. Gates's credentials."

"What?" Harper nearly came out of her seat. "What's wrong with Dante's credentials? He's a respected scientist with a doctorate from the same university I went to. Plus, he's not Dr. Gates," she mimicked in a sing-song voice. "Like he's some random guy with letters after his name. You've all known him for years and years."

"He's certainly qualified but he does bring a level of… celebrity that may dampen the enthusiasm of the FDA committee." Cass smiled to soften the message. "And of course this is not a reflection of our personal feelings toward Dante. I'm glad he's here for you."

Harper huffed out an uncomplimentary grumble but having seen firsthand how women fawned over Dr. Sexy, she really couldn't argue. "Fine. But since he's already here, I'm going to show him around the lab and get him acclimated. I have to produce new samples, regardless."

Trinity leaned forward, a crafty glint in her eye. "I think you guys are being too by the book. The only question here is whether we advertise the fact that Harper outsourced creation of the samples to a TV show host." She shrugged. "Who cares how they were produced? Let Harper and Dante play around in the lab. Who has to know?"

"I would know," Cass countered. "We still haven't caught the person who leaked the existence of Formula-47 to the industry."

As reminders went, it was a harsh one, especially since the leak had happened several months ago, starting a cascade of problems that had ended with the tainted samples. Harper had a fairly decent hunch that responsibility for both lay with the same culprit.

And it was someone under her own nose.

"That's why Dante is so critical," Harper threw in. "Because I can't let anyone else get their hands on these samples. He stays, no matter what."

She needed him for moral support, regardless. Her other friends had their own lives—hence the reason she'd decided to have a baby in the first place. Once Cass turned off the television, Alex's image would fade and she'd be inaccessible to Harper. Oh, yeah, they could text and call. Email. But it wasn't the same.

Gage lived in Austin, which meant Cass spent all of her extra time traveling back and forth from Dallas to spend time with her husband and their son from Gage's previous relationship. Trinity—well, she and Harper had never liked the same things, and now that Harper was pregnant, she didn't expect their friendship to get tighter.

Dante was her constant, and she couldn't begin to say how much it meant to her that he'd volunteered for this project. Her righteous indignation over his audacity in kissing her faded. A little. And then a little more. He'd only been trying an experiment. She was the one who'd blown it out of proportion.

As long as she could keep her mind off that kiss, and on the job at hand, everything would be great.

"That's a fair point." Cass stood, effectively ending the meeting because she probably had a million other things on her agenda. "Just keep in mind that the leak could just as likely spill the beans about Dante's presence here. We need to be aboveboard. In everything. Especially now. But I don't have a problem with giving him special temporary clearance to the lab. Ask Melinda to get him a guest badge."

Harper nodded and beelined it to the receptionist's desk before anyone got started on that third degree. The last thing she wanted to discuss was her pregnancy, or rather the reasons she'd elected to have one.

But as she rounded the door of her office, newly minted badge in hand, Dante glanced up from his laptop, his eyes turning that melty chocolate that threatened to liquefy her panties right off her body. What was *wrong* with her?

Correction. The last thing she wanted to discuss was why Trinity had zeroed in on Dante as the man most likely to pop Harper's cherry. Because she feared she'd done a terrible job of hiding the fact that her body had other ideas about what was appropriate behavior between friends.

And if she couldn't hide it from Trinity, she sure as hell wouldn't be able to hide it from Dante. Especially not in the confines of one very small chemistry lab. Well, she'd have to figure it out. They had work to do.

Harper's lab reflected the organized, thorough style Dante had always associated with the woman. Clean white counters, modern cabinetry and cutting-edge equipment invited him to dive in.

Science—real science—went on here and his heart should be leaping for joy over that alone.

Too bad he could scarcely keep his attention on the tour Harper was dragging him through. Who cared where she kept the disposable pipettes when step two had gone well enough that all he could think about was how quickly they could get to step three in his seduction campaign?

The only experiment he could fathom conducting right now involved his mouth, Harper's body and a hypothesis that she would taste better than the ripe peach she smelled like. Only a round of rigorous testing could prove that theory and he was fully prepared to go the distance. In the name of science, of course.

"Dante?" Harper paused in her recitation of the raw materials available in that particular cabinet, one eyebrow arched. "Am I going too fast? You seem a little distracted."

"It's the thrill of being in the lab again," he improvised smoothly. It would not do to get ahead of himself.

The problem was that step three involved a very intricate series of rational arguments designed to lead Harper to the conclusion that she wanted to take things to the next level.

But he didn't want to talk. He wanted action. Progress—and Harper wanted to show him where Fyra stored talc and deionized water. *Distracted* might be an understatement.

Harper smiled. "I'm glad you're thrilled. I wasn't sure if you'd volunteered for this solely to help me, or because you had a burning desire to do some rudimentary chemistry again."

"Both." He grinned back and wondered if it would be out of line to admit he was an enormous fan of Harper in white. Her long coat hid all her curves, but it made him yearn to strip her out of it. "Spending time with you in a lab is my idea of nirvana."

"I'm not kidding about the rudimentary part." She wrinkled her nose. "I'm almost embarrassed at how simplistic some of the formulas are. Someone with your advanced abilities will most likely find all of this…boring."

That hit him right where it counted. When was the last time someone thought of him as a serious scientist—and an advanced one at that? A big wave of Harper spread through his chest, warming him with equal parts affection and something the opposite of friendly.

Given the fact that every nerve in his body was poised to execute his slightest command—as long as the action involved yanking Harper into his arms—boring was not the description he'd have chosen. "It's been a while since I've picked up a test tube. Entry-level chemistry is right up my alley."

And hers. The parallel didn't escape him. Harper still had a ways to go before she'd be comfortable with a man's hands on her skin. Entry-level chemistry all the way around.

He wanted her to enjoy the experience, to have fun. To be unafraid to do anything she so desired. Losing her virginity was a big thing and he loved the thought of being the one to make it great for her.

A few staff members buzzed their IDs and entered the lab, chatting. All three women skidded to a halt when they caught sight of Harper and her guest.

"Good morning, Dr. Livingston," they recited, all three pairs of eyes on him, not the lady in question, likely calculating whether they could fawn over a celebrity in front of their boss.

She waved them over with the tiniest eye roll. "Dr. Gates loves selfies, so don't be shy."

Of course this would be the one time she'd cater to his ridiculous craving for acceptance. Any other day, he'd welcome a vigorous chat with fans. But not when he had an incredibly long and difficult step three to wade through. And a semi hard-on. Long lab coats that hid a man's boner, for the win.

The three lab techs took their sweet time gushing about how much they loved *The Science of Seduction*, throwing out twenty-dollar words to make sure Dante understood they liked it from an intellectual level as well as a practical level. While he appreciated that fans gleaned great tips from his show, he still didn't quite get what about *him* they found so compelling.

Or maybe he was still stuck on why everyone else in the world couldn't get enough of Dante when the woman at his side held him at arm's length, despite knowing very well that she'd been as affected by that almost-naked scene outside his bedroom door as he had. He'd half thought they might skate right through step two and pick up step three right there in the hallway. But she'd taken off instead of responding to the spark.

Patience is a virtue, he reminded himself.

By the time the lab techs had posted pictures of themselves and Dante on their social media accounts and drifted off, his patience had largely unraveled. Virtues were overrated.

The redhead lounging against one of her pristine white counters shot him an amused smile. "Sure you wanna dip your toe back into the lab? Looks like psychology is your field after all."

He scowled, and not just because Harper had pointed out his issue with his new job—it was *psychology*, not hard science. And pop psychology at that. "The show is not my field. It's entertainment. Any idiot with half a brain could figure out how to read a woman's subtle cues without my help if he really wanted to."

Crossing her arms, she cocked her head. "Really? What am I thinking right now?"

Oh, thank God. A perfect segue. And he intended to take full advantage of it.

"That's not a fair experiment," he countered smoothly and swept her with a once-over that held the slightest tinge of heat. "I'm not an idiot and I've known you a long time. I have a lot of practice paying attention to you."

Curiosity filtered through her expression, cascading all the way down to her mouth, which tipped up at the corners. "Yet you're still standing there not mixing samples."

Yeah, yeah. They were here to fix her sample problem. He got it. And they would. Later. His hands already knew the shape of a beaker and how to hold it. He wanted to educate himself on the feel of this woman, what would make her gasp. Laugh. Sigh. Moan. He wanted it all. Samples could wait one more day, at which point he might actually have a shot at concentrating.

That was the goal here, after all. Kill the lightning-hot buzz between them and move on. Been there, done that. Back to being friends and scientists, where they talked for hours about nothing and everything, laughing over shared jokes, being each other's sounding boards.

"Samples, Harper? Is that really what you were thinking about?" Casually, he leaned on the counter, decreasing the distance between them without making it obvious that he'd boxed her in. "Because that's not what your subtle cues are saying."

She glanced at his hand, which happened to be about four centimeters from where her hip rested against the counter.

"My subtle cues might be saying *feed me*," she said with a half laugh that didn't fool either of them. "It is close to lunchtime."

"It's ten thirty." He caught her gaze. "What's really going on is you're thinking about that kiss. You can't forget how it felt. Or all that heat burning up the atmosphere when you were checking out my tattoo. You're thinking you're a little freaked about it."

Guilt flashed through her gaze. Holy hell. He'd only said that to steer the conversation away from samples and toward his ultimate goal. He had not expected to get an immediate reaction.

Intrigued, he did a quick assessment. How freaked out *was* she? Was she freaked because she wanted him to do it again and didn't know how to ask? Or freaked because she was still in the friend zone with no exit ramp in sight?

"I'm not, either." She tossed her hair behind her shoulder. "We talked about it and things aren't weird anymore. What is there to be freaked out about?"

Door number one then, he decided with no small amount of glee. If she wasn't thinking about doing it again, she'd have trotted out her *we're friends and nothing but* excuse.

"Well, that's a very good question." One he definitely planned to get answers to. "I'll answer that with a question of my own. Why didn't you take Cardoza up on his invitation to do the baby making the old-fashioned way?"

"What?" She crossed her arms and used the action as a poor cover for moving her hip an inch further down the counter. Away from his hand. "How did we circle back to that subject?"

"Easy. You want to know why you'd be freaked over me kissing you. I'll tell you. It's the same reason you shot down Cardoza when the poor man obviously has the hots for you."

Imagining the disappointment on the jerkwad's face made a nice addition to the Kick-Cardoza's-Ass box in his head.

"Yes, well, that's too bad for him," she shot back. "I didn't take Tomas up on his invitation because he's not the man I want to lose my virginity with."

Oh, really? Her bold statement ratcheted up the heat a notch as a zing of energy accompanied the sentiment. Obviously she had a name in her head and it wasn't Dr. Cheater.

"Who is?"

Harper flinched, color flooding her cheeks. "No one! That came out wrong. What I meant was, I don't have any interest in sex. I mean, like none. Zero. Nada. It's just a series of chemical reactions that people would pay a lot less credence to if they really understood the way it works."

What was the *Hamlet* quote? The lady protested way too much. Or something like that.

"Pretend I'm someone who doesn't understand how it works," Dante murmured, clenching his hand into a tight fist so he didn't actually reach out to feather a thumb across that pink staining her delicate features. "Explain it to me."

"Don't be ridiculous. We're in a cosmetics lab." Her tone dropped to such a low register it only made sense to lean in. So he could hear her. "Where I work."

What the hell was she wearing that smelled like peaches? It was mind-boggling. Did she actually think she could lace her skin with a scent like that and he wouldn't notice? That he wouldn't want to sink his nose right into the juncture of her neck and shoulder?

Focus, he reminded himself, and soon he'd have all the peach-scented Harper he could take.

Glancing around, he jerked his head toward the open space behind him. The lab techs had gone into another room, leaving them blessedly alone. "Which is empty. What better place to discuss chemistry than a lab?"

"But we're not discussing chemistry," she ground out. "You're just fishing for intel about Tomas. Out of, I don't know, jealousy or something."

This time, her casual use of first names didn't burn a hole through his gut, which allowed room for a genuine chuckle. "What do I have to be jealous of Cardoza for? You didn't kiss him."

"I shouldn't have kissed you, either," she muttered darkly.

"I beg to differ. How else are you going to find out how wrong you are about your conclusions if you don't kiss me?" He gave her a minute and then leaned on that button again. Hard. "That's why you're still thinking about it. That's why you're freaked out. Because you're curious and you can't stop yourself from wondering. What's all the fuss about?"

Her crossed arms said she wasn't backing down. "I know what the fuss is about. People confuse synapses firing with something mythical and otherworldly, which, in turn, colors the experience. Sexual response is no different than hunger pains."

Oh, what an apt comparison. It was time to help Harper find out exactly how ravenous she was.

Five

"Good for you for not denying your curiosity. So, let's talk about that, shall we?" Dante suggested smoothly and Harper did not like the look in his eye.

Thus far today, she'd inadvertently blurted out the pregnancy news to her friends, fallen into Trinity's crosshairs regarding the suddenly hot topic of her virginity and then stumbled into a discussion about sex with the one man she did not want to talk about sex with.

Could the universe just give her a break, for crying out loud? The nightmare of the FDA issues would have been enough to deal with, thanks. And the way Dante kept twisting her words depending how he wanted to play it—all of it was wearing on her.

"I'd rather not talk at all. Samples," she reminded him, and was sure he didn't miss the touch of desperation behind her words. "They are not going to make themselves."

"Hmm," he fairly purred and her spine tingled as he leaned in a little closer, his gaze wandering down her body with a spark of...something she didn't have any clue what to do with. "I'll make you a deal. Give me ten minutes to make my case. Then we'll get started on your samples and I'll shut up. Scout's honor."

She eyed him as he held up two fingers. "I think that's the 'live long and prosper' sign, not the Scout sign. Clock's ticking."

Bad idea. The worst in the history of bad ideas. But Dante was nothing if not tenacious. She'd give him his ten and cut him off cold. They had work to do.

He eyed her right back. "You know I'm going to win. If proving a theory was a competitive sport, I'd get a gold every time. You must want those samples pretty bad."

Ha. He was obviously forgetting that time in grad school when they'd chosen opposing techniques to catalyze the photo-splitting of water. Photoelectrochemical—also known as Harper's idea—had been the clear frontrunner.

"I don't even think *you* know what case you're trying to make. Therefore, it was a calculated risk, weighted heavily in my favor," she countered primly, only to strangle over her statement as the space between them vanished.

Mute, she stared at him, drowning in his big brown eyes. His glasses showcased the riot of colors that created that yummy chocolate hue she'd seen in her dreams last night.

What were they talking about?

"My hypothesis," he began, and his voice dropped, likely in deference to their public proximity, but that didn't make it any less...affecting. "Is that you *used* to believe sex was just a series of chemicals and that you weren't interested. But that's recently changed.

And you're curious about how. Why. You're a scientist, Harper, and this lack of understanding is killing you. Of course you want more data. I'm offering you a chance to get it. It's an experiment."

"Wait a minute. We're still talking about kissing. Only. Right?"

The sizzling once-over Dante slid down her length answered that question, even as he shook his head. "You know that's not what I'm proposing."

Oh, God. She barely wanted to be talking about kissing. When had sex entered the equation? Harper's body woke up instantly, and her blood heated so fast, she saw stars. *Yes. That's exactly what you want*, her newly aroused lady parts insisted.

No. She scowled. That was the hormones talking and when had they gotten so bossy? "That's a hell of an experiment. What if your hypothesis is wrong?"

His smile did all sorts of interesting things in her lower regions and dang it, her brain was off and running. Because yeah, she was curious.

Why now? Why Dante? What *was* all the fuss about? Trinity's comment about denying herself the fun part of getting pregnant couldn't be pushed out of Harper's mind. It looped through her brain on a continual repeat, like an earworm that wouldn't stop bleating, no matter what other songs she sang.

What if she was the one missing something?

"I'm not wrong, Harper." He drew out the syllables, his eyes on her mouth the entire time, and her lips tingled as if he'd actually touched them, but he hadn't, and *oh, God*. She wanted him to.

Insanity.

"There are all sorts of ways what you're proposing can go south," she murmured, and was that her voice?

It had gone all *sotto voce,* too, and the sound of it put a fascinating glint in his eyes. "We have a friendship that I can't lose. What if I hate it? What if *you* hate it?"

Yes. That was the issue here. Kissing was one thing—a huge thing, which, by the way, had already changed their relationship against her will—but sex? That was an unknown that had *giant risk* painted all over it. Too much of one.

By way of answer, he reached out and she nearly jumped out of her skin, but he just took her hand, smoothing his thumb over it like he'd done a million times. Except she had a full-body awareness of it that flowed through her with an amazing, thick flood. Hormones, she reminded herself.

Oh, who the hell cared? It felt good. She liked it. That was his whole point.

Her knees weakened as she watched him watch her and she had a feeling he'd clued in to her minor capitulation. That was an error she could not repeat, not if she hoped to keep him focused on the roadblocks firmly in the way of his insane plan.

"You're right," he said. "We can't lose our friendship. That's why this is so important. If we both hate it, that's perfect. We laugh, chalk it up to Dr. Gates's faulty logic and go on."

"What if only one of us hates it?"

Shut up. This was not the conversation they should be having and she definitely shouldn't be letting on that his careful argument was swaying her. Because it *wasn't.*

"It doesn't work like that," he said.

Really? Dang it, now he'd thoroughly intrigued her. "Why not?"

"Well, that's the best question of all," he acknowledged and his thumb found a particularly sensitive spot on her hand that she'd have sworn he'd touched before, like a quadrillion times. But it had never rocketed through her with something akin to a lightning bolt.

She scarcely held back the gasp.

"Tell me," she choked out instead and his smile made it clear he knew exactly what he was doing to her.

"It's more of a show kind of thing."

Well, that felt strangely inevitable.

His gaze burned through her, which was completely ridiculous. He wasn't a superhero with laser vision. A man looking at her shouldn't cause a physical reaction. Of course, if she planned to hold that line, neither should thinking about him, hearing his voice, stewing about his audacity to speak to another woman or God forbid, remembering his bare torso with the line of crisp hair that disappeared into a loosely tied towel.

Yet *all* of them induced a physical reaction. What would it feel like to introduce corporal stimuli to the mix, but this time, with permission to experiment?

Weary of fighting herself, she shut her eyes and waited for the brush of his lips against hers. Her body bowed up, poised to feel all those luscious muscles rubbing her breasts again, primed for the rush of those chemicals she'd deny to her grave she craved.

Because yeah. Dante wasn't wrong about his hypothesis, not that she'd admit that to him. Her curiosity would be her undoing, apparently.

She waited.

Nothing. No lips. No rush. No Dante.

She cracked one eye open. He hadn't moved from his spot against the counter, and embarrassment replaced some of the desire she'd been reveling in.

"Um, when does the showing start?" she squeaked,

and geez, had he really maneuvered her to the point where she was begging for it?

Nonchalantly, he shrugged. "I don't know."

Disappointment crushed the air from her lungs and she yanked her hand free of his so she could wrap her arms around her stomach. It didn't hold back the tide of confusion. "So you're not going to kiss me?"

For the love of God. After all that? Really?

"Oh, make no mistake," he countered, and a slow, wicked smile spread across his face. "There's going to be kissing, among other things. But you're the one who's going to be doing it. This is your experiment, not mine. Tell me what you want me to do, Harper. Your wish is my command."

A hodgepodge of X-rated scenarios leaped into her mind, like a dozen browser windows had opened all at once and every one featured something not safe for work. She shut it down. Somehow. There was no way she could initiate anything of the kind. She could barely imagine admitting she'd pictured lurid details involving Dante.

And no way in hell would he ever find a way to convince her to kiss *him*. This was his deal, not hers. She was—almost, sort of, maybe—along for the ride.

"That doesn't make any sense. You kissed me first. You're the one who introduced all of this to our relationship." She glared at him and he didn't even have the grace to look chagrined. "I'm making a huge concession here that you might have a point about there being something between us that we need to deal with and you're forcing *me* to be the lead on this experiment?"

His other hand slid across her jaw, tipping her face up and all at once, she couldn't breathe as time stopped, suspending in a hazy glow. Everything in her peripheral vision faded and the fine details of Dante's face imprinted themselves on her soul. The smattering of freckles across his nose. The little nick on his jaw where he'd cut himself shaving at fifteen and it hadn't ever healed. The indentation high on his cheekbone that was almost a dimple but wasn't until he smiled. Details she'd noted a dozen times a day or more, but never as a whole, and they all belonged to the man she'd have sworn she knew inside and out.

But didn't. There were a thousand nuances of his face that she'd never explored. What would the almost-dimple feel like under her lips, for example?

"No one is forcing you to do anything." His gaze speared through her, sending shafts of heat clear to her toes. "I want you to be fully aware of what we're doing, what's going to happen to you. The choices you're making. The boundaries you've set and the lines you won't cross. If you're in control, nothing happens unless you say. That's how you make sure the other person doesn't hate it."

God, that was so up her alley. Of course it was. Because he knew her, knew that would be exactly the right button to push. But then that begged the obvious question. "How do I know I'm not forcing you then?"

That got a gorgeous smile out of him, and she could not tear her eyes away from that ridiculous dimple that she'd never had trouble ignoring before. How dare he come into her lab and flash that thing around, enticing her into fantasies about it?

"I'm good. I know what I'm getting myself into."

"I hate being at the intellectual disadvantage," she groused.

Something else she hated? His insistence that she make the first move. What was that, but some macho ploy designed to feed his ego? Like she couldn't resist him or something. All the other women in the world flocked to his side, but Harper didn't, so this was all a way to get her to cater to his need for attention.

Plus…she had no idea what she was doing. For someone used to being proficient 24/7, that was a hard pill to swallow.

"But that's easy to resolve. Jump in," he advised with raised brows. "You only gain experience from here and who better to experiment with than someone you trust implicitly? I would never hurt you and you already know I care about you. If I'm right, intimacy just makes our already great relationship better."

The reminder poked at her self-righteous stance. Of course she trusted him. He wasn't some random guy looking for a hookup and trying to talk her into doing something she didn't want to do. That was the whole point. He wanted her to make the decision and he wasn't going to force the issue.

"If nothing else," he continued, "resolve your curiosity now. With me. Once the baby is born, you'll be a busy single mom. Moms don't get unique windows of opportunity like the one I'm offering you."

"So I'm just supposed to kiss you? Right now?"

"When you're ready." His thumb stroked over her cheek again and his hand dropped away. "Time's up."

"Hmm. What?" She blinked as the phrase registered.

Give me ten minutes.

He'd made his case and now he was done. Instantly, the raw, achy places inside got rawer and achier as his heat faded from her skin. As her body started to cool, her temper flared. Oh, so that was how he wanted to play it. Lay out the premise that she could experiment to her heart's desire, set boundaries, be in control. How *dare* he appeal to her sense of logic and reason? That was dirty, through and through.

"That wasn't ten minutes," she informed him with a toss of her hair.

His brow lifted. "It wasn't?"

"Not even close." There was no clock in this part of the lab and both their phones were deep in their coat pockets. It could totally have been seven or eight minutes. How would he know? "I'm not done here."

Dante leaned back against the counter, arms crossed. "I've got nowhere else to be."

There was too much Irish in her blood to put up with all his feigned nonchalance. He'd started this and he was going to finish it. "In case you've forgotten, I have no idea how to kiss a man. I've never done it before. Seems like I should find someone to practice with. Maybe Tomas is free."

Instantly, Dante stiffened and something wholly feral streaked across his expression. "Maybe you can forget that idea."

Not so calm, cool and collected now, are ya, Dr. Gates?

And was it terrible that she liked provoking him? It was only fair. He'd been doing that to her since she got off the plane in LA. "Seems like you threw out some ground rules that sounded an awful lot like I was supposed to be doing all the kissing. You were just going to stand there and look pretty."

He processed that with a gaping fishmouth that warmed her competitive soul. If she did nothing else today, she'd prove that he was wrong. That she wasn't curious, that she wasn't freaked out, that she had no desire to experiment on him or anyone.

"I explained my reasons for allowing you make the first move," he ground out. "For your own peace of mind. What do you want from me?"

"I want you to kiss me," she fairly shouted.

"Yeah?" A wicked smile flashed across his face as he jerked his head. "Come and get it. I dare you to."

Red stained her vision. He didn't think she could do it. What a...*man*. Who was wrong. Of course, that was redundant.

That smile decorating his smug face needed to go. Harper grabbed his lapels and yanked.

His mouth landed on hers with enough force to drive her backward against the counter and his hands took possession of her hair. Moaning, she fell into the kiss with every ounce of pent-up frustration and longing and hormonal imbalance rioting through her body.

God, it was glorious. His mouth. *His hands*. The heat and pressure built until she thought she'd explode.

Something snapped inside and *poof*. No more thinking. This was supposed to prove something but her brain had melted and all she could do was cling to Dante's shoulders, marveling at how solid they were under her fingers.

Tilting her head, he drank from her, his mouth a conduit that pulled all of her strength from her body, weakening her knees. She nearly collapsed into a little puddle of nothing but nerve endings.

But he caught her in his strong arms, holding her tight against his torso. All the delicious hard planes of his body aligned with hers, and *oh, my*. The sensations flooded her. *More, more, more*. And he gave it to her, heightening the dizzy spiral inside until she feared she'd incinerate in his arms.

His heat inflamed her skin, sensitizing it, and she needed...something at her core.

Hips tilting of their own accord, she sought it blindly, until she accidentally hit the steel length of what had to be Dante's erection. Mortified, she froze, but his hand snaked down her back, leaving a trail of fire as it went, until he cupped her bottom, fingers nipping in.

He shoved her mound hard against him, circling until he groaned, and the raw, sensitive place at her core lit up. It was too much. *He* was too much.

Harper tore out of his arms, leaving most of her composure on the floor near his feet.

Torso heaving, she shut her eyes against the wholly affecting sight of Dante's kiss-stained mouth. Her body had other ideas about the distance, swaying toward him in hopes of getting all that lovely sensation back.

"I'm sorry," she whispered. "I can't do this."

That had been a complete and total mistake, because now she couldn't pretend she had no interest in kissing him.

Except she hadn't known he was going to make her feel like *that*. Or touch her in places that had never been touched.

Embarrassment filtered through her, coalescing in all the places Dante had filled her moments before. And now everything was weird again. Had she actually believed that they'd laugh about this and go on?

"Hey." Suddenly, Dante was there, his warm hand on her shoulder, familiar and comforting. "I'm at fault here. I goaded you into it before you were ready. I'm the one who's sorry."

"I made the choice. Like you asked me to." He'd played her exactly right. Ridiculously well, actually, and she was not happy about it, especially since she couldn't even blame him. "You were just indulging me in my experimentation."

"God, Harper, seriously? Did you not feel what you do to me?" He huffed out a frustrated breath, cursed and pinched off his glasses to rub at his eyes. "I goaded you into it because you make me crazy and I wanted you in my arms. And I'm not going to stop wanting more."

Sex. He meant sex. That was the "more."

Her heart froze, refusing to beat and she struggled to drag air into her lungs. If this was the aftermath of a simple kiss, what would it be like if they'd done…other things? Touched each other? Put their mouths against bare skin? Her stupid hormones had pushed her out of her comfort zone, pushed her into a place she did not want to go. Her pulse jump-started again, stumbling over itself in a race to catch up.

Shaking her head, she did some backing up herself. "No. That's not what I want. I…hated it. I was trying to figure out how to tell you."

He put his glasses back in place and cocked a brow at her, clearly unconvinced. "Don't do that. If you're scared, it's okay."

"It's *not* okay."

And I'm not scared.

But she couldn't keep lying to him in that moment any more than she could fly. She was terrified that if they did go down that path, their friendship would disintegrate in a vast sea of weirdness, that she'd do more shameless things in the heat of passion, that she'd be unable to look at Dante without thinking of his hands on her. Without imagining all the wicked things she'd done or would do or wanted to do.

Most of all, she was scared of how easily he could make her stop thinking. That was the real danger, because then what would happen? She'd always relied on her brain to guide her. The body's baser needs were not a reliable source of direction.

Dante cupped her jaw with both hands, forcing her

to look at him. "Harper, I understand that this is strange and you're nervous. No more pushing, no deals. I swear to you I will let you go at your own pace. If you want to kiss me, do it. If you want to strip off all my clothes, have a ball. If you don't, then don't. But don't deny what's happening between us because that *will* hurt our friendship."

With that warning ringing in her ears, Dante glanced around the lab. "Where do I start?"

The chemistry required to make cosmetics was relatively simplistic in the grand scheme of things, but Dante could hardly see through the haze of sexual chemistry painting his vision. Good thing Harper wasn't asking him to do something really difficult, like walk and chew gum at the same time. He'd be screwed, and not in a good way.

Who was he kidding? He'd been screwed since the second the words *I want you to kiss me* left Harper's mouth. That sweet phrase had wound through his blood and gotten him so hot and bothered that he'd thoroughly ruined all the progress he'd made thus far.

If Harper hadn't been freaked enough before to run scared, she certainly was now. It bothered him. A lot. He hated being responsible for upsetting her, because he did care about her—more than anyone else on the planet.

The problem was that he wasn't doing a great job of helping her see how things could only get better between them.

Dante held the test tube in his shaking fingers and willed Harper not to turn around. She'd taken a spot at the lab table near the window, while he'd chosen the furthest seat away from her. The last thing he could afford to do was let on how difficult it had been to let her stop that kiss. How he was still caught in the throes of it, his mouth watering to get her into his arms again.

But he couldn't push her—he'd made a promise. And he should definitely be shot because all he could think about was breaking it. She was his friend and that was not how you treated one.

"Got that reaction under control?" Harper called over her shoulder.

Not even a little.

Bobbling the test tube, Dante firmed his suddenly slick fingers. Practicing her mind reading, was she? Or was the fact that no blood had returned to his brain more obvious than he'd hoped? "I'm good."

"Great." Harper faced forward again, concentrating on her own task. "Those nanoparticles have a tendency to be volatile. We don't want any accidents."

He nearly groaned. Truer words had never been spoken, but he'd bet every last million in his bank account that the double entendre was completely lost on her.

What was the matter with him? This was a God-honest lab, with exciting technology at his very fingertips. He had free rein over every last piece of lab equipment and a well-funded corporation backing it. If he said he needed a different electron microscope, Harper's lab manager would procure it within twenty-four hours, as Harper had generously explained.

Hard science, exactly as the doctor ordered. What was he doing with this golden opportunity? Watching Fyra's chief science officer as she bent over a scale, measuring…something.

Her backside had been firm and sweet under his palms, and he'd ached to sink into her. She'd been hot and ready. And then he'd obviously made a serious blunder by taking things to the next natural level.

Okay, he hadn't been thinking with his brain when he'd ground against her, but who could blame a guy for losing his marbles when a hot redhead tilted her hips against his blazing erection? And then she had the audacity to lie to his face about hating the kiss, when she'd been a hair's breadth away from a fully-clothed orgasm. Which he would have gladly given her if she hadn't stopped.

But she had. He'd respect her boundaries no matter how certain he was that death might be preferable to being forced to shut it down like that again. Not only that, he'd had to soothe her through the remnants of her freak-out. Watching the genuine fear skitter through her expression had cut like he'd swallowed broken glass.

Not to mention the fact that he needed her calm so they could actually get some work done.

Or rather so she could. His attention was fully engaged in hashing out step four: get Harper used to his hands on her. Without breaking his promise.

She needed a little more encouragement, a little more space and a lot more reminders of how off the freaking charts their chemistry was. At great personal expense, as his aching groin liked to remind him.

All at once, he didn't feel like so much of an expert. Apparently seduction was much easier when the female in question started out interested in sex.

Harper pulled away from her scale and set aside the vials she'd been working with in favor of peering over Dante's shoulder. Her breasts brushed his back and he nearly dropped the test tube as all the air in the lab vanished. Good thing. If he breathed in right now, it would smell like peaches and he didn't think he could take that at this moment.

Of course she thought nothing of getting close to him

like this. Because he'd done everything in his power to set things back to rights between them after that fiasco of an experiment.

"I thought you said you had the reaction under control," she tsked. "Those particles have almost completely absorbed the dye. You were supposed to keep them separate."

"Oh, yeah," he said hoarsely. "I was curious if it would change the consistency of the lotion."

She frowned. "I worked on this formula for two years. It's sound."

Crap, he hadn't meant to insult her. Maybe fate had steered him away from hard science for a reason—he'd lost his edge. Or Harper was slowly draining him of every ounce of his intelligence. "Of course it is. This was more for my own curiosity."

The word pinged around inside him, reminding him of the last time he'd said it…when he'd been pushing Harper to absolve hers. In his arms.

All at once, he realized why his seduction skills weren't working like he'd expected them to. He was going about this all wrong.

Harper was a scientist, sure. But she was also a woman. And he'd done absolutely nothing to romance her. Episode twelve of his show had featured that exact subject and at the time, he'd covered a lot of ground regarding the things normal women liked: flowers, moonlight, fine wine.

The woman he wanted would never be impressed by stuff like that. If he hoped to have Dr. Livingston draped naked across his bed any time before the next century rolled around, he needed to get off his ass and figure out how to woo her properly.

Six

By dawn the morning after The Lab Kiss, Harper had slept maybe two hours total.

When she'd invited Dante to stay in her guest bedroom—because hotels were for strangers, not best friends—she hadn't realized she'd develop a sixth sense that allowed her to hear him breathing through the walls.

Nor would she have guessed his presence would induce an achy restlessness she could not shake no matter how many times she recited the periodic table. The problem was that she couldn't forget Dante's parting shot…that to deny the spark between them would affect their friendship.

She got the point. The moment they started lying to each other was the moment they had no trust between them. That scared her more than anything. It had never occurred to her that *she'd* be the one to mess up what they had.

So she'd given herself permission to try out the idea

that she was attracted to Dante. That it was okay to think of him as sexy in every sense of the word. That her base reaction to him had nothing to do with her brain and everything to do with the way his mouth set her core on fire.

Hence the achy restlessness with no relief in sight.

Oh, she had a pretty good handle on how the logistics of that relief might come about. It wasn't like she'd been absent the day they taught human sexuality. Hell, she'd sat through more than one R-rated movie with Dante filching her popcorn as they watched the on-screen couple get it on.

What she did not have a handle on was her own reactions. Because sex was all she could think about. What it would feel like. What Dante might look like under the towel. She had a great imagination or she'd never have come up with something as revolutionary as Formula-47…but the odds of her mind conjuring anything close to the real deal when it came to specifics of sex? Not a chance.

Of course, the second she decided to get a glimpse of the doctor's naked body, she had explicit permission to start unzipping his pants whenever. That was also something she could not envision.

Which put her firmly at square one. Dante had sworn to keep his hands off her from now on. All the balls were in her court and he'd demanded only one thing of her— be truthful about her feelings, no matter what they were.

She'd rather jump off a bridge.

The clock blinked 6:30 a.m. Groaning, she rolled out of bed and trudged across the hardwood floor to the cavernous, lushly appointed bathroom that had been one of the main reasons she'd bought this condo in Victory Park. She showered the grit from her eyes well enough to see, but lacked the proper skill set to also eliminate the grit from her brain.

Why did everything have to be so hard?

When she got out of the shower, she stood naked in front of the floor-to-ceiling mirror in her hundred-square-foot closet, objectively cataloging her body. Soon, her belly would expand, rounding with the child she'd longed for. She'd hoped some of the changes might have started already but everything appeared to be exactly the same as last month and the month before.

The mess with Fyra and the FDA had robbed her of the chance to have a girls' night in with her other pregnant friends so they could compare notes, talk about delivery methods, eat a gallon of ice cream because they were all going to be fat anyway—or already were in Alex's case. She was carrying twins and had ballooned a few weeks ago.

Of course, Harper had only seen that secondhand on a Skype screen because Phillip didn't want Alex to travel unless it was absolutely necessary. And nothing fell in the category of "necessary" where her husband was concerned.

Girls' night in had become a pipe dream. Harper couldn't relax with her friends anyway, not until she'd fixed the problem that she'd caused for her business partners by failing to detect the switched samples.

Yesterday, she'd gotten zero traction. Today had to be better.

Dante stood in her kitchen holding a press pot full of Gyokuro Imperial Green Tea. He smiled when she walked in as if everything between them was A-OK, except his eyes were glowy with something new, or maybe she'd just never paid attention to how beautiful he was. All at once, her heart fell out of cadence.

Great. Now she'd developed an arrhythmia in addition to an awareness of Dante.

"Good morning," he said cheerfully.

Of course he was cheerful. He'd probably slept all night, content in the knowledge that he'd had Harper's number the whole time. Her mood soured.

"It will be a great morning if I can get some workable samples done today," she snapped and immediately regretted her cruddy attitude when he nodded as he poured a cup of tea, hustling her to the table in the small breakfast nook adjacent to the kitchen to sit her down with the mug.

"Then consider it done," he said and shot her another smile that shouldn't have made her as suspicious as it did.

"What, like you're going to put your nose to the grindstone instead of coming up with new and inventive ways to distract me?"

She flinched at her tone. He was being super nice to her, even after she'd barked at him. What was her problem?

"Yes." He settled into the opposite chair with his own mug of tea. "I told you. Next move is yours. In the meantime, you asked for workable samples by the end of the day. I'm going to give you that or bleed while trying."

Her brows arched involuntarily. "You can't bleed in my lab. That's a health code violation."

His dark, rich chuckle spread through her like honey, dang it, and her greedy, hormonal, Dante-starved body soaked it up, begging her to find 187 other ways to get him to laugh like that again.

It was just a laugh. He'd laughed at her jokes in the past. Nothing to see here, she advised her lady parts and scowled at Dante.

Who promptly held up his hands. "No bleeding. Yes,

ma'am. I was merely demonstrating my commitment to the project using figurative language. I note the boss is not a fan. We will stick to literal language the rest of the day, then."

She rolled her eyes. "I'm not the boss of you."

Something sizzled through his expression that heated her already jazzed body. "Oh, but you are. I'm ready, willing and able to be commanded at a moment's notice."

And yeah, she still had enough working brain cells to be quite aware they were no longer talking about samples. She cleared her throat. "I'll keep that in mind."

Which, she had a feeling, had been precisely his intention. And of course, her creative brain had no trouble following that lead. She'd have to watch it or her highly independent mouth might accidentally spill one of those fantasies and he'd take it completely the wrong way.

Dante drove Harper's Mercedes to Fyra because, as he insisted, she should take advantage of having a slave around and relax. Who could relax with all the shimmery electricity arcing between his fingers on the gearshift and her bare knee, mere inches away?

"Let me take you shopping on Saturday," he commented out of the blue.

"For what?"

He shrugged. "Baby stuff. A new car. Groceries. Whatever you need or want. I'm here to help."

"What's wrong with my car?" She'd just bought the cute two-door Mercedes less than six months ago and she loved it. It was sporty and...oh. No backseat. She hadn't gotten that far in her pregnancy planning because she had plenty of time. But she wouldn't have Dante around at her beck and call for more than a couple of weeks.

In a few months, she'd be doing all that baby stuff solo. In a new, more mature car.

That blackened her mood further. Not that she wouldn't give up her cute car for something more sedan-like—she'd gone into the idea of being a mom with a totally open mind—she just didn't like that Dante had been the one to think of it. And make her tea, like he was her personal lackey, ready, willing and able to be told what to do, no matter what her suddenly X-rated mind came up with.

Sinking down in the seat, she crossed her arms and glared out the window because it wasn't Dante's fault her pregnancy hormones had turned her into a lunatic. Instead of craving meat or orange juice, like normal women, she craved Dante. It was totally not fair.

The lab, typically her refuge, reminded her of the kiss from yesterday and reminded her that anytime she wished for a repeat, the man at her side would be totally on board.

But then she'd have to admit that she wanted him. Because in the crazy, mixed-up world she lived in now, their friendship depended on her being honest about that.

Somehow, she focused long enough to get into a rhythm. At first, she'd been leery of letting her guard down long enough to get comfortable with Dante, but soon they were side by side, knee-deep in ingredients, equipment and sheer bliss.

"Did you check on the sodium caseinate?" she muttered to him at one point. "It's about time for it to come out of the homogenization process."

"I did just a minute ago," he confirmed. "It's done."

That was the beauty of working with him. His analytical process mirrored hers and they rarely had to talk through a concept. Things were easy between them, like they had been in college, and when Dante glanced at his watch and noted with surprise that it was lunchtime, the real surprise was that she had indeed relaxed.

And she and Dante had made huge strides toward her goal of working samples. They'd gotten far more accomplished than she could have done on her own. "This has been very productive. I'm a little in awe."

Dante elbowed her good-naturedly. "You say that like you're shocked. I had a chemistry set when I was ten, I'll have you know. This makeup stuff is easy."

She laughed and it felt good, especially in light of her crappy mood from earlier. Dante stood, held out his hand to help her off her stool, and announced that he was taking her to lunch.

Gratefully, she nodded and clasped his hand without fear. She didn't let go, and wonder of wonders, he didn't comment. He just held her hand companionably as they strolled through the building. Like it always had been between them. And she nearly wept at how much she'd needed that in the midst of everything going on in her life.

"Thank you," she choked out around the lump in her throat as they settled into her car. "For being here."

Instead of starting the car and driving, like she'd expected, he turned to meet her gaze, his hand settling into place against her jaw. "I will always be here. We both need that constant."

Something passed between them as she absorbed his touch into her skin. Not heat, not the precursor to a kiss. Something else that was warm and safe and tender, and she reveled in it.

His hand fell away before she was ready and he chatted as he drove. The sound of his voice washed over her, soothing her, and she stopped listening halfway through his conversation. Her head drifted back against the seat. A long sleepless night crashed into her and that was all she wrote.

The car lurched, startling her awake.

Blinking, she oriented herself. "Did I fall asleep?"

Dante ruffled her hair. "Yeah. In the middle of my scintillating conversation, no less. If I didn't know that pregnant women needed more sleep than normal, I'd be offended."

"How do you know that?"

He shrugged. "I did a lot of reading about it. Can't be too prepared when your best friend is pregnant and you've never so much as held a baby. I also know that you're not supposed to eat sushi, certain kinds of fish and we're going to avoid things that are high in sugar because it's far easier to develop glucose intolerance when you're pregnant."

Oh, no. There went her heart arrhythmia again. Speechless, she processed his casually thrown-out admission that he'd researched her condition. Surreptitiously, she rubbed her heart to get it to start beating normally again. Except she was worried she might need defibrillators because when he came around to her side of the car to open her door and help her from the low-slung seat, she glimpsed the sign near the parking lot he'd pulled into.

"You brought me to the Perot Museum for lunch?"

"Is that okay?" He apparently took her earlier hand-holding concession as gospel because he didn't release hers as he guided her toward the crosswalk. "The café is run by Wolfgang Puck and the menu sounded pretty good when I looked it up earlier. They give away a free dinosaur mask with the purchase of a kid's meal. I'll let you have mine. You know, since you're masking for two."

As black-mood lifters went, dinosaur masks might be her new number one favorite. Especially when Dante put one on and then stuck his glasses back on his face over the top of it. Harper couldn't hold back the giggles and before long, he had one tied around her stomach, too. Out came his phone so he could take pictures and she couldn't help but feel a little smug that her selfie with Dr. Sexy included evidence that he'd well and truly accepted her pregnancy with good humor. And that they hadn't lost the ability to have fun together.

The picture was precious. In more ways than one.

After lunch, Dante pulled her toward the mezzanine where they sold tickets to the museum itself. "Take thirty minutes and walk through the exhibits with me. I haven't been here yet and you know science museums are my crack."

That made her grin. She liked that he could be silly with her, no holds barred. And she liked the museum, too.

Since they'd made so much progress on the samples—and she genuinely didn't want the great mood he'd teased out of her to vanish—she nodded. "But I'm paying. You sprang for lunch."

He waved it off. "I picked this date. You pick the next one and I will generously allow you to pay."

She blinked at his back as he handed his black credit card to the clerk behind the counter. This was a date? Like a really real, God-honest date and somehow she'd missed the memo?

Surely he hadn't meant it that way. It was just a word, one they'd both used before to describe an activity, like *I've got tickets to the new Star Wars movie. Wanna be my date?*

But that had been before he'd kissed her. Before she'd

kissed him. *Way* before she'd allowed her attraction for him to come out to play…

Maybe she could just roll with it and stop being so neurotic.

"Ready?" Dante put his hand at the small of her back as he guided her to the escalator, then kept it there as they maneuvered through the crowd.

It should have been weird, given all the other stuff swirling between them. They were physically connected and she was aware of it, but instead of convincing herself it was friendly, or worrying that it sent the wrong message, she eased into it.

Dante didn't seem to notice that she'd basically adhered to his side. They talked about the dinosaur skeletons, pointed out their favorite birds in the bird hall and stood in line for the earthquake simulator, cracking jokes and laughing.

After Dante made a big deal over ensuring that it was okay for a pregnant woman to ride the earthquake simulator, they wedged onto the platform near the railing. Twenty or so other people crowded around them, forcing them face to face. Or rather, her face to his shoulder, which she didn't mind, even when Dante wrapped his arms around her.

Especially then.

"Just in case," he murmured in her ear and his lips nuzzled her in a way that seemed totally casual and highly suggestive simultaneously.

"In case of what?" she muttered back. Spontaneous combustion? Because that seemed likely the longer she stood in his embrace with heated flares jumping through her abdomen unchecked.

But then the simulator started up, jolting the platform. She nearly lost her balance but Dante's arms tightened as he shifted to take her weight. Somehow, her thigh ended up between his in an intimate press that rubbed her in all the right ways.

God, that felt good.

"In case of *that*." His voice rumbled in her ear over the virtual earthquake sounds. "I live in LA. Earthquakes are a thing. Suspected you might not be ready for what was coming."

Understatement of the year.

"Yeah, didn't see that coming," she agreed readily and imagined what it might feel like if she rubbed against his leg a little harder. Or better yet, if she admitted she liked it and asked him to touch her there.

Lust jackknifed through her so fast and so hot that her vision hazed.

"It's okay. I've got you," he said.

Yes, he did. And when she glanced up into his eyes, the answering heat reflected there nearly undid the fragile seams holding her together.

But he didn't close that tiny gap between them. Didn't ease his lips onto hers for a slow, wicked kiss that would be oh, so amazing given the fact that the earth was already shaking beneath their feet.

He didn't because he'd promised her he wouldn't.

And she had ample evidence digging into her stomach that he was as turned on as she was. The iron will he'd been exerting thus far deserved a medal.

Or maybe they both deserved something. But she needed a little bit of help to get there. Otherwise, the sheer terror coursing through her veins would win. Again.

When they got back to Fyra, she gave Dante a few pointed instructions about some tasks he could perform without her oversight and ducked out mumbling about a meeting. Which wasn't exactly a fib. Then she tracked down Trinity in her office, which was a little like bearding a lion crossed with Lady Gaga in its den.

But there was no one else Harper could turn to in her hour of need than a woman who regularly got top marks for her sex-capades.

"Ms. Forrester, are you in?" Harper called and rapped on the open door, which was kind of a joke between them. Trinity hated being called Ms. Forrester because it made her feel old, so of course Harper teased her about it.

Trinity's dark hair swung back from her left cheek as she glanced up. The right side of her hair had been sheared close to her scalp in an angular cut that fit the woman to a T. Last week, she'd colored it all purple but had quickly grown tired of it. That was one thing Harper admired about Trinity—she never let the grass grow under her feet.

And the woman was fearless with a capital *F*.

"S'up, girlfriend," Trinity said with a grin. "Do I sound like a part of the millennial intelligentsia who can sell cosmetics to teenagers?"

"More like a desperate marketing executive staring down the barrel of thirty and none too happy about it."

With a scowl, Trinity stuck out a wrist to show off the new butterfly tattoo she'd gotten a couple of weeks ago. "I'll have you know this thing marks me as super cool when I go to career day at Hockaday."

"Hockaday is a private girl's' school that costs more than my doctorate did," Harper countered and plopped into Trinity's visitor chair. "I'm not sure that demographic is going to give you the most balanced viewpoint into what's hot among seventeen-year-olds."

Out came Trinity's pierced tongue in defiance. "Did

you want something? Something other than to watch my self-esteem slide onto the carpet like yesterday's trash?"

Harper rolled her eyes. "As if that would ever happen. Which is kind of why I'm here."

And now that she was, she couldn't figure out how to actually bring up what she wanted to talk about. They'd been friends a long time, but they had so little in common. Mostly Harper looked to Trinity for fashion advice, especially as it came to what was hot, trendy or was already passé. Together, they'd come up with some of Fyra's most well-received product lines.

It was a little more difficult to lay out a personal problem. Especially one that Trinity would no doubt laugh at.

Trinity laced her fingers together and planted her elbows on her desk, then rested her chin on the ledge she'd created. "You're here because you need dating advice."

Blinking, Harper sank down an inch or two in the chair but only succeeded in wrinkling her pantsuit as opposed to disappearing. "Am I that transparent?"

"Sweetie, I'm not blind. I see what's going on between you and your hot lab partner. The real question is, do *you*?"

Oh, yeah, Harper saw it all right. In living color. In her dreams. When she caught sight of Dante from the corner of her eye and couldn't help but watch him as he measured acrylate into a beaker.

"Maybe," she muttered. Did everyone know that Dante had kissed her and vice versa? Was she walking around with a big neon sign on her back that said *pregnant lady with hormonal imbalance finally discovers her libido*? "It's…confusing."

And private. Embarrassing. Ridiculous. No one else had trouble coming right out and telling a man they wanted something from him. But what if she let her hormones rule and it turned into a disaster? She couldn't deal with that.

"Lay it on me. Wait!" Trinity jumped up and closed her office door, an act of mercy that Harper dearly appreciated, then she sank into the other visitor's chair, rubbing Harper's arm sympathetically. "Clearly we're going to skip the birth control lecture. So what do you need to know?"

Her friend's wry tone actually made Harper smile. Which meant she'd come to the right place for help. "So that's part of the problem. I guess my body reacts to conception a little differently than Alex's or Cass's."

"You've got an influx of hormones, do you?" Trinity chortled. "That's classic. I believe that's known as irony."

"Yeah, hilarious. Dante isn't helping."

"That's a flat-out lie." Disdain made her friend's carefully plucked and penciled eyebrows shoot up. "He is nothing but interested in helping. I can read males from three hundred yards and that man is into you. Always has been. Which is a crying shame, because I'd have tapped him years ago otherwise."

An image of Trinity and Dante together settled into Harper's stomach with a sour lurch. Except he'd slept with lots of women and likely would in the future. Which was none of her business. "I don't own him."

"Please." Trinity snorted. "That doesn't matter. He wouldn't look twice at me, not when his googly eyes are so firmly fixed on you. Do I need to kick him in his very fine backside? How is he not helping?"

By breathing, eating and sleeping in close proximity to Harper. Being sexy and understanding and logical and fun. That was the opposite of helping because it made her yearn for things she'd never realized she could yearn for. Things she didn't know how to ask for. "He's insisting that I make the first move."

"That rat bastard. How dare he?"

"This is not funny," Harper spat back as the reality of the situation overwhelmed her. "I have no idea what I'm doing, and everything is so confusing. How can I make a rational choice when my hormonal state is so unreliable?"

"Honey, if you think rationality is the goal here, you're doing it wrong." Crossing her arms, Trinity leaned back and put Harper under the microscope of her arresting blue eyes. "How does he make you feel?"

"Like I licked Satan himself," she said without hesitation. "Hot, sinful and wicked."

A purely blissful smile lifted Trinity's lips. "Aww, yeah. That's when it's the best. So make the first move. What's stopping you?"

"I just don't want to mess up our friendship."

That was the bottom line. Once that line had been crossed, they could never go back.

Trinity shrugged. "Then don't mess it up. You know what messes up relationships? Emotions. Letting your heart engage is a sure ticket to misery. Emotions aren't a part of sex. Ever. Take all that noise out of the equation and let that man make you feel good. It's a woman's right to have as many orgasms as humanly possible before death."

Emotions. Harper processed that. It made a certain sort of sense. She'd been scared of losing their friendship because…she didn't know why. But it seemed like people who had romantic relationships ended up crying in the break room when they ended. And they always ended.

How had she never seen that the key here was to separate the body from the heart and mind? This was no love affair with the potential to go wrong, leaving broken hearts scattered in its wake. She and Dante weren't romantically involved and never would be.

She could love Dante as a friend but sleep with him as a woman—and be as shameless at that as she wanted to because they'd leave their hearts at the door.

It was sheer brilliance. And humbling. Some scientist she was. Dr. Livingston sure hadn't analyzed that one correctly. At all.

But her friend wasn't done with all the startling disclosures.

"I'll tell you a secret that Cass and Alex told me," Trinity leaned in like someone might overhear, even though the office was empty save the two of them. "When you're pregnant, there's a lot of extra blood flow to your lady parts. Sex is apparently out of this world."

Not that Harper would have any basis for comparison. But that made sense, too. She'd often wondered if something was wrong with her because she'd never been tempted to "see what all the fuss was about," as Dante so succinctly put it—until she got pregnant.

It was almost a relief to hear that pregnancy might be affecting her body in a completely normal way. That made it acceptable to indulge herself, didn't it? Not just acceptable. Practically required. "You don't say."

Trinity nodded. "I have it on good authority. It's kind of a shame I'll never get to experience that."

"Not jumping on the pregnancy bandwagon?" Harper didn't blame Trinity. Every woman had to make her own choices.

The look on the other woman's face could have scalded milk. "Are you out of your mind? Could you imagine *me* as a mother? Besides, I dare any man's swimmers to get past three kinds of birth control. So, are we good here? I answered all your questions?"

"Oh, no." Harper shook her head, renewed in her determination. "I'm just getting started. Tell me how I get Dante into bed."

Something wholly wicked stole through Trinity's expression. "I thought you'd never ask."

Seven

When Harper had finally returned to the lab after a two-hour meeting, she'd wasted no time in announcing to Dante, "I have an idea. For our next date. You, me and dinner. At my place."

And his concentration for the day left the building.

Dinnertime took approximately four hundred years to roll around, but once the antique clock on Harper's wall chimed seven, Dante had the strangest lack of appetite. For food.

Apparently Harper had liked the idea of dating. Better than he would have ever guessed, especially since he hadn't meant it like *that*. The science museum had been a spur-of-the-moment thing designed to get him the hell out of the lab before he busted something.

"Are you sure I can't do anything?" he called to Harper in the kitchen.

She'd unceremoniously ordered him out of the way because, as she put it, this date was her pick. And she owed him for the science museum. Not that he'd felt any particular need to be repaid when he'd been lucky enough to get her into his arms during the monumental shift in their relationship that had somehow happened in the middle of an earthquake simulator. She'd not only welcomed his touch, but melted into his arms. He couldn't have conceived a more perfect way to put a cap on step four than that.

He'd call that serendipity but he'd worked too hard for what he hoped would be the culmination of the evening to chalk it up to fate.

This was his woman to lose. And he didn't intend to.

"I've got it." Harper breezed through the entryway between the kitchen and the dining room, plates extended in both hands, then placed them on the table. "See? All done."

"Yeah, I see." But his eyes were on her.

How could food capture his attention more thoroughly than Harper, when she'd changed out of her snappy work pantsuit and donned a flowing ankle-length dress the color of sunset? She'd left her hair unbound and brushed it out somehow so it waved down her back instead of springing up in curls.

His body stirred to life in apparent appreciation, and the date—particularly the torture part—was officially underway.

Before she could sit down, he leaped up to pull her chair back because an erection was not an excuse to forget his manners. He got her all arranged and pushed her chair up to the table without touching her, though he had little hope he'd have that strength again. She smelled divine, like peaches with a hint of something sharp, like alcohol. Which reminded him of how much he enjoyed the lab and did not help matters down below.

"I'm sorry I didn't have time to cook," she apologized unnecessarily. "We left Fyra too late."

She worried her bottom lip with her teeth, oblivious to the enormous sexiness of the sight. Or maybe she knew exactly what she was doing to him; after all, she'd announced plans for a second date mere hours after they'd finished the first. During that amazing earthquake simulation—which, by the way, felt almost nothing like the real thing—his erection had been happily squished up against her soft stomach and there was no way she'd missed it. And her response? Dinner.

He considered that a huge step forward.

"I don't expect you to cook for me," he told her as he picked up his fork. "We were doing something much more important in the lab. By the way, if I haven't already told you enough times today, Formula-47 is brilliant. I'm not just saying that to get into your pad thai."

They'd stopped at one of the Thai restaurants near American Airlines Center and brought the takeout home. The extent of dinner prep had included heating up the food and plating it, but Dante did not take a hot meal for granted, even after three years of being able to order everything off the menu at the priciest five-star restaurant in LA.

Harper laughed as she dug into her own food. "Thanks. That means a lot coming from you."

"Yeah, because Dr. Sexy's scientific opinion is sought after worldwide." Wow. He hadn't meant for that to come out with such bitterness. But facts were facts. He had changed fields, thanks to Cardoza, and few people cared about Dante's chemistry knowledge.

And psychology, while fascinating in and of itself, was not his first love. Growing up, he'd found his escape in chemistry when no family seemed to want him long-term, not even his own. Formulas made sense, were the same today as they were tomorrow, and base elements always reacted precisely as he intended when the right catalyst was introduced.

Being in the lab again… only sharpened that ache to return to real science. Before lunch, he'd have said that was the highlight of the day. But as this was shaping up to be a stellar evening, he'd reserve judgment on his favorite part until tomorrow.

"Stop it. You're still you." She smiled at him with a touch of fondness that splashed through his chest, mixing with the physical reactions he could never quite keep under control around her.

The blend felt nice.

"I had fun today," he told her. "It was a nice reminder of why we're still friends all these years later."

Her eyes fairly glowed as she put her fork down. "I was thinking the same thing. Except I realized something. Maybe our relationship has evolved and I've been trying too hard to stick to the past. Maybe a little experimentation isn't a bad thing. How else are we going to figure out what's happening if we don't embrace the changes?"

His heart froze, jamming up all the blood in his veins. Because… holy hell.

"What are you saying?" he asked cautiously, in case her point wasn't anything resembling what he hoped it was.

She shrugged, but her gaze never wavered from his, bless her. *That* was the fearless, no-holds-barred woman he knew and loved.

"We've been friends a long time. Because we have a lot in common, and we prioritize our relationship. We care about each other. I've been scared I would lose that. But in the last few days, I haven't seen any evidence of that changing just because your mouth feels like pure electricity against my skin."

The atmosphere heated instantly as she dragged her tongue across her bottom lip, and he couldn't help but follow the trail. Because that electricity wasn't only on her side. "That's what I've been saying all along."

The conversation caught in his throat and it tasted a lot like victory. Harper was finally coming around. Why hadn't he started out with the science museum?

He started to speak but she held up a finger. "You just have to promise me that things won't be weird. Nothing is going to change. Right?"

"Not one thing." What would he change? Everything was perfect between them. Or at least it would be very soon.

"There's just one problem," she said casually and his pulse fell off a cliff.

"What? No. No problems," he countered in a rush.

They had enough problems that he'd spent an inordinate amount of time untangling. His body had already latched onto the original premise: Evolution. Experimentation. Mouths. Electricity. He wanted all that. Now.

"I'm being serious. I'm used to having at least a working theory before I start an experiment and with all of this—" she waved to encompass the condo at large but she really meant the chemistry that burned up all the oxygen between them any time they were in the same room "—I'm not the expert. You are."

"Seems like I've mentioned that a time or two," he murmured, mystified about where she was going with all of this.

"Yeah, but you're insisting that I go at my own pace. I have no idea what my pace is. What to do, how to do it, where to start. Show me."

That beautiful phrase made a perfect little bow of her mouth and Dante officially lost interest in dinner, the dining room table and anything that resembled respect for his hostess's effort toward feeding him.

He hoped she'd forgive him.

If that speech wasn't a green light, Dante needed to work on his ability to read a woman.

Pushing back from the table, he wordlessly held out his hand to Harper and waited for her to grasp it, then drew her to her feet so he could lead her outside onto the balcony that overlooked Victory Park. Downtown Dallas twinkled in the dusk to the left of Harper's condo and in the distance, the Mid-Cities sprang up out of the Texas prairie, marching toward Ft. Worth.

But he focused all his attention on Harper, who needed something from him. Instruction, guidance, reassurance. All of the above.

And he was going to give it to her.

The balcony was Harper's favorite spot in the whole house. Normally. The view always got to her—but she scarcely noticed the twilight-tinged skyline. Her heart climbed into her throat as she stared at Dante, nervous as hell about what she'd gotten herself into by laying it all on the line.

Were they about to put on a show for the entire I-35 corridor?

Or had he just taken mercy on her, realizing that she wanted something, but lacked the skills to properly articulate exactly what it was she wanted?

That had been the crux of Trinity's advice. *Tell Dante to take the lead.* As that fit with her inexperience, she'd approved that plan. Heartily.

"So here's how this is going to go," Dante began, but

before Harper could get her brain started again, he pulled her into his arms and stroked a lock of hair behind her ear. "You're going to remember that part you said about how we care about each other. And then you're going to stand here with me until I say you can move."

His arms encircled her like they had at the museum and she greedily leaned into him. His heart thumped against her chest in a thrilling experience of connection that she wouldn't have guessed would feel so intimate. "And then what?"

"I'll let you know," he murmured. "The point of this part of the experiment is to feel. That's it. What happens next is up to you. But don't worry, I'm going to give you choices."

"Oh, really? Like a test?"

Despite her nerves, her inexperience and the swirl of uncertainty, she laughed. If nothing else, she appreciated the validation that admitting she wanted to explore the spark between them hadn't ruined everything. They still could have fun together. Because Dante was still Dante, no matter what else happened.

This was going to work. And everything inside went taut with anticipation.

He nodded. "But the best kind of test because there are no wrong answers. And it's multiple choice, with an all-of-the-above option you may invoke at any time."

"I like the sound of that. What's the first question?" Her voice had dropped a couple of notes and it darkened his eyes. Deliciously. Why did it make her so shivery to have that melty gaze on her?

"Do you want me to keep holding you like this?"

Easy. "Yes."

"See, you're a pro," he said and dipped his mouth closer to her ear, like he had at the museum, and his breath stirred along her skin, sensitizing it. "Next, I'd like to touch you. Name a spot."

"You're already touching me," she pointed out breathlessly and gave herself a mental kick. He meant somewhere else on her body. And was asking permission because she had a habit of freaking out.

God, did his patience ever end? It was a little dizzying to know he could so carefully devise a way to assuage her fears. And not for the first time. This was, like, the fourth tactic he'd effortlessly switched to, all in the name of progressing their relationship.

All at once, she wanted to reward him. Boldness stole over her, encouraging her to take charge of this one small aspect of the long evening she hoped was in store.

"I like your hands on my back," she whispered. "I think I might like you to touch me other places. But I have some questions of my own. Like where you want me to touch you."

He sucked in a breath, heat simmering in his expression, and against her skin where they connected. "That might be a little too difficult a test at this moment."

Because she affected him when she touched him. Affected him by simply *talking* about touching him. That was thrilling. "What if I said that was what I needed? Show me what to do."

A groan rippled through his chest. "Fine. Put your palms on my chest. Explore to your heart's content. But then I get to do the same to you."

A wicked thrill shot through her at the thought of Dante stroking her in all the achy places under her filmy dress. "Okay. But—"

"No buts. Shhh." Dante put his palms over hers, and dragged them down his chest in a slow, careful sweep. "Touch me like this. There's not a wrong way to do it."

She took that at face value and let her fingers do some exploring. Amazing. There wasn't a part of him that wasn't hard and she reveled in the unadulterated lust that accompanied her perusal. Little firecrackers turned into bigger ones as he leaned into her palms, seeking deeper contact, which she would gladly comply with. Except there was too much fabric between her and the man.

No time like the present to jump in with both feet.

"Can I unbutton your shirt?" she asked, a little shocked that she'd actually gotten that whole sentence out. But holy hell did she want to see that dragon again, touch it, lick it maybe. If he would let her.

"No," he ground out hoarsely as his eyelids shuttered in response. "That's why we're outside, so nothing goes too far."

Her heart swelled a little. Even in this he was thinking of her. "Why do we need to worry about things going too far? Am I not being clear enough that I'm ready?"

"Ready?" The back of his hand came up, knuckles grazing her jaw as the crackle in the air grew to a fever pitch. "In the course of a few hours? Based on past experience, I'd rather make really sure. Like extra, extra sure because I do not have the strength to let you go again."

That set her back. She had been overly wishy-washy, hadn't she? The frustration in his voice wasn't directed at her, just at the situation, and that squished at her heart just as much as the realization that he'd been carefully leading her through her reservations. Which wasn't supposed to be happening. Had she forgotten all of Trinity's warnings about allowing emotions into the middle of this?

But how could Harper push away the fact that he'd had a place in her heart for ten years? Dante was only demonstrating how much he cared about her. That's what friends did, and she'd expect no less. Wasn't it possible that being together like this might actually make their friendship stronger?

"Then don't let go," she murmured. "I heard a rumor that sex is better when you're pregnant, so you don't even have to be very good—"

Dante cut her off with a growl, swinging her up into his arms, caveman-style, and she couldn't even squeak because holy crap, where had that come from?

He carried her into the house through the double French doors, taking care not to bump her, and set her down in the living room, forcing her to slide down the length of his body until she was locked against him.

That's when he kissed her, taking her mouth in his with almost savage possession and she could only cling to him as his tongue licked through the opening she'd given him. Her skin ignited under his hands as they raced across her back, nothing slow about it this time, caressing every millimeter he could reach.

At which point he started a trail of sensation down her bottom, to her thighs, gripping one in his strong fingers to draw it upward. Snugging their bodies closer together.

He lifted his lips long enough to mutter, "Now you can unbutton my shirt," but then he didn't give her a chance to say her fingers had gone numb. His own fingers tangled around the collar of his button-down and he ripped it sideways, pulling the fabric from between them. Half the buttons bounced to the floor, yanked unceremoniously from their moorings, and then the shirt drifted away, baring the sun-bronzed, dragon-enhanced, gorgeous torso that she'd seen in her need-soaked dreams.

Lightning forked through her core as she greedily drank him in and then she couldn't stop herself from tentatively reaching out, running her nails over the green tail where the dragon wound around his bicep. His hot-eyed gaze followed the movement, his muscle flexing along the trail she painted.

"Would it—" She cleared her throat, shocked at her broken speech, but she recognized it as the product of desire. Not fear. "Could I...taste you?"

In response, he groaned. "If you hurry."

That didn't sound very fun to her, so she took her sweet time, laying her lips on the dragon and then dragging her tongue up the scales of his back to where he spread across Dante's shoulder. His flavor exploded in her mouth, part excitement, part salt and all man. She had to stand on her tiptoes to keep going around the back. He accommodated her by dipping down, but she wasn't so involved in her perusal that she didn't notice his legs were shaking.

From her mouth on his flesh? That was so exciting she could hardly stand it.

Emboldened, she licked into the hollow of his collarbone, kissing him with little nibbles because he was delicious and she liked the way it made her feel, until he growled her name.

Before she could blink, he'd spun to capture her in his arms again, nuzzling against her ear in the way she'd come to truly enjoy.

"That was enough. More later."

"How can I go at my own pace if you won't let me experiment?" Seemed like there were a few more buzzwords he'd tossed around in his quest to get them to this point. Oh yeah, how could she forget? "I believe I was promised the opportunity to be in *control*."

Stressing the word did not have the desired effect of letting her continue her exploration. Instead, he backed her up to the couch, sat her down and knelt between her legs, his hands stroking up her thighs suggestively as he parted her knees.

"That was before," he informed her. "When I wanted to be sure you were on board. I've devised another method to figure that out, so we're just going to do that."

The wicked gleam darkening his brown eyes almost made her afraid to ask. But even in this, she preferred to get the data. "Which is?"

"I'm going to show you. As the lady demanded."

Without further ado, he hooked the hem of her dress with both thumbs, then gathered the fabric as he slid upward, baring her legs to his predatory scrutiny. That thrilled through her, sensitizing her core as he traveled oh, so leisurely up her calves, brushing her skin with the pads of his thumbs. His gaze roved over the flesh he'd uncovered as if he couldn't look his fill.

Except he'd seen her legs before. Lots of times. But never with this kind of appreciation. It puckered her skin with prickly goose bumps, but whether from the sudden chill of being bared, from his touch or simply having his full, undivided attention, she couldn't say.

Maybe it was all three. And it was strange, wonderful, nerve-racking. Slow. Way too slow and her nerves stretched taut the higher he went. Over her knees. To her thighs. Which quivered as he thumbed them and all at once, he stopped. Because he'd noticed that she was quivering.

He glanced up at her over the tops of his glasses, evaluating, and the sight of him at her feet, checking in with her when he so clearly wanted to keep going filled her with a different kind of warmth.

"It's okay," she whispered, and meant it. "That's my excited shake."

He flashed a smile that deepened his dimple and then

smoothed his palms over her thighs, leaving her dress bunched at the juncture of her legs. But instead of stopping, like she'd half expected, he bent and placed his lips on the inside of her knee in a long kiss that he didn't seem to be in any hurry to end.

Heat gathered under his lips and he spread the wealth as he mouthed her inner thigh, working slowly toward the bunched fabric covering her panties. His faint five o'clock shadow scraped her, and shot sparks up her leg.

She gasped, nearly twisting off the couch, but Dante apparently had anticipated that as his hands gripped her waist, smoothing downward to hold her hips steady as he added his tongue to the action along her thighs in a long slow lick. Dampness soaked her panties as she watched his tongue move closer and closer to her secrets.

He would stop before he got there. Wouldn't he? It would be weird if he—

Her lungs hitched as he gathered her dress in one hand, twisting the fabric high on her stomach, revealing her low-slung pink panties.

Dante licked at the hem in the crease of her thigh and flicked his gaze sideways to catch her watching him. "I like pink."

Hands fisted against the couch, she dragged air into her body, torso heaving as she processed that. "You're not going to…you know. Are you?"

Those gorgeous lips pursed and he nearly kissed the dampest part of her underwear. That didn't help the breathing situation. Because she ached for his lips to connect, for his magic mouth to relieve the restless achiness all of this was invoking. And she had a pretty good idea that he could accomplish that.

But to touch her *there*…with his tongue? She'd never get that image out of her head. Ever.

"Depends," he murmured and his breath brushed across her sensitive thighs, sending a spiral of white hot heat through her. But with his free hand, he gripped her hip in anticipation, keeping her in place on the couch. "What's *you know*?"

"Don't tease me," she shot back. "I'm not well-versed in all the lingo and it doesn't sound very sexy to use the clinical term."

"Not teasing you. Not yet," he clarified with a wicked smile. "I'm just gathering enough data to answer the question. Because there are several things I can do to you here. For example, I can touch you."

To demonstrate, he lifted one index finger and ran it down the flat of her stomach until he hit the dead center of her damp panties. Her thighs quivered again and clamped together involuntarily, but he just pushed them back apart easily with one firm hand to her knee. Opening her up, and it was decadent. Wicked. Unbelievably affecting.

"Or I can lick you."

Before she could move, he followed the line his finger had traced with his tongue, licking at her panties with little tugs that enflamed her and her hips rolled toward his mouth automatically. Her chest heaved as she blindly sought more.

"And I can do both at the same time."

His thumb eased under the hem of her panties, shoving aside the fabric. Cool air burned against her heated, exposed core as Dante's mouth covered her sex. She forgot to be embarrassed as his lips claimed the hard nub, teasing it as he nibbled and one finger toyed with her folds, finally plunging in.

Oh, my.

Her body bowed as he pushed her higher and higher,

sending her soaring on a flight to ecstasy until she saw pinpricks of light exploding across her vision. The reaction built on itself, her hips circling involuntarily, accepting his fingers deeper until the pressure pushed her over the threshold and the greatest sense of relief and release burst across her center as her muscles clenched and rippled.

Her first orgasm. She cried out with it, might have mumbled his name, might have been talking nonsense. And then she went limp, utterly spent and unable to get her brain to form thoughts. Words. Anything.

Dante covered her with her nearly ruined panties and kissed her thighs, once on each side of her still throbbing core.

"I guess that's a *yes*," he murmured. "I *am* going to."

"Was that one of those 'all of the above' deals?" she choked out, breathless, awed, a million things at once. "Because my answer is that. From now on."

Eight

Dante had never seen a more gorgeous sight than Harper post-orgasm. And she was still fully clothed. His body throbbed with the promise of diving in. But he couldn't stop looking at her

Cheeks flushed, hands limp at her side, eyelids at half-mast. *Yes.* Exactly as he'd envisioned her a million times or more. He couldn't lie—being the man she'd let between her legs, the one who'd tongued her to that amazing finish, the only one ever to do so—it was a hell of a rush.

Best of all, he had a whole night of firsts ahead of him. He nearly felt like a virgin himself, with a raw sense of anticipation that he didn't recall from any of his sexual encounters.

With the honeyed taste of her still fresh on his tongue, he stood and held out a hand to her. He'd lost count of the number of times he'd done so, issuing invitation after invitation for her to follow him to a new place. Every time, she reached back and it thrilled him.

This time was no different. So trusting, she laid her hand in his and allowed him to pull her from the couch, then lead her to the bedroom. The master suite had a million-dollar view of downtown Dallas, lit for the night by this point, so he left the room's lights off, allowing the full wall of glass to provide the illumination he needed to get this woman naked as soon as humanly possible.

"Harper," he murmured, drawing her knuckles to his lips, and she looked at him, her eyes still warm and sated.

His breath tangled in his throat, freezing everything in his chest until he thought all his organs would burst from the pain of how simply stunning she was.

"Dante." Her throaty response thrummed through his erection. "Is it later? Because I'm ready for more."

Seems like he'd said something along those lines out on the balcony. She was asking for a turn to explore him in kind, but that was before she'd nearly taken him apart with her cries and sweet taste. "No. Definitely not. I'm not done with you."

She shuddered and he used that as an excuse to kiss her again, because clearly she needed his warmth. Her mouth opened under his, eagerly, her tongue already meeting his halfway because his darling did not hesitate when she forgot to be self-conscious. That was unbelievably hot and his groin let him know exactly how much by straining against his pants. He'd hesitated to strip off any more clothes than just his shirt—she'd already seen him without one—but since he'd touched her as intimately as possible and she hadn't fled…maybe it was time to take it up a notch.

"I'm going to take off your dress," he told her. "I want to see you."

She nodded and held still, allowing him to kneel at her feet to gather up that hem again, but unlike the last time, he didn't have the patience for a slow reveal. Drawing it upward, he kept going past the creamy expanse of her thighs, which nearly drove him insane a second time, past the pink panties that had frankly been as hot a shock as how quickly she'd come.

Watching her body in the throes, feeling her close around his fingers…highlight of the night, thus far. But he was keeping an open mind in case something else edged out her sharp responses to his tongue for the number one spot.

Finally, he got the fabric free of her body and let the dress float to the floor. Harper stood naked before him save the panties, and every drop of blood rushed from his head as he took in the perfection of her breasts. Tight, hard nipples stood at full attention begging for his mouth, but he couldn't, not yet. Not when she dropped her arms to her sides, letting him look his fill without flinching, and it practically choked him up.

How had he gotten so lucky as to gain this opportunity with such an amazing woman? Yeah, he'd been campaigning for it on and off for years, and in earnest over the last week. But still. Now that it was happening, he didn't actually believe he'd done one blessed thing that had turned the tide. This was one-hundred percent her choice and it humbled him.

"I need to touch you," he whispered and his voice ground out across vocal chords that had forgotten how to operate.

No problem. Everything else still seemed in working order. His erection pulsed with the promise of finally being free of its confines. Quickly, he pulled the condoms from his pocket, because there was no point in pretending that he hadn't hoped to need them, and threw them on the bed. Her eyes flicked toward the packages, questioning.

"Safety equipment is the first rule of any experiment, right?" he told her. It was also the first rule of anyone who had a major aversion to accidental pregnancies.

"But I'm already pregnant," she reminded him with a smile.

As this was not a good point to start discussing reasons why people should use a condom every time they had sex no matter what, he dropped it. All the reasons were on his side anyway, and he'd already forgotten every woman on the planet besides this one.

New subject. His pants hit the floor and she wasted no time checking out his briefs, which frankly weren't big enough to fully contain him, especially not when she reached out to trace the waistband. He sucked in a breath as she grazed the tip of his flesh and his hips jerked backward involuntarily.

"Maybe we'll save that," he ground out through clenched teeth.

"Why? You keep saying that, but this is my first time." Her lashes swept downward as her gaze lit on his crotch. "I want to do all the things."

"Because all the things will be over if you keep that up," he advised her, not even a little ashamed how desperate he sounded. "I'm skating on thin ice here and doing what I can to hold it all back."

"You didn't let me hold back. Why do you get to?"

Always the scientist. He couldn't help but laugh. Even in this, she had to question everything, seeking to understand. He didn't mind. Her curiosity was what had gotten her here. Finally.

"Fair enough." And he didn't even strangle over his surrender.

Eagerly, she let her fingers rest on his pecs before sliding the tips downward, her nails scraping across his skin with fire that threatened to undo. He groaned as she fingered the waistband of his underwear, dipping inside, then shifting around to the back.

And then without warning, she pulled them down, letting them drop to his ankles. Baring him to her hot gaze and his pulse bobbled as she looked at his erection with a sense of wonder, awe and pure fascination.

That was nearly the brink. His sanity was holding on by a thin thread and if he didn't slow things down, her first time would be disappointing indeed.

Before she could make good on the intent in her posture, which he was pretty sure meant her mouth was headed in the direction of his groin, he swept her up in his arms to deposit her on the bed, whether she liked it or not.

He liked it, especially as she rolled to her back and one knee fell to the side, opening her thighs. But not open enough. That pink underwear needed to go. So he stripped it off and took his time settling next to her on the bed, gathering her up in his arms.

"I know it's your first time. Trust me," he murmured, nuzzling the sweet flesh of her ear with his nose because that was where it smelled the most like peaches. "Let me make it good for you and then you can do whatever you want to me. All night. I will willingly submit to your every fantasy. But not right this minute."

She nodded against his neck, her lips grazing his skin. "I trust you."

And then she tipped her head up to take his lips in

a kiss so sweet and unassuming that he fell into it. Fell into her.

Rolling her onto her back, he went with the motion, snugging their bodies tight, and then he let go of his rein on his desire. For so long he'd been forced to temper it, but not now. There was no pretending he wasn't aching for her, no ignoring his need. This woman was his.

He kissed her with every ounce of his pent-up longing, which had been building for a decade. Her firm body under his vibrated with excitement and he groaned as her hands ran down his back, across his bare butt, down his thighs as if she couldn't get enough under her fingertips.

He chunked his glasses onto the bedside table, blessing his nearsightedness. Meant he could see Harper in all her glory just fine but the rest of the room was a blur. Perfect. He had exactly what he wanted to see in his field of vision.

Blindly, he fumbled for the condoms, managed to pull away from her for an eternity while he rolled one on and then he was back against her, tongues clashing in a battle of heat and raging desire. His body screamed to slide into her tight channel, which had never held another man before, and he could not hold back another second. She'd been so wet and swollen for him earlier; he had no idea how he'd stopped himself from taking her right there on the couch. Only a strong determination to give her a memorable end to her virginity kept him from it.

But he wasn't leaving that to chance now.

Ripping away from her lips, he trailed open-mouthed kisses down her throat in a straight line to her nipple, then sucked one between his teeth, rolling it gently as he tongued it and, yes, it did taste like heaven.

Harper's hips bucked against the mattress as he switched to the other nipple and she moaned with the sweetest little sound. Too bad he couldn't hang around doing *that* for another couple of hours. He was about to lose his mind as it was and those moans were sexier than all get-out. He kissed down her stomach until he hit the nirvana between her legs, spreading them wide to give him the full access he hadn't been granted earlier.

Dante groaned as he swiped his tongue across her nub, then dipped into her nectar. She was as hot and wet as she'd been earlier. Amazingly so, and as much as he wanted to bring her to another shattering climax this way, he wanted to be inside her with every fiber of his body so much more.

Shaking with need, he crawled back up her length, gathered Harper in his arms and gave himself the longest-denied pleasure of his life. Slowly, he notched his length at her entrance and caught her gaze in his so he could watch her expression as he pushed into her.

The ecstasy of it swamped his senses. She was tight, but so slick with her desire for him that he slid all the way in before he'd realized the resistance he'd felt was her maidenhood. She froze. Cursing, he fought his instinct to possess her, instead giving her a minute to acclimate.

"Okay?" he whispered.

Harper exhaled and her body relaxed under his. And then she nodded, allowing his heart to start beating again.

He meant to let his body go, let this fire between them rage to its natural conclusion. But all he could do was brush a thumb across her temple tenderly as they stared at each other, locked intimately in a timeless, hazy moment that forever imprinted on his memory as he made love to Harper for the first time.

But definitely not the last. Oh, no. He'd vastly underestimated how many times they'd have to repeat this experiment before they could even think about calling the spark extinguished.

The clear, bottomless depths of her gaze wrapped around him, holding him captive as surely as her body did.

"Dante," she breathed and the whisper floated over his skin, where he absorbed it like water on parched earth. "I'm sorry I held out for so long. I...needed this. So much. Needed you."

That made two of them. He nodded, too overcome to put the overwhelming emotions pounding through his blood into words. So he showed her instead.

Slowly, he withdrew and eased back in, watching her carefully, gauging even the slightest nuance of her expression so he could adjust the pace. He'd never done this with a pregnant woman, had no idea if he should change anything. He had to be careful.

She sucked in a breath and her eyelids drifted closed, her mouth partially open as he repeated the rhythm that felt so good, so right, that it nearly brought tears to his eyes.

Her hips rolled, meeting him on the next thrust, driving him deeper and pulling a gasp from her throat. Oh, she liked that, yes she did, and he was happy to give her more where that came from. Faster now, they came together, and he couldn't help but go a little further each time, pushing her limits with each stroke. And still she met him, fingernails biting into his back in a sweet burn that spurred him on.

He sought her center with his thumb, wedging his hands between their undulating bodies, and fingered her until her eyes went glassy. She bucked her hips faster, finally clenching around him in a tight glove, and he lost his fragile grip on the release he'd been fighting for an eternity.

In tandem, they climaxed, and he pried his lids open to watch her face as she came with him deep inside her, emptying himself as she cradled him. It was so beautiful that it bordered on spiritual.

Enlivened, he stroked her flushed face, drawing a smile from her that speared him right through the gut.

"I can unequivocally say that I now know what all the fuss is about," she said with a contented sigh.

He laughed and his heart wrenched as he lay there still half inside her, still wrapped in her arms. Still wrapped in the utter perfection of the emotional high being with her had created.

That was really, really...*not good*.

He shut his eyes but the feeling didn't go away.

As experiments went, he'd call that one an utter failure. Because nothing he'd hypothesized about the experience of being with Harper Livingston had been true. It wasn't a onetime thing, it definitely hadn't been "just sex," and they weren't going to wake up tomorrow and be friends again like nothing had happened.

None of this had been about one-upping Cardoza, or Dante beating his chest with territorial pride. He'd wanted more from her, more from their relationship, and used any means at his disposal to get it.

Because Dante was hopelessly and utterly in love with Harper.

When he'd taken her virginity, she'd taken something just as precious and unrecoverable—his heart. He needed her like he needed oxygen. She wasn't the closest thing to love he'd ever felt; she was it.

He loved Harper. Of course he did, and had for a decade. But he hadn't realized he was *in love* with her until this moment. Hadn't even realized it was something he was capable of or that it existed in such a pure form.

The sheer disaster of it swept over him, souring the gorgeous moment of clarity.

For the first time in his life, he had a woman in his arms that he could envision a future with, a relationship of equals. Maybe even put a ring on that third finger one day—like tomorrow. Why wait? They'd been moving toward this for a long time.

Except there was no happily-ever-after on the horizon here.

Instead of making their relationship better, he'd ruined it. But how could he have known the complications would arise after it was too late to start scouting for the rip cord?

His newly lost heart squeezed as her hand drifted across his face in a caress, and she shifted against him, stretching her back with a sexy lift of her breasts. He should be thinking about sinking into her again, letting her have her turn. Living in the moment of pleasure because that was all he could possibly hope to get out of this relationship with Harper.

When morning came, she'd still be pregnant with a baby Dante didn't want, who'd been fathered by a man he hated. And Harper didn't believe in love. What had she called it? *A nebulous emotion warped by greeting card companies.*

Before tonight, he'd totally agreed. Now he completely understood how faulty that logic was.

Somehow, he was supposed to pretend none of this had happened and find a way to get back to being friends. He'd promised. Multiple times. And after being let down by people time and time again as a foster kid, keeping his word meant something to him. His friendship meant something to Harper.

How had the simple decision to kiss Harper at the airport turned into his worst nightmare?

Harper took Dante's advice and hightailed it to the bath to soak her sore body in hot water. She'd half hoped he'd join her but he'd just smiled and said they had plenty of time for that later.

Always later. Dante had teased, licked, and rubbed not one, but two orgasms out of her, and it had been glorious. Really, the experiment had been a huge success and now that she had some data, she wanted a hell of a lot more.

Because while she had very little experience, she wasn't completely ignorant. There were a lot of things they hadn't done yet, all of which she wanted to do. The floodgates had been opened.

As she lay in her marble bathtub, the hot water soothed her raw places. Tipping her head back, she closed her eyes and let the images and memories assault her. And it was an assault in every sense of the word because...*wow*.

Hard and fast, all the incredible sensations Dante had elicited buzzed through her mind, and it was fascinating how even imagining him kneeling between her legs, his tongue hot on her sex, induced a similar physical reaction. A powerful lick of heat rippled through her core and she arched with it.

God, he wasn't even in the room and he could still affect her.

But the beauty of it was that she wasn't scared of those feelings anymore. He'd smashed all her barriers with his sweet patience and then taken her to places she'd never dreamed existed. The expert indeed.

And she couldn't wait for her turn to explore his beautiful, mostly unknown body. Find ways to pleasure him as he'd done her. Oh, yes, there was so much more he could teach her and she was a willing student.

When the water grew too cold, Harper climbed from the tub and pulled on a robe. She thought about getting dressed again but why be shy? Dante had seen everything she had to show. And besides, it was kind of wicked to be wandering around her condo naked except for a sheer robe as she searched for the man she hoped to spend a very long night with.

Dante was in the kitchen. Both of their forgotten dinner plates sat on the counter.

He flashed her a smile, but left off the dimple and she missed it all at once.

"Hungry?" he asked. "We never finished dinner. I was going to heat it."

"Sure. Gotta keep up our strength." She winked but he'd already turned around to stick one of the plates in the microwave.

No finer sight than that of Dr. Gates' extremely tight butt. He made khaki pants a work of art. And his shoulders... That dragon lay in exactly the spot she'd discovered tasted the best on his body. Emboldened by the activities of the evening, she put both hands on his back and slid her palms upward, exploring. Because she could. Because she wanted to understand his body better, wanted to please him. And he was hard, delicious and so masculine under her fingers.

Didn't matter if he was clothed. At some point, they'd pick up where they left off. No reason they couldn't indulge in a precursor while dinner heated.

Except he stiffened under her hands. Somehow, she'd envisioned touching him would be pleasurable for him.

That he might melt under her palms and make little noises of appreciation that would tell her she was doing it right.

"Dante?" He didn't answer or turn around. "Is everything okay? Am I not allowed to touch you like this in the kitchen? If there are rules, you better tell me now because I do not want to make a faux pas like stripping off this robe to show you that I'm n—"

"It's fine." His chuckle sounded forced and she wished he'd turn around so she could see his face. "You're allowed to do whatever you want. Your house, your rules."

She blinked and let her hands drop from his shoulders. "Well, in that case, there are no rules. If you want to walk around naked, I'm heavily in favor of it."

"Noted."

The microwave beeped and he made a huge show of removing the first plate and replacing it with the second. As soon as he pressed the start button, she waited for him to make a joke about her walking around naked in kind. When he didn't, a funny tickle started up in her throat.

She was making huge concessions here. Did he not realize that? At one point, she'd have been mortified by the idea of anyone walking around naked. This was all new to her, but she was willing to learn, to try new things, and he'd offered to be her guide. She needed that.

"I was thinking that it might be nice to go to the Kimball this weekend," she offered. Maybe a subject change would dispel the odd tension in the room that she'd somehow caused by touching him. "There's an ancient Egypt exhibit there for a limited time and I hear the mummies are cool. Of course, it's technically your turn to pick the date."

"That sounds great."

And then they stood in awkward silence and the

longer it stretched, the pricklier the back of her throat got. Was this some kind of post-coitus thing men went through? Like a withdrawal that was biologically necessary to replenish their strength?

But his reticence, especially in the face of the monumental experience they'd just shared, struck her oddly.

She opted to let it go. For now. What was she supposed to do instead? Besides, the scent of hot food was making her mouth water and that physiology was easy to interpret. She hadn't eaten dinner and Dante had stirred up all her juices.

Dante took both plates of warmed pad thai to the dining room table and settled in without another word to eat his own dinner. She shoveled noodles and chicken into her mouth as fast as she could, and let the silence stretch until she couldn't stand it any longer.

"This is the best date I've ever been on."

He glanced at her, and his eyes softened behind his glasses, turning that melty chocolate. "I'm glad."

"You didn't ask. But it was amazing."

His eyelids flew shut and he swallowed, clearly struggling, which was a little alarming. But then he looked at her dead-on for the first time since they'd untangled their bodies from each other. "I'm sorry. I should have checked in with you. It *was* amazing, more so than I was expecting. Much more. And my expectations were pretty high."

That put a warm glow in her chest. And other places. Which she liked, maybe a little too much. The glow spreading in her core was about to get out of hand very quickly now that she knew it was just the tip of the iceberg. "I didn't have any. So you definitely exceeded mine."

The smile he flashed her wasn't the wicked one he'd

adopted recently. The one she'd always reacted to and pretended she hadn't. And the tension hadn't fled one iota despite the break in the silence.

Her heart thumped in her chest and not in a good way.

"I am the expert," he intoned and she had the impression it was supposed to be a joke. She didn't feel like laughing all at once. This strange mood was starting to scare her.

"Dante?" She put her fork down and folded her hands. The appetite she'd developed had completely fled in the face of this whatever-it-was that laced the atmosphere. "Remember when we were on the balcony? I asked you to promise that things would not be weird between us if we slept together. I may not have a lot of know-how in the bedroom, but I do know you. And you're making it weird."

At least she thought it was him. A sense of foreboding prickled her spine. Or was this totally on her? Had she messed up by giving in to the lure he'd dangled in front of her?

All her misgivings, the hesitation—she should have listened to her brain, not her body.

Oh, God. He'd *promised*. She couldn't lose him, not now. Not after everything, with his incredible help with the samples, his support for her pregnancy despite not totally being on board.

Not after the cataclysmic lovemaking they'd shared.

Instantly, his face blanked. "I'm not trying to."

The panic sped up, zooming through her veins. "Well, you're not trying *not* to either. I was looking forward to having my turn. You promised me that, too."

He shoved his chair back and stood, gathering both of their plates. "Yeah, I guess I did."

Was that it then? The naked part of their relationship

was over? If so, it didn't bode well for their friendship because it sure seemed like that wasn't going so well, either, if he couldn't talk to her, couldn't even look at her.

All this time she'd thought she would be the one who wouldn't be able to look him in the eye after doing things to each other that she'd only had a vague awareness of after years of watching movies. And that education had been poor indeed compared to reality.

The prickling at her spine flared into full-on temper as she followed him to the kitchen. How dare he make things weird between them? How dare he call an end to the benefits side of their friendship before she was ready?

She needed him to help her understand all the strange, wonderful sensations, the rush of tenderness she'd felt when he touched her. She needed *him*.

"What if I want my turn right now?" She dogged his steps as he headed to the sink, temper rising the more agitated she got. "Right here in the kitchen. What if I wanted to untie this robe and rub myself all over your body?"

The plates clacked into the sink with a little more force than necessary. Dante spread his arms wide, gripping the counter as if holding himself up. His knuckles turned white as he stared at the mess in the sink. "How can that possibly be considered part of your turn?"

Exasperating, frustrating, stubborn, stupid *male*. "Because, Dante! I want to experiment. To see what makes you hot, to see if I can make you feel good like you did for me. How do I know what turns you on unless I try it? I want you to tell me, to teach me."

"The thing is—" He cursed, but kept his back to her. "That was a onetime deal, so we could burn off the spark, remember? We did and we're done."

Her brows came together. What the hell was he talking about? If he thought for one second the spark had been snuffed, there was something sorely lacking in her education on the matter. And the only person who could help her understand was turning her down. A chill crept through her blood.

"Turn around and say that to my face."

"What?" he growled. "Why?"

Because I need you.

She'd always needed him for emotional support, intellectual challenge, even just to make her laugh, and then he'd gone and added a brand-new, complex layer that was one hundred percent physical need—which might be the strongest need of all. For the first time in her memory, she didn't feel like she could express her consternation out loud and that scared her most of all.

So she went with logic. "My house, my rules."

Slowly, he turned, resting his butt against the countertop, arms crossed as he met her gaze. Instead of being blank as she'd fully expected, a thousand things darted through his expression—and all of them labeled him a liar.

They were not done. The spark was not snuffed. And in that moment, she learned he could still convey an enormous amount of affection for her through his melty chocolate eyes when he wanted to.

Her breath caught. "Dante."

He struggled to swallow and suddenly, she didn't care what the rules were. Her heart ached in a way her body never had or could and she wanted all of the weirdness gone. So she stepped into the space between his legs and wrapped herself around him despite his crossed arms because that wasn't anywhere close to enough of a barrier to keep her out.

Immediately, he dropped his defensive posture and

crushed her to his chest, holding her so tight she could hardly breathe, but she didn't mind. Emboldened, she snugged her face into the hollow of his shoulder, the spot she'd discovered earlier where it smelled most like him.

"I'm sorry," he said simply. "No more weird."

Her world tilted back into place as he rested his cheek against her head. Relief rushed into the cold, jagged holes inside, invigorating her, draining all her temper. All her fear. *Everything was okay.*

God, she needed this, needed his strength and his wit and his unique take on life in general. He felt good in her arms, divine under her palms. She spread her fingers to get more of his back muscles against her flesh.

His lips grazed the hair near her temple, his breath stirring against her scalp and it put a tinge of awareness into the embrace that snagged her body's attention.

She turned her head into his mouth, seeking a stronger connection. And was rewarded to feel a very prominent bulge in his pants. Languorously, she tilted her hips against it and his heart rate increased instantly, thumping against her cheek.

Well, that was just lovely.

Nuzzling his neck, she let the moment build, until the anticipation grew so heavy on her shoulders that she could hardly breathe. She wanted him to kiss her, to take her back to bed and light her up again. But there was so much more to explore.

So she did. Her tongue fit nicely in the dip where his throat met his torso and she traced the line of his collarbone. Dante groaned and it rumbled against her breasts, teasing them. She could get used to that. Nibbling her way upward, she concentrated on his earlobe and judging from his sharp exhale, she'd hit a good spot.

"Is this okay?" she asked softly in case he'd really

meant it about being done. He deserved the opportunity to say no.

"More than."

His hands spread across the small of her back, holding her in place and it was delicious, especially given his strange mood earlier. That had completely fled and she reveled in the rush of sensation, of feeling secure in their relationship again. In knowing that they could navigate bumps in their friendship.

"What can I do to pleasure you?" she whispered in his ear and he turned into her mouth, sliding their cheeks together.

"Everything," he murmured, his voice broken and raw against her skin. "Everything is pleasurable when you're in my arms."

And then their mouths connected and he kissed her, but it was so much more than just a kiss. She accepted it, desperate to fall into the connection they'd shared once already this evening.

Hustling her backward, he kissed her and guided her at the same time until she felt the hardwood floor of her bedroom under her feet. Perfect. She pulled away from his mouth—somehow—and backed toward the bed with a smile, shedding her robe as she went until she finally stood naked. Waiting.

He didn't make her wait long. Depositing his glasses on the bedside table, he then shed his own clothes and snugged her into his body as he rolled her onto the bed. She stared up into his beautiful eyes and experienced an odd moment of intimacy as she touched his bare face. Dante without his glasses was almost more intimate than when they were joined, as if she'd gotten a glimpse of him the rest of the world never saw.

And then he proceeded to shatter her a third and

fourth time, carefully avoiding her sorest spots like a master, as if he knew her body better than she did. Her soul sang with the pleasure. But afterward, the weirdness in the kitchen haunted her and despite the major exhaustion of her body, and the gorgeous man holding her, sleep never came.

Nine

Dante woke in the morning still tangled with Harper and it was the most bittersweet experience imaginable. He'd like nothing more than to gather her close and whisper all the things in his heart. It sure as hell wasn't what he'd envisioned he'd want if he got past the threshold of her bedroom door.

And he doubted that she'd like to hear it anyway, especially since half of what was going on inside him was consternation over the permanent roadblocks between him and what he wished could be the next steps. But there were no more steps. No more stages of seduction. This could *not* go on. That was part of what he wanted to tell her, too.

As he blinked the sleep from his eyes, he stared at the ceiling, contemplating the spattered texture, looking for order in the chaos in hopes it would settle his racing mind.

Didn't work. And then Harper stretched against him,

clearly awake and looking to get a little closer. That second time last night had been the worst sort of concession, one he'd schooled himself against and then had been too weak to resist. He'd have to do better today because he truly did not think he could take the barb through the chest again.

"We should get going," he muttered and kissed Harper's temple in apology, though it was a distant second to what he'd rather be doing. "The strides we made yesterday on the formula were great, but we still have a lot of work to do."

"That's a switch. That's usually my line." She rolled to face him, her hair spilling into her face, and he couldn't stop himself from fingering the strands.

She was just so beautiful and perfect and responsive. His body had absolutely no problem adding additional complexity to Dante's anguish, springing fully alert as she slid a leg against his, snugging a thigh tight against his erection.

Oh, who was he kidding? When it came to Harper, he had zero will, and there was no way he could get out of this bed without a wholly conflicted heart anyway, so why not indulge in her sweet, tight body as long as he could?

Rolling her to her back, he dove into an open-mouthed kiss that she instantly responded to and within minutes, she'd moaned her way through a gorgeous climax that nearly pushed him off the edge.

He should leave it at that and get out of Dodge. Nothing wrong with going into the lab still sporting wood. Hell, lately, it had been his constant state, so he certainly had plenty of practice hiding it.

But she arched against him, her fingers questing until they hit his groin, then closed around him. A curse tangled in his throat as she eagerly explored his shaft, lithe fingers stroking the flames higher and higher until he couldn't stand being apart from her a second longer.

Sheathing himself, he slid into the heat at her core, nearly coming instantly, but he battled it back because this was the sweet part. The intimacy of being inside Harper surrounded him and he let his heart fly, unabashed, since this was the only time when he could.

She wrapped her legs around his waist, drawing him deeper, her eyes shiny as she watched him. And his pulse stumbled. There was no way he could give this up. Not anytime soon.

A powerful wave of emotion swamped him as he considered what compromises he could make to keep Harper in his arms. Maybe they could make a deal to be lovers until she had the baby. That gave him time. Eventually he might sate himself enough to go back to a platonic relationship. It could happen.

With that, his body shuddered and he came in a rush, closing his eyes as he let the emotional and physical reaction combine in a swirl of Harper that he couldn't have stopped at gunpoint.

Finally, they rolled from bed and got dressed for work, then drove to Fyra to spend several hours doing his second favorite thing—chemistry. Just after lunch, Harper popped over to his lab table and slid onto the next stool, her expression cluing him in that she was hoping for his undivided attention.

"I have a huge favor to ask," she began and then hesitated.

Which was silly. After the scene in the kitchen last night, he'd obviously lost the ability to deny her—or himself—anything. "Whatever it is, I'm pretty sure the answer is going to be yes."

"Will you go to the obstetrician with me?"

The bottom dropped out of Dante's stomach. He should have waited to hear the favor, obviously. "That's not something you'd rather do with Cass? You guys can compare notes."

There was literally nothing he'd enjoy less than sitting through a doctor's appointment where the major point of discussion would be the largest obstacle between him and bliss.

Harper shook her head. "She's in Austin for the rest of the week. It's Robbie's birthday."

Cass's husband and son lived in Austin and he knew she split her time between cities. Unfortunate timing. And Alex lived in Washington. "Trinity?"

The derision in Harper's snort came through loud and clear. "I'd have a better shot asking Trinity to come with me to get matching root canals. Please, Dante. I know it's not a guy thing, but when I came to LA, this is precisely what I meant when I said I needed you. I don't want to go by myself."

Holy God, if only his objection had anything remotely to do with whether he'd feel masculine enough while sitting in a roomful of pregnant women. "Plenty of guys go with their wives to the doctor's when they're having a baby. We're not married and I'm not that guy."

"Is this because we're...sleeping together?" Her voice dropped to whisper the words, her eyes darting to the two lab techs working on the other side of the room.

Which was frankly ridiculous when he was pretty sure everyone at Fyra knew what had happened between Dante and Harper last night. And again this morning. Trinity had even high-fived him in the breakroom earlier and offered a hearty, *Congrats. Took you long enough.*

"Of course not."

It had everything to do with that, along with the fact that Trinity's comment still stuck in his craw. If only he'd made a move sooner, he could have kept Harper happy enough to forget all about the idea of having a baby.

"It's okay. I'll drive myself." She shrugged, her mouth turning down. "You know, I drove Alex to the doctor and she can't even return the favor because of her own difficult pregnancy. Figures. I got pregnant at the worst possible time, I guess."

Her unhappy tone lanced through him and he groaned. Yeah, he should have just said yes from the beginning and shut up. There was no point pretending she didn't have him wrapped around her finger. "Forget I said anything. I'll take you."

She lit up, which hit him right in the solar plexus. "Thanks, I owe you."

And the gleam in her eye gave him a pretty good idea what she intended to use as currency. Which made the ride to the doctor's office uncomfortable for reasons beyond his emotional turmoil.

There were more than a few fans of Dr. Sexy in the waiting room, judging by the whispers and furtive looks, followed by mad texting. No one approached him for pictures or autographs, a rarity that Dante appreciated given the sensitive nature of their location. Though he wouldn't be surprised to get a couple of calls from his manager and publicist asking if there was something he'd like to tell them about his new girlfriend's condition.

The truth was so much less interesting than speculation, as he well knew. But Harper didn't, and he made a mental note to make sure she understood the downside of celebrity and how being in his orbit would undoubtedly lead to unwelcome exposure.

For now, he held her hand as she nervously beat out

the can-can against his chair leg with her sandaled foot. He distracted her with some funny stories about his TV crew, which only worked about half as well as he'd have liked, and somewhere in the middle of it, his manager called. That was fast. And an easy message to ignore.

Finally, a nurse called Harper's name and he followed her through the warren of hallways to an exam room.

The stark decor reminded him why he'd gone with chemistry instead of biology. He didn't like the idea of poking around in humans and he liked the idea of strangers doing the same to Harper even less. His protective instinct reared its ugly head and suddenly, he was glad she'd asked him to be here.

Especially when the nurse told the mother-to-be to put on a gown, then left the room so Dante could watch Harper strip. That was an unexpected bonus he wouldn't have been granted if they hadn't begun the "experimentation" phase of their relationship.

The doctor bustled into the room, introduced herself and asked after Cass. Huh. Harper hadn't mentioned she'd be seeing Cass's obstetrician, but of course the ladies would share recommendations.

"I'm Dr. Dean. And you must be the...?" The doctor stuck her hand out, eyebrows raised expectantly as she waited for him to fill in the blank to explain his role here.

Wasn't that the million-dollar question? "I'm the uncomfortable one who knows far less about this than he would like. But you can call me Dante. Or Dr. Gates if you like to stand on protocol."

The doctor smiled. "I thought I recognized you. As I'm sure we'll be seeing a lot of each other in the next seven and a half months, I'll stick with Dante. Welcome to fatherhood."

Dante didn't correct her, because all at once, it became an uncomfortable and unwavering fact of his current circumstances that he might very well be the closest thing to a father the baby would have.

God, what was he doing here in this sterile room? A picture of a woman's reproductive organs stared him in the face from the poster on the wall.

Things got even worse when the doctor announced that she'd like to do an ultrasound to determine Harper's due date. Pretty sure he was going to need brain bleach before the appointment was through, Dante gritted his teeth as the tech rolled the equipment from the corner and then gooped up Harper's stomach.

The technician rolled the wand over Harper's abdomen and a strong, strange sound emanated from the machine. *Wha-wha-wha.*

"That's the baby's heartbeat," she said with a smile and pointed at the blotchy screen. "And there's your little jellybean."

Transfixed, Dante gripped Harper's hand and stared at the black-and-white monitor. Would you look at that? It was really in there. The fetus did resemble a bean, or more precisely an ameoba, especially as the tech rolled the wand around to capture measurements, causing elongation of the image.

Out of the corner of his eye, he noticed Harper's flinch. He glanced at her. Tears streamed down her face in silent, powerful emotion and his heart twisted to the point of pain.

Wordlessly, he wiped the tears away and kissed her temple. But she didn't take her eyes off the screen.

"Look," she whispered. "It's my baby."

The rawness in her voice scraped at his soul. "I know, sweetheart. I see it."

And in a snap, it was real. Harper was going to have

a baby. She'd need someone to take care of her as she rounded with it, someone to help make decisions about things, to hold her hand when she went into labor. And then she'd have a baby, one who would also need a lot of care for a very long time.

God, when had he developed such an overwhelming urge to raise his hand and volunteer?

What a disaster that would be. He couldn't be anyone's father. His own crappy childhood had branded him, rendering him incapable of parenting. And even if he had the slightest inclination to figure out a way to get over that handicap—because Harper was totally worth it—what if he somehow transferred his hatred of Cardoza to the baby?

It was too big of a risk.

Harper deserved so much better. She needed someone for the long-term and Dante would only be in the way of that. Wow, if that wasn't a stick through the gullet, he didn't know what was. But it didn't change facts. He would have to encourage Harper to find someone else to be the baby's male influence because he wasn't the right man for the job.

They would have to go back to being friends with no benefits much more quickly than he anticipated and that was so physically painful that he feared his chest might explode from it.

But he had to fight through it. He had to be here for Harper because she'd asked him to come to this doctor's appointment and he was not going to fail her.

Harper let Dante run with the rest of the sample creation. They were almost done, which meant she could focus on the original tainted samples. Or try to focus.

The ultrasound still had her shaken up, even though it had been several days ago.

Pregnancy had merely been a state of being thus far, but she'd somehow divorced it in her mind from the actual, physical baby. Seeing it in 3-D had been one of the single most defining moments in her life, the others being when she'd received her doctorate, the day she, Cass and Alex opened the doors of Fyra, and the night she'd lost her virginity to her best friend.

All of those events shared a common element—they represented the start of something wonderful. And like all of the others, seeing the baby had given her the deepest sense of joy.

She'd made the right decision. The timing was perfect, especially with Dante by her side. All her doubt had instantly fled in that moment.

She hadn't expected the ultrasound to be administered at that initial appointment. Dr. Dean hadn't given Alex an ultrasound that early in her pregnancy, but as the doctor had explained, the fact that Alex had been carrying twins had caused her to change her policy.

Harper was glad. It had spurred her to start thinking about the future a great deal sooner than she'd intended to. Which meant she was trying desperately to figure out what she was going to do when Dante went back to LA in just a few days. Of course they'd see each other. They always had. But everything was different now that they were sleeping together—in every sense of the word.

She went to bed with him at night and woke up to his melty chocolate eyes every morning, something she'd never have dreamed she'd want or grow to crave. Unfortunately, it had an expiration date because of course he had to get back to his home in California.

It was going to suck.

The weeks and weeks ahead loomed long and cold as she'd most certainly be navigating the rest of the pregnancy alone. Ironic that one of the reasons she'd originally decided to have a baby right now was to have something in common with her friends, and they were so busy with their own lives that the only female friend who had time for her lately was the non-pregnant one.

The whole thing depressed her so much that she had to stop thinking about it. Her distraction of choice: throwing herself into the project of deconstructing the original lab samples. If the samples had been altered or substituted, she could prove it by pulling apart the molecular structure and analyzing it against what her formulary said was supposed to be in them. The work was tedious and difficult.

But she couldn't trust this to anyone else.

She'd already done some of the initial analysis back when the FDA first announced suspension of the request for approval. That was when she'd developed the theory that the samples were not the ones she'd submitted—because they weren't. There was no way. Her formula was sound. And she'd prove it.

Hours later, she had her answer. Dumbstruck to have the black-and-white evidence of sabotage, she stared at the data on her computer monitor, her stomach twisting with nausea.

Dante, bless him, must have sensed her distress because he glanced over at her from his lab table and immediately dropped whatever he was doing to cross the room. The warmth of his hand on her shoulder bled through her and she absorbed his presence as he came up behind her.

"What did you find out?" he asked quietly.

The answer was so huge and so overwhelming the

only thing she could do was swivel on her stool and bury her face in his chest. His arms encircled her, holding her close. She'd lost count of the number of times he'd done that over the years and the familiarity of it was the only thing that held her together.

"The samples are different," she said into his shirt and wasn't at all surprised when tears pricked at her eyelids. "Sabotage, for sure. This is *my lab*. My entire career. And someone undermined two years of my life with this stunt."

"I'm sorry, sweetheart."

He stroked her hair and let her cry on him because that was what he did. He was her rock, her go-to guy for everything. Miraculously, their relationship had gotten better and deeper with the addition of sex. Because she knew him so much more intimately now, and the depths blended with their history in a way that was great. Unexpectedly so.

Thank God he was here to soothe the jagged places inside.

She took a deep, shuddery breath. "I have to clean house. I can't trust anyone right now."

That was the worst part of this. She had twelve employees, all highly qualified technicians and scientists whom she'd handpicked way back when they'd started this company from nothing. All of them had been with her since the beginning, and one of them had *betrayed* her. Betrayed the entire company, including the women who were Harper's friends and business partners. It was unforgivable.

"Let's go home," Dante advised, drawing back a touch, and the concern and tenderness in his gaze nearly pulled apart her seams. "You can't do anything more today. You need to get out of here and take some downtime to process. Let me draw you a bath and then I'll take care of dinner."

Her eyelids slammed shut as gratitude washed through her. *Yes*. That sounded like exactly what she needed. Dante was her rock because he paid attention to her. Understood her. Knew what she needed often before she did. He'd always been like that but she'd never fully appreciated it. Until now. Why had it taken her this long to realize how much it meant to her?

She nodded. "That would be perfect. Except I have to tell the others. They need to know."

It was professional courtesy, of course, to inform the members of Fyra's C-suite what she'd discovered. But it was also personal. She'd brought this on Fyra and it was her responsibility to fix it.

Harper asked Melinda, the receptionist, to call an emergency meeting. Trinity, wonder of wonders, breezed through the door first, a neon-pink stripe decorating a lock of hair closest to her face.

"Hey, honey." Trinity slid into a chair and laced her fingers. "I'm guessing by the look on your face that this is not the meeting where you're going to announce that you and Dante are getting married."

Harper's pulse froze as the notion pinged around inside her. "Married? Why in the world would you say something so ridiculous?"

Marriage had never been on Harper's agenda, and she'd never heard Dante so much as breathe the word.

Trinity's expression grew crafty as Cass strode in and set up the TV to call Alex in DC. She fiddled with the controls until Alex's face popped up.

"Cass," Trinity called in a singsong voice. "Why in the world would I expect Dante and Harper to get married someday?"

Cass glanced at Harper with a smirk. "Because they've been in love with each other for like a million years."

Alex clapped. "Oh, did Harper finally figure that out? Is this an announcement?"

Her friends had all gone insane, obviously. "I'd ask if pregnancy hormones have melted all of your brains, but Trinity doesn't have that excuse. So instead, I'll say shut up. I am not in love with Dan—"

But suddenly, she couldn't say it as her throat closed. Romantic love was a chemical reaction gone really wrong at best. It was the psyche's way of putting a framework to sexual response. She'd swear it under oath.

But glancing at Cass and Alex, who were both happily married to amazing men who clearly would move heaven and earth for them…maybe things weren't as cut and dried as Harper had always made them out to be. Still…

"It's okay, honey. Give it a minute," Trinity said soothingly.

What was going on with this conversation? After all, Trinity had been the one to convince Harper that emotion-free was the only way to fly. "You said emotions have no place in sex. I heard you!"

She shrugged. "I told you what you needed to hear. You were letting your feelings for Dante get you all messed up."

"There's nothing like that between us!" Harper cried. "I do love Dante, but not like you're all talking about. Besides, if you really thought that was true, why hasn't anyone said anything before now?"

If they had, she'd have shot it down. The whole concept was ludicrous. Especially when you threw in the part about Dante being in love with her in return. The man had girlfriends coming out of his ears. Hot supermodels who probably knew way more than Harper did about how to please a man, in bed and out, one of whom he'd probably marry at some point if he was going to marry anyone.

Out of nowhere, her eyes started stinging as she imagined him twined with another woman.

Hormones. They were going to kill her.

Alex rolled her eyes. "This is one of those ruby slipper type deals. If we'd told you, you wouldn't have believed us. You have to learn it for yourself."

Sinking down in her seat, Harper thought about banging her head against the table. "Dante is not the reason I called this meeting. Can we please get back on track?"

Voice shaking, Harper told her friends what she'd found in the lab, and spent the next hour talking through the next steps. Grim-faced, they agreed to submit to the FDA the new samples that Harper had been keeping under lock and key. Then they'd do a careful analysis of the staff. Cass wasn't totally on board with a total sweep of the department due to concerns over severance costs and such, but she made a note to talk to Mike, their lawyer, as soon as possible.

Finally, Harper escaped the conference room and hustled Dante out of the lab to take her home, as his plan to put her in a bath and handle dinner was the only sane thing she'd heard in the last ninety minutes.

The bath went a long way toward making her feel human again, as did the back rub and medium-well steak Dante had delivered from Perry's. But of course the highlight of the day came when Dante took her by the hand and led her into the bedroom, then proceeded to undress her. When he kissed her with exquisite thoroughness and care, she nearly wept.

Off came his glasses, and her body flooded with so many feelings at once she could hardly stand under the storm. Which worked out well because Dante swept her up in his arms and rolled with her onto the bed, tangling their bodies so tightly together, it was hard to tell where one started and the other ended.

His gorgeous body…she couldn't get enough of it under her fingers, touching, marveling, letting the heat of his skin heighten her raging need. Then came her favorite part, when he finally entered her, sliding home as if he'd always been there. Her body accepted him easily as he filled her all the way to the brim. As he built the pressure and heat to the boiling point, she caught his gaze and stared into the depths of his gaze while he made love to her. The vastness of what he made her feel overwhelmed her and all at once, the conversation from earlier couldn't be ignored.

If every other female in her life saw something more here than friendship, why didn't she? Or was all of this huge and wonderful depth *exactly* what they were talking about?

Dante kissed her again as he touched her intimately in that way that never failed to make her body erupt with a thousand ripples, but this time, the contractions traveled all the way to her heart, squeezing it so tightly, she feared it might burst. He followed with his own climax—which was an amazing thing to witness, to know she'd had a part in bringing that exquisite expression to his face as he came.

Maybe she should start calling her heart arrhythmia by its proper name and stop pretending she didn't know why the thought of him leaving made her want to cry. She'd chalked it all up to hormones but maybe there was more here she'd been too afraid to examine.

She loved Dante. Always had, without reservation, without fear. He made sense in her life in his role as her friend. Until it made far more sense to be with him like this, and the transition had exceeded her expectations. But the one thing she'd never done was examine whether the emotion she'd always explained away as love for a male friend might be the same as the romantic kind she'd categorically denied existed.

She'd gotten pregnant solely because she'd thought a baby would fill a void in her life that no man could fill, when in reality, no other man could ever hope to compete with the one who already had a piece of her heart.

For someone so smart, she felt really stupid.

The whole concept made her want to curl up in a ball. Figure out unquantifiable emotions, especially after she'd *already* assigned them an ordered place in her mind? She could no sooner do that than she could turn invisible.

Ten

Dante's manager finally got his attention the next afternoon with a pointed text message that someone claiming to be his birth father had been contacting him via his social media accounts. Dante never looked at those things. That's what his publicist was for.

A quick text message back took care of that problem: I don't have a birth father.

Likely it was yet another ploy to get sticky fingers on Dante's money. That had begun happening with alarming frequency once he'd hit the big time and it was one of the many aspects of being a celebrity that he did not enjoy. People had gall, that was for sure. As if he owed anyone money because of some sob story—and yet the sob story weighed on him. Because what if it was true? It haunted him to think he had so much and others had so little.

So he gave money to charities and went on. The benefits of having success, even in the field of psychology, offset the negatives. For now.

At loose ends, Dante prowled around Harper's condo, alone and not happy about it.

They'd finished the samples yesterday and Harper had flown to Washington, DC, to personally hand them over to Alex. Then Alex's husband would present them to the FDA approval board and that would be that. Filming started up on *The Science of Seduction* in three days, and his role in Harper's life would return to what it had been. Friends with fifteen hundred miles between them and a date for lunch in a couple weeks when he connected through the DFW airport on the way to God knew where...*if* their schedules coincided.

He wasn't ready for what had happened in Dallas to be over.

The thought of giving up the lab again was bad enough. But having to leave Harper behind, pregnant and probably scared, definitely gorgeous and funny and so amazingly sexy all the time...that was killing him.

Nor was he ready to talk about the reasons why he had to get on a plane to LA. It was critical that Dante separate himself from Harper and the baby before bad things happened.

Because he couldn't help himself, he pulled out his wallet and fingered open the folded ultrasound picture he'd charmed the technician out of when Harper was talking to Dr. Dean. The little blob had no features whatsoever. It was nothing but cells and a heartbeat. But half the DNA of that blob came from a man who had essentially destroyed Dante's long-term affair with chemistry.

It would be easy to envision a scenario where Harper eventually gave birth and the baby came out with dark hair and Spanish features. Because Cardoza came from strong bloodlines; otherwise Harper wouldn't have chosen him.

A little whisper that had started up at the doctor's office plagued Dante: *if only Harper had asked Dante to be her donor.*

Madness. Why hadn't she asked him? If she had—and he'd said yes—he wouldn't at this very moment feel like his soul was being torn in two.

Also madness. If she'd asked him, he'd have said no. Not just no, but hell no. For exactly the reasons he'd told her that he didn't appreciate being forced into the "male influence" role she'd delegated to him without his consent.

Babies were leagues away from his area of expertise. He had no business being a father. People who jumped into having kids could never be fully certain they'd continue to want kids, and by the time they figured it out, it was too late. The kid already existed and it was far too easy to dump one into the system. The pain of that experience would never leave him, even if he wanted to find a way to be there for Harper and her baby. He saw that now.

Cardoza was no longer the biggest reason Dante couldn't do this. Maybe that had never been the reason and Dante had used his old rival as an excuse to ignore the real issue—he couldn't get past his childhood.

He had nothing to offer Harper or her baby—no parenting skills, no role model to glean advice from. What if he tried and messed up? He'd ruin a kid's whole life.

The longer Dante stared at this picture, the worse the wash of emotions became. The catch-22 was brutal. He couldn't stay, but he didn't want to go back to Hollywood.

Maybe he could find a third option. What good was it to have a healthy bank account if he couldn't buy whatever he wanted? Once upon a time, he'd have given his right arm to have a benefactor fall in his lap who could fund his lab, and he wouldn't have minded one bit if that benefactor popped in occasionally to play around in the nitty-gritty details.

Before he could change his mind, he sat down with his laptop and spent two hours querying everyone he knew in hopes of getting a lead on projects outside the university system in need of quick cash. Grant proposals had too many strings and oversight. Private was the way to go.

Within thirty minutes, four different responses appeared in his inbox. Dante got on the phone and talked to some great people he hadn't touched base with in years. It was cathartic to learn that the scientific community as a whole hadn't shunned him and there were still labs out there hoping to change the world with a big breakthrough. All they lacked was funding.

On his third call, he connected with Val Gochnauer, a guy he'd worked with during his dissertation. Val had landed at a think tank in his native Switzerland and needed an infusion of cash desperately, or the doors would close within thirty days.

Harper's key rattled in the lock and she breezed through the door just as Dante was wrapping up with Val. He cut it shorter than he would have liked because he had a gut feeling Val's setup was exactly what Dante had been looking for. Of course, he'd have to fly to Switzerland to find out. Today. He was due back on the set Monday, so the timing was perfect.

Except for the part where he had to tell Harper he was leaving. His chest hurt already. How was he going to get through a whole conversation?

But as she set down her suitcases and flew into Dante's embrace, the scent of peaches nearly put him on his knees. Instead of pushing her away, like he should, he gathered her close and breathed her in for what was probably the last time.

If he funded Val's lab, he'd probably end up spending all his free time in Switzerland. The situation was tailor-made. If Dante was on another continent, he couldn't tempt himself with a quick side trip to Dallas to spend the weekend in Harper's bed.

"I wasn't expecting you back so soon, or I would have picked you up," he said gruffly into her hair. "I thought your return flight wasn't until tonight. Weren't you going to having dinner with Alex and her husband?"

Nodding, Harper pulled back just enough so he could see her face. "I was supposed to but Phillip had an unexpected thing come up. The busy life of a senator. I don't know how Alex does it."

Good. And not good. It would have been easier if he could have left before she got back. But that kind of cowardice didn't sit well anyway. Now he had a chance to come clean, especially about the part where he was going to opt out of being here during the pregnancy and birth. "I'm glad. I missed you."

That was so not what he'd meant to say.

"I missed you, too." She smiled and it ripped through him with jagged teeth.

Now came the hard part.

God, he did not want to disappoint her. But what was he supposed to do? Hilarious how she'd fought so hard against his seduction campaign because she didn't want to lose their friendship, and he'd been the one to convince her that would never happen because of how important she was to him.

Someone with as many advanced degrees as Dante sure as hell should have predicted the outcome of that a little better. But how could he have seen that he'd end up deciding to remove himself from her life *because* of how much he cared about her? The last thing he wanted was to negatively affect their relationship because of unalterable circumstances surrounding her child. It was much better to drift away, lose contact eventually like so many friends did.

"I have something to tell you," he muttered and dropped his arms far too quickly.

"Funny," she commented brightly. "I have something to tell you, too. I may have slightly misrepresented the thing Phillip had. They actually invited me to come with them but I wanted to come home. I had a lot of time to think about us on the flight and—"

"Us? Is there an us?"

Hope filtered through his heart greedily, and in two seconds, his mind whirled through a series of compromises that sounded incredibly selfish the longer he contemplated them.

Her expression froze and took his pulse along for the ride as she carefully picked her way to the long sofa overlooking the patio, where he'd given himself the first taste of her. She sank down on the cushions. "Well, of course there's an us. We're friends, silly."

She hadn't meant it the way he'd taken it. Harper wasn't looking for anything from him other than friendship. "Yes, always. And because of that, it's important that I tell you mine first. I'm…leaving."

Her brow wrinkled. "I know. On Sunday. That's what I wanted to talk about actually, because I have another doctor's appointment in two weeks and I'm kind of hoping you might be able to get away—"

"Today. In a few hours." He shut his eyes as the reality of it swept over him. She'd been about to ask him to be her official doctor's appointment hand-holder, probably for the remainder of her pregnancy. And he had to say no. "I'm going to Switzerland. There's an amazing opportunity there for me to get back into the lab. So I'll be splitting my time between LA and Zurich for a while. I don't think I'll be able to make it back to Dallas for your appointment."

The first bit of unease moved through Harper's gaze. "What are you talking about? I didn't know you were looking for a lab. What about your TV show?"

"I can do both." He shrugged. "There's a regular direct flight between LAX and Zurich, so it's pretty convenient. I just won't have time to come back here very often. I'm sorry."

She scowled. "Dante, what is going on with you? You promised to be here for me during this pregnancy. Couldn't you have just said no to the Switzerland deal?"

And here came the part where he had to twist the knife because she clearly wasn't getting the full, brutal point of the situation. "I've wanted to get back into the lab for a long time and working with your samples only solidified that. I can't say no because it's my deal. I put it together."

All the blood drained from Harper's face. "You did this on purpose? Help me understand. I want to be supportive of your career, but…this is coming from out of nowhere. What about us?"

"There is no us, Harper, that's the whole point," he said and yeah, it had come out a little more harshly than he'd intended. "I know you were expecting me to be involved in your pregnancy and with the baby, but it's… not going to work out."

She flinched as if he'd smacked her in the face. "You

don't even plan to be around later? After the baby is born? Switzerland is, like, a long-term thing?"

"Afraid so." He crossed his own arms in hopes that it might seal up his insides before they spilled out all over her pristine beige carpet.

"What if…things between us were different?" she whispered, as she stared at a spot on her skirt. "What if we were a couple?"

A couple of what? Idiots who thought that sex wouldn't complicate everything to the point of ruin? "But we're not. That's not even something you want. Right?"

Stupid, stupid, stupid. Why tack that question onto the end, as if the answer would make a difference?

But then she glanced up, tears gathering in her eyes, and said, "I think I'm in love with you."

Oh, my God. His insides fell out anyway, leaving a huge, dark hole where his vital organs should be as his soul processed the words he'd never have imagined falling from her lips. Words that could have made everything better—*should* have made everything better—but didn't. It was so much worse. Now he had to break both of their hearts. Push her away, hurt her, and do it well enough that there was no chance she'd hang onto the hope that her confession changed anything.

The irony. Harper had finally come around to what he'd known for a long time—they were perfect for each other.

Except for the part where they couldn't be together.

That was it—as open and as honest as Harper could be with another human being and all Dante had done with her declaration of love was sit down heavily on the floor, his head cradled in his hands.

"Did you hear what I said?" she repeated softly.

Admitting she was in love with Dante was a huge concession. One she hadn't made lightly and then only because her entire world was sliding away and she'd grabbed on with both hands, clawing back the destruction in the only way she knew how.

"I heard," he muttered. "Maybe *you* didn't hear what you said. You think you're in love? You *think*? I'm supposed to hang my life on the hope that you'll eventually be at least, what, seventy-five percent sure? Can I cross my fingers for ninety?"

"I don't know." Mute, she stared at him. He was angry. At her. For daring to say something so bold and huge as *I love you*. "I'm trying to—"

"You can stop trying. It doesn't matter because I don't believe you anyway."

"You don't—" She faltered. Had Dante just thrown her shaky admission back in her face and called her a liar at the same time? "You think I just randomly go around saying things like that? How dare you."

Dante rose up on his feet then, his expression black. Fierce. "Harper, you don't want to push me right now."

"I don't want to push *you*?" The Irish in her blood stirred and she leaped to her feet in kind, skin pricking with anger she'd never have guessed Dante could provoke. "I just flew three hours home from Washington after being on the ground a total of ninety minutes. Because I wanted to see you. To talk to you about how great things are between us. How becoming lovers is the best thing that ever happened to me. And you're *mad* about it. Please tell me how I'm pushing you."

All at once, he deflated, growing visibly weary as he slipped off his glasses, rubbing the bridge of his nose. "I'm not mad. I'm… I don't know what I am."

The sight of his bare face nearly undid her and she

wrapped her arms around her stomach, hoping to stem the wave of nausea that had risen up almost instantly as she realized she might never see him that intimately again. "You're my friend. Always. Me being in love with you doesn't change that. Isn't that what we've said all along? Becoming more only enhanced what we already had. I don't understand how everything just fell apart in the space of one afternoon."

Bleakly, he shook his head. "It didn't. It's been falling apart since you told me you were pregnant. Back in LA. I tried, Harper. But I can't be your baby's male influence."

The starkness in his expression sliced through her. Since LA. Since she'd flown to *Los Angeles*? That was a gut shot she'd never recover from. He'd not only rejected her love, he wasn't on board with her pregnancy. And hadn't been from the beginning. So what was all this? Simply a way to get her into bed? No. She could never believe something so monstrous.

"What are you saying? That you've been pretending all this time?"

"Yeah. Pretending there was a way this was all going to work out, when in reality, I'm the worst possible person for you to depend on."

"*That's* the lie, Dante," she whispered. "You've always been there for me. There's no one else in my life that I depend on more than you."

"In this, you can't. Not with a baby on the way. For a lot of reasons. But mostly because of who the father is."

His eyes burned like dark coals, unrecognizable. Unyielding. Because she'd asked Tomas to donate sperm.

And that's when her temper snapped. This boiled down to professional rivalry, nothing more. And *oh, my God*. Really? "That's a low blow, Dante. Never mind the loss of what I thought we were headed toward as we took our relationship to the next level. So we can't even be friends anymore? Because you can't get over the fact that a million years ago some guy beat you out for a prize?"

Wrong thing to say. Too harsh. Too much truth.

But her whole body ached with grief and disappointment and a dozen other things that she couldn't voice. She'd never done anything like this before, had no idea how to deal with the blackness swirling through her chest. Dante was her rock. He was supposed to make everything better, bearable. Not tear her apart with nothing more than a few words.

Dante's hands clenched and unclenched. He stretched his fingers out, examining them as he tried to find a measure of calm. But he just stood there and when he exhaled, his angry vibe hadn't diminished at all.

The look in his eyes scared her. She'd stepped way over the line.

"I can't," he finally ground out through clenched teeth. "The thing is, I tried. Don't you see how hard I tried? I don't tell you this because it makes me happy. It's killing me. I would have kept on trying but…"

His voice broke and took her heart with it. She ached to cross the small expanse of carpet because no matter what, he was still Dante, precious and special, and he'd always comforted her. But she didn't think he'd accept the same from her.

"But *what*?" she murmured. "Tomas? That's really so much of a deal breaker?"

If only… But filling in that blank was the path to madness. There was no *if only* in this scenario. She'd made an adult decision to have a baby and now she had to be an adult about the consequences of that decision.

Dante's nod was so imperceptible that it was hard to

fathom how that one small jerk of his head could bring her entire world crashing down.

Dazed, she fell back onto the couch. "So that's it then. You're done here. With me, our intimate relationship. With our friendship as a whole, I guess."

"Not because I want to be," he croaked. "Because that's the only way. I chose Switzerland on purpose, so there was no confusion."

The unfairness of it...the sheer injustice nearly overwhelmed her. "I didn't know I was going to fall in love with you when I asked another man to father my baby. Doesn't that count for anything?"

His brown eyes blinked shut for a moment and it was like all the light in the room vanished. When his lids opened, she knew the answer before he said it. "Sometimes we have to lie in the bed we made, no matter how lonely and cold it is."

And then Dante walked out of her condo, the place where he'd opened her world, introduced her to her first experience with physical pleasures, which in turn had become that much greater because her feelings for him had grown as a result. Only to ultimately give her the first taste of a broken heart.

Eleven

Switzerland had been everything Dante had hoped for. Lab—check. Thousands of miles away from Harper and her baby—check. A large, multi-year project in the works that would definitely be a distraction from the morass of emotion weighing down his entire body—check.

Val was a great guy who deserved the funding Dante would provide. The whole team had welcomed him with open arms—no mystery when you packed your checkbook—but the marked lack of fans sold the deal. No one had even looked at him twice as he walked the halls of the think tank's building in an industrial section north of Zurich. The summer weather was similar to LA, so that even worked. He'd worry about the snow when it became a factor.

Best of all, *The Science of Seduction*'s producers had loved Dante's proposal to film a series in Europe that focused on new strategies he'd developed on the plane.

Nothing said romance like the quaint villages and breathtaking mountains of Switzerland.

Too bad Dante's enthusiasm was entirely faked. Looked like he'd learned to be a fairly decent actor while spending the better part of three years in front of the camera. No one had guessed that he'd left a large chunk of his heart behind in Harper's condo as he'd turned his back on the tears streaming down her face, a necessity because he couldn't be the man she needed. Couldn't be the father figure her baby needed. No matter how much he might want to.

Leaving had been, hands down, the most difficult thing he'd ever done. Even two weeks later, it still haunted him nightly. In the shower. At random moments when he should have been paying attention to a thousand other things. Because as she'd so eloquently pointed out, falling in love hadn't changed the fact that she was still his best friend. He'd lost far more than merely the woman he was sleeping with.

Ten times a day, he reached for his phone to text Harper a funny joke Val had told him, or lament the boredom he faced so frequently on the set as he waited for a costume change or makeup. But ultimately, he always put the phone back in his pocket.

He didn't know how to do life without Harper.

After two weeks back in LA to finish filming the current spate of episodes, Dante had the weekend off to pack and give Mrs. Ortiz some final instructions. Production was moving to a space the studio had found near the think tank and by this time Monday morning, Dante would be living in Zurich. For the next six months and more if he could swing it.

Harper would be late in her last trimester of pregnancy by then, and he did not have any intention of being near the States for the whole of it. Because he very much feared he'd run back to Dallas, desperate to see Harper again, to touch her, see her belly grow as the baby gained features, fingers, toes—things he'd never dreamed he'd want to witness until he'd already given up his right to do so.

But how could he be so selfish as to insinuate himself into Harper's life, and ultimately her child's, when he had no clue how bad of a father he'd be until it was too late? The risks were still too high. Nothing had changed just because he was miserable.

Dante's phone buzzed as he and Mrs. Ortiz wrapped up discussion on the relatively short list of things he'd given her to handle while he was gone. Funny how he lived in this house day in and day out but it didn't seem like much would change with him gone.

It was Howie, Dante's manager. Again. He'd been pestering Dante for a solid week about contacting the man claiming to be Dante's birth father. "What now?"

"It's about this guy, Edgar Gates," Howie said. "He traveled to LA to see you. I know you don't want to hear it, but before you leave for Switzerland, I really think you should talk to him."

Dante's lip curled. After the third round of unsolicited contact, he'd asked his lawyer to discreetly check into the story and there was every possibility that Edgar Gates was indeed Dante's birth father. But why the man thought Dante would give him the time of day was the real mystery.

Obviously this problem wasn't going away anytime soon, and it wasn't fair to his team to continually subject them to this nuisance. A restraining order sounded like the most expedient solution. But suddenly, Dante had an inexplicable urge to face down the man who was the reason he'd had a miserable childhood.

"I'll talk to him. Tell him to meet me at Tango's on Santa Monica."

Dante ended the call. That was stupid. Why pick such a public place in the heart of LA to meet his supposed father? There'd be pictures galore plastered across the tabloids in no time flat. Too late now. And it was probably for the better. Odds were good Dante would think twice about making a scene.

This was the part where he'd normally call Harper. She'd tell him everything he needed to hear, that it didn't matter what this man said, Dante was still amazing and she was in his corner.

But he'd given up her friendship. For her own good. For her baby's good.

Dante arrived ten minutes early because he believed in being prepared. Still, his pulse jackhammered in his temples with no relief in sight, especially as a dark-haired man with a weathered face shuffled in the door. Dante recognized him instantly. Not because he'd met him before. But there was a certain familiar element to the man's features. His carriage. The way his gaze roamed over the crowd and then connected with Dante's—it jolted him into a near cardiac arrest.

Edgar Gates. No question about the man's claim. Dante didn't need a DNA test to know he and this man shared blood. But he didn't stand as his father loomed over the table, didn't offer to shake hands.

"Thanks for coming," Dante said politely because he had manners that he'd taught himself.

"You look just like you do on the TV." Edgar Gates stared at him as if he'd seen a ghost. "I watch you all the time. I thought I was imagining how much you look like your mother."

The man's voice coated Dante's stomach with thick nausea. He shook his head and bit back the years of anger, hatred and disappointment that had surged to the surface hearing this horrible human being speak of things he had no right to talk about. But really, what had Dante expected the outcome of this meeting to be?

He'd prepared himself for the possibility that it was a hoax. An extortion scheme. He had *mistakenly* thought he'd also prepared himself for the alternative, but that was far from true.

Swallowing the bile that had accompanied the surge of emotion, Dante waved at the opposing seat. "Please, don't hover. The time to be a helicopter parent has long passed."

"You're very successful." As he fell heavily into the chair, Edgar Gates's gaze roamed over Dante's face, taking it in but what he was looking for, who could say? "I would like to be proud of that."

"But you can't be," Dante broke in. "Because you had nothing to do with it. What do you want? You have five minutes to lay it out and then I'm leaving."

Success. What was the measure of that in Edgar Gates's world? Money? Fame? A Nobel Prize? Loving a woman until death do you part and raising a family with her because that's what people with honor, character and respect did?

Edgar nodded, wringing his hands. "I've got some medical problems—"

"And you want money." Dante nodded grimly. "How much? I'll write you a check and then you forget my name."

That was the easy part. His "father" would probably

do that the moment he walked out the door. It was Dante who would lay awake at night, wondering why he'd been unworthy of that simple family where he could thrive. Be loved.

"No." Edgar's lips trembled and his face turned ashen. "I wish it was that simple. You have to understand I'm here because I'm desperate. I got no right to be here, to ask anything of you."

"Agreed. So why are you here?" God, his arms wouldn't stop shaking. He crossed them and stuck his hands under his biceps, squeezing until he got the trembling mostly under control.

"I need a kidney. Or I'll die. Soon."

"That's almost too poetic for words. You're here because you suddenly remembered you have a potential match running around loose in the world. What's a dying man to do but look up the son he treated like garbage? It's been thirty years. What's a trip through the foster system between blood relatives, huh?"

Edgar didn't blink, accepting every harsh word as his due, which didn't earn him an iota of Dante's respect. "Is that what happened? Your mother put you in the system?"

"You don't know?" Disbelief squeezed what little civility remained in Dante's chest. "I was told by my caseworker that you left and she couldn't handle being a single mom. So yeah. Into the system. Until I was eighteen."

Why was he rehashing this? There was no changing it, no absolution. No reason to still be sitting here. Dante stood and Edgar followed him with his gaze, holding up a hand to stop him from storming out. It shouldn't have worked. But Dante froze in his tracks anyway.

"That's true." Misery pulled at Edgar's expression,

which was no less than he deserved. "I didn't do right by you or your mother. I took off. Had no interest in being your dad, but that had nothing to do with you. It was all on me. And I've paid for that, over and over."

"Oh, really. Your idea of absolving that debt and mine differ by leagues." His temper spiked, which was the only reason he was able to get the rest out over the knot of emotion in his chest. "No interest in being a dad, hmm? Guess what? It doesn't work that way. You don't get to decide whether you want to be a parent when the kid already exists. You man up and figure it out."

That was the rub. The thing he'd nursed in his gut for ages. And now he'd finally said it to the man who'd needed to hear it, which had been cathartic in a way he'd never expected.

A sense of calm came over him then, allowing him to sit back down so he could settle this once and for all. "Here's the thing. I'm pretty attached to my kidneys and I don't have a spare available for the man who was one half of the reason I never had a home."

Even now he didn't have one. The Spanish hacienda in the Hills had been so easy to walk away from because it wasn't his home.

Harper had been so hard to walk away from because she was.

Dante's temples throbbed as he stared at the man who had given him life but had nothing to do with who Dante had become. His success was all on him. Dante had made difficult choices, risen to impossible challenges, to create his own version of success. He'd studied enough psychology to know you didn't get pottery worth a crap if you didn't put it through the fire, and he could be man enough to accept that his childhood circumstances had driven him to succeed. Perhaps had even been the sole reason.

But he wasn't sure if he was man enough to admit he'd walked away from the only home he'd ever known because he didn't know how to succeed at loving Harper and being a real father to her child. Not because of Cardoza—that was a concern he'd almost gotten over. But because he had little faith in his ability to be a good parent because of how he'd been raised.

He'd chosen to let his pride and a fear of the unknown trump everything instead of letting the past go. That was on him, too.

Edgar nodded bleakly and stood. "I had to try. I appreciate your time. I won't bother you again."

"That's it? You came all this way, I say no, and now you're leaving? No, 'let's have a drink for old times' or 'maybe you could spare me a twenty to tide me over?'"

"I don't expect anything from you. I don't deserve anything. But I'm scared enough of dying that it was worth a shot."

This man was a coward. Through and through. The revelation thumped Dante between the eyes. It was the one thing they had in common—and Dante did not like thinking of himself that way.

But what else could he call a man who walked away from a pregnant woman, forcing her to be a single mom? The differences between Edgar's situation and Dante's weren't as vast as he would have said five minutes ago, and what Dante had done might actually be worse…because he'd done it to his best friend. A woman he loved more than anyone on earth. A woman who didn't have anyone else to lean on as she raised her baby.

Was he really going to choose fear over happiness?

Perhaps he might take his own advice and man up.

No, her baby wasn't biologically his. But if he made the choice to be a father, that would make all the difference. Who cared if the baby had Cardoza's DNA? Evidence that DNA didn't make the man lived inside Dante's own body and he would remember that he and Edgar had *nothing* in common every time he looked in the mirror.

Because Dr. Dante Gates, PhD, was not a coward.

In one of life's great ironies, Dr. Harper Livingston could not go into the lab at Fyra, the place she'd built from scratch, also known as her refuge. She could not walk through the door.

Too many memories. Too much association.

Chemistry and Dante had intertwined to the point where she couldn't separate one from the other, no matter its form. Her body cried for his touch as much as her soul missed his voice. They'd never gone more than a couple of days between phone calls.

She missed him keenly, in a way she never had before.

Morning sickness had walloped her the day after Dante left. Or as she liked to call it, *mourning sickness*. Because every fiber of her body felt black and sticky with grief. Why not throw an upset stomach on top, like the misery cherry on a desolation sundae?

The crackers and ginger ale Alex had recommended sat untouched on her desk. When Alex had gone through the horrific rounds of morning sickness, Harper had been the one to go to 7-Eleven to fetch whatever her friend had asked for. But Alex was on bed rest, and she'd already set the expectation that she'd take a six-month maternity leave. She wouldn't be around to fetch crackers for Harper. In fact, she wouldn't be around, period.

It wasn't that Harper needed someone at her beck and call—she'd been taking care of herself for a long time. It was the emotional support she'd hoped for. Long lunches where she shopped for baby clothes with her friends. Baby showers. Inclusion in the inner circle of motherhood.

Except Cass was spending more and more time in Austin and had started talking to a real estate agent about buildings near Round Rock. Of course the four founding members of Fyra would make the decision together, but everyone knew Cass hoped to move Fyra's headquarters to Austin before her and Gage's baby was born. Harper didn't have any particular ties to Dallas, and Austin was closer to her parents, not that it mattered. They'd never been an overly tight family.

Normally when she got in a mood like this, she'd call Dante and spill her heart about how lonely she was. He'd tell her a joke and say she would always have him to lean on. That small bit of encouragement would make her smile without fail.

Despondent and utterly helpless to change her attitude, Harper sat in her office and clicked through a few emails with zero enthusiasm. They hadn't heard back from the FDA committee about her new samples and the lure of creating something new in the lab had completely vanished.

She had enough new creation going on in her womb, thank you very much.

That thought cheered her slightly. It didn't matter if her friends weren't around. This baby would be her family. Always. The baby would be solely hers and wouldn't drift off to other relationships, other jobs, other cities.

Cue the waterworks. Pregnancy had thoroughly wrecked her. Or maybe it only magnified the reality of losing her best friend over the baby she'd conceived with the best of intentions. A woman with an analytical mind and zero ability to understand her own emotions had to create her own bonds in this world.

Harper sniffled into a tissue and when she looked up, the one man she'd never expected to see again filled her doorway.

"Dante."

Even saying his name hurt, rasping across vocal chords raw from morning sickness and crying jags that lasted until 3:00 a.m. She blinked but he was still standing there, watching her from behind his glasses, his eyes soft and tender. Completely unlike the last time she'd seen him.

"Can I come in?" he asked and when she nodded, he entered and shut the door behind him, leaning against it.

Hungrily, she took in the small details. New lines around his mouth and eyes that begged the question—jet lag? Or was he miserable, too, unable to sleep, unable to function without an anchor in his life?

"Of all the cities you could be in, this isn't the one I was expecting," she said and it almost didn't sound bitter.

He nodded, his spiky brown hair sweeping with the gesture because he needed a haircut but was probably too busy running around the globe to take the time. "I sold my house in LA."

That bobbled her pulse. "What? Why? Did you stop doing the show?"

"No. We're filming in Zurich now." He crossed his arms, his own gaze roaming over her in kind. "How are you? How is the baby?"

The laugh she managed wasn't the slightest bit amused. "Still in there. Still not fathered by someone acceptable."

"What if he or she could be?" he asked. "What if I said I wanted to be its father?"

The words hung in the air, laden with a promise that felt just out of reach.

"What are you talking about? You're an amazing scientist but gene replacement therapy is experimental, and even then only for the treatment of disease. You can't remove the Tomas Cardoza from my baby."

Nor would she if it was possible. She loved the baby the way it was already. No, this was a decision she'd made that Dante could not accept and everyone had to live with it. No matter how hard it was to see him again, to have him in her office, within touching distance.

He shook his head. "That's so far from what I'm saying. I don't want to fix anything about this situation. I want to embrace it."

Startled, she met his gaze and it burned through her with so much implication she couldn't interpret, but her breath caught because something had shifted. What, she couldn't tell, but the room no longer felt like Dante had sucked up all the oxygen when he'd breezed into her office.

"Embrace it?" That sounded an awful lot like he was saying he'd reevaluated…and had come back to tell her he'd changed his mind about them. But to what end—like he wanted to be friends again? Lovers until he jetted off to Switzerland? "How?"

He crossed the room in a flash, rounding her desk and then stopping short, as if not sure she would welcome his touch. In fact, she burned for him to take her into his arms and melt away all the dark, sticky places inside that he'd left behind.

"One hundred percent," he said huskily and leaned back on the desk as if he planned to stay awhile. "You. The baby. Us. Love. This is one of those all-of-the-above deals, in case I'm not being clear."

Something bright flared to life in her chest, nearly overshadowing everything else. But not quite. Because things were never that easy, not when it came to the unquantifiable. She had too much caution ingrained in her now. "You left, Dante. I told you I loved you and you threw it back in my face. You have no idea how hard it was for me to say that when I barely understand it myself."

Dante took that in stride without flinching and somehow, that broke the barrier. He reached out and slid his fingers into hers, then pulled her hand into the hollow of his thigh, trapping her palm against his heat, and holy hell did her Dante-starved body like that.

"I thought I was doing the right thing. For both of us. I tried to make it about Cardoza, but this was about my failings, my insecurities. My past. The problem is that I don't understand love, either. Obviously." His gaze caught hers, holding, evaluating. "Will you let me explain?"

She nodded and he told her the story of his birth father contacting him and how meeting him had surfaced so much anger about Dante's childhood. Some of which she knew about, of course, but she'd never realized how being in the foster system had poisoned him. His reaction when she'd told him she was pregnant made a whole lot more sense in that context. And her heart ached for the little boy who'd never been loved.

Which only made her love the man he'd become twice as much.

Dante concluded his confessional. "I should have stuck around and insisted we figure out how to interpret our emotions together. Instead, I left you. Alone. Because I was so scared of messing up fatherhood for your baby. That was a cowardly move and I'm sorry. So sorry," he murmured and lifted her hand to his cheek, kissing her palm so tenderly that tears sprang to her eyes.

"I forgive you." That hadn't been in question. She could never hold a grudge in any way, shape or form. "But I still don't understand. Why did you come back? If it was so easy to embrace all of this, why did you leave in the first place?"

His short laugh was anything but amused. "None of this is easy. The only thing that changed is that I figured out that you're worth the effort of leaving my past in the past, where it belongs. Being a father scares me. But being without you is worse. I tried that. It didn't work."

And that did it. The tears spilled over, falling down her cheeks as he smiled gently, wiping at her face with his thumb. Totally ineffectual when her hormones were driving the bus. Besides, they were happy tears. "It didn't work for me, either. Turns out I'm not a fan of sleeping alone. Who knew? That's what happens when you experiment. Sometimes you get results you didn't expect."

With a growl, he pulled on her hand until she came out of her swivel chair and fell into his arms. "I wasn't kidding about embracing this. I plan to spend a good chunk of the next six months in bed with you. Once the baby is here, we won't have much time to ourselves."

"I like the sound of that," she said, her voice muffled against his shoulder as she snuggled into his body.

"Which part?" he murmured in her ear.

"All of the above." And then she turned her head, just a little, until she got her nose right in the hollow of his throat, where it most smelled like him. Her insides quivered with unfulfilled need, but there was—apparently—plenty of time for that later.

"Harper?" Dante waited until she pulled back, brows raised, before continuing. His melty chocolate eyes speared her to the core as he looked at her and said, "I love you. Feels like I always have. And I know I always will."

Her heart filled so fast she almost couldn't stand under the force of it. But Dante had her tight in his strong arms, and he didn't let go. "The only question I have now is whether you're in the market for a permanent lab partner. Because I am."

"Depends," she said with a mischievous smile. "Do I have to wash all the beakers?"

He laughed, flashing his dimple. "I would be happy to hire as many beaker washers as the lady of the manor desires. I just want to be with you. For the rest of our lives. I want to wake up next to you and call you Mrs. Gates and put my name on our baby's birth certificate so he knows he's loved from the moment he's born."

Oh, God. That was the most romantic thing he'd ever said to her. She didn't even mind the tears so much anymore, which was a good thing since they didn't seem to have an end in sight. "In that case, yes."

"One additional small thing. Minuscule, really." He hefted her deeper in his arms, smoothing a hand over her back, and she felt it clear to her toes. "How do you feel about Swiss prenatal care? I hear they have one of the highest rated medical systems in the world."

Her eyebrows shot up. "Are you asking me to move to Switzerland with you?"

"I kind of already moved there. Before I knew I was going to ask you to marry me." He eyed her. "See, there's a think tank and I fully funded it for the next six months and our research is going so well, that I—"

"Yes." If Alex could live in Washington, Harper could live in Zurich. And if not, then when Cass moved the company to Austin, she'd sell her share in Fyra to the other three girls.

Nothing was more important to her than Dante and the baby they were going to have together. *Together.* It was nearly miraculous, nearly impossible to grasp how much she'd wanted that and had been afraid to hope.

"Yes? Just like that?" Dumbfounded, Dante gaped at her and she giggled at his fish mouth.

"I love you. I always have. You're everything to me, my whole world. No matter where you are, that's where I want to be, too. So you're stuck with me." The crackle in the air sent a shiver down her spine as he devoured her with his gaze alone. "Keep looking at me like that, Dr. Sexy, and you might find yourself naked in about four seconds."

"Oh, yeah?" he growled and, instantly, buttons started flying as he tore out of his shirt. "I like a woman who knows what she wants."

As they came together in a firestorm of passion that she'd never imagined would be so tender and meaningful, she murmured in his ear, "I forgot to mention that pregnancy does something wicked to me. I can't get enough of you."

"So," he mouthed against her throat as they slid together perfectly. "We're talking ten, maybe twelve, kids then?"

"Keep talking. I like what I'm hearing." And what she was feeling. *Loved.*

What an amazing series of chemical reactions, all of which had come together to make her a part of something—a family.

Epilogue

When Harper got the text message from Cass, she almost ignored it. After all, it might be 3:00 p.m. in Dallas, but it was ten o'clock Central European Time and she had a hot date with her husband. Who walked in the door from the lab at that precise moment, draining her mind of everything but him.

"You work too much," she scolded with a smile, only for Dante to sweep her into his arms with a growl. "Careful. The doctor said you can resume normal activity next week. Not a moment before."

"If I'd known donating a kidney would limit how much sex I can have with my new wife, I'd have waited," Dante said with a mock frown.

"No, you wouldn't have. Your father was in bad shape and your heart is too big to have ignored his need." That was her favorite part of Dante's decision to become the father of her baby. He'd proven he had truly put his past behind him by offering something precious to a man he should hate for a lot of really good reasons. But the fact that he'd so generously given Edgar Gates the chance at life…it tugged at her heart. Dante was going to be a great father in spite of his lack of a good example.

Her phone beeped again and then again. She started to turn it off but then caught sight of the message. "Oh! Cass is calling a meeting. The FDA approved the samples."

So many emotions rushed into her chest as Dante whooped, hauling her close for a tight embrace. Tears of relief and happiness welled up at the corners of her eyes. And here she'd thought marrying her best friend in a small ceremony the week before had been the pinnacle of bliss.

Harper settled into her desk chair, and flipped on the computer to pull up the online meeting software, and the conference room at Fyra blinked into focus. Trinity was the lone C-suite member at the conference room table, but she owned it with a saucy toss of her head.

Cass popped up in a separate video window, her husband, Gage, also in the picture most likely because they were at home together. Then Alex's window appeared and of course Phillip had elected to attend as well since he'd been navigating the FDA meetings on Fyra's behalf.

"It's done," Phillip said without preamble. "The FDA approval is official. Full steam ahead."

Everyone clapped and Dante kissed Harper on the temple with a murmured, "Well done, sweetheart."

Trinity nodded. "Formula-47 never would have happened without you, Harper. You rocked this. Now let's tell the world about our product and watch all our hard work pay off."

"Yes," Cass agreed enthusiastically. "This is the best part, where everything comes together. The marketing campaign we've been working on can finally come to fruition. About that…"

She hesitated and Trinity's eyes narrowed, apparently honing in on that small blip in Cass's normally polished delivery. "What about that, Cass? This is my thing. I've got it."

"Well, the negative publicity over the tainted samples is a problem. Like we've discussed." Cass glanced at Gage, who put his arm around his wife in a sweet gesture that made Harper's heart happy. "I found a publicity consultant that I think we should speak to. Just to get some additional thoughts on how to mitigate the bad press."

Steam shot out of Trinity's ears and she nearly came out of her chair. "A consultant? I'm the CMO, hon. You can consult with me all day long."

"Trin, let the woman talk," Alex cut in mildly. "She's not saying you're not in charge. She's saying we need some damage control and why not outsource that while you focus on the campaign for the formula. That's all."

Cass chuckled. "No need. That's exactly what I was going to say."

Arms crossed, Trinity fumed a bit more and then said, "I'll listen to what the consultant says. But I get final say on everything suggested. Period."

"Cass?" Harper hated to bring it up, but it needed to be said. "We still don't know who was responsible for all of this. I think it's safe to say it's a lab employee and I'm too close to it to be objective. Thoughts?"

Whoever it was had a personal agenda, and they'd hurt all of these people in earshot. One way or another someone needed to pay for that.

Everyone grew quiet and finally Cass sighed. "That's on me. I need to close that down once and for all. Give me a day to come up with a plan of attack."

They talked for a few more minutes and then signed off in deference to Harper's pointed comments about the time difference.

And then she let her gorgeous husband take her to bed where he kissed her belly and murmured to their baby while she stroked his hair. The chemistry between them did indeed come with a hell of kick—in the heart.

* * * * *